T0245868

Created

THE TALENTED SAGA

Talented (Talented Saga # 1)
Caged (Talented Saga # 2)
Hunted (Talented Saga # 3)
Captivated, A Talented Novella
Created (Talented Saga # 4)
Exiled (Talented Saga #4.5)...June 2014
Inescapable (Talented Saga #5)...Fall 2014

NIGHTMARES TRILOGY

Pawn (Nightmares Trilogy #1)
Sacrifice (Nightmares Trilogy #2)...December 2014

BLIND BARRIERS SERIES

Blind Barriers (Blind Barriers Volume #1)
Courting Chaos (Blind Barriers Volume #2)
Fragile Façade (Blind Barriers Volume #3)
Haunted Haven (Blind Barriers Volume #4)...June 2014
Idol Identities (Blind Barriers Volume #5)...July 2014

For Mary Jane Belle—
the best creation there is.

Chapter One

MY PULSE WAS racing and beads of sweat lined my forehead like a damp bandana, as I climbed aboard a sleek transport hoverplane bearing the Coalition's insignia. The hot California sun had set over an hour ago, but the summer night air was still thick with heat.

My boots sounded deceptively heavy, thudding against the metal rungs, echoing the pounding in my head. The synthetic suit that Ian Crane, President, had given me was identical to the ones his soldiers wore, and marked my new allegiance to the *Coalition of Rebel States*: California, Nevada, Utah, Arizona, Colorado, New Mexico and Texas, known as the Coalition. It was strikingly similar to the adapti-suits worn by the *Talented Organization for Extremely Interesting Citizens* (TOXIC) operatives. The lightweight material clung to my body like a second skin, and, while it had temperature-regulating capabilities, my skin still felt clammy underneath.

I tried to tell myself this was just another mission, just like the ones I'd been on while pledging the Hunters. Except that wasn't true; this mission was personal. I wasn't going to retrieve information that meant nothing to me. I wasn't going to quiet a rebellion I naively didn't understand. I was going to save what was left of my world. TOXIC and Mac had taken so much from me: my parents, my childhood, my health, my blood, and the love of my life. Erik was the only item on that list I had a prayer of reclaiming. And I fully intended on doing so, or die trying.

Long metal benches lined both walls of the hoverplane's main cabin. Harnesses dangled above each individual seat, ready to secure their passengers into place. Coalition soldiers, many I recognized from the strategy meetings, occupied the benches. Most were male, but several women broke up the rows of testosterone. A female soldier, Janelle Longpre, was wedged between a guy with a shaved head, red face, and one brilliant black eye and a thin boy with caramel skin and a mop of dark curls. Janelle smiled up at me as I passed, her marbled irises twinkling with unabashed anticipation. The guy with the black eye, Jared Holton, scowled his displeasure, screwing his full lips into a snarl.

A tiny bit of the tension stiffening my shoulders eased as I grinned back at Janelle. She was one of the few friendly soldiers. Jared, on the other hand, had made it very clear he was not my biggest fan. That was okay, though, because I wasn't here to make friends. Besides, he had me to thank for that shiner.

When I'd first arrived at Crane's cottage—better known as Coalition Headquarters on this side of the border—three days ago, my welcome had been anything but. On the trip there, I'd decided my best chance at survival was to surrender to the first soldier I encountered and cross my fingers he didn't use me for target practice. Jared had been that soldier. After the butt of his gun had jabbed into my kidney one too many times, I snapped. In hindsight, starting a fight when I was so seriously outnumbered had been poor judgment, particularly because it ended with me eating dirt.

Watching Jared wince and tentatively finger his bruised cheekbone made the memory a little more pleasant, though.

My sudden appearance in the woods threw off the normally regimented day-to-day business at the cottage. The offer I made Crane, my inside knowledge of TOXIC in exchange for rescuing Erik, had nearly started a riot. Absolute loyalty to their President was the only reason that Crane's soldiers hadn't mutinied when he announced his intention to attack Tramblewood Correctional Facility, the prison where TOXIC Director, Danbury "Mac" Mc-Donough, was holding Erik.

I'd felt the skepticism in our first strategy meeting. Few of the soldiers had understood why Crane was willing to risk so many lives to save just one. Even after he'd explained that, in addition to Erik, we'd be rescuing the soldiers TOXIC had taken hostage during the Coalition's attack on Rittenhouse Research Facility to save Penny, only a handful thought the pros of the strike outweighed the cons. It was hearing Penny's story that had erased their doubts and replaced them with fierce determination. The torture she'd suffered at Mac's hands, and the reasons behind that torture, were strong motivators.

There was an open seat across from Janelle, Jared, and the curly-haired boy, whose name began with an M. I think. As much as I liked Janelle, I had no desire to spend the cross-country flight absorbing the spitefulness leaking off of Jared. My nerves were already frayed from the never-ending parade of horrific images of Mac beating Erik unconscious that I saw every time I closed my eyes. Any additional ugly thoughts were likely to sever them completely. So, I continued up the aisle towards an empty space at the end of one row, closest to the cockpit.

A moment later, I regretted my decision when Frederick Kraft squeezed in beside me.

"Not too much longer now," he said as he lowered the harness over his head.

I ignored his attempt at idle conversation and stared straight ahead.

Frederick had arrived at the cottage a day after I had. To my complete shock, his appearance had been met with warm smiles and claps on the back. He was on a first-name basis with many of the soldiers, as well as Crane.

From the time we'd met in D.C., when Henri—the captain and third member of mine and Erik's Hunter team—first introduced us, I'd liked Frederick. He was kind and gentle and had a way of putting those around him at ease. Over the past two years, I'd come to think of Frederick as more than just Henri's boyfriend, but as my friend too. Then he'd risked his life to help me and Alex, Donavon's son, escape from TOXIC. He'd used his position as a conductor on the Underground to get us safely out of the capital and halfway across the country. Realizing that Frederick wasn't a schoolteacher like he'd told me had stung. The lie was a betrayal of my trust and our friendship. But had that been the extent of his deception, I would've gotten over it already. It was the fact that Frederick had known that Crane was as eager to talk to me as I was him, yet never told me, that caused my anger to spike whenever I thought about it. Frederick had even tried to dissuade me from crossing the border and seeking out Crane. He had agreed to take me into Coalition territory, but made it clear he wasn't thrilled about doing so. His reluctance was part of why, in the end, I'd gone ahead without him. The other part was because I'd been scared for him, worried that traveling with me would paint a target on his back.

My reaction to Frederick's arrival was not one of my finer moments. Even now, while my anger was still festering, I was slightly ashamed of the way I'd blown up and all but attacked him. If Penny hadn't been there to calm me down, the situation would've escalated out of control. I was furious that Frederick could've saved me the trouble of sifting through my own diluted memories to find the cottage, that we could've reached Crane days earlier had Frederick just told me the truth, and most of all, that Erik's suffering had been prolonged because of his failure to do so.

When Frederick tried to explain he'd withheld the location of the cottage because I hadn't told him why I wanted to see Crane, my temper flared. It had felt like he was blaming me for his omission, like our mutual communication failure had been solely mine.

I'd resolved to put my personal feelings aside for the time being. As a Viewer, Frederick had a vital role in this rescue. His Talent was extremely strong, and TOXIC had trained him to use it to track people. Already he'd been viewing Erik at the prison, which was how we knew for certain that Erik was still alive. Crane's spies had provided us with holographic blueprints of Tramblewood with Erik's exact location plainly marked. I'd committed them to memory. Still, this wasn't my first mission. I'd been on enough of them to know that once we were on the ground and the fighting began, I'd be lucky if I could find my way out of a paper bag, let alone through the maze of identical hallways and staircases. I needed Frederick. More importantly, Erik needed Frederick.

"It's not too late to change your mind and stay here," Frederick said softly, mistaking my silence for concern over the rescue mission.

"Not a chance," I said coolly.

This wasn't the first time someone had suggested I stay behind. My answer never changed.

Crane and the pilot, a middle-aged woman with a long, blonde braid named Donna, were the last to board. The two of them trooped up the center aisle together, covering last minute details as they went. Crane gave me a tight smile and a small nod on his way to the cockpit.

"Doors closing," a mechanical voice announced from an unseen speaker overhead.

The whine of metal sliding against metal as the ladder retracted made me cringe. The opening in the underbelly of the hoverplane ceased to exist, and there was a faint thud when the wheels folded up into their compartments.

"Securing safety harnesses," the same androgynous mechanical voice informed us.

Air whooshed near my ears, followed by dozens of clicks as the buckles engaged. My stomach flip-flopped as the hoverplane shot skyward with gravity-defying speed. Suddenly lightheaded, I closed my eyes to stop the spinning sensation.

"Tal," Frederick began. His nervous energy made my skin tingle, and I almost felt sorry for him. Not so sorry that I was going to make this second apology any easier.

"I understand why you're upset," Frederick continued, pitching his voice low in an attempt at privacy. The gesture was pointless since his words bounced off of the rounded ceiling to find the soldiers' perked ears.

I made a very un-ladylike grunt of acknowledgment.

"I should've told you I worked with Ian. There's just so much you still don't know and—"

"Like how you were there the night my parents were murdered?" I hissed.

I opened my eyes, and finally met Frederick's sorrowful gaze. A little of my anger ebbed away. This was another point of contention between us, the one I should've been most upset over. Frederick had been part of the extraction team who, on Mac's orders, had stormed the hotel room where I was staying with my parents. The lone TOXIC survivor, Frederick had traded his silence for release papers. That was when he'd joined the Underground movement.

Calling the string of safe houses located throughout TOXIC territory the Underground was slightly misleading. Only one station was physically underground: the one in the tunnels beneath Washington, D.C. The rest of the stations were communities. Some were suburban developments with cookie-cutter homes and a façade of normal life. Others were campgrounds where inhabitants lived in tents and fed off the land. All had one agenda: protect and hide those wishing freedom from TOXIC's rule.

In my peripheral vision, I caught sight of Janelle pretending to have a conversation with the curly-haired boy—Marcel? Her head was turned so that only her profile was visible. With her rich mane twisted into a flawless bun, I was able to see her ear twitch as she eavesdropped on our exchange.

Frederick blew out a long breath. "Ian tell you that?"

"No," I said, miffed. "I worked it out on my own. Your little bedtime story about going after a child who wasn't under TOXIC's jurisdiction had me curious. I did the math and realized that mission would've been right around the time my parents were killed."

Frederick had told me the story when we were at his home at the Underground station in Kentucky—in one of the suburban neighborhoods. Had I not been so preoccupied thinking about how I was going to rescue Erik and keep Alex safe, I would've realized then that the child he'd mentioned was me. I wanted to hate him for leaving me, for letting Mac take me, for standing by while his team murdered my mom and dad. But I knew what a difficult position he'd been in. I'd been in that same position when I'd extracted Bethy, a powerful Visionary, from her home in rural Pennsylvania, and again when Mac sent me to collect Alex. The only reason I'd chosen to run with Alex was because his mother,

I must have fallen asleep, because his voice startled me. I rubbed my eyes with two balled up fists.

"Right, okay," I replied sluggishly, peering up into Crane's iridescent blue-black eyes. He returned my gaze with a blank stare. He had his game face on. "You're leading our team, right?"

We'd already been over this, of course, but I felt the need to say something, and nothing more intelligible came to mind.

"I am," Crane confirmed. "Brand has team two."

Automatically, I growled at the sound of Brand's name. Crane pretended like he hadn't heard me, but a nearly imperceptible tightening of the skin around the corners of his mouth told me he had.

Being that Brand was so young—not even thirty yet—it had surprised me to learn how heavily Crane relied on Brand's opinions, how much he trusted the younger man, how much power he'd given him. From the Coalition soldiers, Brand commanded respect and generally reeked of authority, which probably had a lot to do with why so many of many of them disliked me. Our brief acquaintance had begun just after I'd foolishly attacked Jared, right around the same time I landed face first on the ground. Things only went downhill from there. Brand ordered the soldiers to take me inside the cottage to some place he referred to as "the cage." Deciding that a cage sounded a lot like a cell—exactly what it turned out to be—I started to struggle again. For my efforts, I was rewarded with a syringe full of sedatives. When I finally regained consciousness several hours later, I was, indeed, in a cage. Brand had made good on his threat.

From there our antagonistic relationship progressed, well, antagonistically. Snarky verbal exchanges escalated to pointed barbs, which then led to physical altercations. More than once, Crane or Penny had intervened before either or both of us inflicted an injury more long-lasting than a bruise or scrape. But it was only a matter of time until one of us—me—snapped. With the Creation drug coursing through my veins, infecting my bloodstream, filling me with unnatural power, I was like a live landmine, and Brand had one foot poised and ready to set me off.

Today, though, we had a truce. The rescue mission was too dangerous for the two of us to be at odds. Crane had helped to keep the peace by assigning Brand and me to different teams, different hoverplanes, and even different missions once inside Tramble-wood. My team was responsible for rescuing Erik who, according to Crane's spies, was being held separately from the general prison population. While we were doing that, Brand's team would be freeing the soldiers taken hostage during the Coalition's attack on Rittenhouse. So, if all went well, our tenuous truce wouldn't be tested.

"You want to go over the plan one more time?" Frederick asked, drawing me back to the present.

I shook my head no. Brand had repeated it in our last meeting, over dinner the previous night, and again on the ride to the hover hangar. During the meeting, he even called upon a male soldier to repeat parts of it when Brand caught him playing with his communicator. The guy was more anal than my teachers at school. And, thanks to his unrequited crush on Penny, my limited down time at Coalition Headquarters was spent in Brand's company. Spending time with my best friend also meant spending time with the biggest pain in my ass.

The fighter jets would be the first wave of attack. Once they took out the four guard towers that ringed the prison's perimeter, the transport planes would be clear to fly in. Both teams were to rappel onto the bridge that separated Echo section—the auxiliary building where Erik was housed—from the main facility. At that point our team would head towards Echo section and Erik, while

Brand's team would go in search of the Coalition's imprisoned soldiers.

While only twenty people, twenty-three if you included Crane, Brand, and me, had been in the tactical meeting, over thirty soldiers had boarded the two transport hoverplanes. Not all of them were going to be part of the ground attack, though. Each transport hoverplane had a five-person medical team in place and ready to tend to the injured.

"Come up front with me." Crane gestured to the cockpit.

I pressed a large green button in the center of the safety harness. Simultaneously all of the buckles sprang open and I was free to wriggle my way out of the contraption. With Crane already on his way to the cockpit, I shoved the harness upward and hurried after him.

The aerodynamics on the plane were amazing, the flight was smooth, and navigating the walkway between the metal benches was easy. Lucky for me since my legs were like hot rubber and even the slightest bit of turbulence would've sent me sprawling.

The cockpit was a gleaming silver mobile command center with enough blinking lights in red, blue, green, and yellow to give me a headache. Two chairs, one for the pilot and one for the co-pilot, were in the very front behind a semicircular dash and rounded plexiglass windshield. The dash was enormous and fitted with a barrage of screens and electronic dials and gauges. I recognized the navigation system and the radar, but had no idea what the other gadgets or screens were for.

On both the far left and far right sides of the cabin were four seats—two facing forward directly across from two facing back-ward—with a square table in the center. All were empty. In the very center of the cabin were two swivel chairs and a flat screen monitor.

Crane slid into one of the swivel chairs and tapped the center of the screen. I stood next to him, peering over his shoulder. The monitor hummed to life, a blue background with two white boxes appeared on screen. Crane pressed both of his index fingers to the white boxes, holding them firmly in place for a three count. "Authorized" blinked white on the blue background before quickly being replaced by a blueprint of Tramblewood. Crane tapped the screen twice, and a holographic image of the prison shot towards us. This one was a little different than the one Brand had shown us in our strategy meetings. It had pulsing red dots crawling all over the place like fire ants.

"Heat signatures," Crane explained. "Each dot indicates one person."

"We're still like 200 miles away!" I exclaimed. TOXIC had similar technology, but nothing with quite so far a range.

"See how some of the dots are brighter than others?" Crane asked. He pointed to one blindingly bright dot that nearly burned my retinas, it was so intense.

"Yeah," I said uneasily.

"The software searches for Talent-related power surges. The stronger the Talent, the brighter the signal. It's able to locate exceptionally strong Talents from hundreds of miles away. This area is sparsely populated with very little interference, so even weak Talents register on here."

"This one," he continued, tapping that insanely bright dot again, "is most likely Erik."

I swallowed hard. Right. Erik's dot was glowing like a damned supernova because he, like Penny, had been injected with multiple Talent signatures. His power dwarfed that of those around him. I prayed he'd be able to control that power, instead of letting it control him.

I did the same with mine. "We have one job: free the Mimic. Once he's been secured, we get out. No heroics. Let Meadows and his team worry about the other hostages. This mission is dangerous enough. I don't want anyone taking unnecessary chances." He looked from one face to the next, searching for understanding in each.

"Doors open in thirty, twenty-nine, twenty-eight," the mechanical voice said over the loudspeaker.

Let the game begin, I thought. The first move was ours, and we had to be the first to score, otherwise we'd be playing catch-up. I knew enough about strategy to understand that luring your opponent into a false sense of security was a good one, and this was the closest we'd get to doing just that. After this attack, Mac would know I'd joined forces with the Coalition, with Ian Crane. He would know to expect the unexpected.

Janelle began securing ropes with carabineers to hooks dangling from the ceiling. I felt my palms grow clammy underneath the suit. My heart raced, and I tried to calm the rising hysteria in my chest. I took deep breaths through my nose and blew them out through my mouth. Frederick grabbed a newly-hung rope and offered it to me. I took it without thanking him, and secured the rope to the knife belt at my waist.

"You know how these work, right?" Frederick asked.

I nodded. I'd never rappelled out of a plane for a mission, but had learned how while pledging the Hunters.

"Ten, nine, eight," the voice called overhead.

Erik, Erik, Erik, I chanted mentally. I could do this as long I kept his face front and center in my mind. I could kill whoever stood between him and his freedom.

I positioned myself on the seam of the plane's floor. Frederick stood on one side and Crane on the other. Janelle stood directly across from me. I met her gaze. She smiled and gave me a thumbs up. The gesture made me grin. Fire burned in her marbled eyes; the flickering flames danced higher and higher the harder her adrenaline pumped. She was excited, drunk on thrill and anticipation. I opened my mind to her. I hadn't established a connection with her, but I could still touch her emotions. I drank in her exhilaration until it drowned out every last fear about what awaited us down below.

"One."

Chapter Two

THE PLANE'S UNDERBELLY burst open in a rush of cool air. Wind whipped up through the chasm with a deafening roar. Beside me, Crane jumped. Janelle followed a split second later, winking a marbled eye at me as she did. On my other side, Frederick nudged me with his elbow before making the leap. I stared down into the black abyss, squinting to locate the bridge below. The main building was aglow with orange fire from the fighter jets' missiles, but only the hoverplane's lights illuminated my target. Now or never, I told myself. Without further hesitation, I stepped over the edge and released the catch on the rope.

I dropped like a stone; the cooler air from the high altitude quickly gave way to the humidity the southern states were known for. I pursed my lips and scrunched my eyes to keep from inhaling the suffocating concoction of smoke and dust wafting from the main building of the prison. The free fall was exhilarating and for a moment, I longed to Morph into a bird and fly away from the chaos below. But before I knew it, my body jerked to an abrupt halt, my head snapping back painfully.

I blinked my eyes open. My feet dangled two feet above the slanted roof covering the bridge. A yard to my right, Crane and Janelle were crouched low with their hands protectively over their heads. I quickly unhooked the carabineer and dropped the short distance. I landed on all fours, scrambling to grip the smooth stone surface with gloved hands. Just as I'd become convinced I wasn't going to slide over the edge, a grenade detonated. Large chucks of stone erupted from the roof like a geyser. Pressing my cheek to the roof, I closed my eyes and prayed nothing would hit me in the back of the head. Bits of rubble rained down, coating the back of my suit and hair.

"Talia? You okay?" Crane's voice asked in my earpiece.

Not wanting to risk losing my tenuous grip by freeing one of my hands to respond in kind, I sent my reply mentally. *"Yeah, I think so. Nothing big hit me."*

Fingers closed around my wrists, and I was being hauled to my feet. Other hands were patting my head, dislodging dust and debris from my curls. Once I was standing, I stared up into Frederick's worried brown eyes. "You good?" he asked.

"Fine," I snapped, even as the smell of burnt hair filled my nostrils.

"Just a few singed strands," Janelle informed me. "Nothing that can't be fixed."

Great, I thought, the first time Erik sees me in a week—whoa, had all of this really happened in a week?—and I was going to look like a burn victim. I shook off the ridiculous thought; my appearance was the least of my worries.

"Let's go. Ian made a hole." Frederick began heading towards where Crane was lowering himself through the jagged opening he'd made in the roof.

Jared and the curly-haired boy—definitely Marcel, I decided—were close on his heels. The larger of the two, Jared, had trouble squeezing his wide frame through the opening and managed to snag his suit on a pointy edge. He swore loudly before dropping out of sight.

"Let me go first. Then Talia. Then you, Janelle," Frederick said, glancing to Janelle for confirmation. She nodded and Frederick descended without another word.

I opened my mouth to argue for no better reason than I was feeling disagreeable, but then remembered this wasn't about me. Every second I spent being obstinate was one more second Erik was locked in a cell.

I heard Frederick's boots hit the concrete floor with a thud a second later.

Dropping first to my knees and then my stomach, I slithered over the edge feet first and pushed off. The distance from roof to ground was farther than I'd estimated, and bolts of pain shot up through my knees when I hit bottom. There was no time to assess myself for damage because Janelle was already on her way down. Quickly I moved out of her way, my eyes sweeping the corridor for signs of trouble. Crane, Jared, and Marcel were already moving towards Echo tower, their guns drawn. Frederick stood several feet to my right and was waving me forward. I glanced over my shoulder at Janelle, who was tentatively rotating her ankle. She gave me a thumbs up, which I took to mean she wasn't actually injured.

My earpiece crackled with static. "How's it look down there?" Brand asked.

The doors to Echo section burst open, and black-clad TOXIC operatives exploded onto the bridge.

"Hostile," I hissed in reply as the firefight began.

Bullets whizzed through the air, one so close to my head that I actually heard the whistle. I dropped into a crouch, instinctively repelling the projectiles with my mind. Realizing that my efforts were doing those in front of me no good, I expanded my Talents,

"Talia, you and Frederick go. Get to Erik. We'll hold them off as long as we can, and then follow," Crane's voice filled my head.

"Affirmative," I sent back before relaying the order to Frederick.

Together, we sprinted for the doorway. As we approached, Frederick slowed and drew his gun, gesturing for me to do the same. He held one finger to his lips in the universal sign for "be quiet." I let him take the lead as we crept forward. I focused on my senses, expanding all of them simultaneously. The slight shuffling of nervous feet on concrete, heavy breathing, accelerated beating of several hearts. Four guards. I tapped Frederick on the shoulder and held up four fingers to let him know. He nodded that he understood. Then he pointed at the automatic weapon still strapped on my back. Rotating the gun, I placed my finger on the trigger and flipped the safety.

Fredrick picked up a piece of ceiling that had broken off when I'd blown up the other half of the bridge. He threw it through the open doorway and into the darkened hallway beyond. Two guards materialized immediately. They fired without hesitation, but I caught the bullets with my mind before they came anywhere close to me or Frederick.

Frederick returned fire, but apparently I wasn't the only telekinetic in this fight. His bullets didn't reach their targets either. I opened my mind and latched on to the two men I could see. They both fell to their knees, clasping their ears. I knew the pain they were experiencing was horrendous. One curled into the fetal position and writhed in agony. The other met my eyes, his baby blues holding my purple gaze. He reminded me of Donavon.

A sick feeling started in my stomach, rising to my chest and gripping my lungs. These were TOXIC operatives. I'd already sent so many to their deaths, and now I was staring into this prison guard's eyes and torturing him. Was I really any better than Mac? Wasn't I abusing my power as a means to an end?

A trickle of blood leaked between the blue-eyed guard's fingers from the ears he was cupping. I did the most merciful thing I could think of: I took over his mind and made him pass out.

The other two guards I'd felt moved into view as Frederick and I passed through the doorway. Recognition slapped me across the face: one of the guards was Desmond.

I'd met Desmond the previous week. Erik had introduced us. They had been friends at school. Rage consumed me. Knowing that Desmond was one of Erik's jailers made me physically ill. I charged past Frederick as gunfire erupted in the corridor. I threw the bullets aside and let loose an inhuman scream as I launched myself through the air at Desmond.

"Tal, no!" Frederick screamed behind me.

I ignored his plea. In that moment nothing mattered but avenging the betrayal. When my hands collided with Desmond's chest, they were actually paws. I had Morphed into the wolf. Primal instincts took over, and I snapped at his face and neck. I should've been more concerned about the other guard, but I wasn't.

Desmond was strong, and recovered quickly after his initial shock at seeing me Morph. He threw me off of him. My back collided with something hard, a wall, I thought. Pain shot up my spine, and stars danced across my vision. I raised a hand to my head and realized that I'd changed back to human.

Desmond advanced towards me, his gun pointed at my head. I froze. Time seemed to stand still, silence deafened my ears. My eyes narrowed on the barrel, and suddenly I was back in the basement of Crane's Nevada home. I couldn't think straight. Part of me knew what I had to do, but my muscles didn't want to work. Instead, I sat, frozen as an ice sculpture.

The crack of gunpowder shattered the silence, and I screamed: a bloodcurdling, window-shattering scream. Pain shot out in a starburst from my side. My hands flew to the wound, hoping to staunch the flow of blood. I continued screaming, despite the raw feeling in my throat.

Strong hands pulled mine away from my wound.

"You're okay, Talia," a voice whispered soothingly in my ear. "You're okay."

I looked down at my side. The material was still intact. No blood soaked through my suit. I looked at my shaking hands. They were dry too.

"You're okay," Crane repeated, pulling me to my feet.

I peered over Crane's shoulder to where Janelle, Marcel, and Jared stood. Marcel was scratched and bleeding, and had what looked like fang marks on the side of his throat. Jared had added a lot more bruises to the collection I'd given him. And Janelle was favoring her left leg. But they were still alive. I was shocked by how relieved that made me.

Frederick crossed from where he'd been kneeling next to Desmond's body. "He's dead," he said flatly.

Get a grip, Talia, I chastised myself. That lapse in composure had nearly cost me my life. Had Crane hesitated before firing, I'd be dead. I shook off the thought. No time for what-ifs. Move forward.

Erik was so close now. Just as I'd told Crane I would, I felt him. The overabundance of power he'd been given was calling to me. *"I'm coming, Erik,"* I sent, just in case he was listening.

"There should be a stairwell ahead on the left," Crane said. He had out a portable communicator and was consulting the prison's blueprints. "Talia, can you tell whether there are more guards nearby?"

I took a deep breath and concentrated. There was a lot of brain activity in Echo section. Most of it in the lower levels, though. Above us, there were only a handful of minds. Five, maybe six or seven. It was hard to be sure since the signals I was getting were fuzzy, like the reception was bad or my antenna needed fine-tuning. But one signal came through louder and clearer than all the rest: Erik.

My heart was so light I felt like it would float right out of my chest. He was alive. I started to run in the direction of the stairwell Crane had indicated.

"Talia?" Crane called after me.

I didn't slow. Erik was drawing me to him like a magnet, and I wouldn't have been able to change direction had I wanted to. But I didn't want to. All I wanted was to see him, touch him, hold him.

"Talia?" Crane called again.

Four sets of feet were running down the hallway after me.

"No guards," I called over my shoulder. "I'm pretty sure it's only prisoners from this level up. The brain patterns feel like the people are drugged or something."

The door to the stairwell was exactly where Crane thought it should be. I jogged up the two flights with Crane and the others trailing close behind. The closer I got to Erik's cell, the stronger the pull was. Exceptionally powerful Talents always had this effect on me. Truthfully, they had this effect on a lot of people—Talented or not. But I'd never felt a pull this strong. It was like I was a fish who'd taken the bait and was being reeled in, hook, line, and sinker.

Part of me knew this attraction to Erik wasn't normal, and that fact should've scared me. Being a Mimic, he didn't emit an essence the way I did. It was only because Mac had injected him with so many Talent signatures that he did now. I tried not to think of the implications of that.

At the landing, I reached for where the door handle should have been, and came up empty. The door was one solid sheet of metal. No window and no handle. Next to the door, at roughly eye-level for someone of normal height, was a retinal scanner. The stairwells were designed so anyone could enter, but only authorized personnel could exit.

"Shit," Jared swore.

"Maybe it will work for Natalia?" Marcel suggested.

"My clearance wasn't high enough before I left. No way that door will open for me now," I said, trying not to sound as defeated as I felt.

"If it does, we're walking into a trap," Janelle pointed out.

I glanced over my shoulder and met Crane's dark gaze. Contemplative was the only way to describe his expression. Curious, I swiped his mind. He was mulling over our limited options. He dismissed one idea, discarding it into the improbable pile. I, however, thought it was genius, and wanted to make an attempt.

"I can do it," I sent him confidently.

Crane's thoughts were doubtful, which irritated me until I realized why. In his eyes, I was still the little girl who'd witnessed her parents' murders. My irritation dimmed a little.

"Ian, I can do it," I repeated, more forcefully this time. I also didn't give him the opportunity to disagree.

Exhaling, I plucked an image from my mental database – one I knew as well as my own reflection. Eyes the color of the sky on a cloudless day filled my mind. I concentrated all of my energy on duplicating those baby blue eyes—Donavon's eyes—down to the minutest detail. The Morph was small, so slight that only a faint pressure in my eye sockets told me it was taking place.

I stood on tiptoes in front of the retinal scanner, and tried not to blink while a thin, red beam scanned from left to right and back again across my eyeball. At first, nothing happened. My heart sank. God, I really sucked at this Morphing thing. Then, to my astonishment, the airlock released and the door swung outward.

"Impressive," Janelle whistled when I turned to grin stupidly at the group. The victory was small, but outsmarting Mac felt empowering. And Janelle was right. The Morph might have been small, but it was impressive, particularly since the Talent was new to me. Human to human Morphs were, for whatever reason, extremely difficult for most Morphers. In fact, I didn't personally know any who'd managed it.

I blinked three times in rapid succession, and the pressure returned for a split second while my irises darkened to their normal deep purple.

Strangely, there was no one standing on the opposite side of the door. No guards. No Mac. Their notable absence sent shivers down my spine. Did I dare hope we'd gotten lucky?

The room beyond the door was small and circular. Five doors lined the walls, and yet another hallway branched off at an angle. Immediately Frederick ran to one of the doors.

"He's in here," he said excitedly, tugging on the handle.

This one didn't budge either. But there were no biometric security measures in place here. It was an old-fashioned lock and key door. Of course, we didn't have a key, but that was not necessary.

I stepped forward to join Frederick and concentrated my energy. Within seconds the door exploded. Splinters of wood rained down on me, but I didn't care. I didn't hesitate. I burst into the small stone room. I recognized it immediately; it was the same room I'd seen in the drawing Alex had made while we were at the Underground station in D.C. My eyes darted around the darkened space, seeking out Erik's dark hair. A strangled yelp that sounded much like a dying animal escaped my lips when my gaze landed on a small cot pushed against the back wall. Equal parts relief, joy, and fury filled me.

Erik was lying with an arm flung over his head, the visible skin dark with a mixture of filth and bruises. Dirty hair hung in clumps over his face, shielding it from view. He didn't so much as stir at the onslaught of light and visitors to his cell. Intuitively, I knew he was alive. I felt him, felt his off-the-charts brain activity. Yet, it wasn't until his finger twitched that I truly believed I wasn't staring at his corpse. Tears sprang to my eyes, and I didn't wipe them away. I didn't care if Crane or whoever else saw me crying and thought me weak. I'd never been so happy in my life.

No one had followed me inside. Whether this was out of respect or they worried I'd lose it if he was dead and didn't want to be in such confined quarters with me should that happen, I didn't know or care. I heard the opening and closing of doors and muffled grunts from the circular room, and paid no attention. Whatever was happening out there no longer concerned me.

Slowly I approached the bed so as not to startle him. I knelt beside it. As gently as possible, I brushed the matted black hair back from his forehead. I nearly swallowed my tongue when I saw his face. A jagged cut ran the length of his brow. One eye was so swollen that it looked like a golf ball protruded from the socket. His bottom lip was torn completely through.

Tears poured down my cheeks, blurring the battered face that was still beautiful, if only to me. I ran my fingertips over his cheek, pressing my lips to his temple. I stroked his hair and moaned his name. The wounds will heal, I reminded myself. At least, these physical ones would.

"Am I dreaming? Because if so, this is the worst dream yet. Usually you're naked."

"Erik!" I exclaimed, pulling back to look at him. His better eye opened, a slit of turquoise peeking out from under the swollen lid.

"Shhh, don't talk, Tals. The good ones never last long," he mumbled, managing a grotesque imitation of a smile. He put an arm around me and weakly tried pulling me onto the bed with him.

"Erik, you need to get up!" I yelled. "We have to go."

"Just come here," he begged. "I never get to hold you."

He thought I was a dream, or a vision, or a hallucination. I had to make him understand. I needed to get him out of here. Had his face been in better shape, I might have slapped him into consciousness. As it was, I worried that would only injure him further.

"Erik, look at me," I demanded, taking control of his mind now that he was fully awake. He obeyed, staring at me with one unfocused eye. *"I'm here to get you, but I can't carry you. Can you walk?"* I didn't need for him to answer; I already knew he couldn't. Somewhere in his head he knew that at least one of his legs was broken.

"Frederick!" I screamed. I needed help. Erik couldn't walk, and I couldn't support his weight alone. "Ian! Jared!" Honestly, I didn't care who came to my aid as long as someone did.

"I'm here, Tal," Frederick called from the ruined doorway.

"Help me!"

I heard footsteps, and then hands pulled me away from Erik. I looked up: Crane.

"We'll get him. Go help the others," Crane told me.

Frederick and Crane grabbed Erik under the armpits. I arranged Erik's arms around their shoulders. His eyes had closed again, but he mumbled something incoherently. I put my ear close to his mouth.

"Talia, Talia, Talia," he moaned my name over and over again.

"I'm right here," I promised him. Fresh tears poured down my face and dripped from my chin. *"I love you."*

"Go, Talia," Frederick ordered. I didn't want to leave Erik. He needed me. Frederick must've seen the hesitancy on my face. "We won't make it out of here if you don't cover us," he said gently. I knew he was right, but I almost didn't care. I just wanted to touch Erik, be close to him.

I kissed Erik's forehead, tasting the blood from his cut. Then I turned and went to check the main room. Marcel, Janelle, and Jared were attempting to break down the other cell doors.

"Stand back," I ordered and concentrated my energy. Four doors burst apart in unison, just as Erik's had done. Prisoners stumbled out of the rooms in varying states of disarray. Some were just dirty and frail, but others sported bruises and cuts of various ages. All looked dazed and disoriented.

Jared offered one of his spare weapons to a man clad in a dingy gray jumpsuit with a number stamped on the front, who he addressed as Tad. Janelle began unsheathing knives from her belt and handing them out like party favors to all of our new recruits. I wasn't sure whether any of them were Coalition soldiers, but she didn't discriminate.

My earpiece crackled to life around my neck, and I expected to hear Brand screaming angry nothings at me. "Alpha team, I need an ETA," came a woman's distant voice. "I'm in position above Echo tower. Enemy is launching a counter airstrike. I can't hold the position long. Repeat, I can't hold the position long."

I looked to Janelle, Marcel, and Jared for guidance. Janelle touched her earpiece. "Donna, we're on our way now. Five minutes. Can you hold for that long?"

"Affirmative. Five minutes," Donna responded.

Janelle turned to Jared. "You and Marcel take the prisoners and head to the roof. I'll stay behind with Talia in case there's company. Get everyone on the hover."

Jared and Marcel both nodded and headed for the stairwell. I watched the group of vagabond soldiers go. None of them appeared to be in shape for a fight, but they were determined; I felt that radiating off of all of them. Hopefully, they wouldn't encounter any trouble between here and the roof.

Frederick and Crane emerged from the cell with Erik still between them.

"Let's head for the roof." Crane looked at me. "Talia, you take lead. Janelle, cover us from behind."

I nodded. This arrangement was not ideal. With Frederick and Crane indisposed, Janelle and I would be the only defense. Unfortunately, this was our only option.

The five of us moved as quickly as we could manage up the stairs. I expanded my senses again so I'd be alerted at the first sign of company. Faint screams were coming from somewhere deep within the walls. I stopped at the first landing and closed my eyes to better focus my energy and locate the source.

"What is it?" Crane asked from somewhere below me.

"I hear someone," I replied, without opening my eyes. "Not guards," I added quickly. "I... I think it's another prisoner."

"There are a lot of other prisoners. We don't have time to get them all," Frederick grunted.

I nodded. He was right. The deal had been for Erik and Crane's people, nothing more. I started climbing to the next level. The screams grew louder, the words more distinct. I wanted to block them. Guilt at leaving this person behind was eating away at my gut. He, and I knew it was a "he" by the timbre of his voice, didn't deserve to spend the rest of his life in prison. He chanted his name over and over again, and there was no longer a choice for me. I had to free him. I owed his sister that much.

"Janelle, switch places with me," I called over my shoulder.

"Talia, we don't have time for this," Frederick said.

I glanced to where Erik's head was lolling against Crane's shoulder. No, we didn't have time for this. But Cadence had helped Erik rescue his family. There was no way I'd be able to live with myself if I gave up the opportunity to repay the favor.

Janelle was already brushing past Frederick, Crane, and Erik to assume the lead.

"Go. I'll be right behind you," I told them.

Crane was reluctant at first, but I'd put enough force behind my words that he soon complied. I waited until all four of them had reached the next landing. Then, I placed my hand on the cold stone wall and opened my mind. I felt a strong buzzing deep within. The prisoner was calling for help. "My name is Randy Choi. Please don't leave me here," he screamed over and over again.

His cell was not close to the stairwell the way Erik's had been. Rather, it was deep within the maze of hallways. As much as I wanted to free him, navigating through the prison would take too much time, and I was unwilling to leave Frederick, Erik, and Crane without backup.

I made a snap decision. One that I wasn't even sure was possible. I would try, though. Concentrating every ounce of energy I possessed on my telekinetic powers, I closed my eyes, envisioned blowing a hole from where I stood, through tons of stone, concrete, steel, and whatever else, to Randy's cell. Power, hot and electrifying, traveled from my mind, down my shoulder, until it reached my hand. It burst forth from my fingertips and into the wall with a sharp crackle and pop. The air seemed to still for just a second before a terrific explosion of stone and concrete erupted beneath my touch.

I stared down at my hand, shocked and relieved that the gamble had paid off.

"Talia?" Crane screamed in my head. "What happened? Are you okay?"

"Fine, Ian," I sent back. "I'm on my way up now."

The rubble and dust settled, and a gaping hole now stood where my hand had been moments earlier. Slowly, a dark form materialized in the blackened depths of the opening. The closer it came, the larger it got. I didn't move, even though I knew I was wasting time. Finally, the person was close enough that the stairwell's dim light illuminated his Asian features. I swallowed hard.

"Randy Choi?" I asked, knowing full well he was. I'd have recognized him from his personnel file even if he hadn't been chanting his name along with his plea for rescue. He had a dark, scraggly beard that covered gaunt, sunken-in cheeks. His gray jumpsuit hung loosely on his too thin frame.

"I'm a friend of your sister," I added for good measure. Not that I truly thought he cared who rescued him as long as someone did, but I hoped the news would light a fire under his butt and he'd move a little faster.

"Cadence." His voice was hoarse, most likely from the combination of screaming for the last however long and disuse.

I nodded and offered him a small smile. "Yeah, Cadence," I said. Then, I turned and headed for the roof, calling over my shoulder, "We need to hurry."

Randy fell in step with me halfway to the next landing. His legs were much longer than mine, but I was still surprised he was able to move so fast. I doubted a four by four cell allowed for any type of exercise and judging by Randy's pallor, he hadn't seen the sun in quite some time. I refrained from comment. I didn't want to waste any breath talking.

Two flights later we reached an open door leading out onto the roof. It was propped open with cinderblock, and warm air was blowing in from outside. Absently, I noticed that this door, too, was devoid of a handle. I considered that, and filed it away under things to worry about later.

I stepped through the doorway first, followed closely by Randy. Frederick had Erik strapped to him, and Crane and Janelle were busy securing the two of them into a harness so that they could be hauled back into the transport plane hovering overhead. Crane looked up when he heard us exit. When he saw Randy, he nodded to him. Whether the two men actually knew each other, I had no idea.

Randy stumbled forward, panting from the run up the stairs, and grabbed a dangling harness, deftly working his way into it.

"Hurry, Talia. The others are already aboard," Crane sent.

"I want to wait until Erik goes up," I replied tightly. No way was I risking a last minute attack. I'd stand guard until he was safely on the plane.

Crane didn't fight me. He seemed to share my concern and waited with me.

Once Frederick had both himself and Erik in the harness, he tugged three times on the rope giving the command to bring them up. Randy followed a moment later. All three of them shooting into the night sky like missiles. As soon as they were gone, a weight seemed to lift from my chest. He was safe. I'd done it. No, I corrected myself, *we'd* done it. Without Crane, this wouldn't have been possible. I owed him.

Crane and I started securing ourselves into the remaining harnesses when a figure burst onto the roof. His gun was drawn and aimed directly at me. I froze. This time, not out of fear.

"Talia, go!" Crane yelled.

I ignored the order and stared into the clear blue eyes of Donavon McDonough. He wouldn't hurt me, I knew that without a doubt. The gun he held was for show. His finger wasn't even on the trigger. I reached out to him mentally, and scanned his thoughts.

Indecision warred in his mind, but the choice he was trying to make wasn't whether to shoot or not. He wanted to come with us, wanted to run away from the life he'd been born into. But obligation and duty to TOXIC and his father had been hammered into him since birth, and leaving this life behind was not a step he was ready to take.

"*Donavon, please come with us,*" I urged him. I considered using my will to force him into submission, but that felt wrong. Going against his father was a decision he needed to make for himself. He certainly wouldn't thank me for taking the choice from him.

"*Get out of here, Tal. Get out of the country, if you can. They'll hunt you to the ends of the earth if need be.*"

"*Donavon,*" I pleaded again.

He shook his head and pursed his lips. "*Go, Natalia.*"

I felt Crane's gaze on me, silently questioning what he should do. Instead of verbally responding, I tugged my rope and began zipping upward. I kept my eyes locked with Donavon's as long as possible, and then continued to stare down at his shrinking form once eye contact was no longer possible. He stood on the roof of Tramblewood, watching me walk out of his life for yet another time. There was a finality that hadn't been there before. He'd made his choice, and I'd made mine. We would fight on opposite sides in this war. I hoped when it was over we'd both be able to live with our decisions.

Chapter Three

THE METAL DOORS clanged shut and the plane was darting forward before I had a chance to untangle myself from the harness. My fingers felt too thick, were too clumsy, and the process took longer than it should have. Cursing, I tripped over the jumble of ropes before finally freeing myself. I raced to the back of the plane, shoving past Janelle and Jared in my haste to reach Erik.

Thin, yet shockingly strong arms circled my waist from behind.

"Get off of me," I growled.

"Let them do their job," Frederick replied calmly, his mouth so close to my ear his breath tickled my neck. I struggled against his hold, kicking and clawing like a wild animal. "You'll just be in the way," he muttered.

Part of me knew he was right. But I could ease Erik's suffering, dull his pain, like he'd done for me on so many occasions. No, I decided, the best place for me was by his side.

While Frederick was stronger than I'd given him credit for, he was no match for either my strength or my manic need to touch Erik. A well-placed boot heel to the side of Frederick's knee and I was able to break free. The medical team was crowded around Erik's stretcher, one young woman barking orders with the authority of a drill sergeant. Machines and contraptions were produced as if by magic as the team assessed the situation.

An explosion rocked the plane, and I stumbled sideways, my shoulder slamming into the wall of the aircraft. My brain barely registered the pain, my nerve-endings unreceptive to any sensation that interfered with my need to reach Erik. The medics blocking my view shifted with the plane, and I caught my first glimpse of Erik in the harsh neon glow of the overhead lights.

I gasped at the sight of his naked torso. Erik's chest looked like a black and red checkerboard, complete with misshapen lumps for playing pieces. Bands of shiny, raw skin ringed his biceps and wrists from where he'd been restrained with ropes or too-tight metal cuffs. Track marks covered both of his hands, his wrists, forearms, and even the side of his neck, creating a giant constellation of red stars across his ashen skin.

A second eruption, this time from below, sent me pitching forward several paces, and into the back of a short, squat medic readying a syringe. He grunted as the female medic who appeared to be in charge grabbed my arm to steady me. Any other time I would have thanked her, at least acknowledged her. Not then, not when my eyes were glued to Erik.

"Oh god, no!" I cried, reaching past the medic with the needle to take Erik's limp hand.

"You need to stay back, miss," the woman in charge told me. She wasn't unkind, but the tone of her voice suggested that disobedience wouldn't be tolerated.

Ignoring her subtle warning, I curled my gloved fingers around Erik's. Through the thin suit material, his skin felt normal, but the easy way our hands slid apart when the woman drew me backwards told me it was clammy with sweat.

42

Daring to pull my gaze from Erik, I looked up at the female medic and snarled. We were nearly the same height, my boots bringing me almost level with her hazel eyes. I gave her a withering glare, anticipating she would wilt like the delicate flower she appeared to be. Only, like me, her size was misleading. Despite being a waif of a woman, when she straightened her spine and said, "Do you want him to die?" I was the one who wilted. Her tone wasn't cold or impersonal, just matter-of-fact.

"Then go sit up front," she continued when I didn't answer her rhetorical question.

With one last glance at the love of my life, I turned to go, praying that this no-nonsense woman was as capable a doctor as her confident demeanor suggested.

"Tals?" His low, raspy whisper was music to my ears.

I spun to see Erik, eyelids fluttering spastically as he made a feeble attempt to sit up. Alarmed by the sudden movement, the medic that I'd crashed into aimed his needle towards the crook of Erik's elbow. In response, Erik's hand shot upwards, and his fingers clamped around the man's windpipe. I watched in horror as the same fingers that were always so gentle when they touched me, so soft when they held me, squeezed until the short man's face turned beet red and his dark eyes bulged like a frog's.

"Erik, no," I breathed, even as he lifted the medic off of the ground far enough that the man's feet dangled in empty air.

The female doctor and I reacted in unison. She went for her colleague and I went for Erik's mind. Frantic, terrified thoughts raced through his head: fight, protect, kill. All around him, Erik saw danger. Each of the medics in their scrubs reminded him of the doctors at Tramblewood. My presence wasn't having the calming effect I'd hoped for. Instead, it thrust Erik's protective instinct into high gear.

There was no time to be gentle. I took complete control of Erik, mind, body, and will. Being so weak, the fragile resistance he put forth was easier to squash than a bug. Different factions of his brain played tug of war with one another, with no one faction being strong enough to fight the intrusion. I forced him to release his grip on the medic's throat. The man dropped to his knees, gulping air by the lungful. Erik's adrenaline was pumping so fast that *my* hands started to shake as a result. His heart pummeled his ribs from the inside, as if demanding to be set free. I began siphoning his panic, drawing more and more of it into me until I felt his emotions start to go numb. My own pulse spiked. I allowed my canines to lengthen until their tips pierced my bottom lip. The sharp burst of pain, mingled with the iron tang of my blood, helped me to remain focused.

Meanwhile, the female doctor had freed the needle from the medic's hand and prepared to stab Erik with it. Trembling from nerves, she tried to maneuver the syringe into position over a vein in his arm. She met my gaze over the stretcher, silently asking whether he was going to attack her too. I shook my head and moved closer to the stretcher and Erik's side. His turquoise eyes were cloudy with confusion, and when he repeated my name, it came out as a question.

"I'm right here," I assured him, my voice choked with emotion.

His eyes darted frantically from left to right and back again, never lingering on any one thing for more than a nanosecond. Strong-willed and prideful as Erik was, he began to fight me for control of his mind. Agitation and anger over being stripped of his free will caused him to emit a guttural growl that sent the female doctor scurrying backwards. While I was fairly confident that Erik was no match for me mentally, I didn't want to test that theory.

"Do it," I hissed at the female doctor, nodding towards the needle she had clutched in her fist.

Mustering a smile for Erik's benefit, I leaned down and smoothed back the dark hair clinging to his forehead. "It's okay," I soothed. "You're gonna be okay." With my touch, I willed him to relax further.

"You came," Erik murmured, the two words slurring together to become one. "He said you would."

I had a good idea of who "he" was. And I hoped "he" was kicking himself now. Despite Mac's best efforts, I'd still rescued Erik. The smug satisfaction I felt was lessened when I recalled the lack of security surrounding Erik's cell. I had a bad feeling that I might be the one kicking myself soon.

"I'll always come for you," I sent Erik.

I held his gaze, wanting my face to be the last thing he saw before he lost consciousness. Erik's eyelids began to droop and like a child fighting bedtime, he tried to hold them up. The doctor inched forward and with a practiced hand finally inserted the needle. Erik winced slightly as she depressed the plunger, injecting a strong sedative into his bloodstream. The drug took effect instantaneously. I'd become so immersed in Erik that warmth seemed to spread through my veins, followed by a leaden sensation that made my limbs feel heavy and my mind sluggish. Erik and I both welcomed the chemical haze and the brief moment of drug-induced euphoria that occurred just before his eyes closed and the connection severed.

My knees buckled, and I had to grip the stretcher with my free hand to stay upright. My brain ricocheted off the sides of my skull like a ping pong ball. I clenched my teeth as a powerful wave of dizziness crashed over me. The mental energy it had taken to control Erik was more than I'd realized. Being strong-willed, Erik's barriers had been harder to break down than most. All I wanted was to sit and make the room stop spinning.

"Talia! Are you okay?" Crane exclaimed, coming to my aid. He looped his arm around my waist to support me.

"We've got it from here," the female doctor added, nodding encouragingly.

I let Crane drag me back from the stretcher, but I refused to turn my gaze from Erik's bruised face. Pain caused my stomach muscles to spasm uncontrollably. I doubled over, crying out. Crane's grip on me tightened, and I leaned against him.

I watched as the medics began peeling away Erik's remaining clothes. That word didn't even really apply to the tattered scraps of material left on him. His body had gone limp, his muscles unresponsive. It was for the best, subconsciously I knew that. Still, seeing him so helpless made my chest ache.

"Come on, let's go sit down," Crane said gently.

I didn't want to leave. I wanted to stay with Erik, but knew I'd only be in the way. For the time being, I'd done all I could do to help him. Now, he was in the medics' hands. Their ministrations and Erik's will to live would have to be enough.

Crane led me past the metal benches, now lined with Coalition soldiers and refugees from Tramblewood. A Coalition man I didn't know was bent over Frederick, applying something that smelled like disinfectant to the gashes on his face. He gave me a small half-smile as I passed. Next to him, Janelle winced as Jared spread burn cream over the right side of her neck. Others had first aid kits out tending to injuries that, while not life threatening, needed medical attention.

Instead of placing me in a seat in the main bay of the plane, Crane led me to the cockpit and gestured to the sitting area to the left of the entrance. I settled into a cushy armchair, letting my head fall against the headrest. I closed my eyes, now heavy with exhaustion, and silently prayed to anyone listening to save Erik's life.

I felt Crane's presence as he eased himself down beside me. I was no longer on an adrenaline high, and I'd used so much mental energy that I couldn't have erected my mental walls had my life depended on it. However, I also found that I really didn't care if Crane knew my thoughts. My display beside Erik's sickbed had clearly shown everyone watching where my head was.

In the cockpit, the soldiers' voices were muted, and most of the sound came in the form of beeps and buzzes from the navigation system. It was hard to concentrate on any one conversation, and more than anything I needed a distraction. I'd have liked to lose myself into the sweet oblivion of sleep, but my mind was humming too loudly for that to be a viable option. So, I decided to talk.

"Have you heard from Brand? Was his team able to get all your people out? Did they encounter a lot of trouble?" I peppered Crane with questions. My eyelids felt too heavy to hold open, so I let them droop as I spoke.

Crane sighed, measured his words. "Things could've gone worse," he said finally.

When the Coalition President failed to elaborate, I pressed. "How much worse?"

"A lot. Brand's team landed in the main courtyard just fine. It took them longer than anticipated to reach the cell block with our people. The route they took had more obstacles."

I cringed. The cell block with the Coalition hostages was in the rear of the main building, close to the bridge. The bridge I'd destroyed. That was why both teams had planned to land there originally.

"There were causalities," Crane was saying gravely.

"Who?" I asked, the pain in my stomach intensifying under the heavy guilt weighing it down.

At least now Brand had a legitimate reason to hate me, I thought dryly.

"Pat Asure and Link Mahoney," Crane said.

Neither name sounded familiar. I tied to recall the faces of the soldiers who'd gathered in the command center for our strategy meetings. Regret mingled with the guilt when I realized that I hadn't bothered to pay enough attention then to conjure up a single image now.

"Good men," Crane added.

"Ian, I'm—"

"You don't have any reason to be sorry, Talia. They knew the risks. Mahoney even volunteered for this mission. Besides, at least five of my people are going home to families who thought they'd never see their loved ones again." He paused, and I felt his eyes burning holes through my suit. "But it's not just about the people we rescued from Tramblewood, Talia. This mission has far-reaching implications. Tonight, we showed TOXIC we are serious, that we won't let them bully us any longer. And, we're one step closer to proving to the world that TOXIC has been using the Creation drug, which means we're one step closer to stopping them."

His sentiments eased my lingering guilt. Crane was right. With Erik, Penny, and I, the Coalition had irrefutable proof that TOXIC was creating Talents.

Proof was the second reason Crane had agreed to the rescue mission.

After Penny recounted her appalling tale of torture and testing while in TOXIC's custody, Crane had given me a history lesson on the Creation drug.

The United Nations International Talent Education Division (UNITED) had banned the use of the drug over a decade ago, after their own research hit a brick wall. Unlike Mac, their primary concern hadn't been over the short period in which most recipients exhibited Talent, but rather the long-term side-effects.

Natural Talents learn to cope with the power that accompanies their gifts, from a young age. Even before Talents truly manifest, you know they're there, just below the surface, separated from you by an invisible barrier that you can't seem to cross. And while it has never been proven, I've always believed that the Talented are born with an extra gene or whatever that helps them control the power. Sometimes the combination of genetics and learned behavior isn't enough, and your Talent is your undoing. The power builds and builds inside of you until you think your skin might rip open to release it. With no outlet, the abundance of power begins to erode your mind, and eventually there's nothing left in your skull but mush.

Nearly a century after the Great Contamination, it was rare to find a Talent strong enough that the whole brain mush phenomenon was a real concern. Well, rare to find a natural born Talent with that much power, anyhow.

UNITED referred to them as the Created, the man-made, genetically engineered Talents who resulted from the Creation drug.

UNITED had encountered the same problem with the Creation drug that Mac's medical research team had. Knowing no better, they administered repeat injections to their test subjects to see if that made the Talents stick, so to speak, for longer. It worked, sort of. The recipients' Talents lasted for weeks after the second injection, months after a third, and so on and so forth. Soon though, UNITED's research team realized a direct correlation between the number of injections and brain deterioration. Even the subjects injected just once had holes in their brains. It was determined that their bodies weren't equipped with the ability to handle the manufactured power.

Switching gears, UNITED had next enlisted Talented test subjects to see whether they fared better with the drug since they were already Talented. This, too, sort of worked. The hybrid Talented-Created showed less deterioration and sustained their engineered powers for longer, but they still weren't completely immune to the side-effects. It was after this avenue lead nowhere good that UNITED shut down the project and banned the drug.

Crane had strong allies within UNITED, many of whom were only too happy to help bring down TOXIC over the use of the Creation drug. But, they needed proof that they were using it. Penny and I alone were probably proof enough, but Erik would be icing on the cake.

Once we provided them with proof, UNITED would intervene and Mac would have to answer for illegal experimentation, genetic engineering, and generally being an asshole.

But will he have to answer for killing your parents? a voice in my mind asked. Once UNITED became involved, I worried my window for revenge would close. Sure, Mac would serve time in prison for his crimes against humanity. Was that enough, though? After my parents' murders, I'd vowed vengeance: a life for a life. How would I feel if that never occurred?

"Ian?" a high-pitched female voice called, dragging me out of my thoughts. Crane and I both turned to look at her.

She appeared young, no more than twenty-five, with pale jade eyes and hair the color of wheat. She wore a gray scrub top over black and white camo pants and heavy combat boots. I thought she might have been one of the medics attending to Erik, but wasn't positive.

"Can I speak with you?" she asked. Her eyes darted pointedly in my direction, and I knew whatever she had to tell him was not good news.

Ian followed her line of sight, his gaze steady when our eyes met. "You might as well tell me here, Cheryl," he said, but he didn't break eye contact with me.

"Sir, I really think that—" Cheryl started to say, but Crane cut her off.

"She's a mind reader with exceptional hearing," he inclined his head in my direction, "There's no point in us speaking privately."

Cheryl seemed unconvinced, but didn't argue further. She swallowed hard, and seemed to measure her words before she spoke. A cold sweat began to spread across my skin, coating first my face, then my arms and legs with a thin layer of ice.

"Four of his ribs are broken. The internal damage is... extensive. But it's the blood loss that's really troubling. He needs a transfusion," she finally said. Cheryl looked at Crane, and Crane looked at me.

"Will he be... okay, until we get back to California?" My throat was so tight that I was surprised the words squeezed out. He had to make it, he had to make it.

"I'm not sure. The longer it takes to get him treatment..." Cheryl's voice trailed off, but the unspoken words rang in my mind. If Erik didn't get treatment, he would die. All of this would be for nothing.

I felt the tears teetering on the edge of my eyelids, I didn't want to cry. Not again. It seemed like that was all I'd been doing lately. I bit down on the inside of my cheek until a coppery taste filled my mouth. The pain dampened my desire to sob, but I wasn't sure how long I could fend off the inevitable. Crane's sympathy leaked into me, and the tears fell.

"There's an Underground station in Tennessee; we can be there in less than an hour. Do what you can for him until then and be ready to move once we're on the ground," Crane instructed her in a low, even voice.

"Yes, sir," Cheryl replied, and without another word she retreated.

Crane hit a button on the arm of his chair. "Get me a line to the other plane. I need to speak with Brand." He was no longer wearing his earpiece, and Brand probably wasn't either.

"Right away, sir," the reply came from a speaker that I couldn't see.

Crane reached towards me as if to take my hand, but thought better of it at the last minute. Instead, he patted my shoulder once then drew back. The gesture was nearly lost on me, though; no amount of empathetic gestures would console me.

"Meadows," a voice crackled through the unseen speaker.

"Change of plans. We're going to land in Gatlinburg. I need you to take the soldiers from our plane back to base. The fighters will accompany you."

"What's wrong?" Brand's staticky voice asked.

"We need don't have adequate medical supplies aboard. Gatlinburg is the closest camp."

"It's too dangerous, Ian," Brand said. "It's only a matter of time before they launch a counterstrike. We were followed out of there. We need to put more distance between ourselves and their fighters."

"We are landing in Gatlinburg. That's an order, Captain Meadows." Crane's tone held so much authority that it reminded me of Mac.

"Yes, sir," said Brand, his words punctuated by a burst of white noise. Then the connection broke.

Thanking Crane seemed like the right thing to do, but I found I lacked the strength. The icy sensation that had come over me left my outsides numb and my insides hollow. The tears flowed freely and I no longer cared. I wanted to tuck my knees to my chest, close my eyes, and pray that I would wake up and find this had all been a bad dream.

"He needs you right now," Crane said softly, startling me out of my misery. "The blood loss alone might be too much. I over-estimated how much TOXIC wanted to keep him alive."

I hugged myself, trying to quell the trembling wave starting to make its way through my body. I tucked my chin to my chest and rocked slowly back and forth.

"But, I've seen men come back from worse," Crane continued. "You know what separates the ones that make from those who don't?"

I said nothing.

"Strength of will. If Penny is any indication, McDonough will have done everything in his power to break Erik's."

I shook harder.

"Good thing for him, you have more than enough for both of you."

I finally looked at Crane, astounded. "I can't will Erik to live," I said incredulously.

"No, but you can give him the strength to want to."

Chapter Four

TWENTY MINUTES LATER, the hoverplane touched down in Gatlinburg, Tennessee. The medics and Erik deplaned as the wheels were still skimming the grassy runway. They were already hurrying him towards a large tent with a white cross by the time I made my way down the gangplank. I started to run after them, but Frederick stopped me.

"Have a little faith, Tal," he said quietly. "Those guys are good at what they do."

"You should get those looked at. They might need stitches," I replied, pointing to the shiny red marks on his cheeks.

"I put some disinfectant on them. They'll heal on their own," he responded dismissively.

Several feet away, Crane and Brand were arguing in low, heated voices. Crane was insisting Brand take the rest of the soldiers and return to the cottage in California. Brand didn't want to leave Crane here unprotected. A quick glimpse into Crane's mind told me the Underground stations held mostly civilians. While most,

CREATED

this one included, had weapons arsenals, few of the residents were trained in combat. We'd be sitting ducks if TOXIC attacked.

I surveyed the landscape. Green, brown, and beige tents were interspersed among tall trees. The area was extremely rural and, judging by the thin air, located in the mountains. The tents were likely supposed to be camouflaged to blend into the surrounding nature. Except like many remote areas of the country, Gatlinburg still bore the effects of the Great Contamination. The tree bark was knobby and black, the leaves a vibrant, almost neon, green-yellow. The ground was thickly packed dirt, with swatches of spiky, blue grass sprinkled throughout. The blades looked sharp as razors, and I made a mental note not to walk around barefoot.

"Talia?" a startled voice asked, pulling me from the haze.

I turned. The guy walking towards me began to jog with a pronounced limp. His legs were so long that he covered the distance in seconds. My heart grew wings that fluttered in my chest: Henri. Alive, safe, and not permanently damaged.

"Henri!" I threw my arms around his neck, and buried my face in his thin shirt. He wrapped his long arms protectively around me, making me feel truly safe for the first time in a long time. Relief washed over me as I squeezed him tighter. I'd been so worried about Erik that, after Frederick informed me that Henri was alive, I didn't fret too much over his well-being.

Henri released me much too soon. When he put me down, he was no longer looking at me, but rather over me. A smile slowly spread across his drawn face, the dimness in his brown eyes disappeared. He'd obviously seen Frederick.

"What are you guys doing here?" Henri called to his boyfriend.

Frederick, trailed by Crane and an irate Brand, joined us. Henri and Frederick embraced, both boys seeming to relax now that they were together. Crane came to stand firmly by my side; he was careful not to get so close that we touched. Brand crossed his arms over

55

his chest, thrust one foot forward, and refused to look at me. He looked like a child who'd been scolded instead of Crane's second in command. It was immature, particularly at that moment, but I had to work to suppress a giggle.

"We needed a decent medical facility and this was the closest one," Crane answered Henri.

When Henri and Frederick drew apart, Henri looked weary. He rose to his full height, which was quite impressive, and his muscles tensed. Frederick placed a hand on his boyfriend's shoulder. The gesture was meant to calm him, but had little effect on Henri.

"You can trust him," Frederick said in a low voice.

Well, that answered one question, I thought. Henri had no idea the true nature of Frederick's job. This made me feel a little better. At least I wasn't the only one who'd been left in the dark. Then again, I hoped the omission didn't ruin their relationship like it nearly had mine and Frederick's. Trust was vital in any relationship, and Frederick had clearly violated Henri's. Now more than ever, they needed each other.

"What are you doing here with him?" Henri demanded, shrugging Frederick's hand off. "Frederick, what the hell is going on?"

Okay, so maybe this wasn't going to go as smoothly as I'd hoped.

I stepped forward; the last thing we needed was a scene. "Henri, why don't we go sit down and talk about this?" The calm tone in my voice surprised even me. I wasn't prone to being rational, and after the past week, I was shocked that I had the capacity to act so now.

Henri backed away, looking disgustedly between me and his boyfriend. Frederick reached for him, but Henri swatted at his hand, accusation and hurt mingling in his brown eyes.

"I need some air," Henri declared, despite the fact that we were surrounded by nothing but fresh air. He turned on his heel, and practically ran for the wooded area surrounding the clearing.

Both Frederick and I moved to go after him.

"Let him go," Crane said quietly. "He needs time to come to terms with everything before you drop another bombshell."

Frederick started to protest, but I cut him off. "He's right. It's a lot to take in."

"Besides," Crane continued. "We need to make a plan right now. Brand, you take all the soldiers except for Talia, Frederick, and Janelle. We'll stay here until Erik is strong enough to travel, then we'll meet up with you at the cottage."

Incredulity distorted Brand's features, and he opened his mouth to make what was certain to be an argument. Crane held up one hand, halting the words in Brand's throat.

"That's an order, Soldier," Crane said, his voice pure authority.

My eyes ping ponged between Crane and Brand. They looked like two unmovable bookends, Frederick and I trapped between their blockades. I wondered how close their relationship really was. I couldn't imagine that just any soldier would challenge Crane's authority, yet Brand was openly doing so. Their staring contest reminded me of the battle of wills that had been going on between me and Mac for years.

"Affirmative, *Mr. President*," Brand finally spat.

"Dismissed, Meadows," Crane said.

As if to prove a point, I had no idea to whom, Brand remained where he was for a pregnant moment before spinning on his heel and stalking off towards the planes.

"Why don't you two find the Station Manager and make sleeping arrangements?" Crane suggested after a long silence where the three of us stood staring at one another.

"I want to be there when Erik wakes up," I protested.

After the way Henri had reacted to Crane, I needed to be there to explain. The last thing I wanted was for Erik to wake up among strangers and believe he'd traded one captor for another. God forbid he tried to strangle another one of Crane's medical staff. Once was excusable, given the circumstances. A second time? Well, that might not go over so well.

"The best thing you can do right now is get some rest. You haven't slept in what? Twenty-four hours?"

Longer, I thought. It felt like years since I'd had a good night's sleep.

"I'll personally come find you the minute he regains consciousness," Crane promised as if sensing I was about to put up a fight.

I sighed. I really was exhausted. "Okay," I agreed.

Frederick and I set off in search of the Station Manager. We found Walter Gains in a large beige tent in the center of a cluster of smaller tents. He was sitting at a makeshift table in one corner, surrounded by loose papers, and typing furiously on a portable communicator. His bald head shot up when we entered.

"Ah, Frederick," he said, "are you the source of all the commotion?" Oversized wire-rimmed glasses slid down his pointy nose as he spoke. He pushed them back into place only to have them slide down again a second later.

"Hey, Walt. Yeah, sorry, we had to make an emergency landing. One of the men we freed from Tramblewood is in pretty bad shape. The medics thought it best to stop here and get him patched up before returning to Coalition territory."

I shot Frederick a surprised glance. I hadn't realized our rescue mission was public knowledge.

"Sorry to hear that. You're welcome to stay as long as you need. Were you followed?"

"Briefly. The fighter planes were able to neutralize the situation before we were too far from the prison," Frederick said tightly.

Translation: the fighters had shot them down. I shuddered. More dead TOXIC Operatives. I prayed Donavon hadn't been among them.

"I see," was all Walter said and returned his attention to the communicator.

Frederick cleared his throat, drawing Walter away from his work for a second time. "This is Natalia." Frederick jerked his head in my direction. Water's thin eyebrows shot up, and he didn't try to conceal his surprise when he finally took the time to look me up and down.

"Lots of people looking for you, Ms. Lyons," he said.

I gave him a tight smile. "I know, sir. I don't want to cause any trouble for you or the others here. I'll be gone as soon as Erik is stable." I really didn't want to draw TOXIC forces to the station. Enough people had died today already, and the sun had yet to rise.

"This organization is devoted to helping people like you. I, and the other people who live here, are accustomed to risk. Every day that passes without a TOXIC raid is a success in my book. You're welcome here as long as necessary."

I gave him a more genuine smile this time, relieved he hadn't insisted I leave immediately. His generosity reminded me of Adam—the Station Manager at the Underground stop in the tunnels beneath D.C.—and I wondered how he and his people were faring since my departure.

"Thank you," I told Walter sincerely.

Feet shuffled on the dirt floor behind me, followed by the rustle of canvass as the tent flap opened. I whipped my head around, and watched as Crane entered.

"Conductor Gaines," he greeted Walter with a quick nod of his head.

"Mr. President," Walter replied respectfully.

"Talia," Crane said, turning his attention to me. "There is someone who would like to see you."

Relief washed over me, causing my muscles to become limp as wet noodles. Erik was awake. "Oh, thank heavens!" I exclaimed. My feet were already in motion when Crane held up his hand in warning.

"Not so fast. It isn't Erik." The bubble of hope in my stomach burst. "I think you'll be happy to see this person, though."

I stared at him quizzically. Who would I possibly know at an Underground station in Tennessee? Let alone be happy to see?

Crane motioned for me to follow him. Slowly, I started walking again. Crane held the tent flap open for me to pass through, and then nodded his head to the right. He stayed close to me as we wound through the tents. His arm twitched a couple of times, and I thought he was deciding whether to wrap his arm around my shoulders. He had an undeniable urge to comfort me; I felt that. But a quick swipe of his mind told me he feared overstepping his bounds. His parental instincts where I was concerned were touching, but I was reluctant to trust them. For the life of me, I didn't understand where they came from.

He led me to a small tent with a white cross emblazoned on the triangle top. Four cots lined each canvass wall, with several more littering the earthen floor in the center. All were empty except for one. The moment I laid eyes on her, I knew Crane had been correct. I wasn't just happy to see Cadence Choi, I was elated.

Her short, dark hair poked out in every direction, reminding me of a porcupine. Underneath the thin white blanket, one of her legs appeared three times the size of the other. The arm slung across her stomach was wrapped in a bubble of hard blue plastic. When she turned her head, I noticed that half of her face was bandaged with white gauze. She'd seen better days, that was for sure. But she was alive, and I felt like celebrating.

"Cadence!" I exclaimed, and started winding through the cot-maze to get to her. Had someone told me a few weeks ago that I'd practically jump for joy at the sight of her, I'd have told him to have his head examined. Now, though? I wanted to throw my arms around Cadence and tell her how much I'd missed her. And I had missed her. Until that instant I hadn't realized how much.

She grinned. At least I was pretty sure it was a grin. The gauze obscuring the right side of her mouth made it hard to be sure. "Hey, Talia," she mumbled.

I knelt next to her bed and reached for her good hand. She flinched when I touched her, and I noticed that the fingers of her "good hand" were swollen into fat, red sausages. My heart sank a little lower in my chest. I knew she'd been hurt, but I had no idea her injuries were so extensive.

"How ya feeling?" I asked, and instantly regretted the question. Obviously she felt awful. I wanted to smack myself for being so insensitive.

"Been better." She tried to smile again, but her expression quickly turned sour.

I wanted to comfort her, but I was afraid to touch her again for fear of inflicting more pain. So instead, I did the only thing that I could think of. I dampened her suffering.

Cadence's body relaxed into the thin mattress. She sighed and her visible eye fluttered several times. As with Erik, absorbing her pain brought about an instant ache that consumed every inch of my body. A sharp, leaden quality tinged the pain, making my head woozy and my vision unfocused. Painkillers, I realized. She was higher than a hovercraft.

"Thanks," she mumbled.

I eased into a sitting position, my legs beginning to throb and my fingers burning with Cadence's pain. Even with the narcotics, she was extremely uncomfortable. Mostly they made her not care so much. I bit the inside of my bottom lip to keep the torment out of my expression. Hers was a bearable pain, at least.

"I hear you found Randy," she continued, her voice a little stronger now. "Is he... okay?"

"A little thin, but otherwise appears to be okay," I said honestly. Besides the malnourishment, I was pretty sure Randy was physically fine. Mentally, I couldn't even imagine the extent of the damage. He'd been locked away for six years. His crime had been a serious one, as far as TOXIC was concerned anyhow. Helping a Coalition woman escape prison had landed him a one-way ticket to Tramblewood—the same prison where he'd been a guard. That Coalition woman had been Penny's mother, Crane's sister.

"Better than you," I added as Cadence fought the tears causing her dark irises to swim.

"Mr. Crane says he's on his way to a Coalition safe house." I was shocked at how easily she'd adjusted to Crane's presence. I'd actually forgotten he was in the tent until she'd said his name. I turned to find him standing quietly in the doorway.

"I want to go, too. When I'm healthy," Cadence continued, drawing my attention back to her.

"Of course," I promised without asking Crane; although, I doubted he'd mind.

"Visiting hours are over. Ms. Choi needs her rest," a stern female voice said from behind me.

I glanced back. Now standing next to Crane was a short, pudgy woman. She wore her dark red hair in a severe bun at the nape of her neck. It pulled at the skin around her hairline, making her cat-like eyes appear even more feline.

"I'll sleep here, in one of the empty cots," I replied. I wanted to stay with Cadence. I needed to do something, feel useful. I was no medic; my minimal first-aid training was limited to bandaging scrapes and, in a pinch, suturing wounds. Erik's level of injury was beyond me. Cadence's was not. Shouldering Cadence's pain might even distract me, or tire me out enough to actually fall asleep.

"This is a medical tent," the nurse replied. Her tone suggested my request was ridiculous.

"Please, let her stay," Cadence sniffed next to me.

While the tears and sniffling were byproducts of the overwhelming relief she felt about her brother, Nurse Crotchety didn't know that. The emotional display smoothed the woman's puckered lips.

"There's no harm in it," Crane said, turning what could only be explained as charm on the nurse. "The beds aren't being used."

The nurse smiled up at Crane with enough sugar to make my teeth hurt, then glared at me. "I suppose we can make an exception this once. But no talking. Ms. Choi needs to rest if she is going to get better."

"Thank you," I told her in as polite a tone as I could manage.

"Would you mind finding Ms. Lyons some clean clothes?" Crane asked the nurse in that same charming tone.

That was when I realized I was still wearing my suit and it was covered in dirt, dust, and blood. Gross.

"Of course, sir." The nurse patted her bun as she crossed to a small chest of plastic drawers in one corner. Her back was to me, so I couldn't see what she was doing. But when she turned around, she held a pair of clean green scrubs in her hands. I happily took the clothes, but decided it was best to wait until Cadence and I were alone to strip.

"I'll be back to check on you in a little while, dear," the nurse told Cadence.

"Night, ladies," Crane said.

The electric lights lining the tent's ceiling buzzed loudly then made a popping noise, which was followed by darkness. I made quick work of shedding the filthy suit and replacing it with the scrubs. Not only were the clothes clean, they smelled like sunshine as if they'd been hung on a line outside to dry. They probably had been, I realized. While there was electricity here, I doubted it was wasted on such trivial machines as clothes dryers. Not when they needed to power medical equipment. Gatlinburg was definitely one of the rural-live-off-the-land stations.

A shower would have been welcome, and much needed just then, but the new clothes made me feel refreshed. At least I wouldn't wake up with the remnants of the mission clinging to me.

The cot mattress proved to be as thin as it looked and as soft as cardboard. Bedsprings poked into my back as I tried to make myself comfortable. My sense of time was out of whack from traveling across so many time zones and back in such a short time period. No light peeked through the split between the tent flaps, so I guessed sunrise was a ways off.

A thousand questions swirled in my mind, all fighting their way to my mouth. I wanted to ask Cadence about what happened when they went for Erik's parents, and how he'd been captured in the first place. I wanted to know how she and Henri had escaped from TOXIC while Erik had been captured, and then become separated from Erik's father and brothers. I wanted to know what life at this station was like, because it was very different from the ones I'd seen. Here, the Station Manager seemed to know and like Crane. The D.C. Station Manager, Adam, hadn't known Crane at all. He didn't believe TOXIC's party line about Crane and the Coalition hating Talents and wanting to end our existence, but he hadn't seemed to trust him either. Yet both stations had the same goal. Maybe Crane's actual involvement with the Underground movement was a need-to-know type of thing.

I asked her nothing. She was exhausted, and bombarding her with questions seemed mean. Her defenses were down and I could easily read her mind. So, I knew the medical staff here had a limited supply of painkillers, and after the first couple of days she'd begun to refuse medication except at night to sleep. Now all she received on a regular basis were anti-infection injections. I breathed in more of her suffering.

"You don't have to do this for me," Cadence whispered. Her words came out garbled, and she was close to drifting off into dreamland.

"Just until you can fall asleep," I replied.

In a weird way, her pain comforted me. Weaving so much of Cadence's mind with my own made me feel less alone. For those blissful minutes, her problems seemed to trump mine. Tomorrow's to-do list consisted of sitting up and eating without assistance. She worried about Randy and whether he was really okay as I'd promised. She regretted that he'd been so close and she hadn't been able to see him. A part of her was grateful for that too, though. Cadence hated the idea of wearing plastic and gauze for their first encounter since she'd provided the testimony that had damned her brother to Tramblewood. She worried he hated her for that testimony.

"Thanks, Talia." Cadence's voice was in my head this time. She didn't have enough energy to speak the words aloud, but knew that thinking the message was just as good. *"For everything."*

Moments later, my hold on her mind began to wane before disappearing completely. I stretched my kinked limbs and let the buzz of mosquitoes serve as a lullaby.

Smoke fills my nostrils, burning my throat and searing my lungs. My eyes begin to sting, and heat crawls over my arms and legs like thousands of fire ants. I want to scream, but the sound sticks in my throat, unable to push past the knot blocking the passageway like hair in a drainpipe. When I pry my eyes open, I discover all the color has been washed from the world. Either that or I've gone blind to it. Gray. Everything is gray. I blink my eyes, but nothing changes. The cots and dressers are blobs of darker gray in a sea of gray.

The air is so thick that I think it will take a machete to cut my way through. A throbbing in my head makes it feel too big, and when I try to stand, my equilibrium is off. The room feels like it's tilting, but I can't be sure since I am lost in the strange gray clouds. Instinctively I drop to the ground. My knees slam into the packed earth and I wince. Disorientation soon gives way to horror when I realize that I am not only colorblind, but deaf, too. I am surrounded by complete silence. I scream. In my head, the shrieks could crack glass, but in reality they don't penetrate the blanket of smoke that is now smothering me.

I shot upright in the hospital bed, instantly aware that the nightmare was not entirely in my head. The hospital tent was hazy, as if a giant gray cloud had drifted inside and swallowed us in its thick embrace. Only, the air was sizzling like we were too close to the sun. Frantically, I stumbled over the side of the bed and felt my way to Cadence. I shook my head to clear the cobwebs that blocked my eardrums. When I did, I heard terrified screams from somewhere close by. The earth began to quake and I fell, catching myself at the last second before slamming into the railing of Cadence's bed.

"Cadence?" I whispered. "Cadence, wake up!" I didn't want to shake her if I didn't have to.

"Talia?" she asked. "What's going on?" Her was voice was groggy with sleep.

"I don't know," I started to tell her as another explosion rocked the tent. "Can you move?"

"I can try," Cadence answered timidly.

She was in bad shape, and I didn't want to risk moving her until I knew for sure that it was necessary. "I'll be right back," I told her.

"Hurry," she pleaded, now sounding panicked.

I ran to the tent flap and thrust my head out. The air out here was at least ten degrees warmer and filled with a curtain of thick, dark fog in every direction except up. The night sky was alive with blinding light, and I had to squint against the harsh glare. People-shaped blobs hurried past the tent without slowing. When my eyes adjusted and some of the fog had dissipated, I noticed the lights above were from hovercrafts. Large black shapes were dropping to earth like avenging angels, spraying liquid fire as they descended.

Several nearby tents were ablaze with blue-green flames. Chemical bombs, my brain registered after a moment. Not good. Immediately survival instinct kicked in and I covered my mouth and noise with my scrub top. The thin fabric was a poor filter for the hazardous smoke, but it was better than nothing.

"Talia!" a man yelled. His voice was muffled, probably by a crude air filter just like mine, but I was pretty sure it was Crane. "Talia!" he screamed again. I spotted him, running against the flow like a lone salmon swimming upstream. With the two automatic weapons strapped across his chest and the manic expression across his face, Crane looked more like a shark, predatory and out for blood.

"Ian, what's going on? Are we being attacked? Where's Erik?" I asked, stupidly. Of course we were being attacked. Gunfire was popping through the air, eliciting more terrified screams from the refugees weaving through the tents. Bomb after bomb rained down from the crafts overhead.

TOXIC had found me.

"We need to go, now!" Crane exclaimed, freeing one of the rifles and offering it to me. "All the critical patients and medical staff have been evacuated. Erik's already on a transport plane."

I stared at the gun for a moment too long before accepting it. I was in no shape for another fight.

"What about Cadence?" I demanded, as Crane tried to pull me away from the tent. "We can't leave her!" Crane looked like he wanted to argue, but I planted my feet and refused to move. She had risked her life for me. She was lying in a hospital bed because of me. There was no way I was leaving her behind.

Crane pushed past me into the tent, and I hurried to follow. He was at Cadence's bedside, pulling her to her feet by the time I reached him. Cadence looped her injured arm around Crane's waist and one around my shoulders. I tried to give her a reassuring smile, but my heart was in my throat, and I knew that it wasn't very convincing.

The three of us stumbled awkwardly out of the recovery tent and began moving way too slowly in the direction that the others were running. We had only made it a couple of yards when Cadence's nurse and another man joined us. They were wheeling a stretcher. I eyed it dubiously. As a threesome, we weren't making much progress. But the stretcher was slow and awkward to push over the grass.

"Don't worry, this'll protect her," the nurse said, even as Crane scooped up Cadence and placed her on the stretcher. The instant she was settled, a metal shell sprang up around her prone form, leaving only her head uncovered. "Six inches of titanium," the nurse added, tapping the top of the shell. And then, the wheels retracted and Cadence was floating.

I nodded mutely, intrigued by the contraption.

Bending down to meet Cadence's eyes, I said, "You're going to be fine."

She smiled up at me as best she could as the nurse and her assistant began guiding Cadence away. Crane took hold of my arm and dragged me forward. Together, we wove through the tent city until finally reaching a clearing. Twenty yards of chaos separated us from a shallow outcropping of trees, just beyond which sat the escape hoverplanes.

Neither of us broke stride, quickened our pace if anything, as we shot into the clearing. I'd only taken a handful of steps when I heard, "Halt!" screamed behind me. There was no need to turn around to know the command was meant for me. Laser crosshairs pricked the exposed skin at the nape of my neck. Crane's left boot hooked around my right ankle at the same time the heel of his left hand jabbed me between the shoulder blades. I lurched forward as a bullet whizzed so close to my head it singed a stray curl. Crane caught me before I fell, and was indiscriminately firing over one shoulder as he urged me towards the trees.

"How did they find us?" I asked, practically screaming to be heard over the cacophony of blasts and shouts.

"They put a tracker in Erik," Crane yelled back. "Medics did a body scan on the plane and didn't see one. TOXIC masked it well. Dr. Eicher found it during surgery. The attack began minutes later."

A tracker? Damn it, why hadn't I thought of that? Mac had anticipated my rescue attempt. Of course he had, that was Mac: his contingency plans had contingency plans. Even if he'd been 99.9 percent sure I'd fail, he'd have wanted a backup plan. Implanting Erik with a tracker had been that backup plan.

Fortunately I had little time to dwell on my own naiveté.

Ten feet in front of me, the earth opened up, sending a cloud of dirt and chemicals flying. In favor of freeing my hands to hold the weapon, I no longer had the makeshift mask of my scrub top secured over my mouth and nose. Immediately my eyes began to sting, and my lungs burned liked I'd swallowed hot coals. I doubled over to retch at the same time the wind was knocked out of me from behind. Those spiky blades of grass I'd noticed earlier sliced my cheeks and arms, impaling me like hundreds of tiny swords.

For a second time in as many seconds, the air raced out of my lungs as something heavy landed on top of me.

"You're a walking bullseye," Crane sent.

I had no time for a smartass comeback. No sooner had I started breathing again, Crane had me on my feet and on the move. My knees ached, and my lungs felt like they were going to burst free from my chest. I covered my mouth and nose with the bottom of the scrub top, using it to filter the acrid air once again. Squinting, I tried to get my bearings in the haze of chemical smoke

"Do you know where we're going?" I sent Crane.

"Keep your eyes shut and trust me," he sent back.

A zipping sound from above caught my attention. I looked up just as more black-clad operatives dropped from the sky in front of us. My stomach roiled when I realized we were about to be surrounded. I gripped Crane's hand tighter as a black circle formed around us. Slowly, the circle began to shrink. Like they'd choreographed the routine, the operatives moved inwards as one.

"Calm," Crane sent. It was a warning of sorts, maybe more of a reminder. Crane was reminding me not to lose my cool.

"Always," I sent back. Grace under pressure was in my skillset, even if I rarely used it.

All around us, muffled voices commanded us to "stop," "drop your weapons," and "surrender." Neither of us moved.

Three large figures materialized directly in front of us as if they'd been conjured by some invisible sorcerer. Crane did move now. He moved his finger to the trigger of his gun and pulled. The operatives' protective gear bore the brunt of the attack, but Crane was an excellent shot. Three well-placed bullets in their throats had our assailants immobilized, permanently.

I sucked in a sharp breath.

"It's us or them, Talia," Crane shouted and charged towards the three-man-wide hole in the circle.

I followed without thinking, trusting Ian Crane to lead the way to safety. I had to jump over the dead operatives. Nausea swept through me, and I covered my mouth with my hand and gagged. Thick, blonde hair was sticking out from beneath one of the helmets. No, please not Donavon, I prayed. I crouched to pull the helmet free, but Crane yanked my arm so hard I thought it might dislodge from the socket.

"No time," he hissed in my head.

Regretfully, I glanced over my shoulder. Not Donavon, I assured myself. Just like with Erik, my mental connection to Donavon was solid. If he was here, I'd feel him. If he were dead, I'd know.

The air was less contaminated in the mini forest of trees. I could see more clearly, and what I saw was a beautiful sight: an operative-free path to escape crafts. I exhaled with relief. The odds of survival just tipped in our favor. Operatives were pursuing us from behind, but the trees afforded us some cover. A ragtag group of men and women were stationed at the gangplank of the hoverplane, increasing our chances of making it out of this alive by firing on our would-be attackers. None of them were as good a shot as Crane, but their efforts were slowing Mac's operatives. I could feel the gap between us and them widening.

Fifty feet until we reached the hovercraft. Hope of making it out of this nightmare alive made my feet move faster. Forty feet. Screams of the dying assaulted my ears, and, as guilty as it made me feel, I prayed the pleas were coming from the lips of TOXIC operatives. Thirty feet. I heard the soft hum of a hovercraft overhead, and I braced myself for another earth-moving explosion. Twenty feet. I stumbled forward, fighting gravity to remain on my feet.

"Get on the plane!" Crane screamed.

I glanced to my right, where Crane had been running alongside me, and realized he was no longer there. He'd stopped, and was now taking aim at the newest wave of operatives rappelling from above.

"Go!"

I hesitated. I was so close to the escape hovercraft. Ten feet now and I'd be at the gangplank. No, I decided, no way I was leaving him behind. I turned to join Crane.

"Natalia Lyons." The sound of my name reverberated through the air with physical force, drowning out all other noise.

I stopped dead in my tracks. Slowly, I raised my face to see the TOXIC attack plane looming over me like an alien ship ready to beam me aboard.

"On your knees, Operative Lyons," the same voice boomed through the loudspeaker. A spotlight snared me in its beam and I fought to breathe.

"We have you surrounded. Surrender now and we will let the others go," the voice said.

Suddenly images of tents aflame with blue-green fire and bloody civilians pleading for their lives at the feet of uncaring operatives filled my head. Innocents are dying, I thought. I saw a line of men, women, and children lying on their stomachs as an executioner claimed one victim after the next. Guilt twisted my intestines into a pretzel. My fault, I thought, this is my fault.

"Only you can end this," the voice told me, only I wasn't sure whether the voice was in my head.

"Fight it, Talia," a second voice commanded. This one was definitely in my head, and it was definitely Crane's. *"You're stronger."*

Stronger than what? I thought, as, slowly, I lowered the gun I still held in my hands to the ground in front of my toes. Feet, I now realized, that were sticky with my blood. I almost laughed. I'd forgotten to remind myself not to run around barefoot.

I raised my hands, palms out. Images that I'd seen in Alex's visions invaded my head. Except, they were slightly different than before. Maybe from a different vantage point?

"Talia, don't!" Crane again. He sounded angry. No, not angry, I corrected myself, scared.

I was too numb to be scared. Would Mac torture me the same way he'd tortured Erik? Would I become his newest test subject? None of that mattered. Only I could end this standoff. My freedom for countless innocent lives. Seemed like a fair price.

I opened my mouth to say the words, *I surrender.*

Chapter Five

BEFORE BREATH PASSED my lips, there was an explosion that sounded like cymbals crashing inside my head. Then, it felt like fingers were digging into my skull, down through bone and muscle to rip my brain in two. Flashes of bright golden lights collided with one another behind my eyeballs, and spilled sparks across my vision.

Cradling my head between my palms, I fought the excruciating pain threatening to consume me. Wave after wave washed over me, and I pushed back harder and harder with each one. More golden lights popped and fizzled behind my eyes. I shoved with all of my will, finally expelling both the pain, and the cause of it, from my head.

I blinked, relieved to find the blinding lights were gone, but alarmed to find myself standing in the middle of a dense, white cloud. I blinked again, and the world started to come into focus.

There was no sea of death or hordes of operatives claiming victims right and left, as I'd expected. Gone were the trees, the hoverplanes, and Crane, replaced by a large sterile room that reminded me of the cafeteria at school.

Young, wide-eyed children, clothed in hospital gowns and strange paper booties, formed row after row of perfect lines in front of ten evenly-spaced tables. One by one, the children were called forward and directed to insert their arms into plastic tubes similar to the one Cadence had around her arm.

Instinctively I knew that they were being injected with the Creation drug. Not just one injection either. The tubes were lined with needles, each attached to a vial containing a different Talent signature. After the injection, each child was escorted from the room by an armed guard. A skinny girl with milk chocolate skin and eyes the color of sunflowers passed in front of me with her guard. When our gazes met, hers began to glow. Her nose and lips appeared to melt before my eyes, and her square teeth became jagged points. Only her head Morphed, which alone was odd and unnatural. But the truly disturbing part was that the animal-form was unrecognizable. She had reptilian eyes over an avian beak and her skin was leathery and gray like an elephant. She snarled and spit in my direction, and then vomited yellow goo.

I was nearly knocked off of my feet by the fist of agony that struck the interior of my skull.

Only you can save them. TOXIC will let them go once we have you. Surrender now. Join us.

"Talia!"

My name ripped through me, tearing me from the vision of the children and blotting out the silky voice urging me to capitulate.

I felt the intrusion immediately. Someone was in my head. Someone was scrambling my brain like an egg. Someone was man-ipulating my emotions, playing on my vulnerabilities. I wasn't the only Mind Manipulator alive today, but I was the only one with enough power to control another Manipulator. Or so I'd been led to believe.

I slammed my mental walls into place, evicting the interloper from my head. Now, more than anything, I was furious. TOXIC had just tried to beat me at my own game.

"You have until the count of ten," the disembodied voice informed me. This time the message was definitely not in my head.

I met Crane's dark gaze as he took down another of his opponents. I didn't need to hear his order; the communication came through loud and clear in his expression: Run.

"Ten. Nine. Eight..."

Indecision glued my feet firmly in place. Not because I was still considering surrender, but because I didn't want to leave Crane.

"Talia!" a male voice screamed a second time.

I swiveled around. A tall figure was charging towards me from behind the escape hovercraft. Henri. One of the operatives surrounding Crane turned his attention on Henri, following his movements with the barrel of his gun. Terror ripped through me, shattering the one-dimensional world that I'd been living in since I heard my name. Henri appeared blind to the threats as he sprinted to reach me, and I knew that even if I called a warning it would be too late.

Without thinking, I summoned the gun from where it lay at my feet. My finger found the trigger as if pulled there by a magnet. I leveled it at the operative about to shoot Henri, and fired. I was too late. Henri jerked wildly as the bullet lodged into his shoulder, and he fell to the ground.

"NO!!" I shrieked. My feet moved of their own volition. My only thought was reaching Henri. I pulled the trigger over and over again, emptying the clip into the man who had just shot my friend. The fury that I'd felt moments earlier was replaced by a blinding rage. Wind whipped my hair free from its ponytail as I knelt down beside Henri. Gusts of air swirled around where I sat, tearing nearby operatives' weapons from their vice-like grips. The closest operative stumbled back, throwing his arm across his face like a shield. He wasn't the only one, either. Crane's attackers were caught in my windstorm.

Henri had his hand pressed against the wound, blood seeping through his splayed fingers. I gently pulled his hand free to assess the damage. I gasped when I saw the jagged edges of the bullet hole. His shoulder was a bloody, fleshy mess. I wanted to look away from the grotesque sight, but I didn't. I swallowed the rising bile, and pressed my hand to Henri's shoulder.

"You're going to be okay," I promised him, nodding vigorously as if that would somehow make the statement more true.

"It's just a flesh wound," Henri replied through gritted teeth. His face was ashen in the floodlights of the plane overhead. The winds spiraling around us were keeping any further attacks at bay, cocooning us in a torrent of flying dirt and rocks.

"We need to get you to the plane," I told him, helping him to his feet.

Henri placed the hand of his good arm on my shoulder and pushed himself to a stand. I kept us safely ensconced in the funnel cloud as we moved towards the belly of the waiting hovercraft. When we were only a couple of feet away, I let go of the winds. Henri stumbled forward as several people moved to help him aboard. I knew that I should go too, but I also knew that the disembodied voice from the plane overhead was right. We were outnumbered and outgunned. The likelihood of escape was diminishing by the heartbeat.

Invigorated by the blood still boiling in my veins, I focused on Crane's attackers. I latched onto their minds, bending and manipulating their wills to mine. The reaction was almost instantaneous.

All three dropped to their knees, then crumpled to the ground like robots whose plugs have been pulled.

"Ian, come on!" I called to Crane.

He hesitated, and I thought for a minute that he might take the opportunity to kill the operatives in cold blood. But he didn't. He ran to join me instead.

"Operative Lyons, we will be forced to shoot the hovercraft down if you board it," the disembodied voice declared. I didn't know whether they would follow through with that threat, but I wasn't willing to gamble with so many innocent lives.

"Come on, Talia," Crane said, trying to drag me the last several feet to the gangplank.

"Get on the plane, Ian," I replied calmly.

"Whatever you're considering doing, don't."

"Get on the plane," I repeated. When he still appeared hesitant, I added, "I have no intention of surrendering." Dread bubbled up inside of me at what I was about to do. Us or them, I reminded myself. Definitely us.

I summoned the images of Erik battered and bleeding; Erik being tortured; the horrible wound in Henri's shoulder; Cadence lying on the cot; Randy Choi's emaciated body. I thought about Penny and the flashbacks she'd been experiencing. Mac had damaged her mind. And then he'd taken the fragments and smashed them for good measure. All the psychological glue in the world might not make Penny's mind whole again.

I didn't try to control my emotions. I let the anger and hatred engulf me, turning my emotions into physical beings.

Fat raindrops pelted my face, plastering my hair into a helmet on my head. The wind gusts were deafening, blocking out the final countdown from above. Energy coursed through my veins until the power became too much and it broke through my skin and the suit to form a pulsing aura outlining my body. I felt wild and alive and invincible. In that instant I truly understand why Gretchen had warned me against abusing my Talents. The power was addicting.

The first bolt of lightning struck the tail of the overhead craft, and a chunk fell to earth in a smoldering heap of twisted metal. I could envision the pilot fighting for control of the spinning hoverplane. The second bolt struck the nose, and the floodlights winked out of existence like a giant beast closing his eyes. The plane dipped dangerously low on the left side until it was ninety degrees off center.

I felt Crane's physical presence behind me. He was smart enough not to try to force his way into my mind. His light touch on my arm barely registered through the suit, but the nervous tension he was projecting came through like a national news broadcast alert. The lives of the TOXIC operatives on the hovercraft that was plummeting at record speed were inconsequential to Crane. He preferred casualties. They sent a message: the Coalition was serious. What worried Ian Crane was how their deaths would affect me, particularly since I'd be the one responsible. After I came down from my power high, he believed I'd regret crashing the plane.

I didn't want to kill the operatives aboard. Well, maybe the one who'd made my head his playground, but not the others. Guilt was already starting to eat away at my gut. So many people had died in the last twenty-four hours. There was no need to add to the death total.

"They won't be able to chase us," Crane said. "Let's go before reinforcements show up."

The TOXIC plane sank lower and lower as I finally followed Crane up the gangplank.

The doors were closing as we passed through, and without warning, the hoverplane launched skyward. I flew backwards into the metal doors, spine first. The sharp burst of pain made me instantly more alert. The main bay of the hoverplane came into focus. Pained whimpers and frightened ramblings met my ears. Fire and smoke, chemicals and gunpowder, blood and sickness, clogged my nostrils and I fought the bile pushing its way up my esophagus. Everywhere I looked, soldiers and civilians alike were patching bullet wounds, splinting broken limbs, and applying cooling creams to varying degrees of burns.

"Come on, Talia," Crane said gently as he gestured towards the front of the hoverplane.

The craft was older than the ones I'd flown on while with TOXIC and far shabbier than the hoverplane that had brought us to Gatlinburg. Time and exposure to the elements had allowed the metal walls to rust in places, and a grayish putty-like substance had been used to plug the holes. Loops of cracked leather served as handholds to help navigate the wide aisle between two rows of scratched benches. Many of the safety harnesses were frayed or torn and some were missing altogether.

Turbulence and poorly-maintained equipment made the flight bumpy. Being so short, I couldn't reach the handholds and had to use Crane to steady myself and keep from falling on the other passengers littering the aisle.

As the anger and fury died down, I started to feel weak and shaky and in desperate need of juice to up my blood sugar. Expending more power than I had to give had exhausted me. Black spots dotted my vision, and I blinked them away.

Just a couple more hours, I promised myself. Once we make it to the cottage, you'll be able to rest.

Near the cockpit I noticed Henri wedged into the small corner between the end of the bench and the wall separating the two areas of the hoverplane. His eyes were closed and his face was a sickly shade of green.

"Get me a first aid kit," I said to Crane. He nodded and left to find one without comment.

I sank down on my knees in front of Henri, and smoothed his sweat-dampened hair back from his forehead. "How ya doing?" I asked, even though I knew it was a stupid question. Talking was always a good distraction.

A ghost of a smile flitted across his dry, cracked lips, but he didn't speak. The hand he was using to apply pressure to his wound was streaked brown and red with blood and dirt. I feared an infection was in his future. I looked down at my own hands, which were also caked with grime. Better not add to the risk, I thought. Instead, I summoned energy from my nearly-tapped reserves and absorbed as much of Henri's pain as I could bear.

"Did they get Erik out?" he asked, his lips barely parting as he spoke.

"He was one of the first people evacuated," I replied and relaxed a little with the knowledge. At least Erik was safe. Unless, of course, that plane had been shot down. I didn't let myself dwell on the thought; I had to remain optimistic. The only thing keeping me together was the belief that at least Erik was out of TOXIC's reach.

"Good," Henri whispered.

"Have you seen Frederick?" I asked tentatively. I glanced around the plane's cargo bay, but I couldn't find Frederick's angelic face among the crowd.

Henri went rigid and I instantly regretted asking. He was a strong Projector anyway, but his resistance to my Talents was further weakened by his physical condition, and I read the remorse etched in his mind. Henri hadn't seen Frederick since their fight earlier. He had just resolved to go talk to him when the attacked started.

Crane cleared his throat behind me. When I looked up, he held out a small white box with a red cross painted on the top. "The medical supplies on the plane are limited, but there should be stuff in here to get him cleaned up."

"Thanks," I said, gratefully accepting the kit.

"I'm going to check on the status of the other planes, make sure they got off okay," Crane told me. "I'll be back when I know more." He squeezed my shoulder once and was gone.

Inside the medical kit, I found towels, scalpels, gauze, thread, needles, sanitizing creams, burn ointments, and several bottles of distilled water. I used the water to clean the filth off of my hands the best I could. Next, I gently pried Henri's hand away from the bullet wound. Even though I'd already seen it, the gruesome sight made me blanch.

"I'm sure I can hang on until someone else is free," Henri said. He'd opened his eyes, and saw my reaction.

I swallowed hard. I could do this. I had to do this. Everyone else on the plane was busy tending to themselves or to the other injured; I had no choice.

"What, don't you trust me?" I tried to joke to lighten his mood.

"With my life, Tal," he whispered.

"Good, then be quiet so I can concentrate."

I found the sharpest scalpel and used it to cut away the fabric surrounding the entry wound; it was sticky and I had to peel the material away from his skin. He winced, and I drew a little more of his pain into me.

"Don't, Tal," Henri muttered. "You need your wits about you right now."

He was right, but I hated that without me dulling his sensations, he would feel every move my clumsy fingers made. I took a deep breath and released his mind.

I wet one of the towels with the distilled water and dabbed at the blood and dirt surrounding the wound. Henri grimaced but didn't complain. Once his shirt and the excess blood were out of the way, I was able to tell that the bullet had gone clean through his shoulder. The metal had left the space close to his armpit a mess of torn flesh and tendons. I swallowed my revulsion, not wanting him to see how hard this was for me. If I thought seeing the injury was bad, I couldn't imagine how he must be feeling. Actually, I could. Yeah, I definitely had the better end of the deal.

"This is probably going to hurt," I said as a disclaimer. Then without giving him time to respond, I poured the sterilizing serum over his injury.

Henri jerked back, slamming his head against the bench. A solitary tear leaked out from beneath one closed lid. I let him rest for several long seconds before gently easing him forward and repeating the process on the exit wound. His hand shot out and gripped my thigh so tightly that I thought he might actually break the skin. I kept my face expressionless. If I couldn't use my Talents to lessen his pain, letting him use my leg like a stress-reliever was the least I could do.

"Breathe," I coaxed him. "Just breathe. It'll pass." We both knew that while the sharp bite of the sterilizing serum would pass, the worst was yet to come.

Once his skin was clean and sterile, I threaded the needle and prepared to stitch his wounds. During my time with the Hunters, I'd learned how to stitch wounds, but this would be the first time I'd actually done it.

"Ready?" I asked when his breathing evened out. "I'll be quick," I added when he nodded.

"Don't be too fast. I don't want to have a scar," he replied through tightly clenched teeth.

I smiled at his attempt at a joke. We both knew he was going to have a nasty scar. He'd be lucky if his shoulder ever worked right again. TOXIC doctors, and probably Coalition doctors, too, would be able to reattach any torn tendons and muscles, but with my limited medical training, he'd be lucky if the stitches were remotely straight.

The task of pulling the skin on either side of his injuries closed was much harder than I'd anticipated. He ground his back teeth together while I worked, but remained otherwise stoic. When I was finally finished, I clumsily wrapped gauze around his chest and shoulder to keep the stitches clean.

"Thanks, Tal," he muttered.

"You did this for me once," I replied. It was Henri who had stitched a knife wound on my side when I was a Pledge. Only his steady hand had produced a perfectly sewn line that would've left a small scar had TOXIC not used lasers to remove it.

Henri settled back, trying to make himself as comfortable as possible on the hard floor. I looked around the cabin, thinking that I should try to help the others with their injuries. But the critically injured outnumbered the relatively healthy, and I didn't know where to begin.

A small boy with blond hair and pale skin caught my eye. He was sitting in his mother's lap, and she was cradling wet towels to one of his small arms. When I looked closer, I noticed blackened holes in his clothing, exposing reddened flesh beneath.

I quickly rose, and carefully staggered my way to where he sat.

"Did he get burned?" I asked his mother.

She met my gaze with hollow brown eyes. There was a deep gash just above her right eyebrow, causing rivulets of blood to snake down one side of her face like a morbid tattoo.

"Yeah, it's pretty bad, too," the woman replied dully.

She's in shock, I thought.

I gently tried to remove the towels, but the fabric clung to the boy's skin. I was afraid of tearing it and causing him further damage. The anger from earlier resurfaced, scalding me from the inside out. He was too young to be exposed to such atrocities. It wasn't fair. He should be playing with his friends, coloring, making those weird noodle pictures like Alex had done for me when we were in D.C.

Alex. Another little boy whose innocence and youth had been stolen.

Don't think about him now, I told myself. He's safe with Erik's father and brothers. That's all that matters.

Returning my attention to the here and now, I steeled my nerves and slowly began separating fabric from flesh. The skin underneath the towel was raw and blistered, and the temperature of my own skin soared as I absorbed the child's pain. Compartmentalization had always been one of my strengths, and I did just that now. I shoved the boy's suffering into the deepest recess of my mind and locked the door. Tension left my shoulders, and the ache at the base of my skull lessened as I began to slather burn cream over his arm.

"Thank you," he mumbled when I was finished.

I gave him a small smile and willed him to sleep. I couldn't hold onto his pain for him, but at least I could put him out of his misery for a little while.

"Talia?" Crane said, tapping me on the shoulder. I hadn't heard him come up behind me, and I jumped a little at the contact. "I have news about the others."

I nodded, following Crane back through the maze of injured people to the pilot's cabin. There were four hard plastic chairs behind the cockpit, and I sank gratefully into an empty one. Part of me felt bad for not staying to help tend to the injured, but I was also relieved to put some distance between me and their suffering. I hadn't even realized how much their emotions were impacting mine until I was separated from them.

"Is Erik safe?" I asked, as soon as Crane took the seat next to me.

"Yes. The first plane got out shortly after the attack began. He and the other critical patients are en route to the cottage. He's had several transfusions, and so far, his body has accepted the blood. He's still unconscious, but that's to be expected."

I sighed, disappointed that the news wasn't better. But really, what had I expected? The fact that he'd gotten out safely was the best-case scenario.

"Frederick, is he okay?" I asked.

"Fine. He was still in Gatlinburg when we left, looking for Henri. When he saw him get shot, and the three of us board the hovercraft, he jumped on the last plane to get out of there."

I sighed. All my friends were accounted for.

"What about all the people we left behind?" I asked, hating how small and childlike my voice sounded to my ears. By the time Crane and I had reached the escape crafts, only two had been left. I didn't know how many others there had been originally, but probably not enough for the droves of people I'd seen running through the camp.

Crane didn't answer right away, and when he finally did, he wouldn't meet my gaze. "There are caves in the woods about two miles from the camp. The caves have enough food, water, and medical supplies to last several months. There is also a fair amount of weapons, so they'll be able to protect themselves in the event TOXIC pursues them."

"What about the ones who didn't make it to the caves?" I asked, dreading the answer.

"The survivors will be taken into custody," Crane replied evenly.

So, they would be arrested. Their homes were destroyed, their families torn apart, many were killed, and even more were injured, and it was because of me. TOXIC came for me, and all those people paid the price.

"The members of the Underground know the risks, Talia. They understand the consequences if they're caught. You can't blame yourself. If it's anyone's fault, it's mine." Crane slammed a closed fist into the armrest, and I jumped at the rare display of emotion.

"When the doctors on the first hoverplane told me they hadn't found one, I should've insisted they keep looking. McDonough is too methodical, too cunning to leave anything to chance."

Crane's guilt magnified my own. We were both partially responsible for the tracker debacle. Both of us should've known better. I closed my mind off completely. There was no use lingering on things that couldn't be changed, and doing so would only sink me into despair. Forward. I needed to just keep moving forward.

"Where will all the refugees go?" I asked to change the subject.

With the critical patients on their way to the cottage, plus Brand and the other soldiers, Coalition Headquarters—Crane's home—had to be nearing capacity. Even with all of the sublevels, there wasn't anywhere close to enough room for everyone.

"There are temporary facilities where they can stay until we find them permanent housing. Doctors can treat their injuries there, and they can be assessed for compatibility with the Coalition," Crane replied.

Compatibility with the Coalition? That sounded ominous.

"We can't be too careful, Talia. I have spies all over the eastern half of the United States, and some placed in high government positions within TOXIC. McDonough isn't stupid; he's done the same. Anyone seeking refuge in the Coalition's territory has to be thoroughly evaluated before being allowed in."

"I see," was all I said. His reasons made sense, but I didn't want to think about the little boy with the burned arm being "evaluated." It brought to mind the images of those lines of children that had been forced into my mind on the ground in Gatlinburg. I shuddered. That Manipulator had controlled me as easily as a puppet. I didn't appreciate that. No, I hated that. I was done with blind subservience.

"Our procedures are painless, I promise," Crane continued, as though reading my mind. He wasn't. I'd made sure of that. But I was doing little to keep my emotions out of my expression.

"How long before we're back at the cottage?" I asked abruptly.

I wanted nothing more than to see Erik. To sit with him, hold his hand, and tell him that everything was okay. I wanted to tell him about flying to California, convincing Crane to help us, and the rescue mission. I wanted to tell him Penny was alive, and that together the three of us would provide UNITED with the proof they needed to take action and stop Mac and TOXIC.

"A couple of hours. We need to drop the refugees off at one of the induction facilities, then we'll fly straight home. Don't worry. He's in good hands until you get there. My doctors are top notch. I have a feeling Penny will personally take charge of his care in your absence. And God help him if he wakes up before we get there and Marin takes responsibility for his care. She is quite the force to be reckoned with." Crane's eyes crinkled when he talked about his supposed housekeeper.

That was how she'd been introduced to me, as Crane's housekeeper, the official headquarters cook, and unofficial Coalition manager. I wasn't fooled. The way Crane and Marin looked at each other, all soft and sickeningly sweet, made it obvious the separate bedrooms were purely for show. And I'd taken the liberty of reading Marin's thoughts, just to be sure I was right—know thy enemy and all that. Neither Crane nor Marin was my enemy, but they were unknown entities, so I thought the proverb still applied.

"What about Henri? Are you going to make him go to an induction camp?" I really hoped not. He was already wary of Crane and after being shot, I didn't trust his wellbeing to strangers.

Crane scrutinized my face as I gave him, what I hoped, was an earnest smile. I thought about summoning the strength to compel him to agree, but I wasn't sure I had it in me. Old-fashion begging, however, I was plenty capable of.

"He's Frederick's partner, right?" Crane asked, clearly stalling for time.

"Yes, and he was my team captain when I was with the Hunters. You can trust him."

"Trust is a strong word, Talia. You shouldn't use it lightly," Crane replied, giving me one of his penetrating gazes.

"I don't," I snapped, suddenly irritated that he was treating me like a child.

"Do you trust me?" he asked, surprising me.

Did I trust Ian Crane? I knew he hadn't killed my parents and he'd helped me rescue Erik. But did that mean that I trusted him? So many people had violated my trust. So many people had lied to me. Some had done it to protect me, others not so much. Crane wasn't one of those people.

"Yes," I whispered. "I think I do."

Pure relief flooded Crane's features, causing the iridescent blue-black irises to swirl. He cleared his throat loudly before speaking. "If it means that much to you, then Henri may come back to the cottage. But I'm warning you, if he turns out to be a spy, you'll be answering to Brand." Crane was at least partially teasing me, but the thought of being at Brand's mercy made me shiver.

I elected to return to the main cabin after my talk with Crane. I didn't want Henri to be alone, and wanted him to know Frederick was safe.

The steel flooring of the cabin was uncomfortable and my butt soon went numb. I insisted Henri lie down, and had him rest his head in my lap while I applied a wet towel to his clammy forehead. I relayed the good news about Frederick, and it went a long way towards relaxing him. He slept fitfully for the remainder of the journey. I felt horrible for him. In one week, his entire world had been turned upside down. He'd been hurt rescuing Erik's family, and then shot in the raid on the station. He had really believed in TOXIC and what they stood for; he was loyal through and through. Yet, his loyalty to the Agency had been usurped by his friendship with Erik. He'd risked his life to help Erik save his family, and he was paying dearly for it. Henri would never be able to go home again, never see his sister, or his parents.

At some point, a young girl with sloppy pigtails and wide-set eyes brought me damp rags and insisted I tend to my feet. In caring for Henri, I'd forgotten how beat up they were. I thanked her, and wiped them clean as best I could manage without jostling Henri. Thankfully, the scratches were all superficial. As long as they weren't already infected from stepping in so much grossness, I'd heal quickly.

The stop at the induction camps to drop off the refugees was short, and I declined Crane's offer to inspect them for myself. I knew he only suggested it to allay my fears that the process was unpleasant. Admittedly, I was extremely curious. I was also extremely tired, to the point that even the slightest movement was a chore. Every inch of me, from my eyeballs to my pinkie toes ached with fatigue. Lack of decent sleep was the biggest contributor, but using my Talents repeatedly hadn't helped either.

The little burned boy's mother thanked me for helping her son before deplaning, and it took every ounce of self-control I possessed not to blather on about how sorry I was that I'd brought the war to her front door.

While Crane talked to the soldiers at the facility, I helped Henri lie down on one of the vacated benches so that he could stretch out. When Crane re-boarded, he handed me a paper bag and two bottles of fresh water.

"You both need nourishment," he told me.

I hungrily dug into the paper bag and discovered two sandwiches. The meat was from an animal I couldn't identify and the bread was grainy with an odd consistency, but I devoured mine in three bites, and then drained half my bottle of water. I woke Henri, and insisted he try to eat his meal. He only ate half of the sandwich, which didn't appear to sit well with him. I worried that maybe I hadn't cleaned his wound well enough, and infection was already setting in.

It was late afternoon, West Coast time, when we finally landed at the cottage. My bones creaked when I moved, my vision lacked focus, and I was practically sleepwalking, but the moment my scratched feet hit the pebbled driveway, I knew I was home.

Chapter Six

"TALIA, THANK GOODNESS you're alive!" Penny cried, bursting through the front door and flying at me in a blur of bright red hair and pale limbs.

The heaviness surrounding my heart lightened at the sound of her voice. I returned her tight embrace, still finding it hard to believe she was alive herself.

"Penny?!?" Henri exclaimed.

When I turned to look at him, he was pale as if he'd seen a ghost. In a way, he had, I supposed. "You're... alive?"

"It's a miracle, I know!" she replied, releasing me in favor of him.

Henri awkwardly returned the gesture the best he could with only one working arm. His torso was still bare except for the gauze I'd wrapped across his chest and injured shoulder. When Penny stepped back, he reached for her again with his good hand, lightly fingering her bright red hair as if checking to make sure she was corporeal and not a hallucination.

"What? How? They said that... " Henri seemed at a loss for words.

Not that I blamed him. My reaction at seeing her in the flesh that first time had been nearly identical.

"Not that Talia didn't do a great job patching you up, but I think one of my doctors should take a look at you right now. I'm sure one of the girls will explain everything after you've had some rest," Crane interjected, steering Henri towards the door. He didn't protest, but kept stealing glances at Penny over his shoulder.

Penny linked her arm through mine and led me inside the cottage. I leaned gratefully into her for support, more emotional than physical.

"What happened?" she asked as we walked. "Brand got back and said you guys had to stop so that Erik could get medical attention, and then Erik and like three other people showed up on a hovercraft. The pilot said something about the Underground station being raided? And then we started to get all this chatter about it. The word on the airways is that there are a ton of casualties, and that both you and Uncle Ian had been spotted! And why aren't you wearing shoes?" In typical Penny fashion, she didn't take a single breath. I smiled, the familiarity of it easing a little of my tension.

"How's Erik? After I see him, I promise I'll tell you all I know," I said.

"Oh! I'm such a bad friend. Of course you can see him first!" She squeezed my arm affectionately.

"You're not a bad friend, Penny. You're the best friend that I could ask for," I told her, meaning every word of it.

We'd fallen back into our friendship easily. I'd apologized for exposing her as a Coalition spy and she'd apologized for not coming clean with me. Each of us had insisted the other had nothing to be sorry for. I truly believed she didn't. Sure, I wished she'd told me who she was and why she was there. And no matter her proclamations to the contrary, I knew she wished I hadn't outted her as a spy.

Over mugs of orange blossom tea, Penny had told me exactly why she'd been sent undercover to the school.

The Coalition had spies all over TOXIC. From prison guards to the unseen cafeteria staff at school to medics at Elite Headquarters, Crane had eyes and ears nearly everywhere. His spies had watched me and reported their findings to him. So Crane knew Mac kept me close to him, and dating Donavon brought me closer still. He knew Mac had given me a pseudo family, a boyfriend, and a facsimile of a normal life. Well, normal for a Talent, anyway. What Mac hadn't given me were friends. Besides Donavon, I was close to no one my own age. Crane had thought filling that gap with Penny would prove easy. He'd overestimated how much I cared that it was empty.

Penny told me she'd tried to get close to me while we were both still at school, but despite being almost friendless, I was also almost never alone. We had none of the same classes, and I spent my weekends with Donavon, and after he'd left to pledge the Hunters, Gretchen and Mac.

The day she'd approached me in the Hunters' Village was fortuitous, Penny had said. It had been the opportunity she'd been waiting for. She'd been excited she was finally making progress on her mission to befriend me. Once she did, however, she realized convincing me to leave TOXIC wasn't going to happen. She saw how loyal I was to Mac, and knew I wouldn't believe her if she told me that Mac, not Crane, had killed my parents.

Instead of scrapping the mission altogether, Penny and Crane had devised an elaborate plan to bring me face-to-face with Crane. Once I talked to him, they thought, surely I'd see the truth. And, eventually, I had. Just not soon enough.

"Stop, you'll make me cry," Penny teased, pulling me back to the present.

I smiled at her, and suppressed the urge to apologize for the umpteenth time.

At first glance, the cottage that Crane and Penny, among others, called home was an adorable rustic cabin. Built on the very edge of cliffs that stretched one hundred feet above the Pacific Ocean, the one-level structure boasted an impressive view of the beautiful body of water. The lush redwood forest surrounding the cottage on the other three sides provided protection from prying eyes. Of course, the heavily armed soldiers patrolling that forest also prevented unauthorized individuals from getting too close.

The single above ground level was Crane's living quarters. It had a small foyer, a small study to the right of the doorway, a short hallway with three small bedrooms to the left of the doorway, and a ridiculously large kitchen occupying the entire back half of the cottage. In the center of that small foyer was a trapdoor, which led to the first of ten subterranean levels built into the cliffs beneath the cottage like an inverted skyscraper. Those subterranean levels—sublevels, really—made up Coalition Headquarters.

Penny accompanied me through the trap door, down the metal staircase, through the atrium, to the elevator bank, and finally to sublevel five: the medical ward. The air in the corridor was chilly on account of it being so far underground. The walls were smooth stone, and the electric lights looked modern and out of place in comparison. I worried about Erik being down here in the drafty space.

Brand stood, surly as ever, outside the door to Erik's room. He looked bored until his piercing green eyes caught sight of me. Then he gave a whole new meaning to the phrase if looks could kill. Despite my exhaustion, I straightened my spine, rising to my full sub-five feet, and met his challenge head-on.

"What, are you guarding him?" I demanded. "He isn't a danger to you."

Brand gave me an exaggerated eye roll. "No, I'm babysitting him. Ian wanted to be informed the minute his condition changed, so I've been relegated to sitting in his room watching him sleep. The doctor is in there now, and he asked me to wait in the hallway."

"Oh," I said, the fight going out of me. "How is he?"

Sympathy flashed across Brand's face, but it was gone in an instant and I thought I might have imagined it. "You'll have to ask his doctor," he said.

I looked from Penny to Brand. "Can I go in?" I wasn't sure since Brand had said the doctor asked him to leave.

"Probably. I assume you've seen him naked, so it won't be an invasion of his privacy."

I let the barb go. I had seen Erik naked and didn't care if Brand knew it.

"Brand, be nice," Penny chastised him. "Go on, Tal. I'll wait out here," she said to me.

I slowly turned the knob and pushed the door open, trying to make as little noise as possible. My fears about Erik being uncomfortable down here were put to rest immediately. The room had the same stone walls as the corridor, but the floor was covered in soft white rugs. A bamboo dresser sat on one wall, a matching desk on another. A comfortable-looking overstuffed couch lined the third. And the fourth wall was entirely glass and overlooked the ocean below. I'd been down to the beach several times since my arrival at Casa de Crane, and knew the exterior of the windowpane was coated with camo spray to make it indistinguishable from the rock face surrounding it.

A dark-skinned man in a white lab coat stood next to Erik's bed. He used an electronic pad to record all of the vitals from the monitors hooked up to Erik. The doctor looked up when he saw me, the irritated expression he wore quickly melted into a kind smile.

"Ms. Lyons, I presume?" he said. His accent was thick, but his English was perfect.

"Um, yeah," I replied, surprised he'd addressed me by name.

The doctor waved me forward, and I slowly crossed the stone floor to join him at Erik's bedside.

"Dr. Patel," he said, offering me his hand.

Tentatively, I shook it. The doctor radiated warmth and caring, and I was immensely grateful that this was the man treating Erik. All of my doctors were cold and impersonal, and I rarely got the impression they cared about me so much as they were fascinated by me. But Dr. Patel was not like that at all.

"It's nice to meet you," I told the doctor honestly.

"You as well, Ms. Lyons," he said, and I got the distinct impression he really meant it, too.

"How is he?" I nodded my head towards Erik.

The quilt on the bed was pulled down, exposing Erik's body from the waist up. His abdomen was so swollen that it puffed out like the bellies of malnourished children I'd seen pictures of. Bruises in various stages of healing colored his chest black, purple, blue, green, and yellow. A thin line of stitches ran through his bottom lip to the point of his chin. A blue plastic cast, identical to the one Cadence wore, encased his right arm from the tips of his fingers to his armpit. Underneath the quilt, there was a huge bulge where one of his knees should've been.

Someone had taken the care to wash his hair, and it was shiny and still a little damp, and smelled like pine. I longed to run my fingers through the thick strands. All the dirt and blood had been scrubbed from his skin, which only made his injuries that much more visible.

"He had a great deal of internal bleeding. A broken rib punctured his lung. Bones in his arm are broken, as is his knee cap," the doctor said matter-of-factly.

I inhaled a shaky breath. "Is that all?" I mumbled, the words coming out more sarcastic than I'd meant them to.

Dr. Patel gave a short laugh. "Yes, he has been through quite an ordeal. He has lost a lot of blood, but his body has responded well to the transfusions. I have him sedated right now." The doctor paused, and I felt the weight of his gaze assessing me. "Ms. Lyons, how long was Mr. Kelley imprisoned?" he asked finally.

"Around a week," I said absently.

"Was he injured prior to his imprisonment?"

"No," I said, growing uneasy. "Why?" I tore my gaze away from Erik to appraise the doctor.

"The breaks to his bones do not appear recent. Judging by the level of remodeling, I would posit the breaks occurred several weeks ago. Even many of his bruises appear older than one week."

"He's a Talent; he heals fast," I said with a shrug like it was no big deal. Truthfully, I didn't think it was. Dr. Patel probably just didn't treat many Talents, so he wasn't used to our rapid healing abilities.

"No, Ms. Lyons, there is more to it than that," Dr. Patel replied with a patient smile. "Being Talented, his cells do regenerate more quickly than a non-Talent. But not this quickly."

"What are you suggesting?" I asked impatiently. My head hurt and I was growing tired of this roundabout conversation.

"I believe he was given something, a drug perhaps, to help him heal faster. Nothing came up in his initial blood work, but I have ordered more in-depth testing. I will know for certain shortly."

"So, what does that mean exactly? Is the healing drug a bad thing or a good thing?"

"Too soon to tell," Dr. Patel responded, his words full of false cheerfulness. "Right now, the important thing is that all of his vitals are strong. I am hopeful he will make a full recovery."

"Is there a chance he won't?" I asked.

"As I said, his body has yet to reject the blood transfusions, which is a very good sign."

"But?" I prompted since there was definitely a "but."

"But it is too soon for certainties. There is still a chance his body will reject the blood."

"What will happen if it does?"

"I do not believe you need to worry about—"

"What will happen if it does?" I hissed the question through gritted teeth this time.

"He could die."

Tears sprang immediately to my eyes, spilling down my cheeks before I thought to stop them.

"I have faith, Ms. Lyons. You should, too. The fact he is still alive after what he has been through is a miracle. It would take much less than that for him to pull through." Dr. Patel placed a hand on my shoulder and gave it a light squeeze. "The best thing you can do for him now is be here. Talk to him. Let him hear your voice, feel your touch. The emergency medics said he called your name on the plane. I cannot imagine he won't make a full recovery so long as he knows you are waiting on this side for him."

My shoulders began to tremble, and I had to bite my knuckles to keep from dissolving into a blubbering mess. The doctor patted my back once more then quietly left me alone with the love of my life.

Penny and Brand didn't enter Erik's room right away; they let me cry in peace. When Penny finally did come in, she had clean clothes for me, including soft fuzzy socks. Brand stayed in the doorway, looking uncomfortable.

"There's a bathroom through there," Penny said gently, pointing at a door I hadn't noticed before. "Why don't you take a shower, get cleaned up. I'll sit with him in case he wakes up."

I didn't care about getting clean. I didn't care that I was likely covered in blood, dirt, chemicals, and who knew what else. I just wanted to be with him.

"You really want the first thing he sees when he wakes up to be you, looking like you've been to hell and back?" Penny asked.

"Yeah, if he sees you like this, he'll probably wish he hadn't bothered," Brand piped up from the doorway.

I shot him my own if-looks-could-kill glare, knowing full well that the difference between mine and Brand's was that I was actually capable of killing someone with my stare. Brand recoiled; inwardly, I smiled with satisfaction.

"You promise you'll stay with him?" I said to Penny. "I don't want him waking up alone or with a stranger. It might scare him."

Brand snorted.

"What's so funny?" I snapped, rounding on Brand. I'd had all I could take of his snarky attitude.

"Really? He's been physically and psychologically tortured. His body has taken more abuse than I can even fathom. I don't know how he didn't break, let alone how he stayed sane. And you're worried he'll be scared if he wakes up alone? Give the guy a little more credit than that." Brand's tone was more respectful than I'd ever heard it. Even when addressing Crane, he didn't show such reverence.

"That's enough, Brand," Penny said sternly. "Yes, Talia, I promise," she added, addressing me.

"Thanks, Penny."

I took the clothes she'd brought me from my room upstairs and headed for the bathroom. The hot water stung my face and neck, but it felt amazing and I barely cared. Originally, I'd planned on rinsing off the worst of the grime and then returning to Erik's side. But the desire to rid my body of not just the visible signs of battle, but the deeper, hidden reminders, as well, trumped that.

After dislodging small rocks, twigs, and some questionable metal fragments from my curls, I filled the porcelain tub to the brim with steaming water. I scrubbed furiously at the grossness lodged under my fingernails, between my toes, and in odd places like behind my ears. Pieces of rubble that still clung to my hair sank to the bottom of the tub when I finger-combed the tangles. I used lavender soap to rid my skin of the acrid scent of chemical bombs and gunpowder. I had to empty and refill the tub three times to avoid sitting in filth.

In addition to the lavender soap, someone had left a collection of lavender face wash along with shampoo and conditioner. I made a mental note to thank Penny. Only she would have gone to so much trouble for me.

Being naked, I discovered my feet weren't the only parts of my body bearing marks. Bruises were blossoming on my calf, my thigh, over my right hip, and those were just the ones that had started to turn color. Tender patches of skin along my ribcage promised later discoloration would follow there, too. After more than an hour, I finally emptied the tub for the last time, and wrapped my body in a thick towel. The material was so soft and if Brand hadn't been on the other side of the door, I might've worn the towel to keep my vigil. Propriety made me put on the shorts and t-shirt Penny had brought me.

A collection of gold-handled hairbrushes and combs were laid out on the bathroom vanity. An intricate rose design had been carved into the handle of each utensil. There was something oddly familiar about the carvings, but I couldn't place it.

Clean and smelling a hundred times better than when I entered the bathroom, I finally rejoined Penny, Brand, and Erik. I noticed right away that the couch had been folded out, revealing a sofa bed. Sheets, pillows, and a quilt that matched the one covering Erik were already layered over the mattress. Penny and Brand were seated in the two armchairs.

"Feel better?" Penny asked brightly when she saw me.

"You look better. Not so crazed," Brand said before I had a chance to answer her.

I didn't have the energy to deal with him, so I ignored Brand's half-assed compliment.

"I do. You were right, a shower was good for me," I said, pointedly focusing my attention on Penny. "Thank you for the soaps, the hairbrushes, and, of course, for making the bed."

"I figured you'd want to sleep down here with him." She shrugged, looking a little embarrassed by my gratitude. "Are you hungry? Do you want me to have Marin send some food down?"

"No thank you. I ate something earlier on the plane," I told her, staring longingly at the sofa bed.

"I'm sure you want to get some sleep. Just send a comm up if you need anything, and I'll come see you later," Penny said, having followed my gaze. "Let's go, Brand."

Penny hugged me once more, promising to return later. I watched the two of them leave. I was so tired that my vision kept crossing, and I couldn't think straight. But I wanted to touch Erik, let him know I was here, just as Dr. Patel had suggested. I grabbed the quilt off of the sofa bed, dragged one of the armchairs across the floor, and set it next to the hospital bed. I bent over Erik's sleeping form, kissing him softly on his forehead. He didn't stir. I curled my legs underneath me in the chair, rested my head against the arm, and laced my fingers with his.

"I love you," I whispered, before closing my eyes and giving myself over to exhaustion.

Chapter Seven

SOMETHING WET AND sticky slid over my forehead. It stung and I groaned. When I tried to swat it away, fingers encircled my wrist. My eyes shot open, and I was staring into Dr. Patel's chocolate eyes. I jumped slightly, recoiling from his touch.

"Ms. Lyons, good morning," the doctor said cheerfully.

Morning? Hadn't it been afternoon when I'd fallen asleep? I looked past him at the picture window. Someone must have pulled the curtains shut, because only a small crack was visible between the navy panels. Light sliced through the opening, creating a golden rod across the quilt covering Erik.

"What did you do to me?" I croaked, lightly fingering my forehead. The pads of my fingers came away tacky.

"You have some nasty scratches. I thought it best to disinfect them," Dr. Patel answered pleasantly.

"Thanks," I muttered. I shifted to a sitting position, the springs of the sofa bed groaning softly underneath me. Confused, I looked for the chair that I remembered dragging to Erik's bedside. "Didn't I sleep in a chair?" I asked him.

"You fell asleep in the chair, but President Crane moved you in the night." Dr. Patel straightened, backed away from the sofa bed, and gestured to a small folding table. "Are you hungry? Ms. Marin sent down breakfast."

I inhaled the rich aroma of freshly brewed coffee and sweet cinnamon buns. My stomach growled, and I swung my legs over the side of the bed as I reached for the coffee. The steam wafting over the lip of the mug warned me that the contents were hot, but I took a long swallow anyway. The liquid burned my tongue, but the caffeine jolted my senses awake.

"How is he this morning?" I asked Dr. Patel, who was now busy recording Erik's vitals on his electronic pad.

"Everything looks to be in order," Dr. Patel replied, keeping his back to me.

I grabbed one of the cinnamon buns sitting on the plate and bit into it. Sugary icing and cinnamon pastry filled my mouth as I hungrily devoured the treat. My stomach clenched almost painfully around the food, but I moved on to a second pastry without hesitation.

"Are you treating all of the people who were brought from Gatlinburg?" I asked Dr. Patel. I wanted to know how Cadence was doing. Somehow between my concern for Henri and my haste to get to Erik, I'd forgotten to make sure that she'd arrived here.

"Some of them. Your friend, Mr. Reich is it? He is doing well. His shoulder will require surgery, but you did a fine job stitching the wound."

I breathed a sigh of relief. At least Henri was okay. "What about a girl? She's in her early twenties, small, with black hair and black eyes. She has a broken leg and some other injuries. She should have been brought in around the same time as Erik."

Dr. Patel turned, and shook his head. "I am sorry, Ms. Lyons, no one meeting that description is under my care. She may have been taken to one of the induction camps."

Right, the induction camps. Cadence had probably been taken there since I hadn't been on her plane to advocate for her being brought to the cottage instead.

"I will come by again in a couple of hours. If you need me before then, send a comm and I will come immediately. When you are through with your breakfast," he paused, looking at the empty plate, "Put the dishes in the dumbwaiter and send them up."

"Dumbwaiter?" I asked, looking around the room like that would help me understand what he was talking about.

"Yes." Dr. Patel crossed the room, and pushed a button next to a metal square fixed into the wall. The door slid open, revealing a hollow space. "Dumbwaiter."

I grabbed my empty breakfast dish and joined him. I placed the plate on the tray inside the dumbwaiter. He closed the door and pushed a second button. This one had a small up pointing arrow. A metallic whine met my ears, and instinctively I knew that the plate was soaring upwards. It was like an elevator, for food.

"It is connected with the kitchen. Marin can send food, clothes, whatever you need, using the dumbwaiter. That way you will not have to leave unless you wish to do so," Dr. Patel explained.

"Thank you," I said.

"Comm me if you or Mr. Kelley needs anything," Dr. Patel replied, and then he left.

I took my coffee and curled up in the chair I'd set by Erik's bed the night before. The steady hum of the machines monitoring his vitals was oddly peaceful. His breathing was shallow but even, and maybe it was just wishful thinking, but I swore his bruises had faded some.

"I met your father," I told Erik's sleeping form. I waited before continuing, even though I knew he wasn't going to respond. "He misses you. Your brothers, too." I swallowed down the lump in my throat. "I don't think Edmond likes me very much, but Evan seemed to come around after spending the day with me." I laced my fingers with Erik's, running the back of his hand down my cheek. I swore his pulse quickened in his wrist, but when I looked at his heart rate monitor, it was steady.

"Alex is with them. You'd be so proud of him; he's been so brave. When you wake up," I choked on the words, tears spilling onto our joined hands. I cleared my throat, "When you wake up," I repeated, "we can go see them."

I continued telling Erik about my journey to California, about becoming the bird and the exhilaration of flying. I told him Penny was alive. Then I rambled on about the attack on the Underground station, and how Henri had been shot but was recovering nicely. I left out the part about him needing surgery—only good vibes in this hospital room.

"Believe it or not, I stitched up the wound myself!" I said in a cheery voice.

"Talia?" For one brief second, I dared to hope that it was Erik who'd called my name. I jumped to my feet, sloshing coffee down my nightshirt.

"Sorry, I didn't mean to startle you."

I heaved out a sigh of disappointment. It was only Crane.

"Hi, Ian," I greeted him. I slumped back into my chair as I heard the soft click of Crane's shoes on the stone floor, which became muffled when he crossed over the rugs.

"How's the patient this morning?" he asked.

I had a feeling he already knew and was just making idle conversation.

"Dr. Patel said he's doing okay," I replied absently, stroking Erik's hand.

"He's going to get better." Crane's voice held so much conviction that hope bubbled up in my throat and fresh tears welled in my eyes.

"I know," I whispered.

We sat in silence for several long minutes. The only sound in the room was the intermittent beeps from Erik's heart monitor. Finally, Crane cleared his throat, and I knew that he was gearing up to tell my something unpleasant.

"I've been in touch with UNITED, Talia. They're eager to meet with you, Penelope, and Erik. A handful of the members are on their way here as we speak."

"So soon," I mused softly. I'd known this was coming. One of Crane's reasons for rescuing Erik was to provide UNITED with proof that TOXIC was using the Creation drug. I'd thought I'd have more time to prepare, though. Not that I had any clue what I was preparing for, but still.

"The sooner they get their proof, the sooner they get involved. The sooner they get involved, the sooner we can stop TOXIC. Further delay will only increase the chances of the news about the experimentation with the drug leaking. If that happens, we'll have a world crisis on our hands."

"I understand," I said. "What's going to happen to us, though? I mean, how are they going to determine that we've been injected with the drug?"

Crane's hesitation was long enough to cause me concern. I turned in my seat to look at him. The Coalition President's expression was as blank as unlined paper. A chill rippled over my skin, leaving goosebumps in its wake.

"Ian?" I prompted. "What are they going to do to us?"

His sigh was like that of a man much older than his years. "A blood sample will prove that you've been injected."

"A blood sample? That's it?" There had to be more to it. Crane wouldn't be blocking me from his thoughts—he definitely had his mental barriers in place—if all they wanted was a blood sample.

"They'd like to evaluate the three of you, as well. I'm sure it will mostly involve questions about TOXIC and your experiences since receiving the drug."

"Mostly?" I parroted, honing in on the one word. "Mostly" implied that UNITED wanted to do more than question us.

"They want to do psychological evaluations on each of you," Crane admitted.

I swallowed hard and turned back around. Psychological evaluations. Wow. While not surprising, also not good. They'd see how unstable I'd become over the last year, that my mood swings were out of control. They'd know Penny had been experiencing catatonic episodes, each one lasting longer than the one before it. Who knew what they'd learn about Erik. What then? What if they determined we were too dangerous to roam free? Would they lock us in a medical ward and study us?

"You have nothing to worry about, Talia," Crane said, in what I assumed was supposed to be a reassuring tone, but fell flat. "I'd never have agreed to let them evaluate you three if I thought there was even the slightest possibility any of you would be harmed in the process."

Right, I thought, but being "harmed" and not being locked up were completely separate things.

"You can always opt out. The choice is yours."

I closed my eyes and pinched the bridge of my nose between my thumb and forefinger. Yes, in theory I had a choice. Not in actuality, though. If I didn't go through with the evaluation, then UNITED would still be lacking their proof.

"Penelope has agreed," Crane added softly.

Erik would, too, I thought. Because this was bigger than the three of us. TOXIC and Mac needed to be stopped. It was a small sacrifice on my part. After encountering that Mind Manipulator in Gatlinburg, who I was starting to fear might be Created, I was more determined than ever to stop them. Recalling how easily that person had manipulated me, an Elite-level Talent, I understood what was at stake here.

That person had been given the gift of mind manipulation and was abusing the power. He wasn't using it for the greater good, he was attempting to brainwash people with it.

After a good night's sleep, my brain was functioning better, and I was starting to understand what I'd seen. The vision of those children Morphing into grotesque half-human, half-animal hybrids hadn't been meant for my eyes. I'd reversed the mental intrusion, seen into that manipulator's mind. Those images were real. They were his memories. And that was truly terrifying.

"No, I want to do it," I said. "How bad can it be, right?"

"Right." I heard the smile in Crane's voice.

Neither of us spoke, the silent seconds stretching into silent minutes. I focused on Erik, content to watch his eyeballs flitter under his lids like he was having a fitful dream. The rest of his body remained eerily still. Every so often my gaze flicked to his heart monitor to reassure myself his heart was still beating.

I felt Crane behind me, watching me watch Erik. He was studying me, the back of my head at least. I wondered what he saw. Sure, I could have swiped his mind, but I wasn't in the mood. There was so much going on, Ian Crane's head was probably a troubling place to be. Probably more troubling than my own head.

"We captured a TOXIC operative during the raid. He tried to board one of the escape planes, and not knowing what else to do, the people overpowered him and brought him here. We are holding him in the cage. He hasn't said much, but I think maybe if you talk to him, he'll cooperate with us," Crane said after a while.

He'd been so quiet, the sound of his voice startled me.

"Why me? I'm sure he considers me a traitor. Not likely he'll be any more willing to talk to me than he has been to you."

"It's my understanding that he knows you. Frederick says you two are friends. His name is Harris Daughtery."

"Harris?!" I exclaimed, whipping around to face Crane, all thoughts of the evaluation temporarily forgotten. "Harris is here?"

"Yes, a couple of levels below you actually. I assure you, he is being treated well," Crane quickly added. "Do you think you might try talking to him?"

It was strange to have someone ask me rather than tell me what to do. Like with the evaluation, I had a choice. I could tell Crane to go to hell, and while I was sure he would be disappointed, I doubted he would force me to do his bidding. Then a horrible thought occurred to me. "Does Penny know?" I whispered.

"My niece?" Crane asked, surprised, like there was another Penny lurking around Coalition Headquarters. "I don't know if she does or not. She's been busy with other matters. Why would Penelope care?"

Awkward.

How did I tell Crane that his niece, who was like a daughter to him, had been, um romantically involved with Harris?

A smile tugged at the corners of my mouth when I thought about telling Brand. Man, he'd be *so* jealous.

"They were... close," I said finally.

Crane appeared confused. "She sent regular reports while on assignment, and filed a very thorough one after her return. I don't recall seeing his name."

"Their relationship was personal," I said comfortably, hoping he'd take the hint so I wouldn't have to spell it out. "It wasn't relevant to her mission," I added for good measure.

"I see," Crane said thoughtfully. "Well, in that case, it's probably better I don't tell her just yet. The young man is not well."

"Not well?" I asked. The cinnamon buns began to churn in my stomach.

"You'll understand when you see him. I can't explain it, but hopefully you'll be able to shed some light on his current ... condition." The way that Crane said "condition" made my toes tingle. What had TOXIC done to Harris?

"The UNITED council members will be here by dinnertime. If you're willing, I'd like for you to see Mr. Daughtery before you meet with them. I have a feeling they'll want to evaluate him, as well. But I'd like your take on his mental state before I let them know he's here."

"Okay, sure," I said quietly.

At one time, Harris had been a good friend to me. He'd always been a good friend to Donavon and Erik, somehow managing to juggle the two guys, despite their mutual disdain for one another. Someone had to determine what was wrong with him, and I preferred that someone be me.

"I'll send Brand for you later in the day. I have some things to attend to before the Council arrives, so he will accompany you to visit Mr. Daughtery."

I nodded, considerably less enthusiastic about the visit than I had been a moment before. Which was saying something, since I'd already been dreading seeing Harris.

Penny brought lunch around noon, and the two of us ate and talked while Erik slept. She already knew most of the details of the attack on Tramblewood since she'd been tuned in to the same frequency our earpieces were transmitting on. Brand had filled in the gaps for her. Apparently he was still pissed about me destroying the bridge, and had complained to Penny about it at length. But after some gentle prodding on her part, he'd grudgingly admitted the decision had been for the best. I understood him a little better when Penny informed me it was his job to tell the families of the deceased that their loved ones weren't coming home.

"I saw Cadence," I told Penny.

"Really? How is she?"

I shrugged and poked at the remains of my lunch, stewed vegetables. Bright orange liquid seeped out of an overcooked tomato when I speared it with my fork.

"She'll heal," I said finally.

"That's good. Uncle Ian told me you found her brother, Randy Choi."

The subject of Randy was one I'd been hoping to avoid. In hindsight, bringing up Cadence had been a bad idea.

Randy had helped Penny's mother escape Tramblewood after she'd been caught trying to break into the McDonough School. When I'd first learned about the incident, I thought it strange. Why would the Coalition want to break into the school? I'd thought. Now, well, now I was pretty sure I knew. Me. Ellen Larsen, Penny's mother, Ian Crane's sister, had been sent to rescue me.

She'd been caught and thrown in prison. Randy had been one of her jailers. From the limited information I had, I knew the two developed a friendship, and Randy helped her escape. TOXIC had chased Ellen, shooting and killing her before she reached Coalition territory.

Like so many wrongs in Penny's life, I felt responsible—if indirectly—for this one, too.

"I want to meet him," Penny continued when I didn't answer. "He was the last to see her, you know."

"Penny—"

"It's been a long time, Tal. I'm okay."

But she wasn't okay. The torment was all over her face. Her eyes had a haunted, hollow quality to them. I wanted to say something helpful. I'd have settled for something intelligible. Instead, all I came up with was, "Seeing Randy will help."

Help what, I didn't know. Closure. People always talked about getting closure, so maybe meeting Randy would help Penny get closure. Just like killing Mac would help me get mine.

"I'm just glad you all got out of Gatlinburg," Penny said, switching gears. "Uncle Ian said it was close."

"It was," I agreed, shifting uncomfortably in my chair as I thought about how close I'd come to surrendering because of that stupid Manipulator. "Do you think Mac's already started injecting people with the new form of the drug? The one with your and Erik's blood."

"Yeah, probably. I mean he did use the old drug on people. I'm sure he's using this one to bolster his army."

That was exactly what I'd feared.

"I think I met one. One of the Created."

Voicing my theory that Mac had already succeeded in creating another Mind Manipulator who was as powerful, if not more so, as me, made it more real. If he had one, he probably had more. Maybe he had an entire army of Morphing Mind Manipulators who foretold the future. I'd handed him Bethy, an exceptionally powerful Visionary, on a silver platter just weeks ago. That was plenty of time for him to have stolen enough of her blood to make more just like her.

I told Penny about my encounter with the Manipulator, sparing no detail.

"Wow. So he was as strong as you?" she asked, green eyes wide with amazement.

"Stronger, maybe," I admitted reluctantly. It was stupid, but I was used to being the best, the most powerful, and I hated having an equal in the Talent department.

"No, not stronger." Penny shook her head decisively. "Not possible. A Created Talent is only as strong, at best, as his creator—the blood donor. So, he can't be stronger than you since you're most likely his blood donor."

I choked on my own saliva. "Excuse me?" I stammered, sure I'd misheard.

"You are the strongest Mind Manipulator alive today—"

"That we know of," I interjected.

"That we know of," she conceded. "Which means Director McDonough probably used your blood to make that guy. If he's as strong as you say."

I was torn between being comforted and disgusted by this. Comforted because that meant the next time I faced off with my Talent clone, I'd know I was stronger than him. Disgusted because there was a Created Mind Manipulator out there abusing *my* Talent.

The anger began as a small knot in the pit of my stomach, growing hotter with each breath I took, until finally I was ready to explode. My natural gifts, my Talents that were just as much a part of me as my freckles or my purple eyes, were being exploited. Until that instant I hadn't truly appreciated how infuriating that was.

"Tal?" Penny sounded scared. "Tal, calm down." Her thin fingers were prying at mine.

I looked down and realized my nails had become talons, the skin of my arms leathery and black, and I was drawing deep grooves in the arm of the chair.

"Control, Talia. Remember? We need to stay in control." Her voice was so soothing, her suggestion so reasonable. The anger began to dissipate, leaving a tranquil calm in its place.

Before my eyes, my hands became my own. I shook my head. "Looks like you were given my blood, too," I told Penny.

Her grave silence was answer enough.

Dr. Patel made another visit that afternoon, accompanied by Brand. At first, I was dismayed by Brand's appearance, but it proved beneficial when he told me that Henri was asking for me. Penny said she'd sit with Erik while I was gone. Brand hurriedly offered to wait with her. I smirked at his eagerness.

Dr. Patel escorted me down the corridor to Henri's room, since he said that he needed to check on him anyway. On the short walk the doctor informed me that Henri had undergone minor surgery during the night, and the bullet damage had been repaired. The good news lifted my spirits.

Henri's room was much smaller than Erik's, more akin to a real hospital room than the posh hotel atmosphere of Erik's. He, too, had a window that overlooked the ocean, and Frederick was admiring the view when I entered.

"Hey, Talia," Frederick greeted me, turning at the sound of the door opening. "Doctor."

"Mr. Kraft," Dr. Patel nodded respectfully to Frederick. "And how are you feeling, Mr. Reich?" he asked turning his attention on Henri.

"Pretty good," Henri replied.

I waved at Henri, then moved to join Frederick by the window. I smiled at him tentatively, letting him know my anger with him had lessened. It would be a while before I forgave him completely, but harboring a grudge was exhausting and seemed petty.

Together, Frederick and I watched while Dr. Patel removed Henri's bandages and checked his shoulder. Fresh, precision-straight stitches held together tender pink skin. Henri's color was much better than it had been when we arrived; there was no green tinge to his cheeks anymore. He seemed to be in a good mood.

"Your sutures look good, Mr. Reich," Dr. Patel declared, and wrapped fresh bandages around Henri's torso. "I do not anticipate lasting damage, but your range of motion will be limited for some time. In a couple of days we will begin some light physical therapy. Ms. Lyons, Mr. Kraft, I will see you both later." With that Dr. Patel left to check on his other patients.

I moved to Henri's bedside and gave him a tentative hug. "I'm glad to see you're doing better," I told him.

"Thanks to you," he replied.

"Thanks to Dr. Patel," I said. "He's the reason you'll be able to use that arm again."

Gingerly, Henri wiggled his shoulder and grimaced. "Hopefully." His expression turned serious, and he averted his gaze to his lap. "I'm sorry about yesterday, Talia. I overreacted."

"It's a lot to take in," Frederick interjected. "I should've been honest with you from the beginning. It's my fault, really. You have nothing to be sorry for."

I reached for Henri's good hand, and threaded my small fingers through his long ones. "Frederick's right. It is a lot to take in. I'm still wrapping my head around it all, and I've been here for days."

"In Gatlinburg people were talking about Crane, saying how he's this great person. They idolize him. I sort of always thought TOXIC was exaggerating the whole hating Talents thing, so I wasn't surprised to hear that wasn't true. And Erik told me about the Creation drug and how the Director had used it on Donavon, which is crazy," Henri continued as if I hadn't spoken. "It was just... I don't know, when I saw you two with Crane, I felt like..." his voice trailed off.

"Like you'd been lied to?" I guessed.

Henri nodded miserably. I squeezed his hand affectionately. I knew the feeling all too well.

"Henri," Frederick began, crossing the room in three long strides to join us.

"No, I get it," Henri held up his free hand to cut off his boyfriend's apologies, and winced when the movement irritated his shoulder. "You did what you thought was best. Not confiding in me about your involvement with the Coalition was for the best at the time. I understand that, seriously."

Frederick and Henri exchanged smiles, both boys' eyes glazing over with a warmth that made me feel like I should leave them alone. I patted Henri's hand and was about to politely excuse myself before my presence become intrusive, when Henri asked, "How's Erik?"

"Stable. Dr. Patel thinks he'll make a full recovery," I replied, trying to smile. I wanted to believe Dr. Patel. I needed to believe him. "Has Penny been by?" I asked to change the subject.

Henri laughed. "She stopped by earlier this morning. After all that she's been through, it's nice to see she hasn't changed."

"Did she tell you what happened to her?" I asked, arching an eyebrow in surprise. Besides me, her uncle, and Brand, I didn't think Penny had told anyone.

"No, Frederick did. Poor Penny."

"I read her official report," Frederick explained.

"She's a survivor," I said, thinking about her determination to go through with the evaluation, despite not knowing what that might entail.

Of the two of us, she was the stronger in many ways. Where I was scared of the unknown, she seemed to embrace it. She'd gone undercover in TOXIC fully aware of the consequences if she were discovered. Yet, she had no way to know what she'd find once there.

Now, once again, Penny was ready to do whatever it took to bring TOXIC down. She wasn't concerned with the prospect of being locked away or treated like a test subject, and she had more reason to fear that than I did. After all, she'd already lived that reality. Not for the first time, I vowed to be more like Penny.

"Any news on Cadence? Or Randy?" I asked to break the awkward silence that had descended on our trio like a wet blanket.

"They're both at one of the induction facilities," Frederick said. "I've had their evaluations marked as high priority so they won't have to stay there longer than necessary. With all of the refugees being brought in from the various Underground stations, it will take a couple of days, though."

I nodded. That was the best I could have hoped for. Frederick seemed to have as much clout as anyone besides Crane and Brand, so if a couple of days was the best he could do, then that would have to be that.

I wondered how much either of them knew about Harris. Crane had said that Frederick was the one to inform him of our friendship, which meant Frederick at least knew he was at the cottage. All the mystery surrounding Harris's "condition" had me more than a little curious.

"Have you seen Harris?" I asked.

Frederick and Henri exchanged uneasy glances that set my teeth on edge.

"What?" I demanded, looking from one guy to the other and back again.

Neither answered me, but instead carried on an annoying conversation with eye rolls and face gestures. It was like they were speaking their own language, one I wasn't fluent in. I hated being left out of the loop.

"What?" I repeated, backing the single word with a dose of my will to prevent being ignored a second time.

Finally, Frederick said, "You should really see him for yourself. It's too hard to explain."

Now I rolled my eyes. Why all the secrecy? If I was going to talk to him anyway, why didn't anyone feel comfortable preparing me for what I was going to find? A thought occurred to me: no one knew what I'd find. Whatever was wrong with Harris was unidentifiable. That was why Crane wanted me to talk to him.

"You are going to talk to him, aren't you?" Frederick asked.

I sighed. "Yeah, I told Ian I would."

"Just be prepared," Frederick said.

"For what?" I threw up my free hand in exasperation.

"The worst, Tal."

That deflated me. After all I'd seen lately, I couldn't even imagine what the worst was. I found myself reconsidering the visit, particularly when I remembered Brand was my chaperone.

"Want to go with me?" I asked Frederick hopefully. Maybe I could cut Brand out of the equation.

Frederick laughed. It seemed as though he'd read between the lines of my request. "Give Brand a chance. He's really not so bad."

"Give *him* a chance?" I said incredulously. "He's the one who hates me!"

"He doesn't hate you," Frederick said softly. "Brand's story is complicated. He's been through a lot."

I wanted to argue. Hadn't I been through a lot? I'd seen my parents die, been taken in by their murderer, lied to, experimented on, and who knew what else. And I didn't have a boulder-sized chip on my shoulder. But when I opened my mouth to make a snappy retort, I realized that maybe I did. It wasn't like I had people lining up to be my friends. With a shudder, I considered that Brand and I might be more alike than I cared to admit.

"I'll see you guys later," I said instead. I hugged first Henri and then Frederick, who whispered in my ear that he'd see me in the meeting later. That lifted my spirits a little. At least there'd be one friendly face in the crowd.

Chapter Eight

BRAND WAS SITTING in an armchair when I returned to Erik's room, reading a tattered book. Penny, I noticed immediately, was nowhere in sight. Without the permanent scowl that he normally wore, Brand was actually kind of good looking. The sunlight bathed him in a warm glow, threading golden highlights through his dark hair. He seemed relaxed, calmer than usual, like he was at peace with the world instead of angry at it. I wondered about what Frederick had said. What trauma had occurred in his past to make Brand so hard?

I actually considered asking Brand about himself, extending an olive branch or whatever. Then, he opened his mouth and all thoughts of a budding friendship flew out the door.

"Took you long enough," he grunted.

"Yeah, well... Where's Penny?"

"Not that it's any of your business, but she's resting."

I snapped. Brand had just made one snide remark too many. "Not my business?" I growled. "Penny is my best friend, which makes her my business."

Brand rose, throwing the book he'd been reading onto the chair with enough force that the binding came loose. "Really, *Natalia*? She's your best friend? Do you condemn all of your friends to death? It's a wonder you have any. Oh wait, I forgot, you don't. Isn't that why it took Penny so long to get close to you in the first place? Because you're too good to be bothered with friends?"

His words hit too close to home. It was true. I didn't have many friends. The ones I did have were recent additions to my social stratosphere. My jaw clenched, and I felt my back molars grind together as I tried to contain my anger.

"She only did it, you know, became your friend, because Ian told her to. She was doing her *job* like any good soldier. Sort of like McDonough's son. What's his name? Donavon? Didn't he only date you to make daddy happy? So daddy could keep you close?" Brand hurtled the accusations at me like knives, and I felt each one stab me in the heart. How he knew about Donavon, I'll never know. Maybe he was just fishing until he hit a nerve. Well, he had.

"Get out," I snarled around a mouth full of razor-sharp teeth. I was literally seconds away from tearing into him. At my sides, my hands were fisted into tight balls with my nails piercing my palms.

"Why? So you can run to Ian and cry about how I was mean to you? Come on, Talia, you're supposed to be this badass, a TOXIC assassin. But when push comes to shove, you hide behind—"

I'd heard enough. My right arm shot forward, power cascaded from my fingertips, spraying raw energy like a fire hose. Brand flew backward, his grass-green eyes going wide with shock before squeezing tight against the pain he felt when his head cracked against the stone wall. I advanced on him, beyond rational thought and indifferent to the repercussions of killing Crane's second in command.

Despite the blood I could smell leaking from the back of his skull, Brand was on his feet before I reached him. He put up his fists, like this was some sort of schoolyard fight. I had news for him: in my schoolyard, we'd fought with our Talents. I slammed him into the wall a second time, and his spine bore the brunt of it. Brand's shoulders sagged, and he was attempting to catch his breath since the wind had apparently been knocked out of him.

I smiled, showing my canines and went in for the knockout. Only, I'd been too quick to count Brand out. He charged me from that hunched-over position, landing a shoulder in the center of my sternum and sending me toppling onto my butt. A jolt of pain rocketed up my spine and down my legs before being swallowed by my mounting rage. Brand was good, I'd give him that. He didn't waste the small window of opportunity he'd been given. His fist was like a hammer to my temple. I'd been hit plenty of times before, and by better fighters than Brand Meadows. But never had my assailants' punches packed so much animosity and hatred. I was, probably, the better combatant. Brand was the more emotional one. With every blow, I felt his burning anger. He hated me for what I'd done to Penny. He blamed me for her mother's death. The death of a woman who'd treated him like a son after he was orphaned.

I wasn't the type to allow myself to be a punching bag, even if I secretly felt I deserved many of the hits. I used one arm to shield my face while thrusting the other into his windpipe, causing Brand to arch his neck backward to avoid being cut off from his air supply. His blows started going wild as he flailed against me. Latching onto his mind, I forced him to stop his assault. The guy had a strong will, though, and holding onto his mind was harder than I'd anticipated.

I was able to force Brand off of me, but he fought my manipulation every step of the way. As soon as I was free of his weight, I scrambled to my feet. Sluggish and dazed, Brand tried to stand. I didn't let him. Some of my anger had burned away, but the primal urge to attack was still present. Once again, I went in to finish him.

Not kill him, just make him think twice the next time he wanted to be such an asshole.

"Talia!"

My name stopped me in my tracks. It wasn't his anger or astonishment that brought me up short. It was his disappointment. With TOXIC, I'd been conditioned to please, to seek praise. Having someone I admired be disappointed in me wasn't something I handled well.

There was no need to turn around; I knew Crane was standing behind me, witnessing my loss of control. All at once, the room came back into focus. Brand was on his knees in front of me, looking like he'd gone ten rounds in the sparring ring. Erik was unconscious and oblivious. And Crane stood in the doorway with an open-mouthed Dr. Patel.

Slowly, I turned to face Crane.

"I'm sorry," I stammered, turning my hands over and realizing they were slick with Brand's blood.

One look at my swollen face, and Crane's harsh gaze moved to Brand, who was now staggering to his feet. He swayed a little, but managed to appear defiant.

"I hope you two have gotten your differences out," Crane said. "I will not tolerate this behavior any longer."

"Sir—" Brand started, but Crane cut him off with a wave of his hand.

"I don't want to hear it, Brand. You're both acting ridiculous. This feud has to stop."

Used to being chastised for childish antics, I held my tongue and took the reprimand without comment. Brand, however, seemed to feel the need to defend his actions, and kept trying to interrupt. Crane didn't take kindly to the insubordination, and I got my first real insight into why Ian Crane commanded so much respect.

"If this is going to continue to be a problem for you, Meadows, there are plenty of other soldiers waiting to take your place. I've taken a lot of flak over the years for promoting someone so young over others who are more qualified. Until today, I've never regretted my decision. 'He's mature for his age,' I tell your critics. You just proved me wrong."

I wasn't stupid enough to display the smirk tugging at one corner of my mouth. Crane's ire would turn on me soon.

"And, Talia, you're so worried about UNITED hiding you away for fear you're out of control."

All the blood drained from my face. I was extremely worried about that.

"Are you trying to make that choice easier for them? UNITED has already recommended containment until a reversal drug can be finalized."

My head started to spin. No, no way was I being contained, which was just a fancy way of saying "imprisoned."

"I have their word that it won't come to that unless you prove dangerous in your evaluation." Crane gestured to Brand, who was holding the back of his skull to staunch the bleeding. "Right now, you're proving yourself dangerous."

I bit my cheek to keep from saying something that might damn me further.

"Brand, let Dr. Patel take a look at you. Talia, get cleaned up. I'll be back in one hour to take you to see Mr. Daughtery. Obviously you two need some time away from each other to cool off. This better be the last time I see either of you draw the other's blood. Am I clear?"

"Yes, sir," Brand muttered.

I just nodded. Opening my mouth would've been like lowering the floodgates; a rush of pleas, protests, and profanity would've spewed forth.

All three men exited Erik's room together, leaving me with my wounded pride. Brand's words had angered me. More than that, they'd hurt me. The truth really did hurt. I truly believed that Penny was my friend. At least, now she was. But Brand hadn't been wrong about her reasons for approaching me in the first place. She had gotten close to me because that was her assignment. Donavon had had a similar motivation for dating me. Mac had wanted to keep me close, make sure I never strayed. What better way than to have his son make me fall in love with him?

I continued my pity party as I walked to the bathroom to wash Brand's blood from my skin. One look at my reflection in the mirror over the sink, and I was furious all over again. The left side of my face was all puffy. I looked like a chipmunk that had stuffed too much food into its cheek. I wasn't sure whether to laugh or cry. If he woke up soon, Erik would find a girlfriend with more bumps and bruises than he had. I started to smile but stopped when the gesture caused my cheekbone to sing with pain. Erik would kill Brand if he saw my face.

As happy as that thought made me, I knew I'd have to intervene before it came to that. UNITED would contain Erik if they found him dangerous. No way was I allowing anyone to put him in a cell ever again.

After I was clean, I rang Marin and asked her to send down ice. I was sure Dr. Patel had creams and whatever that would reduce the swelling and prevent horrible bruising, but my naturally expedient healing abilities and ice would work nearly as well. Not even two minutes later, the dumbwaiter dinged its arrival. I opened the door and found two big bags full of ice.

I sat in my chair next to Erik's bed to nurse my injuries while I explained to my unconscious boyfriend all the unfortunate accidents I was envisioning Brand having in the near future. Sure, I knew it was wishful thinking, and that I'd never follow through with any of them. But the little session was therapeutic all the same. I felt a million times better after telling Erik how Brand was going to step on a hornet's nest and get stung one thousand times, or how he might fall out of a hovercraft without a parachute or rappelling harness.

"Ms. Lyons?"

I froze mid-sentence. How long had Dr. Patel been listening to my manic ramblings? Oh no, would he tell Crane?

"Is it okay if I come in? I would like to check his vitals again."

"Of course," I mumbled guiltily, and moved aside to give the doctor room.

Dr. Patel assured me that it was too soon to expect Erik to regain consciousness. Nonetheless, his vitals were strong and the outlook good. Quick scans of his internal organs and bones showed that he was healing rapidly, which seemed to confirm Dr. Patel's suspicion that TOXIC had given him some sort of drug to speed his body's natural healing process. That was likely why Mac and his minions had been so rough with Erik in the first place: they'd known the damage would repair itself quickly.

"Mr. Kelley's blood work came back positive for Veloxics Valencia, a rare drug that increases the rate at which cells and tissues regenerate within the body. At one time, it was used with great frequency, but fell out of favor within the medical community before even I was born." He chuckled like his age was amusing. I wasn't sure I got the joke. Dr. Patel couldn't have been more than like forty.

"Why isn't it used anymore?" I asked, curious. A speedy recovery sounded like a good thing to me.

"Just like with anything that is done in a rush, the healing can be sloppy, for lack of a better word. Bones might be twisted when they reform. Torn tendons might knit back together off-center. That sort of thing. When this sloppy healing occurs, the patient will be very uncomfortable and oftentimes will require surgery to correct the problems. Bones have to be re-broken and reset. It is a mess. The benefits do not outweigh the detriments."

I cringed as the sound of snapping bone filled my mind.

"Mr. Kelley's breaks appear to be healing nicely, though," Dr. Patel added quickly. "All of his scans are promising."

This news did comfort me to a degree. It also sickened me, though. I healed faster than the average human, all Talents did. I'd thought it was a side effect of being Talented. Now I wasn't so sure. Maybe all of the people under TOXIC's control had been given this super-fast healing drug. Maybe that was why Mac was so willing to send us out into potentially life-threatening situations. Dr. Thistler had said my injuries, the ones I'd sustained in Nevada, took an unusually long time to heal because TOXIC hadn't gotten to me soon enough. But maybe they'd just been worse than she'd been willing to admit.

"I am not going to give him any more sedatives," Dr. Patel continued. "Let us see if he wakes up."

For the next hour I watched Erik with rapt attention for even the slightest hint he was ready to rejoin the world. Dr. Patel had told me the sedatives he'd been giving Erik were powerful enough to knock out a two-ton mammal and would, therefore, take anywhere from several hours to several days to wear off. Still, I couldn't help but be discouraged when Erik's beautiful turquoise eyes didn't open immediately.

Crane returned to escort me to Harris's cell. The elevator ride to the prison level was tense and uncomfortable. I stared at the steel doors, at the numbered buttons, at my feet, anywhere except at Crane. I felt as though an apology was in order, but I was still peeved, so I kept quiet.

The prison level was just as cold and impersonal as I remembered it. I shivered at the memory of waking up in a cage after my first encounter with Brand, which made me wish I'd hit him harder.

At the end of the long corridor, two soldiers waited for us. They both nodded to Crane first, and then to me. I gave a small, tight smile in return.

The soldiers showed us into the cage area. The cage had bars on three sides, allowing the inhabitant to be observed at all times. A small cot sat against the solitary wall; Harris was curled into a ball on top of the thin mattress.

"I'd like to go inside," I said to one of the guards.

He looked to Crane for confirmation. When he nodded, the guard unlocked the cage door and held it open for me.

Once inside, I stayed near the door. No one had prepared me for what I'd find, save that there was something "off" about Harris. I had no desire to be within arm's reach if he decided to attack.

"Harris?" I said quietly. He didn't move. "Harris, it's Talia," I tried again. He still didn't budge.

Throwing caution to the wind, I knelt next to the cot so that we were at eye level. The guards outside the cage did have guns trained on us, ostensibly for my protection. If Harris made a threatening gesture, they were prepared to shoot. That idea didn't sit well with me, but at least I knew they had my back.

Harris's expression was blank. His eyes stared through me as if I were invisible. He didn't so much as blink when I snapped my fingers in front of his face. Yep, there was definitely something off with him.

I sank onto the concrete floor, sitting cross-legged. I reached up to touch his cheek. Relief washed over me when he flinched. At least he wasn't completely impervious to his surroundings.

"What have you given him?" I called over my shoulder. Brand had sedated me upon my arrival, and I assumed the guards had done the same to Harris. Maybe they'd given him too much, which would account for his vacant expression and lethargy.

"Nothing," Crane replied. "He's been like this since his arrival."

Okay, so much for that theory.

I'd known Harris for years, and had enough of a connection with him to easily read his mind. If he wasn't going to talk to me, taking a look inside his head was my only option. I took a deep breath, inhaling the stench of his unwashed body and the smoke and chemicals that still clung to his clothes. I reached into his mind.

Harris's most recent memories were of the cage. He remembered being led down the corridor by two armed guards and being locked inside this cell. He hadn't put up a fight, and as a result, the guards hadn't been too rough with him. These images were of no value to Crane, since he likely already knew about Harris's arrival. I wanted to make sure he was being treated well, so I took my time sifting through them. I saw food being delivered, and the guards offering to let him shower. He never spoke to his captors and left the food untouched.

Systematically, I moved backwards on the timeline of Harris's life. His journey to the cottage was uneventful. Like Crane said, Harris ran aboard one of the escape planes and surrendered immediately. He'd been shackled in the corner of the cargo hold, and guarded by a woman in a torn blue dress with a large gun; he didn't fight her.

I moved backward further, to the raid on the station. Harris had been one of the first operatives on the ground. I cringed as I watched him shoot men, women, and even children as they tried to flee. He felt no remorse. It struck me as odd. No feeling, no emotion accompanied any of his memories. He'd been so upset after everything that happened with Penny, so I knew this wasn't ordinary for him.

In all the time I'd known him, he'd struck me as compassionate and fair. Despite the rivalry between Erik and Donavon, Harris had managed to maintain friendships with both guys. He was one of the few of Donavon's friends who had actually liked me, as opposed to being nice to my face and talking about me behind my back.

I went back further still. At least, I *tried* to. His mind was blank before the raid. It was like he'd been born the moment he boarded the plane for Gatlinburg. This was not the first time I'd used this type of mental regression when reading someone's mind. But it was the first time I'd hit a wall such as this.

Scared now, I pressed harder, searching specifically for memories of Penny. His emotional connection to her had been strong, so even if someone had played in his head, images of Penny shouldn't have been easily suppressed. No matter how deep I dug, not one memory of her floated through his head.

I felt my heart starting to pound harder, and my head began to throb with the effort of using so much mental energy. Calm down, I had to tell myself. Concentrate, you can do this.

Eradicating Penny from Harris's memories wasn't unheard of; it was possible. A strong Manipulator, such as myself, could do it. Maybe his grief over her death had become too much, and Mac had ordered some type of mental extraction therapy to help him cope. This, too, was possible, but unlikely. Extractions were tricky, and extremely risky. I wasn't even sure TOXIC currently had anyone on staff capable of performing one.

Switching gears, I tried to locate memories of myself, Erik, and Donavon. The three of us had also played a major role in Harris's life. We'd all been at school together, and Donavon had been on Harris's Hunting team. There were none of the boys, but there was one of me. Just one, though. And it wasn't a memory so much as picture. He saw me as I looked in my official TOXIC photo, and the thoughts attached with the picture weren't what I'd expected. He felt no emotion where I was concerned. My image didn't conjure any sort of resentment or confusion or evoke a single feeling. When Harris saw me, three words ran through his mind: Capture. Don't Kill.

I gasped upon seeing these words flit through his mind over and over again like a mantra.

"Talia?" Crane sounded alarmed. "What's happening? What did you see?"

"Nothing," I said hurriedly.

I would tell him when this was over. Right now, though, I needed to have another crack at Harris's mind. I was in uncharted territory here. Deciding to pledge the Hunters meant I never received advanced interrogation training, but I had taken several classes on the matter while at school. I understood the principal behind delving beyond a block such as the one in Harris's head. I just hadn't expected to ever be faced with the situation.

"Let me in, Harris," I said softly, and put all my energy into making it a command. The more receptive Harris was to the intrusion, the more likely I'd be able to break down his defenses.

Again, I searched for memories from before the raid, and again there weren't any. When I'd tried to infiltrate Crane's mind, I'd been met with a similar resistance. But I'd been able to feel that there was something behind the wall. Harris wasn't like that. He wasn't blocking me; he actually didn't have anything to share. This terrified me.

Had he been robbed of all of his memories, of the life he'd led prior to the raid, his brain would've suffered irreparable harm. His motor skills would have suffered, and he wouldn't have been able to participate in the raid at all. At least, that was what had happened to Ernest, the boy whose memory I'd inadvertently erased.

"What's going on, Talia?" Crane called.

I heard the shuffling of his boots on stone as he shifted from one foot to the other nervously.

"Hold on, let me try one more thing," I called back.

When Mac made me interrogate Ernest, his mind had gone blank, just like Harris's was now. But when I'd tried to put his memories back, it had worked. I wanted to try the same with Harris. I hoped implanting my own memories of our time together would unlock the door holding back his past experiences.

I conjured up images of when we'd spent Festivis Day in D.C. Along with Erik, Penny, Henri, and Frederick, we'd gone into the city to watch the parade and the fireworks. The six of us had drank, ate, and generally acted stupid. That was the night he'd first gotten together with Penny. With his feelings for her having been so strong in the past, I thought this of all nights would evoke a response. The memory bounced off of his mental wall. There was no other way to describe it. All the images I tried to project from my mind into his were flung back at me. I tried again. The same thing happened. It was like throwing a boomerang. Every toss was returned.

Frustrated, I pulled out of his head and stared into his unseeing eyes. What the hell was going on? Why wasn't this working? Was it because I was using memories that weren't his? Because the images weren't through his eyes?

I tried to stand, but my legs were shaky and they buckled under my weight. A firm hand gripped my upper arm, forcing me upright.

"Thanks," I muttered, my voice coming out strained.

"You okay? What did you do to him?" Crane asked.

I hadn't even heard him move into the cell.

"Fine," I mumbled. "He doesn't remember anything before the raid. His mind is blank," I added.

"Blank?" Crane asked. "Maybe he's blocking you?"

"No, he has no mental resistance. It was easy, almost too easy to get into his head. I had no problem seeing everything from the moment he boarded the plane to Gatlinburg until now, but I couldn't access anything before that. There wasn't even anything to access." My voice cracked; I was becoming slightly hysterical. What was wrong with him? What had Mac done to him?

I shrugged off Crane's hand, wanting to throw my arms around Harris and comfort him.

"Don't, Talia," Crane warned. "He might attack you."

"Harris won't hurt me," I shot back, moving towards my friend. Slowly, I sat on the edge of his bed. He didn't move.

"Talia, he doesn't know who you are. He doesn't know that you used to be friends. You might be scaring him."

I mulled over Crane's words. He had a point. Harris didn't know who I was, only that he was supposed to capture me. But he was wrong about Harris being scared. There was no trace of fear in Harris's mind; he wasn't projecting any feeling at all.

Tentatively I placed my hand on his arm. Fast as a whip, Harris shot up, grabbed my wrist, twisted it behind my back, and wrapped his other arm around my throat. The pressure wasn't enough to cut off my air supply completely, but did make it difficult to breathe.

Crane was only a second slower drawing his gun. "Let her go," he demanded.

Crane wasn't playing around. His finger was on the trigger and he was milliseconds away from firing.

Harris said nothing, but his grip on me tightened. I should've been frightened, but he wasn't actually hurting me. Sure, I was uncomfortable, but uncomfortable I could handle. *Capture, don't kill. Capture, don't kill*, chanted Harris in his head.

What did scare me was the fact that Harris wasn't scared. His heartbeat was steady, his muscles relaxed given the circumstances. With Crane standing at point-blank range, ready and willing to pull the trigger, Harris's adrenaline should have been pumping. His natural fight or flight instincts should have been taking over. They didn't, though. He was calm, nonplussed by his current predicament. Even if Crane was a lousy marksman, his bullet would severely injure, if not kill, Harris.

"Lower your weapons," I told Crane and the two guards, who now had their guns trained on Harris, as well. Not one of them complied. "I said, lower your weapons," I repeated in a firmer voice. This time, the guards obeyed. Crane hesitated, fighting my control. On a good day, Crane's will rivaled mine. Today, he was no match. My fight with Brand had left me keyed up and taut as a drum. Crane lowered his gun, letting it drop to hang at his side. I relaxed a little.

"Harris, let me go," I demanded, focusing my energy on him now.

Harris had never been strong-willed, so I was surprised he didn't release me immediately. But with a surge of power on my part, he finally relented.

The instant I was free, Crane grabbed my arm and pushed me forcefully towards the cell door. Without a word and as if nothing had happened, Harris sat on the edge of his cot before curling into the fetal position and closing his eyes.

"What the hell were you thinking?" Crane demanded, once we were safely in the elevator. He sounded more scared than angry.

"He didn't want to hurt me," I replied defensively, stung by Crane's chastising. The stupid comment was harsh, but not unwarranted. I'd known better. My actions, as well intentioned as I'd thought them at the time, could've gotten someone killed. Most likely me.

"How could you be so sure?"

"I'm a mind reader, remember?" I shot back, my tone snarky to mask the slight tremble in my words. "Besides, he was programmed to capture me. Not kill me."

This caught Crane off guard. "Programmed?" he repeated.

"That's what his thoughts feel like. Like he's been programmed. Like his will isn't his own anymore." I shuddered; I couldn't imagine anything worse than having your free will taken from you.

Crane didn't say anything. His thoughts seemed to turn inward. We rode the rest of the way in silence.

Chapter Nine

CRANE AND I parted ways at the medical sublevel.

"Marin was able to procure some nicer clothes for you. The UNITED council members are formal people. I'd like for you to dress appropriately."

"Sure," I agreed, my stomach sinking.

Meeting the mysterious UNITED council was already something I was dreading. Getting dressed up to do so, well, that just made the task even more unpleasant.

In mine and Erik's room, I found a black suit jacket, matching black pants, a white blouse, and black leather shoes neatly arranged in the dumbwaiter. Marin, I assumed from the loopy feminine scrawl, had pinned a note to the blazer, written on thick eggshell stationary.

Hope these fit. I guessed your size.

The clothes actually did fit, sort of. A belt would've helped keep the pants in place at my waist, and the blazer hung like it had been intended for someone taller. All in all, the outfit didn't look half bad on me, I decided as I admired myself in the bathroom mirror. A soft knock sounded on the outer door.

Penny, I thought, winding my curls into a knot at the base of my skull. With her new, Created Talents, her essence was unmistakable. She emitted so much raw power; I'd never felt anything quite like it. Erik would be the same way, I realized.

"Tal? You ready?" Penny called, poking her head through the door.

"Yep," I replied, tugging my suit jacket into place as I walked out of the bathroom.

Penny stepped into the bedroom. She, too, wore business attire. Her suit was navy with a green and blue striped camisole underneath the blazer. She'd smoothed her shoulder length mane into a sleek ponytail, which accentuated her sharp cheekbones. Her appearance projected maturity and confidence, a sharp contrast to the fear she felt inside.

"How are you feeling?" Penny asked.

I shrugged. "Okay. A little nervous," I admitted.

A total lie. I was majorly worried, but she didn't need to know that. Given the circumstances, Penny seemed calm. A quick swipe of her thoughts told me she had complete faith in UNITED and their good intentions. She also believed Crane wouldn't let them contain us. She'd believed him when he said the evaluations were a formality. I, however, didn't share her feelings. UNITED wouldn't hesitate to contain us if they decided we were dangerous.

"Me, too," Penny said. "But I've been through worse. We both have. This'll be a breeze."

"Definitely a breeze," I agreed, mustering a smile for my best friend's benefit.

I kissed Erik on the forehead. His skin felt cool beneath my lips. Then, I followed Penny into the hallway and to the elevator.

She pushed the call button and then stared at the closed doors, managing to look both impatient and anxious at the same time. The elevator came and we boarded. Penny pressed the button for sublevel one. The elevator shot upwards, and she studied my face, her lime-colored eyes narrowing in on my bruises. She pursed her lips into two narrow lines.

"Was physical violence really necessary?" she asked.

Guilt made my cheeks burn. "He provoked me," I said defensively.

"I don't doubt it. But, Tal, he means a lot to me. You both do. I'd really like if you guys could be friends. At least not enemies."

I was about to say I'd play nice when he did, but Penny turned big pleading eyes on me and added, "Please, Talia."

"I'll try," I promised her.

She smiled. "Thanks."

The conference room on sublevel one was already full when Penny and I entered. Brand, bruises and all, sat beside Crane, who was in his place at the head of the oval table. For the occasion, both men had traded their fatigues in favor of charcoal gray suits. Brand paired his with a green button-down that matched his eyes. Even with two black eyes, he cleaned up well. Penny's face lit up when she met his gaze. The feelings were mutual. Brand beamed at her, seeming momentarily dazed by the sight of Penny all dressed up.

My eyes shifted to Crane. For the first time since I'd met him, he actually looked like the political figure he was. With a red power tie adding a splash of color to his otherwise monochromatic ensemble, authority radiated off of him. He nodded approvingly after giving my own outfit a once-over.

Frederick was at the opposite end of the table from Brand and Crane. He looked like a model in his perfectly tailored suit and immaculately styled hair. Ten of the twelve remaining chairs at the table were occupied by three women and seven men I didn't recognize. All of them wore beautiful clothes made from expensive silks and wools; even the leather of their shoes smelled like they'd cost a small fortune. I thought how ridiculous all the pageantry was.

My skin began to prickle from the collective power radiating off of the UNITED council members. I breathed it in, letting it wash over me, savoring the feel of so much raw Talent in such a confined space. I'd encountered numerous strong Talents while with TOXIC, but never so many at once. The effect was intoxicating for someone like me, someone with ability to *feel* other's abilities. I wondered how Penny was handling it. As a Mimic, she must be going nuts trying to process all the different gifts. Then again, with twelve Talent signatures inside of her already, maybe this was nothing new.

I glanced at Penny out of the corner of my eye. She gave no outward sign that the power in the room was affecting her. Inside, butterflies were flapping their wings in her belly. But I thought the fluttering sensation had more to do with Brand than nerves. Brand might've been a total ass to me, but he clearly loved her. That was reason enough for me to keep my promise and try to be civil to him.

I erected my mental barriers, creating a wall to separate myself from the power swirling in the conference room as I slid in beside Frederick. I feared prolonged exposure to the other's energy would make me Talent drunk, and the crazy inside of me might surface. It was bad enough that, to a discerning eye, my bruises and marks complimented Brand's, and the UNITED council members all had discerning eyes. I felt all twenty of them follow my every move. I just hoped no one would ask about the injuries.

Penny eased herself into the chair on my other side, just as Crane cleared his throat to draw everyone's attention his way.

"Ladies and gentlemen," Crane began, rising to his feet to address the table. "As I am sure you all know by now, a Coalition team attacked TOXIC's maximum security prison, Tramblewood Correctional Facility, two nights ago. Despite the loss of four soldiers, the mission was a success. We rescued the men and women taken prisoner during our attack on Rittenhouse Research Facility two weeks ago. In addition, we rescued the Mimic Erikson Kelley." Crane paused, glanced around the table, and met each of our eyes in turn.

The way he said Erik's name with such familiarity sent a chill up my spine to settle at the base of my skull, giving me a cold headache like I'd eaten ice cream too fast. This wasn't the first time Crane had discussed Erik with the council members, I realized. They were all aware of his situation.

I looked around the table at their eager faces. Ten sets of eyes were glazed with anticipation, like they couldn't wait to get their hands on him. To study him, learn from him, dissect him. Not just Erik, I reminded myself, Penny and me, too. Several gazes flicked to our end of the table, turning those ravenous looks on more immediate prey. I swallowed hard. This evaluation was going to suck.

"Mr. Kelley was in need of medical attention, precipitating a stop at the Underground station in Gatlinburg, Tennessee. Using a tracker implanted in Mr. Kelley, TOXIC forces followed us to the station and launched a retaliatory attack. The death toll is still undetermined.

"Up to this point the Coalition has been passive, playing defense in the hopes of providing a peaceful life for those wishing to live outside of TOXIC's rule. But that is no longer an option. I have verified that TOXIC is using the Creation drug, in direct violation of UNITED Mandate 1216.45, which prohibits use and experimentation of the same. You have asked for proof. Today I have asked you here to deliver that proof."

Crane's speech, much like all our outfits, seemed formal.

"All three children have agreed to the evaluation?" an auburn haired woman asked, a strong British accent flavoring her words.

I blanched at her characterization of us as "children." We were hardly children. I'd killed for TOXIC, and now for the Coalition; that definitely classified me as an adult in my book.

"Why don't you ask them yourself, Victoria?" Crane suggested mildly, and gestured to where Penny and I sat.

Victoria turned to stare at us with gold eyes that seemed to shimmer in the fluorescent lighting. She radiated a cool calm that wasn't exactly unpleasant so much as odd when it touched me. I felt that she was kind but clinical, a scientist with a heart. I decided to reserve judgment for later.

Under the table, Penny reached for my hand. I squeezed hers to let her know we were in this together. Apparently she was more nervous about the evaluation than she'd let on.

"If it helps stop Mac, then I'm in," I said, meeting Victoria's gaze with a confident one of my own. At least, I hoped it was confident since nerves were swimming in my stomach like sharks.

"Natalia Lyons, I presume?" Victoria said, making it obvious she knew exactly who I was. This fact did nothing to lessen my fears.

I nodded mutely.

"What about the boy?" a man with bushy black eyebrows and a pronounced overbite asked in German. "Why is he not here?"

My upbringing had involved a lot of travel because of my father's job for the Italian Government. Between that and being a mind reader, I was fluent in a number of languages, including German.

"The boy," I said through clenched teeth, "is still unconscious. While I'm sure he'll agree, you'll have to wait until he wakes up."

The German councilman raised those caterpillars several millimeters to show his surprise at my understanding of his native tongue. His thick lips twitched a little and I thought maybe he was impressed.

"I, for one, would like to hear what the young women have to say," another man added in a soft voice.

I focused on him, smiling a little at the respect he'd shown by calling us "young women." His almond eyes were kind, and I found I liked him instantly.

"There will be time for that in their individual evaluations, Michael," Victoria said.

"Yes, of course, Councilwoman, but not all of us will be taking part in the evaluations. I would like to hear it now."

Twenty eyes turned on us in unison. Crane nodded, giving an unspoken cue that it was our turn to speak.

Next to me, Penny released my hand and stood slowly. She gripped the table with white knuckles. Her arms trembled slightly, but her face remained expressionless.

"Hello, my name is Penelope Crane," Penny began, her voice low and even. The room went silent, everyone giving Penny their undivided attention.

Her story was nearly verbatim the one she'd told the soldiers before the attack on Tramblewood. Every so often one of the council members would politely raise his or her hand and ask a question for clarification. A beautiful olive-skinned woman with startlingly light gray eyes and a faint Portuguese accent was nearly as vocal as Victoria. She recorded Penny's answers on an electronic tablet on the table in front of her. Michael showed the most deference, and any time Penny tripped over a question, he gently prodded her in the right direction. I wondered how much of this he already knew.

When Penny finished, it was my turn. My story was considerably less eventful than Penny's. I carefully edited the encounter with Crane in the basement of his Nevada home. It wasn't really important, and didn't help my case for sanity. Sure, I'd just been acting in self-defense, but my actions could be termed dangerous. I doubted the Council would care that the incident had occurred prior to receiving the Creation drug.

I was shocked and a little relieved to realize that many of the council members found my story as appalling as Penny's. Though, I thought it had more to do with the fact that Mac had infected his son than the accidental transference to me. Honestly, that was what had been hardest for me to digest, as well. How any parent could knowingly put his child in danger was beyond me.

"You were infected eighteen months ago?" Victoria asked me.

"Yes."

"Yet you still have the ability to Morph? Fascinating." While she phrased it like a question, I wasn't sure whether she actually expected an answer.

"I do," I confirmed, just in case she did want an answer. I was doing my best to appear obedient and helpful.

"That is highly unusual," the Portuguese councilwoman commented.

This time, I said nothing. I knew Created Talents faded with time, and was well aware that mine lasting this long was rare. For once, I hated being unique.

"She was Talented to begin with," Michael pointed out mildly. "We know the drug works better in the Talented."

"How many different forms can you take?" Victoria asked me.

"I don't know. All I've attempted have worked," I said.

"And those would be?" Victoria prompted impatiently.

"Um, well, I've Morphed into a wolf and a bird," I said. "Oh, and a person."

This got their attention. Several of the UNITED council members sat up straighter in the chairs. An ancient woman with folds of skin weighing down her eyelids studied me with new interest.

"You have successfully performed a human transformation?" Victoria asked, sounding intrigued if not impressed.

"Sort of," I amended. "I changed my eyes to imitate another's. For a retinal scanner."

"Truly remarkable," Michael said, nodding his head appreciatively.

"Yes," Victoria agreed. "Quite."

From there the questions turned towards my emotions and feelings. The UNITED council wanted to know what made me angry, sad, happy, and had that changed since my infection. I hated how they kept referring to it that way. Infected. It made me feel dirty. Every time someone uttered that word, my temper rose a degree. Constant mental reminders from Crane, and waves of calm from Penny were all that kept me from verbally lashing out.

Exhausted from the rapid-fire questions that felt much like an interrogation, I was finally allowed to sit back down. Frederick patted my leg under the table for support. He'd been quiet through both mine and Penny's question and answer sessions. I wasn't sure why he was there, but I was glad he was.

The council members began conferring among themselves. All of them understood English, but several insisted on speaking in their native languages. I followed the conversation easily, keeping up a running translation for Penny, who wasn't so fortunate.

"*The German guy wants to do our evaluations tonight. But he doesn't want to make a decision before Erik wakes up. The old guy is French, or at least speaks French, but his accent is weird. He wants to bring in reinforcements now. He's heard enough,*" I told her.

"I think that is premature, Barbar," Victoria retorted, addressing the maybe-French guy. "I agree that we have to take action, but I'd like to have a better idea what we are up against. The evaluations will show us that."

"Have not these young women been through enough?" Michael asked.

"We can't know what TOXIC's army is capable of unless we dig deeper," Victoria shot back. "We need to be prepared."

"I am not convinced," a dark-skinned man interjected in clipped English. "I'd like to wait until we have the girls' blood samples. That will be concrete proof."

This debate continued so long my vision went blurry trying to follow the threads. It was hard to tell who was winning. On the one hand, a lot of the Council did think that our stories were proof enough to intercede. Some of those same members still thought the evaluations were necessary. Others wanted to launch an airstrike on Washington, D.C. this very minute. Ultimately, the decision would be Victoria's. She was the undisputed leader, even if no one actually stated that. Hers was the opinion that mattered in the end.

I was on the edge of my seat, ready to interject my own unwanted advice into the mix, when Victoria declared, "This is how we shall proceed."

Penny clammy fingers found mine again. I felt like I was holding hands with an octopus, but I squeezed back with as much reassurance as possible.

"Councilman Neumann," Victoria continued, turning those gold eyes on her German colleague, "you will return to Bern and inform the rest of the Council of our decision to take action against TOXIC. From this moment on, persons associated with TOXIC are wanted for questioning for the illegal use of the Creation drug. Have a formal declaration sent to Director Danbury McDonough, inviting him to voluntarily come before the UNITED Council to plead his case. Should he refuse, which I assume he will, then make it clear the Council will launch an attack." She turned to Michael. "Councilman Tanaka, your job is to, discreetly, meet with the conservative nations. Once TOXIC's use of the Creation drug becomes public knowledge, those countries will declare war. The United States' polices protecting the Talented have not endeared them to the less tolerant nations, who would like nothing more than mass genocide of our kind. TOXIC's violation of Mandate 1216.45 will be used as pretense. Let them know UNITED will handle the situation."

"President Crane, if you would be so kind as to lend us the use of your facilities, I want to have the children evaluated immediately. As I expressed earlier, I want to know what we are up against. I understand the boy cannot be evaluated yet. The girls, however, can be."

"Of course, Victoria. Whatever you need," Crane replied.

"How is your team progressing with the cure?" Victoria asked him. "You are still researching the cure, are you not?"

"Dr. Patel's research had been stagnant until recently. I am confident with Penelope, Talia, and Erik here it will pick up. He will find one soon."

"Wonderful. It will be invaluable. If TOXIC has succeeded in making a Created army, we need a way to deal with them. We cannot have the Created running loose in the world. Whether they have been infected with the beta version of the drug or the long-lasting version, they are too dangerous to be roaming free."

So not the words I wanted to hear. It sounded like Victoria had all but sentenced us to containment. I couldn't keep quiet.

"Not all of us are dangerous," I interjected. "I get it, the power is hard to control for people who haven't had it their whole lives. But what about those of us who have? I'm not a danger to society."

"Debatable," I heard Brand mutter under his breath. I shot him a nasty glare.

"Ms. Lyons," Victoria began in an extremely patronizing tone that suggested I was five, "the drug was outlawed for a reason. Part of that reason was to prevent exactly what TOXIC has done. Injecting unwilling recipients is abhorrent, I think we can all agree on that. Even more disturbing are the long-term ramifications of the drug. The original study showed that even recipients who were naturally Talented were unable to handle the additional power. Without exception, the test subjects' minds slowly deteriorated. The Council was left with a contingent of people who needed to be contained."

"Institutionalized, you mean," I retorted, a mixture of anger and fear bubbling up inside of me. I saw her point. Really, I did. But I wasn't like those people. Penny wasn't like those people. Erik wasn't like those people.

"Yes, Ms. Lyons, institutionalized. For their own good and the good of society."

"So these evaluations are just a courtesy to Ian? You've already determined we're a threat?" I wanted to scream.

"Talia, it isn't like that," Crane said with a warning note in his voice. His mind pushed on mine and I knew he wanted to tell me to cool off before I nailed my own cell door shut. I didn't need the reminder. I was fully aware that openly arguing with Victoria wasn't the smartest idea I'd ever had.

"You, Ms. Lyons, have always been a threat," she said coolly. "Mind Manipulators are the most dangerous of Talents. Katerina knew that. Why do you think she insisted you not parade your abilities in front of others?"

The blood drained from my head, leaving me dizzy and disoriented. How dare she bring my mother into this.

"Victoria, really," Michael admonished.

"No decisions have been made, Talia," Crane said quickly. I could tell by the way his dark eyes went wide, he feared I was about to give the Council members a front-row show of just how dangerous I really was. "Isn't that right, Victoria? I had your word the children would be evaluated on an individual basis. Talia has lived for almost eighteen years without incident."

Victoria's high-pitched laughter was grating to my ears. Another councilperson snorted and someone coughed to discreetly cover a grunt. Apparently the Council had a dossier of my exploits. Not good.

"And they will be, Ian," she said with a smile. "Do not worry, Ms. Lyons, I will be evaluating you myself."

My mounting outrage had caused my mental barriers to drop, and I was projecting like crazy. Or, maybe just projecting crazy. Crane read the words out of my head before they formed on my lips.

"Don't. Let it go. You can trust me, Talia. I won't let them put you in containment," he sent.

I swallowed the nasty retort I'd been about to make and said, "I look forward to it Councilwoman."

Chapter Ten

THANKFULLY, WHEN VICTORIA had said she wanted the evaluations done "immediately," she really meant the following morning. Now I had roughly eight hours before my big mouth got me contained. Awesome.

The meeting had been productive, though. The fact that the Council was taking action against TOXIC was a huge load off of my mind. No, I didn't actually expect Mac to voluntarily appear before UNITED to answer for his crimes, which meant a war was inevitable. But at least the Coalition wouldn't be fighting alone. Mac and his army of Created, if he'd succeeded in making one, had to be stopped, and I wanted to be part of the solution. I needed to be part of the solution. The more I thought about the Mind Manipulator from Gatlinburg, the more sure I was that Mac *had* succeeded. That person had mostly likely been spawned from my blood, which made me feel responsible for his actions. No way was I going to let him wreak havoc in the world.

Brand had shepherded Penny to her bedroom the moment we'd been dismissed, insisting she needed to rest, despite her protests to the contrary. Frederick and I had returned to the medical floor together, him leaving me at Henri's door with the promise to visit me in the morning before my evaluation. I'd thought about visiting with Henri for a while before returning to Erik's room, but decided my time was better spent by Erik's bedside.

I was sitting vigil in my chair, holding Erik's cold hand and telling him all about the heinous Victoria and the other Council members when the soft squeak of the door hinge made me jump. I turned, expecting to see Frederick. Crane stood in the doorway, an oblong triangle of light shining onto the stone floor in front of him, one hand rubbing back and forth against his short hair.

"I figured you'd still be awake," he said softly.

"Too keyed up to sleep," I replied, in a voice slightly louder than the one he'd used. Crane didn't have Morph hearing like me.

"Can we talk?" he asked.

I glanced back at Erik's blissfully unconscious form. As badly as I wanted him to wake up, as many times as I willed him to do so, he wasn't going to tonight. Dr. Patel thought tomorrow at the earliest. Besides, Crane and I had a lot to discuss. I kissed the hand of Erik's that I still held in mine before tucking it safely under the patchwork quilt.

"Sure," I said, gesturing to the other armchair.

While Crane settled in, I dragged my chair over to the sitting area. Crane hadn't changed after the meeting with the Council. He still wore his suit pants, but they'd lost their crisp clean look and were now tired and wrinkled, much like Crane himself. His button-down appeared looser than it had earlier, like he'd shrunk under all the stress. I felt bad for him.

"I know you're upset about the evaluations," he began. His muscled forearms rested on the arms of the chair, and he studied me with his intense eyes.

I shrugged like it was no big deal. "The Coalition can't defeat TOXIC on its own. We need their help. They need proof. The evaluations are necessary for that proof. I get it."

"I meant what I said, Talia. I won't let them contain you. It's in nobody's best interests. You're an asset in this war. You know McDonough better than anyone else on our side. Deep down, Victoria knows that." He paused, waiting for some reaction I wasn't willing to give. Crane sighed. "Mind Manipulators are, by definition, dangerous. But having one as powerful as you on our side is beneficial. She knows that. Just keep calm and answer her questions tomorrow, and you'll be fine. Let her see how strong your Talent is. UNITED recruits the best and the brightest from around the globe. If her desire to have you on her team outweighs the risk you pose, she won't lock you up."

I laughed humorlessly and shook my head. "I see. So she's like Mac. Great. One more power-hungry politician, just what I need."

"Victoria means well. But yes, she is drawn to strong Talents the same way McDonough is. The same way you are. The same way I am."

I averted my gaze and said nothing. I hated being lumped into a category that included Mac and Victoria. Even if the description was accurate.

"You still have a choice—"

"A choice?" I snapped. "What? Run? Because that is the only alternative I see. The choice was taken from me the minute you informed the Council I'd been injected."

The accusation hung in the air like smoke, creating a curtain between us.

"Technically, the Council doesn't have jurisdiction here. This half of the country is not a member nation. I invited them here and I can disinvite them. Once you've been evaluated, yes, the Council can insist you be contained. If you choose not to go through with it, there isn't anything they can do."

Crane had more experience with UNITED than I did. I'd only ever heard vague mentions of them before now, and never actually met a council member until tonight. Still, I had a feeling he wasn't being entirely honest with me. If I refused, they'd bully Crane into turning me over to them. Or worse. They'd withdraw their aid in the fight against TOXIC.

I thought of all the children who had been infected with the drug already. I thought about the army of super-Talents Mac was creating as we sat there. I thought about the Mind Manipulator in Gatlinburg and how little it took for him to control me. I closed my eyes and sighed. The better UNITED understood their opponent, the more likely they were to defeat him. Studying me would help with that. I focused on the bigger picture.

"I'd said I'd do it and I will. Cool, calm, and collected tomorrow, that's me."

Crane actually smiled at that. "I'll make sure Brand makes himself scarce until after the evaluation."

Guiltily I fingered the bruised skin next to my right eye. Yeah, that was probably a good idea.

Several tense minutes passed where neither of us spoke. Since Crane made no move to leave, I figured he had more to say. Yet, he was in no hurry to start up the conversation again. I considered taking a peek at his thoughts, but I wasn't in a hurry either. I had a long sleepless night ahead of me. What were a couple more minutes with Crane?

"The Creation Project is a black mark in UNITED's history," he finally began. "They'd prefer to forget it ever happened. That's part of why they're so eager to contain all the recipients of the Creation drug. Don't misunderstand. What Victoria said was correct. The power, as well as the drug itself, deteriorates the mind. But they don't want their mistake causing chaos in the world either."

"Why did they fund the project in the first place?" I asked. "I mean, why create Talents? It just seems like a bad idea."

Crane smiled. "Now it does. But at the time, studying the genetic makeup of Talents and learning how to create new ones was exciting. No one considered the ramifications. Hell, I'm not sure anyone really believed it was possible. Since the Great Contamination, scientists have been trying to understand why some people are Talented and others aren't. There is no biological component, no gene that is passed on from parent to child. Isolating Talent signatures was revolutionary. The scientists were so eager to see how far they could take it. When they first succeeded in creating new Talents, the Council was elated; it was a huge breakthrough."

I scoffed. Idiots.

"A couple of weeks after the first successful implantations, the team noticed that the recipients' Talents were weakening. They considered it a setback, but no one was terribly concerned. A hiccup, they thought. They injected the first round of recipients again. And again, their Talents weakened within a couple of weeks. It wasn't until the head of the research team discovered that the recipients' minds were devolving that people started to argue in favor of scrapping the project."

"Did they?" I asked. "Scrap the project?"

"No. Not yet. They figured it was only a matter of time before they perfected the formula. The research was only in its infancy, the researchers said. Give it time. UNITED did. Time only produced more failures. Several of the scientists resigned from the project. Dr. Albert Wythe was one of them."

My jaw came unhinged. It took me several long moments before I was able to speak. "You mean, Dr. Wythe, my therapist?"

Now it was Crane's turn to look surprised. "I wasn't aware that was Albert's function within TOXIC, but yes, I suppose it makes sense. He is a very strong Manipulator, both perception and mind."

"Perception? That's rare," I commented. Perception Manipulators were even rarer than Mind Manipulators. They altered their surroundings so that people saw what they wanted them to see. It was an external Talent, where Mind Manipulation was internal.

Crane grinned and the room around me fell away, replaced by sun, sand, and surf. I gasped. Rays of sunshine warmed my arms and legs. Waves lapped the shore, sounding like a soothing lullaby. For a split second, I was relaxed and at peace. Then, it all went away and I was back in Erik's bedroom, staring open-mouthed at a beaming Crane.

"So that's your Talent?" I said when I regained control over my muscles.

"Guilty as charged. Brand, too. He's not quite as strong, though."

I was suitably impressed.

"But I digress. After Albert left the project, the team made another breakthrough. They perfected the formula. The head of research presented his findings to UNITED, with the suggestion that the drug be outlawed. He concluded that the side-effects far outweighed the benefits. The recipients were no longer showing signs of lessening ability over time, but their minds were still devolving. Now UNITED was burdened with dozens of people who were both extremely gifted and extremely unstable. Immediately, the focus turned to creating an anti-drug. A cure, if you will. But... " Crane's voice trailed off.

"But what? If they could invent the drug, how hard could inventing a cure be? And why hadn't anyone thought about that from the start?"

Crane's black gaze turned sad. Sympathy rolled off of him in waves, and my throat tightened.

"The head of research died before he had the chance to finish working on the cure. Even with his notes, the rest of the team has been unable to produce results."

"How'd he die?" I asked, dread forming a pit in my stomach.

"He was murdered, Talia. Murdered because he refused to give the perfected formula to TOXIC."

Murdered because TOXIC wanted his very Talented daughter, I thought.

"I worked on the project with your father, Talia. His intentions were good. He was a scientist. He craved knowledge. Having a Talented daughter, when neither he nor Katerina were Talented, made the research personal for him. He wanted to learn everything he could about Talents." Crane's words cut through the booming in my ears.

Tears prickled at the backs of my eyes. My father had been the one who invented the Creation drug. My father had unleashed this plague on the world. My parents had died because of a stupid, freaking drug. The throbbing inside my head started at the base of my skull before taking over my entire body. Soon my skin was pulsing with the need to release the energy building inside of me. I wanted to scream, to throw the chair I was sitting in, to beat my fists against the wall. Anything besides sit there and think about what Crane had just told me.

"No. No," I moaned. "He worked for the government. He was... he was...," I stuttered, at a loss as to how to finish the sentence. All I'd known as a child was that my father worked for the government. I realized I had no idea what his job had entailed.

"Yes, he was a scientist, a *brilliant* scientist, for the Italian Government. That is why UNITED asked him to head the project. They asked me because I had some of the most qualified doctors and researchers in my employ. I agreed because I was curious. I've always been fascinated by genetics. After your father's death, the project was disbanded for good. Work on the cure has continued, but in general, UNITED has focused on containment. A cure wasn't necessary because the pool of test subjects from the original project wasn't very large. Now, well, now it's imperative. There is no telling how many people have been infected."

I tried to wrap my head around the tornado of information, but all I kept thinking was about how my father's thirst for knowledge had thrown the world into a tailspin, and we were just now realizing it.

"The reason I'm telling you this now is so that Victoria doesn't catch you off-guard tomorrow."

My head snapped up from where I was cradling it in my hands. "Excuse me?"

Crane blew out a long, tired breath. "Victoria *might* bring it up during your evaluation tomorrow to see how you react. She'll use it to needle you, see if she can elicit a reaction. I want you to be prepared."

I blinked and hot tears poured down my cheeks.

"Francis was my friend, Talia. He was a great man, a great father, and a great scientist. Don't let this taint your memory of him. He was the one who insisted the drug be outlawed. He was the first person to understand that nothing good could come of creating Talents. If you want to place blame, lay it on Albert Wythe's doorstep. He's the one who gave the early versions of the drug to TOXIC. Blame TOXIC for using it, despite the risks. But don't think ill of your father. He died trying to do what was right."

Crane stood and came to crouch in front of my chair. He met my tear-filled eyes before he wrapped long arms around me in a tight embrace. At first, I stiffened, surprised by the affection. Slowly, I relaxed and leaned my head against his shoulder and cried.

Chapter Eleven

BEFORE HE LEFT for the night, Crane had Marin send down ginger-infused tea with honey and a plate of sugar cookies. He asked if I wanted him to stay, or to send Frederick or Penny to keep me company. I declined. Erik's was the only company I craved.

With the floral-patterned china teacup clutched between my palms, I returned to Erik's bedside and told him about my father. He'd been here, obviously, but it felt good to repeat the hard truths out loud. I tried to keep Crane's sentiments in mind, about how my father was a good man with good intentions and that Dr. Wythe and Mac deserved all of the blame. But my mind kept going back to that saying about the road to hell being paved with good intentions. If the Council didn't stop Mac soon, there'd be hell on earth.

While I'd been certain sleep was an impossibility, I must've succumbed at some point because next I knew, Frederick was shaking my shoulder to wake me up. My head felt like a ton of bricks had fallen on top of it, and my mouth tasted like Erik's workout clothes smelled. Marin must've put a sleeping pill in that tea, I thought as I tried to will away the pounding in my head.

"Why don't you shower and get dressed? You have about an hour until your evaluation," Frederick told me, and then blessedly handed me a mug of rich black coffee.

"You're an angel," I muttered, stumbling out of my chair to take the coffee.

"I'll remember you said that," he teased.

I sipped the hot beverage, letting the fragrant aroma and bold flavors give life to my senses. Still groggy, but more steady on my feet, I dutifully trooped to the bathroom to get ready for the day. The hot spray from the shower felt amazing as it unkinked my taxed muscles and eased the knots in my shoulders. I wanted to spend time with Erik before the evaluation, just in case Victoria did rattle me enough that I flipped on her and they shipped me off to a containment facility, so I didn't linger too long.

I combed through the tangles in my dark curls as I stared at my reflection in the mirror over the bathroom sink. My face was too angular, my cheekbones too defined. Stress and exhaustion were taking a toll on my appearance. Not to mention the bruises that served as a reminder of what happened when I lost my temper. They looked worse than they had yesterday, the swollen red stung-by-a-bee appearance having given way to swirls of black and blue. By tomorrow, the marks would have faded. I had TOXIC to thank for that gift.

When I returned to the main room, Frederick was in my seat, talking to Erik.

"Henri's going to come by soon. He's worried about you, man. We all are. Talia more than the rest of us. She only leaves your side when she has to. Come back to us soon."

I felt like an eavesdropper as I stood in the doorframe and listened to Frederick's encouraging words. I cleared my throat, startling Frederick. His cheeks flushed to pale pink, which made his delicate features appear pretty, almost feminine. I smiled sheepishly.

"Sorry," I said. "Didn't mean to overhear."

He shook his head, sending light blonde hair fanning over his forehead. "It's cool. Dr. Patel said talking to him might help. Anyway, you ready?"

I chewed my lower lip and nodded. "Can I have a minute with him? Just in case I don't come back."

"That won't happen, Tal," Frederick said confidently. "Ian won't let them take you."

"Yeah, I know," I replied, though, I wasn't sure he would be able to stop Victoria if she labeled me dangerous. "Still, I'd hate it if I didn't get to say goodbye."

"I'll be outside." Frederick stood, smoothed the small creases in his jeans, and headed for the door.

I waited until I heard the soft click of the door shutting before joining Erik. Using the tip of my right forefinger, I traced the contours of his face, committing them to memory, as if that were necessary. His face was what I saw every time I closed my eyes. I placed feather-light kisses on each of his closed eyelids, his bruised cheek, and finally his split lip.

"Cool, calm, and collected," I sent him, even though I couldn't reach his unconscious mind. *"I won't let Victoria bait me."* The promise was more to myself than him, but thinking it helped remind me how important that was. *"I'll be back before you know it."* I hated how true that statement was.

When I found Frederick in the hallway a moment later, he wasn't alone. Henri, arm in a sling, was wrapped in his boyfriend's arms. They both colored slightly when they noticed me, and I realized how rare it was to see them display physical emotion in public. Well, not really public; until I'd intruded they'd been alone.

"I'm going to read to him," Henri said, holding up a leather-bound book with his good hand. "Give me something to do besides twiddle my thumbs. I gotta say, recovery is boring."

I smiled up at him. "Yeah, tell me about it. Try nine months of solitude. It sucks."

Frederick was getting antsy now, shifting uneasily from one foot to the other.

"I guess it's time," I said, his nervous energy compounding my own. I started to sweat, despite the cool hallway and sundress I'd chosen for the occasion.

I'd selected a white sundress over more casual options like jeans or shorts because I wanted to appear innocent. Victoria wasn't likely to be fooled by such an obvious ruse, but it couldn't hurt either.

Henri kissed Frederick lightly on the cheek, a small peck that seemed to express so much more than mild affection. Then he leaned down and hugged me with his good arm.

"Just don't be yourself," he teased, "and you'll be good."

"Thanks," I snorted, only slightly offended, and returned his embrace.

Three minutes that passed too quickly later, Frederick and I were standing outside an unmarked door on sublevel two. This was one of the few floors I'd yet to explore, and I didn't get the chance now. The empty corridor looked much like the others, with its stone walls and floors; it was the atmosphere that felt different. It had a colder, more impersonal feel than anywhere else I'd been in Coalition Headquarters, which heightened my unease.

"I'll be right here when you're finished," Frederick told me.

I nodded mutely, unable to form words. He knocked on the unmarked door. Three sharp thumps that echoed through the sublevel. I heard a whoosh as the airlock released, followed by a small creak when the door swung inward. Without glancing at Frederick, I entered to face my fate.

Victoria sat in the middle of a long, rectangular table. Her hair was neatly styled in a chignon, and she wore a crisp red pantsuit the color of fresh blood. I felt a tug on my heartstrings as I met her golden eyes. Her polished appearance reminded me of Gretchen. Gretchen, who I hadn't given a second thought to since fleeing D.C. How much did she know? I pushed the thought aside before it could distract me from more immediate concerns.

On either side of Victoria were two additional council members. One was the Portuguese delegate, the other a man I'd never seen. Doctor, was my immediate thought. He had that look to him, that superior air of one who thought himself better than others. Immediate dislike sent off warning bells in my head.

"Ms. Lyons, good of you to join us this morning," Victoria greeted me in a regal tone that brought to mind images of a queen addressing her subjects. "Please, have a seat." She indicated the lone plastic chair facing the panel of three.

Head held high, spine ramrod straight, I took my place. Once seated, I arranged the pleats of my white dress so that the fabric hung just below my knees and crossed my ankles to prevent fidgeting. My hair was still a little damp from my shower and it felt heavy, like a wet veil cascading down my back.

"I am Victoria Walburton. This is Councilwoman Amberly Azevedo," she indicated the Portuguese councilwoman with a nod in the other woman's direction. "And this is Dr. Kramer." She gestured to her other side. "We would like to start by asking you a few questions, if that is alright with you?" Victoria phrased it as though she was asking permission, her voice lilting at the end of the sentence to suggest a question mark. I wasn't fooled by her polite tone. We both knew I didn't have a choice.

"Of course, Councilwoman," I said. Two could play this game, I thought.

In the beginning, many of the questions were the same as the day before. I tried not to show how annoying I found the repetition.

They had me recount the story I'd told them the previous day. Instead of asking for clarification on confusing points, they hammered me with question after question until I became so confused that I wasn't sure which way was up, let alone what the truth was. Just when I thought I knew where one line of questioning was headed, one of the council members would throw a wrench in the mix and ask, "And how did that make you feel?" like this was a therapy session with Dr. Wythe.

They asked me about destroying Donavon's cabin when I'd been a pledge, and whether, now that I was older and had had time to reflect on the incident, would I have acted differently?

"No," I snapped without thinking, recalling the rage I'd felt seeing Kandice's long hair spilling over the side of Donavon's bed.

"How many people have you killed, Ms. Lyons?" Amberly asked.

"I don't keep a body count," I replied through gritted teeth.

"Five? Ten? A hundred?" she prompted.

"I said, I don't know." *Calm, cool, collected,* I chanted.

"You don't have many friends, isn't that correct, Ms. Lyons?" Victoria switched gears.

"I have enough," I said uneasily, not sure where this was going.

"Is it because you think you are better than your peers? Because your Talents are superior to theirs?" Victoria urged.

"No," I scoffed. "I've been a little busy to worry about a social life."

My palms were sweating, and I discreetly wiped them on the folds of my dress.

"Busy? Busy planning the assassination of your parents' killer?" Victoria asked.

"Busy training to become a Hunter," I clarified.

"But you wanted to become a Hunter to avenge Francis and Katerina, correct?"

My temper was reaching the breaking point. The casual mention of my parents' names was one brick too many in my wobbly control.

"Yes, I did. Wouldn't you?" I shot back angrily. Cool, calm, and collected were gone.

"You have quite the temper, Ms. Lyons," the doctor said. He'd been fairly quiet up to this point.

"Since the day I was born," I said. Maybe not the wisest remark, but it was true, and I didn't want them thinking I'd developed this attitude after being injected.

"On a scale of one to ten, ten being highest, how much has being injected with the Creation drug affected your personality?" Amberly asked.

I met her smoky gaze and shrugged. "Two," I lied.

My personality shift was noticeable, but manageable. At least, now that I knew the cause it was manageable. While no one called me a liar, the accusation was on all three minds.

"The night your parents were killed, what happened?" Victoria again.

I swallowed hard. This was the first open-ended question they'd asked me. Even the ones about my feelings regarding a particular incident had facilitated one word answers. This, though, this was different. I felt the mood in the room shift and had the horrible realization that this was what they'd wanted to talk about from the beginning. My actions that horrible night were going to be what condemned me to containment, not anything that had happened since the injection.

"Ms. Lyons, answer the question," Victoria said impatiently, tapping one red-tipped nail on the glass table in front of her.

"TOXIC men entered the hotel room where my family was staying, killed my parents, and took me." I shrugged. "End of story."

Victoria smiled condescendingly as she shared a conspiratorial glance with first Amberly and then the doctor. She made an annoying clucking sound with her tongue and shook her head. "No, Ms. Lyons. That is not the end of the story. According to our records, you killed the intruders."

A gust of wind whipped through the room, conjured from nowhere. I sat on my hands and tried to think happy thoughts. Calm, cool, collected. Calm, cool, collected.

"Ms. Lyons, we are interested in understanding the extent of your abilities, both before and after the injection. Now, please, answer the question."

"Why?" I snapped. "Obviously you have the answer in front of you. Do you want me to admit it? Fine, I did it. I killed those bastards and I don't regret it. Are you happy? Does that help you understand how dangerous I am? What a threat I am?"

I could hear Crane's voice in my head telling me to reel it in. Any minute now armed guards were going to bust through the door, sedate and shackle me, and I'd wake up tomorrow in some freaky European psycho ward.

"You were ten, yes?" Amberly asked, amazingly nonplussed by my outburst.

I inhaled deeply, breathing in the calming vibes she was giving off. "Yes."

The three Council members, my judges and jury, conferred with one another using eye movements and head tilts, and had I not known better, I would've sworn they were communicating telepathically. Then I noticed that Victoria wasn't the only one clicking her nails on the table. She was just the one who was the most annoying, but they all were doing it. They were passing messages on the electronic tabletop.

Desperate to know whether bars and hospital gowns were in my future, I dropped my mental walls and started to peek behind Amberly's curtain of resistance. Hers was the weakest mind of the three, also the weakest will. If I had to manipulate one of them, she'd be my target.

"Ms. Lyons," Victoria said abruptly.

I felt like I'd been caught stealing an extra dessert from the school cafeteria. Guiltily, I stared at my lap and willed my burning cheeks to cool.

"Do you still want revenge for your parents?"

I hesitated. Not because I didn't know the answer. Hell yes, I wanted revenge. Did I admit that, though? Would the admission paint me as the bloodthirsty monster they thought I might be?

"Ms. Lyons, Talia, please, honesty is best here." Victoria's voice was gentle, soothing and I wanted to tell her the truth. She wasn't manipulating me, that wasn't her Talent – Morpher by the feel of her brain patterns. Yet, the urge to be honest was like a physical pull, and the words were tumbling out of my mouth like rocks before I could stop them.

"Yes. I want Mac to look me in the eye and admit it was him. I want him to tell me why. And then, when he's finished, I want him to suffer the way I have all these years."

It was hard to determine who was the most surprised by my frank statement and venomous tone. Victoria's gold eyes were large and round. Amberly's normally full mouth had thinned to two white gashes. And the doctor looked, well, frightened. Awesome.

The room was entirely silent except for four beating hearts, no one even breathed. I thought for sure I'd messed up epically. Maybe I had misread Victoria. Maybe she was some type of Manipulator or demon, because I felt like she'd possessed me and forced the truth out.

"I think that will do for now. If you would follow Dr. Kramer, he can begin the physical examination," Victoria said with a smile that could have frozen boiling water.

"Wait, what? That's it? How'd I do? Did I pass?" I asked. "And what do you mean a physical examination?"

"It will be painless, Ms. Lyons. Much less so than this question and answer session," the doctor told me.

Super convincing, I thought wryly.

"We will speak again after the physical," Victoria said. "No determination can be made just yet."

I didn't like where this was heading. I didn't want Dr. Kramer poking and prodding me like an animal. I'd come to hate doctors over the past year and half, and he had yet to prove he was an exception to the arrogant rule. But I had come this far. Besides letting my temper get the better of me once or twice, the evaluation hadn't been so bad. I'd refrained from Morphing and attacking one of the council members— it would've been Victoria if I had—and I wasn't handcuffed just yet. All in all, best-case scenario.

Dr. Kramer rose and I realized he was a tiny man. Sitting, he'd appeared square. Square head, square jaw, square frame. Standing, the statement was even truer. He was as tall as he was wide.

"This way, Ms. Lyons." He gestured to the far end of the room where a door blended seamlessly into the white wall. Only my keen eyesight and the faint outline let me know it was actually there.

I stood and followed him, my sandals flip-flopping on the hard tile floor. The door had no handle or knob, but opened on its own when we were positioned in front of it. The nerves from earlier returned, creating a maelstrom in my stomach.

Dr. Kramer entered first, and I followed a step behind, unwilling to show Victoria and Amberly my hesitation. I wanted to appear confident, even if I felt anything but. Once inside the auxiliary room, I nearly sagged with relief. Dr. Patel was waiting for us.

"Ah, Ms. Lyons, good to see you looking so pretty today. How are your bruises? They appear to be healing nicely," he said.

I touched the side of my face. The Council hadn't asked about them, not that I minded, and I'd almost forgotten they were there.

"Thank you, doctor. They don't hurt at all."

"Good, good. If you would be so kind as to remove your dress and change into the clothes in the bathroom, we can get started." He pointed towards a small nook off of the main area. Bathroom was a stretch for the curtained-off corner of the large hospital-like room. It was more of an alcove with a sink and toilet. The rest of the area was covered in medical machines, monitors, and computers. In the very center was a rubber mat with two foot-prints. On the ceiling above the mat, an ominous-looking clear plastic tube was ready to descend upon its victim and swallow her whole.

I tried not to shudder. Painless maybe. Traumatizing definitely.

I shuffled to the sectioned-off area and closed the partition, cutting off my view of the doctors and theirs of me. Their words were still audible, and as I changed into a pair of white shorts and plain white tank top, I listened to their conversation. Unfortunately, the one language I wasn't fluent in was medical jargon. So, I had no idea what they were talking about. I caught phrases like "neuro-something-something imaging resonance something" and "artificial stimuli inducer."

Yikes, I thought, that sounded creepy.

I didn't linger behind the curtain. I wanted this ordeal over with posthaste.

"Ready," I declared as I rejoined the doctors. "Evaluate me."

"If you could stand on the feet, please," Dr. Patel instructed me.

I complied and tried not to glance up at the tube that was surely about to claim me as its lunch.

Dr. Kramer began affixing electrodes to my chest, neck and temples. Then he wrapped a strap around my ribcage along my bra line. Next, he retrieved a syringe and took three vials of blood from the vein in my left elbow. The sudden blood loss left me dizzy, and I swayed a little.

"That is the most pain you will feel," he promised.

Doubtful, I thought.

Dr. Patel, who'd been fiddling with the dials on one of the many monitors in the room, came to stand in front of me. "We are going to take a look inside your head," he said.

I scowled.

"It will tell us if there has been any deterioration," he continued. "Then, we are going to perform situational analysis."

"Which means what, exactly?" I asked.

"The electrodes attached to your body will send images to your brain, and we will gauge your reactions. It will let us know how your mind perceives threats and how you will react in a given situation."

Oh no, I thought, a test I couldn't lie my way out of.

Both doctors stepped back, and I heard a faint whine from above. I closed my eyes and waited for the tube to engulf me. I heard the low hum as it spun in slow, steady circles around my body. Soft clicking let me know the contraption was taking pictures. As promised, the procedure was painless. I didn't feel a thing except for the buzz of electricity that the machine gave off, but the sensation wasn't unpleasant.

"Now we will begin the situational analysis," one of the doctors said. His voice was muffled by the thick plastic, and I couldn't tell which one it was. My head felt woozy and starbursts exploded behind my closed eyelids. I tried to open my eyes but found only blackness when I did. Panic seized me for a brief moment before I sank into darkness.

My eyelids spasmed uncontrollably like the repeated clicking of a camera shutter. Just as I started to think I was having a seizure, the movement stopped. My heartbeat was sluggish and irregular, a thump thump followed by a long pause before another soft thump. I breathed in and out to calm myself. The plastic tube was just clearing my head, and the evaluation room was visible once again.

"See? Painless," Dr. Kramer smiled at me.

We were face to face, his poufy hair giving him an inch on me.

"Is it over?" I asked, trying to recall the procedure.

"You performed beautifully," Dr. Patel said.

"You may change back into your own clothing, and we can rejoin the others," Dr. Kramer added.

"Okay."

I stumbled when I stepped off of the mat, and Dr. Patel hurried forward to catch me. He guided me to the alcove, but didn't follow me inside. Stripping off the white clothes took longer than it should have since my motor skills were impaired like I was drunk or something. The feeling didn't last long. By the time my dress was firmly in place, I was in control of my body and mind. And I was livid. What had they given me? When had they done it?

The syringe, I realized, it had been coated with a sedative or something.

Thrusting the curtain aside, I stomped forward. "What did you do to me?" I demanded.

Dr. Patel looked sheepish. Dr. Kramer looked first startled, then like I'd offended him by asking.

"Ms. Lyons, a powerful Mind Manipulator such as yourself can alter the results if conscious. This was the only way to get a true reading on your threat level."

I'd been categorized a lot in my life. TOXIC dubbed me a Mind Manipulator at the age of ten. By sixteen I was afforded the honor of Elite. Never once had anyone given me a threat rating. Honestly, I was a little curious. Was I truly lethal?

"And? How'd I stack up?" I asked.

"Let us reconvene with the others."

Hmm, that remark could be taken either way.

When we reentered the big room on the other side of the seamless door, Dr. Patel accompanied us. That lessened my fears for some reason. While I didn't know the man well, I liked him. I thought maybe he'd advocate for me if the need arose.

Dr. Kramer took his place at the rectangular table. Dr. Patel stayed firmly by my side as I sat in my chair, further reassuring me that I had a friend.

"Ms. Lyons, I will make this brief," Victoria began.

Shit.

"Just as I suspected, you are extremely dangerous. Your threat level is off the charts."

I was glad I was sitting because all my bones seemed to melt inside of me.

"Your brain is exhibiting signs of slight deterioration. Nothing irreversible if the cure is found sooner rather than later." She paused for dramatic effect, and had my muscles been functional, I would've leapt for her. "In light of the current predicament UNITED is facing, I believe you are an asset to our cause. Your need for revenge, while violent, will help bring Danbury McDonough to justice. At this time, it is the feeling of the UNITED Council that containment is not necessary. However, I am recommending that you be reevaluated once a month for an indeterminable amount of time."

Now my head spun for an entirely different reason. I wasn't going to be locked up. I was dangerous, sure, but I was free. Crane had been right: she wanted my Talents too badly to contain me.

The council members waited expectantly. I figured they were waiting for a thank you, but I wasn't about to give them the satisfaction.

When I just stared at Victoria and her colleagues with open defiance, she cleared her throat and continued. "The UNITED guard will be arriving in the next several days. President Crane has been so kind as to let us set up a home base in Coalition territory. Should Director McDonough fail to appear before the Council in Bern in the next seventy-two hours, we will be forced to strike. I am offering you a place among the guard, if you are interested."

"I am," I said quickly. No way was I letting them take down Mac without me. And it would come to that. Mac wasn't the surrendering type.

Victoria smiled. A genuine smile that lit up her golden eyes and projected twin rays of sunshine onto the table in front of her. "I thought you would say that. Word will be sent to you in due time. For now, you are free to go about your business."

She didn't have to tell me twice. I was out of my seat and practically running through the door before she finished her sentence. My first thought was Erik. I wanted to tell him the good news. Then, another thought had me changing course and heading upstairs: Penny. Had her evaluation gone as well as mine?

I reached the main atrium on sublevel one, where I ran into Crane as he was coming down the spiral staircase. His expression was grim and his eyes were like endless pools of black tar.

"Ian? What's wrong?" I asked, terrified that Penny had been carted off.

"TOXIC attacked the Underground station in Kentucky," he said.

The temporary joy of freedom gave way to panic. Erik's family was at that station. Alex was at that station. I'd failed. Failed Kandice and Donavon and their son.

"When are we leaving?" I asked.

"Get changed and meet me in the command center."

I didn't waste time responding. I practically flew to the elevator.

Chapter Twelve

AFTER SAYING A hurried goodbye to Erik and Henri, I'd joined Crane and a group of soldiers in the command center on sublevel one. Frederick was among the gathered. Since he'd left the Kentucky station, he'd been using his remote viewing gifts to keep an eye on Alex and Erik's family. During his morning check, he'd seen the quartet being forced from Frederick's home by TOXIC operatives. The four of them were being held captive in a rec center at the station.

"When was the last time you had contact with the station manager there?" Jared asked Crane. He wasn't a fan of the rescue mission. And he wasn't the only one. Several of Crane's soldiers were attempting to talk him out of the plan.

"We haven't been able to get through to them," Crane admitted.

"TOXIC has control of the station," Jared replied.

"Yes, but they haven't started evacuating people yet," Crane said. "We can reach them before that happens."

"And then what? Our induction facilities are full. Where are they going to go?" Jared demanded.

"Hundreds of people died in the raid in Tennessee," Brand pointed out. "You said yourself it was chaos. You barely escaped. I don't think it's worth the risk. We don't have the manpower."

"Not worth it!" I demanded, interjecting myself in the argument. "What if Mac decides to execute them? He's likely operating in panic mode after receiving UNITED's order to turn himself in."

"Talia's right," Frederick agreed. "Director McDonough is desperate and irrational. We need to send help."

"TOXIC is already there," Brand insisted, rounding on Frederick. "You're a Viewer, not a Visionary. You saw something that is happening as we speak. We're already too late."

"If we leave now, we'll be there in an hour," Frederick shot back.

"With minimal forces. Even if every able body here went, we'd still only have thirty, forty soldiers tops," Brand replied.

"All this talking is a waste of time. The longer we argue, the more people die, and the less chance we have of getting there before Mac starts carting the defectors off to prisons." Already on edge from lack of sleep and my evaluation, I felt ready to explode.

"This isn't up for discussion. Brand, you've been in contact with the bases in Denver and Seattle, correct?" Crane asked.

"Yeah. They're ready to deploy on your command," Brand confirmed reluctantly.

"Good. The Denver team should be able to get eyes on the situation pretty fast," Crane said. "Give the order."

After that, everything happened in blur of barked commands. Before I knew it, I was aboard a hoverplane with twenty Coalition soldiers, and outfitted with a mini arsenal of weapons.

The ride to Kentucky was tense, the mood on the plane volatile. The Coalition soldiers weren't used to so much action. Several of the others had been part of the attack on Tramblewood and still sported the evidence. I was glad to see Janelle. I liked her, and she had proved herself a solid soldier in the last attack. She sat next to me on one of the long metal benches. We didn't speak, but having her close by was a comfort all the same. Frederick was also on my plane. He spent the ride lost in a trance, viewing the events in Kentucky as they unfolded. Every so often he'd provide an update to the group at large. So far, all the residents were still being held captive by TOXIC operatives, who were waiting for Mac to arrive.

Crane had insisted that Brand stay at the cottage. He said he didn't want to leave it unprotected, and Brand needed to coordinate the impromptu fight from there. When we'd left, Penny was in the control room with Brand, ready to call the shots from our home base. I hadn't had time to talk to her about her own evaluation, but took it as a good sign that she was still at the cottage.

As expected, the Denver team reached the camp first. They were in constant communication with our team through the onboard communicators. A soldier named Benton provided a running commentary that was piped through the overhead speakers. Using radar, Benton's team had determined that several TOXIC hovercrafts were patrolling the airspace surrounding the camp. The fight would start in the air. Over the speaker in our craft, I heard Brand order the Denver team to wait for our arrival. We were approximately an hour ahead of the Seattle team, but we weren't going to wait for them. Once we rendezvoused with Benton's team, we'd strike.

"Mr. President, we have the enemy crafts on our radar," the pilot's voice came over the loudspeaker. I recognized her throaty drawl. It was Donna, the same pilot who'd flown us to Tramblewood.

"Okay, everyone strap yourselves in. This might get ugly," Crane ordered.

I secured the shoulder harness around my body. My palms were sweaty, sliding over the metal of the gun in my hands. Adrenaline pumped fast and furious in my veins. Nausea rolled through my stomach, making me glad there was nothing in there to throw up. I was still a little woozy from the loss of blood and the sedative from earlier. Deep inhales, followed by long exhales kept me focused. Beside me, Janelle imitated my breathing method, mumbling something that sounded like a prayer.

"Denver team has an enemy craft locked in their sights," Brand said over the speaker. "Denver team, fire in three, two, one." I closed my eyes, expecting to feel the shock waves from the explosion, but we were too far away.

"It's a hit. Repeat, it's a hit," Brand said.

"Alpha team, fire in five, four, three, two, one," this time it was Penny. Her firm, authoritative tone comforted me. I felt better just knowing she was there.

The plane rocked as the pilot released the missile, causing my head to ricochet between the shoulder straps of the harness.

"Negative, hit," Donna shouted over the speaker.

The plane swerved wildly, dipping low on the left side. The maneuver propelled me forward, the harness suspending me in midair. I yelped, clutching frantically to my gun. I checked the safety, relieved to find it engaged. At least if I dropped it, the weapon wasn't likely to go off accidentally. I suppressed the bubble of manic laughter caught in my throat.

"Denver team, fire in three, two, one," Brand commanded over the speaker.

Our plane rocked, and for a brief second I thought that it was a shock wave from another plane exploding too close to us. Then we began to spin, and I knew we'd been hit. One minute I was upside down, feet dangling over my head, the next my spine slammed against the metal seat, only to have the cycle repeat over and over again.

My screams were lost in those of the other soldiers. I squeezed my eyes shut, pressed my gun to my chest, and prayed for the ride to end. It seemed like an eternity before Donna regained control of the plane. The man across from me leaned over and vomited onto the floor. I hoped we didn't start spinning again, I would lose my own stomach contents if his landed on me.

"Alpha team, do you copy? How bad are you hit?" Penny sounded frantic now. "Repeat, Alpha team, do you copy?"

"We're hit pretty good," Donna responded over the speaker.

"Make the drop, and get out of there," Brand barked. "I'm dispatching a pick-up hovercraft now."

"That's our cue," Crane said, and started unbuckling his harness.

My fingers fumbled with the release clasps, and I couldn't seem to focus my eyes. When I was finally free of the harness, I tried to stand, but another jolt sent me crashing to my knees. Pain exploded down my calves. I willed it away, now was not the time to nurse an injury. I used the bench I'd just vacated to push myself to my feet.

"Hatch opening in five, four," I met Crane's eyes across the cabin and he nodded, "three, two, one."

The doors in the belly of the plane drew apart, creating a chasm. The ground was so far below. I swallowed hard and jumped.

I counted to five, then pulled the cord attached to my shoulder strap. The parachute sprang up, yanking me upwards temporarily before allowing me to float downward. The ground rushed up to meet me, not fast enough, though.

Gunfire erupted from below. All around me, bullets tore through the other soldiers' parachutes. Someone close by screamed as his body hurdled towards earth at an alarming speed. I braced myself for the inevitable. A spark of hope ignited in my chest when I was within ten feet of the ground, my chute unscathed. Not wanting to test my luck, I grabbed a knife from my belt and deftly sliced through the shoulder straps, falling the last six or seven feet to the grass below before a TOXIC bullet tagged me.

From above I'd seen TOXIC operatives littering the neighborhood, and had been worried about landing in the middle of them. Thankfully I landed in the backyard of a small home that was devoid of people. I quickly ran for safety and flattened myself against the back of the house, the siding pressing hard into my back. I counted to three, punctuating each number with a deep breath, then I rounded the corner, gun first.

"*Talia,*" snapped Crane in my head.

I pivoted, searching for him.

In the camouflage suit, he was hard to spot in the bushes of the next house over. It wasn't until he raised a hand to beckon me over that I was able to make out his shape among the leaves. As quietly as I could manage, I hurried to join him.

"*We need to get to the rec center,*" Crane sent.

I nodded my understanding.

"*How?*" I responded. I'd lost track of our location during the emergency evacuation.

Crane touched the opening in his ear, and I heard the tiniest crackle of static. "Brand," he whispered. "Brand, it's Ian, do you copy?"

Brand's voice was faint, and I could just make out his reply. "I'm here, Ian."

"Do you have my location? Can you direct me to the rec center from here?" Crane whispered back.

"Affirmative. Stand by." Brand's words drifted from Crane's earpiece.

My heightened sense of sound registered footsteps an instant later. "*Operatives, rounding the house,*" I sent Crane.

"*How many?*"

I listened harder, concentrating my energy on my hearing. Three distinct sets of feet.

"Three, I think. Unless they're running in sync," I replied.

"Are you sure you saw them land over here?" a man's voice sounded over the chaos taking place on the other side of the house.

I held my breath. Three was manageable; Ian and I had the element of surprise. And I could control three minds at once if push came to shove.

"Yes, Jackson, I'm sure. Two people came down back here," a second man replied.

I focused on the second speaker, willing him to recant.

"Actually, I think it was a couple houses down, to the left," he amended his statement.

Ian's earpiece pinged. "Ian, the rec center is approximately one kilometer to the east of your current position," I heard Brand say.

I closed my eyes and urged the operatives to start moving. I knew the only reason that I could hear Brand through the transmitter was because of my heightened senses, but I wasn't taking any chances. The operatives were close, no more than five feet away. If one of them was a Morph, they might hear him, too.

When Crane didn't respond, Brand tried again. "Ian, do you copy?" Crane tapped his ear canal, one short thud, followed by two longer ones, ending with three short ones. A code, I realized.

"Understood," Brand replied.

On the other side of our hiding place, the operatives were already in motion. Their angry voices drifted back as they set off in the direction the guy I'd manipulated indicated. When we were sure that they were gone, Crane crept into the open. He stayed low, crouching as he surveyed the area.

"Let's move," he sent, once he seemed satisfied.

I slid from the bushes, and together we jogged east. I remained vigilant, expanding all my senses simultaneously. I sniffed the air like a dog for the scent of gunpowder and sweat. I listened for the thudding of boots on grass. My eyes darted up, down, left, right, searching for the slightest hint of movement.

The houses provided us cover, but the breaks in between left us vulnerable. We paused, only briefly, at each one. Crane plunged ahead of me to draw any fire in the event that we were spotted. Shouts and the steady staccato rhythm of gunfire wafted from the street. My palms itched with the desire to run out there and help the Coalition soldiers that were fighting to take control of the situation. The prisoners were more important. If we didn't move fast, there was still a chance TOXIC would get them out of here before our people reached them, and then it wouldn't matter who was in control of the station.

I felt the vibration in the air before I heard the hum of the hovercraft. I looked up, searching the clear sky. It was close, and approaching fast.

"Ian, three o'clock," I sent, pointing towards the approaching plane. He followed my finger and nodded. Crane tapped his ear again, and spoke to Brand.

"It's ours, Seattle team," he sent back to me.

We started moving again, and moments later parachutes dotted the sky, coming to aid our efforts. I relaxed slightly, before realizing that they were going to draw attention to our position. I picked up my pace, trying to put as much distance between us and them as possible. Too late.

Operatives poured around the sides of the houses. Between the house behind us and the operatives on our right and left, we were surrounded on three sides. The only option left was the woods in front of us.

"Run," Crane screamed, not bothering to communicate the command mentally. There was no point. We'd been spotted.

I didn't need to be told twice. I took off. My legs burned as I pushed the muscles harder. The sound of my racing heartbeat drowned out the shouts of Mac's people. My ears registered a dozen or so soft clicks as fingers pulled triggers, and I braced myself for the pain that would accompany their bullets piercing my skin. Mentally, I deflected the ones the ones I could identify. One managed to evade my powers and skimmed my right shoulder. The suit took the brunt of the blow, and the smell of singed fabric assaulted my nostrils. I ran harder. Another burst of gunfire erupted behind me. A second bullet struck square between my shoulder blades. Pain blossomed from the point of impact, and I stumbled forward from the force. My knees struck the grass.

Get up, get up, get up, I ordered myself. The woods were less than five feet away. If I could make it there, I still had a chance.

"Hold your fire, it's her," someone screamed behind me.

Run, run, run, must keep going, I thought.

I willed myself to stand, blocking the pain shooting down my spine. Terror propelled me into the woods. I could feel my pursuers closing in, and I started to weave between trees, hoping to throw them off course. I wasn't sure how many of them there were. Too many minds to count. My legs ached and my lungs burned and I knew that I wouldn't be able to run forever. I used the best weapon I had: my mind. I sent misdirecting thoughts over my shoulder, praying at least some of the operatives would be led astray.

It worked. The footsteps veered to the right. I collapsed behind an ancient oak. Gulping fresh air, I assessed my situation. I was alone, wounded, and had no way to communicate with anyone. Panic set in, coming on hard and fast, and nearly crippling me.

You're better than this, I chastised myself. Think, plan, stay alive.

First things first, I needed to see how badly I was injured. The pain in my back had dimmed to a dull throbbing sensation. I twisted my arm behind my back and fumbled for the wound. Instead of a bloody hole, my fingers closed around a warm, misshapen lump midway between my shoulder blades. The bullet hadn't penetrated the suit; the fabric was thicker back there and had snared the metal before it could do any permanent damage. The first flicker of hope broke through. I yanked the bullet remains free and threw it to the ground. Next, I assessed my shoulder. The material was singed, the skin underneath red and tender. I touched the sensitive spot gingerly with one finger. It stung, but the injury wasn't incapacitating.

Now confident that I was going to live, I needed to devise a plan. I needed to get back to Crane and his men. Crane. He was out here somewhere, he had to be. I opened my mind, searching for his. My heart sank when my mental feelers returned no results. They've captured him, I thought.

"Not good, not good, not good," I muttered under my breath. Crane's life was more important than mine. Without his leadership, the Coalition would fall apart. Without him, who knew what Victoria and the Council would do with me, Penny, and Erik.

The crack of a branch turned the sweat covering my face to ice. I went rigid, molding my body against the tree trunk. I tried to latch onto the person's mind. My attempt was met with a brick wall of resistance. Stubborn pride made me try again. The second attempt was as unproductive as the first.

"I don't think she could've gotten this far," a man called. Every fine hair on my body rose; I knew that voice.

"The ground is trampled, she definitely came this way," a woman called back. She was panting, and her voice came from a much farther distance.

Heavy footsteps, no longer trying to be discreet, came next. I tried not to breath, not to so much as twitch a muscle. Maybe they will leave, I thought. No such luck. More branches breaking, more people talking, more operatives coming to join the search.

Think, Talia, I ordered myself. They want you alive. They will take you to where they are holding the other prisoners, probably where they are holding Crane.

I tried to put myself in Mac's shoes. Mac was logical, calculated. He would've ordered his men to take Ian alive, too. He'd want to be the one to end Crane's life to send a message to UNITED. By now, he'd know Crane was collaborating with them. The blow would send a message: Mac wasn't going down without a fight.

Surrendering was contrary to my nature, to every ideal TOXIC had drilled into me. Death was better than capitulation, Mac had taught me that. Death was also selfish. Too many people were counting on me.

I inhaled, long and even, then, before I lost my nerve, stepped around the tree.

"Hello, Captain," I said, my voice steel.

"Lyons," Captain Alvarez replied, not looking nearly as pleased to see me as I'd anticipated.

Guns clicked behind him, but I kept my eyes trained on Captain Alvarez. I might crack if I thought too much about the barrels pointed in my direction.

"Never thought we'd be on opposite sides," the Captain continued.

"I never thought you'd break the oath you took to protect the people of the United States," I shot back, letting too much emotion creep into my voice. I bit my lip to quell the desire to attack.

"Yes, it does seem that *one* of us chose the wrong side," he responded. Something about the way he said it gave me pause. Had he intentionally used "one" instead of "you?" Or was that just wishful thinking?

The operatives behind him became antsy, shifting uncomfortably in their heavy boots. I worried someone might get an itchy trigger finger and shoot me despite their orders to the contrary. My eyes shifted, almost involuntarily, to the guns. As if sensing my discomfort, Captain Alvarez gestured for them to lower their weapons. Most did, but a few held out.

"She's not going anywhere," he snapped. "Talia knows it would be pointless to run *now*." He emphasized the now, and I again wondered if it was intentional. I tried to reach out to his mind again, but just like before, I couldn't get past the barricades. Were my Talents fading? No, Victoria's assessment would've picked up on that.

I shifted my focus to a woman standing slightly behind Captain Alvarez, forced her to her knees, and then ordered her to place the barrel of her gun to her temple. No trace of fear showed on her face, and I knew that her will was mine. Why couldn't I control the Captain?

"Lyons," Captain Alvarez snapped, and I released my hold on the operative's mind. I wasn't really going to make her shoot herself, I was just putting on a show. I wanted the operatives to remember who and what they were dealing with.

I forced out a laugh, like I thought making someone commit suicide was funny. I didn't, it reminded me too much of what I'd done the night my parents were killed.

"Toss me the gun, Lyons," the Captain ordered me. "And the knife belt, too; it's not like you need them." It's not like you need them? Didn't he mean it's not like you'll be able to use them? Or it's not like you'll be able to get a shot off before one of my men shoots you in the head?

"Now!" he barked.

Apparently I was taking too long pondering his words.

Glaring, I slid the gun across the forest floor. The knife belt followed shortly thereafter. Captain Alvarez gestured for the woman I'd forced to the ground to pick up my weapons.

"What now? You hand me over to Mac?" I sneered, surprised at my ability to affect flippancy while being captured. No, I reminded myself, not captured. I surrendered. This was my choice, my terms. Of course, if this backfired, I'd have no one to blame but me. I'd worry about that later.

Captain Alvarez's hard, appraising eyes softened, and a wave of regret hit me. "In time," he muttered. I swallowed hard, my pulse raced on a current of fear. What were they going to do to me before Mac arrived?

"Wilkes, Nichols, take her," the Captain pointed to someone behind him and the woman who'd taken my weapons, the woman I'd so easily controlled.

Odd choice, I thought.

A man with cold blue eyes, Wilkes I assumed, cut through the crowd of operatives and grabbed my injured arm with one beefy paw of a hand. I ground my back teeth to keep from wincing. Nichols didn't move. She appeared to be both mystified and terrified by me, like I was some dark fairytale beast come to life.

"That's an order, Nichols," Captain Alvarez snapped.

Hesitantly she walked towards me, taking hold of my free arm. Nichols' grip was slack, like touching me physically pained her. Wilkes pulled me forward with too much force. I focused on my feet so that I wouldn't give him the satisfaction of falling. He halted next to Captain Alvarez.

"Sir, do you want her with the others?" Wilkes asked.

"No, keep her separate from the general populace. Put her in a room alone, the one next to the Kelleys," the Captain replied. He shifted his attention to me, holding my gaze as he spoke his next words. "Be careful, she's extremely powerful, and not all of us are immune to her Talents."

He knew I'd tried, and failed, to take control of his mind. Something had been done to him, something that allowed him to block me. I boldly stared back, willing him to say more even though I knew my gifts wouldn't affect him. Captain Alvarez's stare became more intense; he was trying to pass a message, I realized.

I let my mental barriers fall, completely opening my mind to the Captain.

"The Director's on his way from D.C. You should have an hour before he arrives. Our orders are to keep all the prisoners contained until he arrives," Captain Alvarez sent.

Relief was overshadowed by dread. I wasn't reading his mind. He was projecting his thoughts into my head, using gifts similar to mine. He'd been infected with the Creation drug. The worst case scenario had just been confirmed. Mac had made his army of super-Talents.

"What then? What does he plan on doing with the prisoners?" I sent back.

"Those he thinks he can control will be injected. The others killed."

No one expletive accurately summed up just how terrifying that prospect was.

"Yes, sir." Wilkes nodded his head in a show of respect. "We can handle her."

The Captain didn't spare the operative a second glance. He tapped his pointer finger once against his temple and nodded, at me. I thrust my chin in the air, defiant and proud.

"The beauty of being human, Captain, is that we were *created* with free will, the ability to choose. One of us has an hour to exercise that liberty. Maybe it's not too late... for one of us. The next time we see each other, one of us won't be so lenient. Tell Mac

I look forward to talking to him," I said, hoping that he caught all the double meanings.

The Captain's chuckle held no mirth. "Unfortunately, Talia, it is too late for one of us."

This time, I was positive the "one" of us he was talking about was him.

"I'm sorry to hear that, Captain," I told him.

He closed his eyes, his chest shook when he inhaled.

"Get her out of here," he ordered my guards.

Wilkes gripped the back of my neck, his fingers digging painfully into the tense muscles. His other hand twisted my arm behind my back as he pushed me forward. Nichols released me, drew her gun, and thrust it between my shoulder blades, in the same spot the bullet had struck me. While there was no visible wound, the impact had left a monster-sized bruise, and the added pressure sent jolts of pain spider-webbing out from the source.

All the force was unnecessary. I was ready to go with them. Here, in the woods and surrounded by TOXIC operatives, I was unable to do any real damage. Alone, just the three of us in a room, now that was a different story.

"You might as well ditch the gun. We both know it's an empty threat," I said to Nichols as our trio tromped over fallen branches and trampled earth. "Capture, don't kill. Those are your orders, right?" I continued when she didn't respond.

I didn't have the energy or the inclination to taunt my captors, but it distracted me from reality. If I didn't find a way to escape, find Crane, and get the hell out of here in the next hour, Alex and the Kelleys—the reason I'd been adamant about this mission— would be at TOXIC's mercy.

Mac would spare Alex's life. Not because the little boy was his grandson; familial ties didn't mean much to Mac. But Alex's Talent, remote viewing, was rare, and his blood valuable. Erik's family wouldn't be so lucky. Mac would kill them. Maybe for retaliation. Maybe to make an example of them. Maybe just because he could. I wouldn't let that happen.

"You heard the Captain. I'm extremely powerful. Aren't you scared to be alone with me?" I continued, making crazy eyes at Nichols over my shoulder. She was definitely the weak link. Her lips pursed together, but she didn't take the bait.

"So what is it Mac plans on doing with all the people here? Public trials? Oh wait, I forgot, traitors don't get trials. I guess he'll just have them sentenced to death then. You do know that the last traitor he supposedly killed is still alive, right? Perfectly healthy, in fact." The lie was hard to get out. Penny was not perfectly healthy. She put on a good face, but the power was affecting her.

"Shut up," Wilkes growled.

I was getting to him.

"Make me," I shot back, turning my attention to him.

His hand shot out with superhuman speed. Stars exploded behind my eyes, and pain shot across my cheek as my head whipped to one side. Crap, that hurt. Blood filled my mouth, and I spit the coppery substance on the ground.

"That the best you got?" I managed to squeak out. I was on shaky ground. Mac might not want me dead, but if I were unconscious, I would lose my chance to escape. I needed to calm down and stop being stupid.

I fully expected him to hit me again. I would've hit me again. But we were out of the woods now and nearing a large building. Operatives were stationed around the perimeter. At first, I wasn't sure exactly what made him hesitate. Then I noticed a tall, broad shouldered figure in a crisp, gray suit striding towards us.

Blood froze in my veins as my stomach hit the grass. I was meeting my maker, literally. Mac had arrived early.

Chapter Thirteen

"DIRECTOR, WILKES SAID. "We didn't expect you so soon." Like a good operative, he straightened and saluted.

Had my muscles not entered temporary paralysis at the sight of Mac, I probably would have rolled my eyes at the ridiculous display.

Nichols too seemed caught off guard and slightly awed by Mac's appearance. She dropped her barely-there grip on my arm and mimicked Wilkes' show of respect. "We have the Lyons girl, sir," she said.

This time, I did roll my eyes. Really? Stating the obvious seemed like a good idea? Did she think Mac had forgotten what I looked like?

"You don't say?" Mac replied sarcastically. When he spoke, his steel gray eyes sought out mine and the look that passed between us was almost conspiratorial.

I blinked to make sure I wasn't hallucinating. No, the face staring down at me was definitely Danbury McDonough. Only, while the cold gaze, sharp nose, and pursed lips were his, the essence radiating off of him was not. The person standing in front of me was warm and caring and extremely worried about me. This person cared about me. This person was also exerting an extreme amount of Talent. Energy leaked from him as he fought to stay in control.

As if all these weren't enough clues that something about this situation was off, his next statement confirmed it. "I'll take Talia from here."

Talia? Mac never called me Talia.

Mac reached for my arm, gently wrapping strong fingers around my bicep.

"She's a mouthy twit," Wilkes said, shoving me forward.

"Yes, Natalia's mouth does get her in trouble," Mac agreed, staring down at me with a very unMac-like twinkle in his eye.

"Captain Alvarez ordered us to escort her to an isolation room." It was Nichols who spoke this time.

I was impressed by her nerve. Openly questioning Mac was a bad idea, and here I thought she was weak-willed. Then again, maybe she sensed there was something off about this Mac, too.

"Last time I checked, the door to my office read, *Director*, not the Captain's." Mac was authority personified. A shiver ran through me. Maybe all the knocking about of my head on the plane had thrown me off, because this felt like the Mac I knew. Maybe before had just been wishful thinking.

"Of course, sir," Nichols stuttered. "I wasn't questioning your authority—"

Mac cut her off with a wave of his hand. "Go. I have the situation under control."

As I watched the two operatives retreat, I thought about swiping Mac's mind. Sure, he'd know I was there, and likely be expecting it, but just in case his defenses were down, I wanted to try. Knowing what he planned to do with me seemed like a good idea. Only before I had the opportunity, he spoke in my mind. And I finally understood what was really going on.

"Are you okay? What the hell are you doing here, Tal? You should be somewhere safe. You got Erik back, why are you still taking risks?" Donavon's mental voice said.

I was so relieved and impressed that I found myself unable to answer him.

Long ago, when I'd first come to the McDonoughs, Donavon had told me that exceptionally powerful Morphers could take *any* other living form. Animals were the easiest and the most natural, for whatever reason. Human shifts were hard to pull off and harder to maintain. Donavon had been trying for years to achieve a human transformation. This was the first he'd managed. Perfect timing, I thought.

Donavon, disguised as Mac, started leading me forward.

"Were you shot?" he asked, gently touching the frayed fabric on my shoulder.

"Yeah, but it's nothing. I'm fine. And I'm here because Erik's father and brothers are here, and he nearly died to rescue them. I'm here because Erik's isn't the only life worth fighting for. I'm here to protect your son," I sent back, growing angrier with each word. *"Where are you taking me?"*

We reached the doors to the rec center. Two guards saluted Donavon and eyed me warily. Donavon's grip on my arm tightened, and I knew he was fighting to maintain his Mac-like shape. The effort was draining him.

"As much as I hate to admit it, I'm glad you're here. I've been trying to figure out how to get Alex out of here since I saw him," he sent as we entered the foyer.

"How's he doing?" I asked.

"Good. I'm just glad I got to see him one last time."

"Don't say that. He needs you, Donavon." I wasn't really sure what I felt for Donavon anymore: anger because he sided with his father; irritation because he was too much of a coward to stand up for what was right; pity because he felt he didn't have a choice. One thing was certain, I was sad for him. Sadder still for Alex, who was certain to lose all his remaining family members once UNITED became involved. Even if Donavon lived through the attacks, he'd definitely be contained. Having been injected with an inferior form of the Creation drug at such a young age meant he'd have needed repeated injections to keep his Talents strong. There was no telling how badly his mind had been affected. And unlike me, he didn't hold enough value for UNITED to decide his potential worth to their cause outweighed the threat he posed. Morphing was the most common Talent.

"No, Tal, you're the one he needs now. He needs you to keep him safe. I'm... I'm no good for him."

"Does that mean that you're going to help me escape?" I asked, hoping that was the case. I needed all the help I could get.

Donavon came to a stop in front of a door marked "Cliff Oswald, Manager," and twisted the knob. He pushed the door open and led me through. It was a small office with a desk and two chairs. He gestured for me to sit in one. Reluctantly, I agreed.

"It's the least I can do," he said.

"You could come with me," I replied hopefully. *"You could come be with Alex."* It had been on the tip of my tongue to say cottage, but I shoved the word back. I didn't want to give away too much. Honestly, I wanted him to come with us, but also knew that was unrealistic.

"No, Tal, I can't. All personnel were implanted with trackers. That's how they found you in Tennessee. They put a tracker in Erik. My father knew you'd come for him. Although, I've got to say, he didn't expect you to show up with Crane and Coalition soldiers."

Donavon actually laughed. *"Not much surprises him anymore. You know how he is, rarely losing his cool in front of people. He popped blood vessels when he saw you and Crane together during the attack. Now this business with UNITED. He's flipping his shit."*

"Was he there?" I asked.

"Yeah. He was watching on the surveillance cameras in the warden's office. He was planning on letting you get far enough inside the prison that he'd be able to trap you. But once he realized you weren't alone, he knew he'd screwed up. He underestimated you. He ordered guards to Erik's cell. When you guys landed on the bridge, though, those guards left their posts to come after you. I was in Echo section when the attack started. Dad sent me after you defeated our forces on the bridge. He was so certain you wouldn't hurt me." Donavon shook his head and rolled his eyes. *"He never considered the feelings went both ways."*

I smiled sadly, recalling how on the roof I'd known without a doubt that Donavon wouldn't hurt me.

"Did you get in trouble for letting us go?"

Donavon swallowed hard, averting his eyes. *"No, I told him you manipulated me. No way to prove otherwise. Only you and I know the truth. I had to go before a tribunal and plead my case. Half voted to arrest me, but Dad backed me up. Argued our connection was strong, and you'd have had no trouble controlling me. Instead they agreed to give me the mental block. Fortunately Dad rescued me again there. He got Dr. Thistler to forge the paperwork."*

"That was nice of him, I suppose," I sent, not sure whether I meant it or not.

Donavon laughed bitterly. *"Not really. He thinks you might try to contact me, you know, mentally. If I got the block, he knows you wouldn't be able to. What he fails to understand is that I wouldn't tell him if you did."*

My heart went out to him. Donavon never had a choice in his life. From childhood he'd been condemned to this fate. This horrible fate of being his father's son. Donavon would be a good father in another life.

"Donavon, please come with me. Crane's men removed Erik's tracker; they'll be able to do the same for you. You don't have to stay. I know you don't agree with what your father is doing. You're a good person. You'll be a great father. Alex needs his father. Please. I'm sure UNITED will grant you clemency if you help lead them to Mac."

Donavon shook his head sadly. *"Erik's tracker was different. It was just a mechanical chip, like the one they put in your hip for your solo mission. Mine isn't. It runs through my blood. In time it will wear off, but that takes weeks. Besides, I know what UNITED does to the Created. I can't live like that."*

The blood tracker must've been why Captain Alvarez told me that there wasn't a choice for him. He'd been injected with the same tracking serum. Mac was reaching new lows. I wondered if he'd used a mechanical tracker on Erik for fear of contaminating his Mimic blood.

"Besides, I'm no good for Alex. That's why I stayed away from him and Kandice in the first place. Dad did have me removed from the Hunters as punishment for giving you my blood. But there was more to it. The Creation drug screws with people's heads. I was starting to forget things, have huge memory lapses. I messed up on missions. I was a liability. Dr. Thistler gives me drugs that help, but it's like putting a band-aid on a bullet wound. I don't have much longer."

My heart broke because he was right. For Donavon to have remained Talented for over a decade, he'd have been given numerous injections. The side effects might not be reversible in his case.

"Look, Tal. We don't have much time, Dad will be here soon. I need you and Alex out of here before he is. Right now Dad doesn't have a strong Viewer to steal blood from to make more. Alex is exactly what he's looking for. Crane's forces have nearly breached the perimeter we have set up around this place. Get Alex, join them, and get the hell onto one of the Coalition hovercrafts. Otherwise, the camp's emergency evacuation planes are approximately three kilometers due south. You should be able to pilot one of the smaller ones on your own."

"Where's Ian?" I asked. No way was I returning to the cottage without him and risk facing Brand's wrath and Penny's grief. Donavon blanched when I referred to Crane as "Ian."

"Last I heard he was leading the charge to break through the perimeter we have set up around the rec center."

"So he wasn't captured?" I clarified.

Donavon shook his head. "Guy's an escape artist."

No, I thought, even better: a Perception Manipulator. Once alone, he'd have been able to hide in plain sight by giving off the perception that he was a TOXIC operative or maybe even a tree.

"Is Alex with Erik's family? Captain Alvarez said they were being held separately from the rest of the prisoners."

"Yeah. I was able to keep them together so Alex wouldn't be scared."

"Where are they, Donavon?"

I met Donavon's cornflower blue eyes, and they were Donavon's eyes now. The years had fallen away, and with them the deepest of the wrinkles and worry lines. Mac's silver-streaked pale gold hair had been replaced by Donavon's darker blonde locks. The gray suit was gone, replaced by an adapti-suit that showed off Donavon's trim frame.

Donavon offered me his hand and I took it, letting him pull me to my feet. He wrapped his arms around me, and I buried my face in his chest. I needed to get moving if I wanted out of here before the real Mac arrived, but I didn't want the moment to end. Donavon had been my everything for so long, and I wasn't ready to give him up yet.

"They're three doors down to the right. There is one guard stationed outside. I'll distract him long enough for you to slip inside. Don't waste time. Get in and get them out. Follow the hallway to the staircase at the end. Go all the way to the basement. There are exit doors from the stairwell that open to the back of the building. There should be five guards back there. I'll radio that we need reinforcements to the front to draw them away. That will give you a clear exit. Don't hesitate, Talia. If you do run into any guards, they won't intentionally kill you, but they are likely to shoot first, ask questions second. I'll give you my gun, use it. You don't have friends here anymore, you hear me?"

"I have one friend here," I told him sadly, tears filling my eyes and wetting the front of his suit. But that wasn't exactly true, I had at least one other. Captain Alvarez had tried to engineer my escape, too. How many others weren't loyal to Mac anymore?

"I love you, Natalia. Always have. Always will."

I pulled back from Donavon, wiping my eyes with the back of my hand. Donavon's eyes glistened, too, and I reached up to wipe a single tear weaving down his cheek. "I love you, too."

Donavon worked the strap of the gun over his head and handed it to me. Then he drew another from a holster at his hip. I slung the larger weapon across my chest, deciding to keep the smaller clutched in my hands.

"Give me two minutes before coming out," Donavon sent.

I nodded, and watched as he turned and left. I counted to one hundred and twenty, forcing myself not to rush the numbers. As the final seconds ticked off, I hurried to the door. I turned the knob, and found it locked from the outside. He wasn't making this too easy on me, I thought dryly. Using my powers, I disengaged the lock, and then eased the door open. My muscles relaxed slightly when I found the hallway empty. Tip-toeing, I counted the doors as I passed until I found the third one. There was a rectangle of frosted glass in the door. I glanced in, making sure that there were no additional guards waiting for me. I could make out several distorted shapes, but couldn't see the entire space.

The door was, of course, locked as well. This time, though, all I had to do was turn the bar. I said a silent prayer that the Kelleys and Alex were alone, and then pushed the door open. Erik's father was sitting slumped over what looked like a school desk. Edmond, the middle of the Kelley boys, leaned against the far wall, cradling one arm to his chest and Alex with the other. And Evan, Erik's youngest brother, was at his father's feet, holding a balled up wad of fabric to his father's thigh. His shirt, I realized, when I registered the fact he was naked from the waist up.

Edmond saw me first. "Talia?" he exclaimed, too loudly for my liking.

Alex's tiny head shot up, and my heart clenched. "Tals," he squealed.

I put my finger to my lips to shush Edmond.

"It's me, baby, but you need to be quiet," I said softly to Alex.

"Quiet," he parroted in his little-kid whisper.

Mr. Kelley's head bobbed, blood dripped down the right side of his face.

"Are you here to rescue us?" Edmond asked, speaking more softly this time.

"Yeah. We need to move. There isn't much time."

Evan scurried to his feet before helping his father from the desk. Mr. Kelley slung his arm around his son's shoulders, leaning heavily on him for support. The wound that Evan had been applying pressure to was a bullet hole.

"Crap," I muttered, moving farther into the room. I knelt in front of Erik's father, trying to assess the damage. I could see bone. Not good. Racking my brain for a way to staunch the bleeding while we made our escape, I came up empty. Then I remembered the tear from my own brush with a bullet. I gripped the tear in my suit and yanked. The fabric ripped, but only a little. Realizing what I was doing, Edmond hurried to join the effort. It took both of us to get the sleeve of the suit free. I deftly used the material to create a tourniquet.

"It's good to see you, Talia," Mr. Kelley mumbled softly. He was losing too much blood too fast.

"We need to go," I said, speaking to Edmond since I figured he was most in control. "Here." I handed him the handgun, keeping the rifle for myself. "You know how to use a gun, right?"

Edmond rolled his eyes dramatically. "Of course I do."

"Good," I replied, ignoring his patronizing tone.

I collected Alex from where he was curled up on the floor. "Can you be brave and walk on your own?" I asked. Carrying him would tie up my hands, and I needed them free to fend off attackers.

He nodded and scrambled to his feet. I gave him a quick once-over, patting my hands up and down his body to make sure he wasn't injured.

"What I need you to do is follow me," I whispered. "Can you concentrate on my mind? View me?" I wasn't sure if he knew what I meant, but he nodded like he understood. "Okay, let's move."

I took the lead, Evan and Mr. Kelley limping awkwardly behind me with Alex clutching Evan's free hand. Edmond brought up the rear. The hallway was still empty, and I sent waves of gratitude towards Donavon, wherever he was. We moved slowly, but managed to get to the stairwell without incident. Once inside, Edmond hurried to help Evan carry their father down the stairs. I ran ahead to scout for threats.

"It's clear down here," I called up, my voice echoing off the walls. I cringed, hoping that it hadn't carried to anyone on other floors.

Edmond, Evan, Mr. Kelley, and Alex joined me several moments later. Edmond looked at me expectantly. "What now?" he whispered, his normal hostility absent.

"There might be guards on the other side of these doors," I indicated the exit. "Let me go first, check it out." To Alex, I sent an order to stay with Evan.

Edmond nodded, but moved forward to put himself between his family and Alex and the doors. I closed my eyes, counted to three, and slammed my booted foot into the door.

Noise blasted through the opening, nearly knocking me back. Soldiers in camouflage suits barreled across the field towards the building. Black-clad operatives stood between me and Crane's men. A number of people had Morphed; a menagerie of animals was interspersed with the humans, claws and teeth seeking exposed flesh. It was impossible to tell whether the Morphers were TOXIC operatives or Coalition soldiers. I stood momentarily frozen, not sure how best to proceed. Bodies were falling right and left, creating a morbid picture of death across the grass. There was no way that I could get Mr. Kelley through the firefight in his condition. I looked to Edmond for direction, but his features were paralyzed in a horrified mask.

As if in slow motion, I turned back to the battlefield. Do something, don't just stand here, I chastised myself. My feet were in motion before my brain could devise a plan. I charged the operative closest to me. The butt of my rifle connected with the back of his skull with a sickening thud, and he crumpled like an accordion. A second operative moved on my right. I spun to face the new threat, and in the same motion brought the barrel of the gun up to eye level. Instead of firing, I whipped the weapon across the operative's face. His head snapped back, causing him to lose his footing and tumble backwards. Using telekinesis, I robbed him of the weapon still clutched between his meaty palms, but recalling Amberly's question about how many I'd killed, left him alive.

Satisfied that he was no longer a threat to me, I glanced up to find my next target. The TOXIC operatives closest to me were preoccupied by Coalition soldiers, and paid me no attention. Across the sea of fighters, I sought out Crane.

"Talia, thank god!" his voice sounded in my head.

My gaze went directly to him, led by the mental thread connecting our minds. Crane's long, lean form was sprinting through the battle, dodging and ducking, bobbing and weaving, as he single-mindedly tried to reach me.

"Ian, Mr. Kelley, Erik's father, he's been shot. He's in bad shape, he can't walk well. I think, I think he might need to be carried. And Alex is with them," I sent, hysteria gripping my lungs like an iron fist. Being in charge had kept me focused, but Crane's appearance meant I no longer had to make life or death decisions. He would know what to do.

"Okay. Let me worry about them. Just get to the plane." Crane pointed behind him, at a waiting hovercraft.

One hundred yards separated me and safety. One hundred yards, and Mac's army of death.

"What about Alex? He's just a little kid."

"I won't let anything happen to him," Crane promised.

Crane managed to reach me without being shot. He was like the invisible man. No one even registered his presence, let alone tried to stop him. He was using his manipulation, I realized.

"Go!" he screamed, and gave me a not-so-subtle shove forward.

I glanced behind me to where Edmond stood in the doorway like an impenetrable force of nature, daring anyone and everyone to make a play for his father or Evan or Alex. I trusted Crane to get

Erik's family and Donavon's son through the fray, but still hated leaving them behind. I debated taking Alex myself. After seeing the way Crane had navigated across the battlefield, though, I knew he was the better option.

Janelle and another soldier broke free from their combatants to follow Crane into the building. Crane and Edmond exchanged words I couldn't hear, and then Edmond finally relinquished his post.

"The soldiers have Dad, let's go," he called, and grabbed my hand. Edmond fired the handgun haphazardly at anyone wearing a black suit to clear our path forward.

We'd made it halfway to the plane when a storm cloud of black descended upon us, blocking the escape craft from view. Edmond didn't slow his pace, charging ahead like a madman on a mission. As the operatives took aim, I used my powers to tear the guns from their hands. Several managed to get shots off beforehand, and I deflected the bullets as they raced in our direction.

Behind us, Crane and his soldiers were in a tight cluster around Mr. Kelley and Evan, shielding them from stray gunfire. Janelle had Alex cocooned in her arms. A plane appeared overhead, bringing with it a fresh wave of reinforcements. I didn't take the time to determine whether the new soldiers were ours or TOXIC's.

"Talia, watch out!" The voice in my head was tight with panic. I yanked free from Edmond, frantically scanning the scene for the cause of the warning.

This time, I had no doubt the man barreling towards me was the real Mac. He wasn't wearing his usual gray suit and impeccably-polished loafers. Today he was the commander of his army, dressed in a black adapti-suit and toting a semi-automatic assault rifle. He wore no helmet, and his short hair was tousled and unkempt, which only added to the crazed gleam in his cold gray eyes. For a man so old, he sure runs fast, I thought as he closed the distance with surprising speed.

The gun was in my hands, but I never thought to raise it. My icy purple gaze found Mac's, and all I could do was watch. Seeing him stirred the pot of anger and frustration churning within me. A million thoughts raced through my mind at once, but I couldn't concentrate on any one. When Mac's finger tightened on the trigger, all those thoughts drained out as if someone had pulled the stopper holding them in. Frozen, I stared at the man I'd thought of as a father, a leader, a friend, and now my killer.

It all happened in a flash of gray fur and white canines. The wolf collided with Mac from the side, surprising the Director enough that he pulled the trigger even though he no longer had me locked in his sights. The crack of the bullet leaving the barrel should have been louder, instead it was muffled, muted somehow when it reached my oversensitive ears. A whimper followed, and the wolf went still. I'd seen him take the shape so many times over the years, the animal was nearly as familiar to me as the human.

Mac shoved the wolf's weight off of his chest, rolling the animal onto its back and exposing matted crimson fur.

"NO!!!" I screamed, as the glue pasting my boots to the grass gave way and I surged forward. "You bastard!" I shot the words at Mac like an arrow as he stood staring down at his son's dying form, no hint of remorse in his expression.

I raised my gun to fire. I pumped the trigger, releasing one bullet after another and screaming Donavon's name over and over again. Several of my shots found their mark, embedding themselves in the suit covering Mac's body. Hot tears obscured my vision, making aiming impossible. I wanted Mac to die. For years I'd thought I'd known true hatred: real teeth-clenching, gut-burning, rage-fueling hatred. Now, I understood that even when I'd thought Ian Crane had murdered my parents, I'd never truly hated him. I'd never had the desire to rip Crane limb from limb, to inflict pain and suffering on him the way I wanted to do with Mac in that instant. Using my Talents didn't occur to me. I craved physical violence, the satisfaction of feeling Mac's life leaking out of him by my hand.

Before I could reach the father and son, Captain Alvarez intervened. He appeared at Mac's side and began dragging him away from Donavon's wolf body. I would have pursued them, had it not been for Donavon's voice in my head.

"Alex. Take care of him, Tal."

More tears. I willed Donavon to fight, hold on just long enough for help to arrive.

"He needs you," I sent back. *"I need you."*

My pleas were met with silence. The connection, my strongest and longest, broke like a branch snapping. I immediately felt his absence. It was a physical hurt, as if a piece of me had been torn off, and it rocked me to my very core. My brain was slower to register the loss.

"Donavon, answer me," I shouted at him. "Damn it, answer me!"

The air near his flattened ears began to shimmer, the disturbance traveling down his body until he was human once again.

I stared into dull, cerulean eyes. "No, you won't die. Do you hear me, Donavon? You will not die!" I slapped him hard across the face, hoping, praying to get a reaction. He didn't move; his eyes still stared skyward. The change from wolf to human was a clear indication that he was gone, but I found the reality hard to accept.

A hand touched my shoulder; I didn't look up to see who it was. I didn't care. Donavon was gone. The hand squeezed, and I thought someone spoke, but the voice sounded far away. I stroked Donavon's cheek where I'd slapped him. No red mark showed on his skin because no blood had rushed to the injury.

"No, no, no," I moaned.

Fingers closed around mine, gently pulling my hand from Donavon's face. Two thick fingers lowered Donavon's eyelids. An arm wrapped around my waist, hauling me to my feet. Pressure behind my knees made me fall back. Someone caught me before I hit the ground. I didn't struggle or protest, just admitted defeat. The person began running, my added weight not seeming to encumber his movements or slow his stride. I didn't bother to glance up to see who "he" was.

"Is she hurt?" someone, Crane maybe, asked.

"No. Just in shock. Do you know, were they friends?" the person holding me said. His chest vibrated when he spoke, and I rested my cheek against him because it reminded me of Erik.

"Yes... friends," the person I thought was Crane replied.

"He saved her life." The guy sounded a little like Erik.

I finally looked up, and saw his face through a blurry haze. Sapphire light glinted behind a wall of tears.

"Erik?" I whispered, confused. The arms didn't feel quite like Erik's, too thin. No sensation of calm or peace washed over me like when I was with Erik.

"No, Talia," Edmond whispered.

Not Erik. Not Erik, because Erik was back at the cottage, unconscious. And Donavon was dead.

"Put her up front, in the pilot's cabin. Have one of the medics give her a sedative. I'll be up there as soon as I'm sure we've gotten everyone," Crane said.

I felt Edmond walking up the gangplank. I was vaguely aware of the others already on the plane, but I stared at them without really seeing. Many were injured, some were grievously wounded, but that wasn't important. Donavon was dead.

Edmond spoke to someone in a low voice; I didn't bother listening. Whatever they were talking about was inconsequential. I felt a sharp prick in my bicep; I couldn't muster the energy to care. Then, darkness.

Chapter Fourteen

MY THROAT WAS raw, and when I tried to swallow, shards of glass seemed to rake against the soft tissue. My eyes felt like they were bugging out of my head, and they stung when I tried to open them. My neck was stiff; I rolled it to release the tension, and my chin rubbed across something scratchy on my shoulder. Gauze, I realized. Why was my shoulder wrapped in gauze? I tried to sit up, but every muscle protested.

"Rest, Ms. Lyons. You must be exhausted," a voice said in the darkness.

"Dr. Patel?" I mumbled, confused. Was I back at the cottage? That wasn't right. The last thing I remembered was... oh God, Donavon.

"They gave you a sedative on the plane. President Crane thought it best. I can give you another if you prefer?"

"No, thank you," I whispered.

"If you change your mind, send a comm and I'll come back. Once you're feeling up to it, there are quite a few people that would like to see you," Dr. Patel said.

I didn't want to see anyone. I wanted to close my eyes and never open them again. I didn't want to live in a world where I had to tell a little boy that his daddy was dead. Alex was now an orphan, like me. Then again, he probably knew. He'd been there, after all. Just like when Kandice was murdered.

"I don't want to see anyone right now," I replied.

"That is understandable. I will let them know." Dr. Patel started to walk away.

"Doctor?" I called after him into the darkness. I couldn't see well, my eyes were too swollen, and I wasn't entirely sure where I was. "Am I in Erik's room?"

"Yes, Ms. Lyons. I wanted to put you in a hospital bed, but President Crane thought this the best place for you to wake up." I made a mental note to thank Ian the next time I saw him.

I waited until I heard the door shut before crawling out of bed. My eyes were starting to adjust to the darkness and by the time I'd taken three steps, they'd adapted. I padded to Erik's bedside. I'd lied to Dr. Patel. There was one person I wanted to see.

The monitors all beeped and hummed steadily, an unpleasant reminder that Erik's condition was unchanged. The chair was still there, but holding his hand wasn't sufficient. I needed to be closer to him. Carefully, I climbed into his hospital bed, cognizant of the IV and the electrodes monitoring his vitals. I wedged myself between the rail keeping Erik from falling out of the bed and his side. Then I draped his limp arm around my waist, and rested his hand on the curve of my hip. I buried my face in his neck, and cried myself back to sleep.

Fingers stroked the scar on my hip from where I'd cut out the tracking device TOXIC had implanted in me for my solo mission. I knew I was dreaming, but I went with it anyway. I imagined they were Erik's, and before long they startled tickling my stomach. Smiling, I kissed the underside of Erik's chin, and he groaned softly.

207

I beamed, I liked it when he did that. I kissed along his jaw, keeping my eyes shut, not wanting to do anything that might bring me back to reality.

The hand stroking my stomach moved back to my hip, gripping my side. My lips trailed kisses towards his mouth. When our lips met, it was pure bliss. The last time we'd kissed felt like ages ago. I rolled on top of him, careful not to hurt him before remembering that in a dream that wasn't possible. His hands encircled my waist, and then began running up and down my sides. His mouth moved to my throat and I tilted my head back, letting my hair cascade down my back.

An irritating, repetitive beeping invaded the happy haze of the dream. My eyes snapped open, and that was when I realized the heart monitor was going nuts. The beeps were so close together now that it sounded more like one, extremely long beep. I blinked my eyes, and stared down at the most beautiful sight in the world. Erik's brilliant turquoise irises were gazing up at me. He was awake.

"Erik." The one word burst from my lips on a wave of emotion.

His fingers were digging into my sides with so much force that I didn't need to pinch myself to know this was really happening.

"Why are you here?" Erik demanded, hysteria making his voice crack. The monitors started to screech, responding to his accelerated pulse and spiking brain activity.

I tried to scramble off of him, but he held me firmly in place.

"What do you mean?" I stammered.

"I mean, why are you here? Did... Did they get you, too?"

Get me too? Oh no, he thinks he's still in prison.

"Erik," I began calmly. "You aren't in Tramblewood. We rescued you. Do you remember?"

"Is this a trick? Are you really her?" Erik demanded, shaking me with so much force my teeth chattered.

"Erik, listen to me. I came to Tramblewood, to the cell, and got you out. Then we brought you here. You've been unconscious for days, but you're safe. You're with me and you're safe."

Confusion and fear flickered in his eyes, and my heart broke. What had Mac done to him? I tentatively leaned closer, until our faces were millimeters apart. "You are safe," I told him, willing him to understand.

Behind me the monitors were screaming for attention. The room exploded in light, as the door burst open. I heard shoes pounding on the stone floor. Erik started to shake underneath me, and the monitors shrieked warnings.

"GET OUT!" I screamed, not bothering to look at the people who'd invaded our space.

Underneath me, Erik struggled to sit up, while at the same time keeping me in his lap as he twisted to position his body between mine and those he perceived as a threat.

"Don't touch her!" he shouted, cradling my head against his chest. His voice was strong and clear, but I felt his fear. He didn't understand what was happening. He was scared for both of us.

"Sedate him before he hurts her," Dr. Patel ordered.

"NO!" I protested, my voice muffled by Erik's chest. The approaching feet quieted with the weight of my command.

"It's okay, Erik. We're safe," I assured him, rubbing his back.

Erik's nerves were frayed, and taking control of his mind was easy. I met Dr. Patel's uneasy gaze over Erik's shoulder.

"Leave," I snapped. "Let me handle this."

"Do as she says." It was Crane who responded. I hadn't noticed him standing in the doorway. "The boy is terrified and he doesn't trust anyone but her. You'll just be prolonging the inevitable if you sedate him."

Dr. Patel looked like he wanted to argue, but stopped himself. The medics he'd brought didn't move.

"I'd suggest backing up slowly. Individually, they are both deadly. Together, they could kill us all where we stand without lifting a finger." Crane's tone was lazy, but when I caught his black eyes, I saw the trepidation. He worried Erik was physically too strong for me to control, and if Crane or the medics tried to intervene, the situation would escalate quickly.

The medics obeyed Crane, backing slowly towards the door. Crane was the last to leave, nodding to me before he closed the door.

Erik released a shaky breath and slumped back against the mattress, taking me with him. I let him hold me. His desire to protect me seemed to clear his head a little. Erik wound his fingers through my hair, tugging on the curls to make sure they were real.

"Erik?" I whispered. "You are safe, I promise. I can't imagine how scared you are right now, but you have to trust me."

Only the too-fast beeps from his heart monitor told me he was still awake. "Erik, talk to me," I pleaded.

"Was that Ian Crane?" he asked, his voice raspy.

I sighed, this was going to be harder than I thought. Not only did I have to convince him that he was safe, but that Crane was one of the good guys.

"Yes. We're at his cottage, Coalition Headquarters, in California. He helped rescue you from Tramblewood. Ian's doctors have been taking care of you. They healed you. Mac..." I let my voice trail off. I couldn't bring myself to add "tortured you," "experimented on you," "nearly killed you," "stole your blood," or any of the million other atrocities.

Erik was still nervous, but his fear had dimmed some. "I'm not at Tramblewood?" He sounded like a child, and I almost wished he were still in attack mode like he had been when the doctors came in. Seeing him so vulnerable made my heart hurt.

"No, you're in California with me. You're safe," I repeated the words, hoping they'd sink in.

Gently he pushed me off of his chest, holding me at arm's length. His muscles quivered from the effort, and I eased myself off to one side. I propped myself up on one elbow without breaking eye contact. He needed to see me, I felt that. Slowly, Erik reached his fingers towards my face, trailing the tips down my forehead, over my eyelids, down my cheeks. He lightly traced my mouth, my jawline, my collarbone. The more he touched me, the more he relaxed.

I sat still as a statue, while he cupped my neck and stroked my arms.

"It was real," he mumbled, amazed.

"Yeah. I'm real," I said smiling.

"No." Erik shook his head, becoming agitated. "Before was real."

My smile faltered. He was babbling nonsense. I tried to reassure myself the confusion was normal. He'd woken up in a strange bed, in a strange room, and then strange people had insisted he be sedated. Of course he was disoriented.

"This is real," I said gently, kissing the tips of his fingers when he brought them to my mouth a second time.

"I saw you with him, with Crane. When I was in Tramblewood. I saw you two talking." Erik squinted like the small amount of light coming through the parted curtains hurt his head. "And Penny was there. And this guy I didn't know." He rubbed his forehead. "Brian. His name was Brian, I think."

"Brand," I corrected automatically.

"Yeah. That's it. Brand. So it was real? You came to Ian Crane for help. Penny, she's alive? It was real?"

I nodded, aware the instant understanding dawned.

Erik stared at me, a mixture of disbelief and longing playing across his features. In his mind I saw the conversations between

Crane, Penny, Brand, and me that Erik had thought were dreams until now. The visions were watery, and had a dream-like quality to them. He had spent all of his alone time viewing me. Watching me, continually, even though he'd thought it was all a hallucination. I blanched as a cloudy image of Donavon materialized in Erik's head. The two had a conversation that Erik couldn't recall, but he remembered feeling better after the other guy left.

"Kiss me," he said suddenly.

I leaned down, bringing my lips to his. I felt him wince as his lips parted. The tear in his bottom lip still hadn't healed completely.

"No," he sent when I tried to pull back to keep from hurting him. The kiss became deeper. His arms snaked around my waist, pulling me closer. He ran one palm up my spine, caressing my hip with the other.

"I'm safe. With you. In California," he repeated my words back, more to himself than me. I tangled my fingers in his thick hair. "I love you," I sent. The kiss became more desperate, and I wanted to lose myself in Erik. I wanted to pretend like we were the only two people on the planet, in the galaxy, with infinite time to just be together.

The hand tangled in my hair pulled my head back a little too hard, and Erik began working his mouth down my throat. At first I reveled in the touch. I never wanted it to end. Erik wasn't being gentle, and I started to get a little uneasy.

"Easy, tiger," I said, moving my hands to his chest and pushing away. "I think we should let the doctor check you out. You know, make sure you're up for this." Erik grabbed my arms, pulling me to him. His fingers dug into my flesh, his knuckles turning white. The intensity of his actions frightened me.

"Erik, stop!" I said, more forcefully this time. I scooted back, putting as much distance between us as possible. His eyes wouldn't meet mine, and an odd aura was coming off of him. "Erik, look at me," I whispered.

When he finally lifted his gaze, I drew in a sharp breath. It wasn't desire in his eyes, it was something more primal, more intense, and it scared me. This wasn't my Erik. I reached for his mind. Angry, dangerous thoughts swirled through his head like storm clouds. I nearly fell off the bed in my haste to get farther away. The sound of me crashing into the chair I'd used for my bedside vigil seemed to bring him out of the trance-like state.

Erik blinked several times in fast succession, trying to clear the fog that clouded his mind. "I'm sorry, Tals," he said hoarsely. "I don't know what came over me. I just can't believe I'm alive and we're together." He looked around the room, confused, like he was seeing it for the first time.

Tentatively I inched forward, taking his outstretched hand between both of my palms. "It's okay, I understand." I tried to smile to reassure him. "Why don't I get Dr. Patel, so he can take a look at you and make sure you're okay?"

Erik looked hesitant, eyes darting nervously around the room again. I squeezed his hand. "You trust me, right?" I asked, putting a commanding edge in my tone.

"Of course I do," he replied automatically.

"I trust Dr. Patel, Erik. He's been treating you for days, and he patched up Henri, too," I added for good measure. Bewilderment crossed his features.

"Henri? He's here?" he asked.

"Yeah, I'll explain everything after you let Dr. Patel take a look at you," I promised.

Erik considered this, staring at me as if he once again thought I might be a hallucination. "Okay," he finally conceded. He shot me the smile that made my heart melt, and the tension mounting between us lessened. Erik traced the veins on the back of one of my hands, concentrating way too hard. He was scared again.

"Will you stay with me? While the doctor is in here?" he mumbled, his words running together in a fluid stream.

I could feel him fighting his insecurities. It pained him to appear so vulnerable, but the thought of an unknown doctor touching him, injecting him with drugs, created a spike of panic the like of which I'd never experienced vicariously through him.

"Anything you want," I promised, offering my own winning smile.

Gently I drew my hands back and went to the wall communicator. I quickly found Dr. Patel's number and typed a short message. I hadn't even made it back to Erik's bed when a soft knock sounded at the door.

"I'll get it," I said unnecessarily. Obviously Erik wouldn't be getting out of bed to greet the visitor.

Dr. Patel greeted me with a friendly smile when I held the door open for him. He must've been waiting in the hallway, I realized. I peered through the door before closing it. Crane, Brand, and two medics were talking in quiet voices. They didn't appear to notice me, so I ducked back into the room and took a seat in an armchair.

"Mr. Kelley, or do you prefer Erik?" Dr. Patel was saying.

"Just Erik," Erik replied. No trace of his earlier vulnerability remained. He was cool and in control, if not detached, now. He'd erected a wall of protection around his mind, complete with flashing signs warning people not to get too close. Unfortunately, I was the only one who saw them.

"Erik, then. You have suffered massive internal bleeding, head trauma, and blood loss. Initially I was worried about whether you might wake up, but it seems my fears were unfounded." Erik didn't respond. "Would it be okay if I checked your injuries?" the doctor continued. "They are healing at a remarkable rate."

Erik's eyes found mine over the doctor's shoulder. I nodded encouragingly, trying to mask the pain I felt at how untrusting he was.

"Sure," he told the doctor stiffly.

I turned my head, staring at the wall like it held all the answers. I felt intrusive watching while Dr. Patel examined Erik's injuries, particularly since I knew that he was practically naked under the quilt.

"Tal?" Erik sent.

"I'm right here," I assured him, and forced my gaze back to the bed. Dr. Patel's form blocked my view of Erik's body. I was ashamed at how relieved that made me. I couldn't handle seeing the bruises and stitched cuts. The last twenty four hours—hell, the last week—had been too traumatizing. I'd seen so much violence, and I really didn't want to be reminded of the torture he'd suffered.

"You are healing nicely," Dr. Patel announced. "How about I give you pain medication to take the edge off?"

"NO!" Erik shouted. Dr. Patel was already reaching into the pocket of his white lab coat, and Erik slapped his arm, sending the syringe flying across the room.

I jumped to my feet, scared of what might happen next. I crossed the room in three long strides.

"I don't want drugs," Erik said, fighting to keep his voice even.

"Of course. If you change your mind, have Ms. Lyons send me a comm. I'll come back and check on you in a couple of hours." The doctor seemed unfazed by Erik's outburst.

"I want the IV out," Erik demanded.

"That would be fine," Dr. Patel said. He reached tentatively towards Erik's arm, then thought better of it. "Would you like me to remove it? Or do you prefer to do it yourself?"

Erik appeared to consider this for a moment before offering the doctor his arm.

I thanked Dr. Patel, and promised to call him if he was needed before his next check. I waited until he was gone before moving to Erik's bedside.

"Are you hungry? Thirsty?" I asked, smoothing the hair back from his forehead. He shook his head.

"There's a bathroom right over there." I pointed towards the adjoining room. "I can draw you a bath." I wasn't sure that was a great idea, since I wasn't sure he could walk on his own, but I was desperate to make him more comfortable.

"Okay," he agreed. "A bath would be good."

I filled the tub with warm water, adding in some of the lavender scented bubbles that Penny had put there for me. While I waited, I laid out towels and washcloths. Once I was satisfied that Erik would have everything that he needed, I returned to the bedroom.

Erik had managed to scoot to the edge of his bed; his feet dangled over the side. His swollen knee was no longer a grotesque softball, more like a large golf ball, occupying the space between his thigh and calf. Only an extremely small pair of boxer shorts covered his more private areas, showcasing the rest of his injuries. I felt a tug in my stomach as I took in the technicolor quality of his skin. Dr. Patel was right about how fast he was healing, but the evidence of his time at Tramblewood was still visible.

As it turned out, Erik couldn't walk on his own. I was too small to support all of his weight, so it took us an inordinately long time to get to the bathroom. Erik's breath came in haggard gasps by the time I helped him settle onto the closed toilet seat. The walk had exhausted him, and a light sheen now covered his face and chest.

"You gonna join me in there?" he asked playfully, nodding towards the bathtub. I almost cried with relief. He was my Erik: silly, inappropriate, sexual, and mine.

"If you're lucky," I shot back, crossing my arms over my chest and faking indifference while he caught his breath.

Erik's laugh came out a wheeze. "Your doctor seems to think that I'm a pretty lucky guy."

"You are," I whispered, all trace of humor gone. "You really are."

When he was ready, I let him lean on my shoulder while he removed the boxers and slid into the tub.

"Yell if you need anything, I'll be just outside the door," I told him.

"Guess I'm not that lucky after all," he teased, but his chest was still heaving, and his eyes were closed now as he rested his head against the back ledge.

"Once you have your strength back," I promised him, leaning over to brush my lips across his.

I wouldn't have gotten in the bath with him in his current condition anyway, but the memory of the way he'd grabbed me, and the off-putting look in his eyes, made the decision easier.

"Tal?" he called when I had one foot through the doorway.

"Yeah?" I sent back.

"I love you."

"I love you, too, Erik."

I kept the door open, figuring that the sound of splashing water would let me know he hadn't passed out and drowned. Despite his instance that he wasn't hungry, I commed Marin and asked her to send down an assortment of easily-digestible foods. Next, I messaged Crane and asked him if he could send clothes for Erik. Crane promised that he would, and asked if I wanted him to bring Alex down. I thought about the change in Erik's personality and decided against it. I would let Erik adjust to his new surroundings before bringing Alex in.

Crane arrived with my ordered food and clothes before Erik was done in the bath. He helped me set out fruits, cheeses, and bread on a tray, but didn't move to leave when we were done.

"I'd like to speak with him," Crane said softly.

"I don't know." I looked towards the bathroom. Erik only let Dr. Patel touch him because I promised him that he was safe. He'd been on edge during the doctor's visit like a cobra ready to strike. Crane interrogating him right now wasn't the best idea. What if he freaked out? Erik might be physically weaker than normal, but even weaker than his normal, he was stronger than the average person. Crane wasn't average, but I had no desire to find out who would win if the two men fought.

"Talia, Victoria is itching to get her hands on him. It's best we prepare him before she does. She's insisting he be evaluated immediately. If I talk to him and explain the situation and he tells me what McDonough did to him, I might be able to hold her off a little longer."

"She can't see him like this," I said emphatically. "She'll never believe he's safe. Ian, please."

Crane held up a hand. "I know, I know. Dr. Patel has already drawn and analyzed his blood, so it's been proven he was injected with the drug. That's not good enough for UNITED. I promise, if he talks to me now, I'll find excuses to keep Victoria and the other council members away. It'll buy him a couple more days."

"I'll ask him," I relented.

Crane was trying to do Erik a favor. UNITED probably knew about Erik attacking the medic on the hoverplane. They seemed omnipresent. It was doubtful they'd be understanding about the incident. Erik needed time to adjust and come to terms with his temporary home at the cottage. A couple of days might not be enough, but it was better than the alternative.

Crane settled into an armchair, and I walked back into the bathroom. Only a thin film of bubbles remained on the water's surface. I felt a hot flush creep up my face, and I barely stopped myself from trying to peer between the gaps. Erik's eyes were still closed, but his hair was wet and his face looked as though it had been scrubbed raw.

"Erik, Ian—" he cut me off.

"I heard, Tals," he said.

"You don't have to talk to him yet. It can wait until you're feeling better." The lie was stupid when Erik had listened to the conversation.

"No, it can't. Does he have my clothes, though? I'd prefer not to talk to him naked."

"Yeah, I'll get them," I said, turning to go fetch the clothes.

Getting Erik out of the water and dressed was a lot harder than getting him in. I considered asking Crane to help, but I could tell how embarrassed Erik was letting me help him. I knew he'd refuse Crane's assistance.

When we hobbled back into the bedroom, Erik insisted on sitting on the sofa bed. I obliged, partly because he was so adamant and partly because it was a lot closer than the hospital bed. Crane watched silently, not offering to help once. He and Erik were cut from the same cloth, proud and too distinctly male to admit they needed someone. Crane probably knew that Erik would crawl before accepting some random person's pity.

"Erik Kelley, it's nice to finally meet you," Crane declared once I'd managed to get Erik situated, a pillow under his knee.

"Not sure I can say the same, but I hear you've been more hospitable than my last host, so I'll reserve judgment." Erik's tone was matter-of-fact, not snide or flippant, and I took that as a good sign. The more time that passed, the more like my Erik he seemed, and I began to relax.

Of course he'd been out of sorts after he woke up. Who wouldn't be? I was sure that the odd sensation I'd gotten from him was just a result of his fear. Fear wasn't an emotion I usually felt from Erik, and I'd just misinterpreted it, I assured myself. A nagging feeling still caused a pit to form in my stomach. Had the Creation drug altered him the same as it had me? What new abilities was his body trying to cope with? Was he going to become irrational and prone to erratic emotions the way I was?

"I can't imagine what you've been through—" Ian started to say, but Erik cut him off.

"No, you can't."

"Would you be willing to tell me? I hate to seem blunt or insensitive, but it's really important. A lot has happened since your rescue from Tramblewood. And the more we know, the better." Crane still sat in the armchair, leaving a wide berth between Erik and himself.

My eyes darted from Crane to Erik. The ball was in Erik's court, and I thought I knew what his next move would be. But to my surprise, he agreed.

"One condition, though," Erik quickly added. "We talk alone. I'd like you to leave, Natalia." He wouldn't look at me when he said my name, and the use of my whole name threw me off. Just an hour ago he'd insisted that he didn't want to be alone with Dr. Patel, but now he was ordering me out of the room.

I was stunned and more than a little hurt. I'd risked my life to rescue him. I'd sat by his bed, holding his hand, praying for him to wake up, and this was how he repaid me? My temper flared as his rejection sunk in. I fisted my hands at my sides, digging what was left of my ragged nails into my palms to keep from verbally lashing out at Erik. With a glare that I hoped spoke volumes, I turned on my heel and stomped towards the door. Neither man tried to stop me.

The stone walls did little to cool the hot anger and humiliation of Erik's dismissal. I rested my forehead next to the door, replaying Erik's words. I wanted to know what he was telling Crane, what he didn't want me to hear. The walls were thick and I could only hear snippets of their conversation. Pressing my ear to the door, I concentrated harder. When I still couldn't make out more than every third word, I reached out for Erik's mind.

"Eavesdrop much?" The words echoed in the narrow passage. I nearly jumped out of my skin. I turned and met Brand's amused face. I hadn't even heard him come up behind me.

"Shhh," I shushed him. "I have a right to know what they're saying." I did, right?

"Oh you have a right, do you? More like an insatiable curiosity. Or maybe all that spy training is just too hard to forget. Or there is always the possibility that you just hate not being in control. I guess it's pretty hard for someone who knows everyone's secrets to be kept in the dark." His tone wasn't malicious, but I felt like he'd thrown a bucket of ice water in my face. Brand didn't know me. He had some nerve speaking as if he did. Incredulous, I opened my mouth to make a snappy retort, but Brand continued before I got the words out.

"Let him have a little privacy, Talia. Did it occur to you that maybe he's embarrassed by what he went through? That maybe he doesn't want the one person that he's gone to the ends of the earth to protect knowing how badly they tortured him? Not to mention the humiliating things they subjected him to? You really are selfish, you know."

I backed away from Brand; his verbal assault felt more like a physical one. Selfish? I wasn't selfish, I was just trying to help Erik. I wanted him to know I was there for him no matter what. There was nothing he could say to change that.

I crossed my arms over my chest, creating armor to protect my wounded pride. "What do you know about what he went through?" I hissed.

"I know what your Agency did to Penny. I know she is broken on the inside, and how hard she tries to keep you out so you won't see it. Penny, Erik, even Ian, they all want to protect poor, precious Talia. Yet you just keep pushing. Everyone is making sacrifices for you and you don't even appreciate it. Erik nearly died, and all he wants is keep the more humiliating details from the person whose opinion he values most. Don't take that away from him."

Fuming, I dug the jagged points of my nails into my flesh. How dare he? Did Brand not think I'd made sacrifices? That I hadn't been hurt in all of this, too?

A nagging voice in the back of my mind reminded me that Erik wouldn't have needed rescuing if I hadn't been so rash in running away with Alex. Had Erik helped me because it was the right thing to do? Or had his love for me blinded him to rational thought?

A thought struck me. Brand was acting like this was about Erik, but it wasn't, I realized. This animosity couldn't possibly be on behalf of a guy he didn't know. I already knew Brand blamed me for what had happened to Penny and for Penny's mother's death. There was more to it, though. I thought about Frederick's words. He'd said Brand had been through a lot. What else could have possibly occurred in Brand's life that he could construe to make my fault?

I latched on to Brand's impossibly green eyes, now blazing furious and hateful. He guarded his mind just like Crane, but his defenses weren't nearly as strong. While he might not be as good at building barriers, he was no slouch either. Sweat began to trickle down my forehead with the effort of invading his thoughts. Brand's eye twitched; he knew what I was doing.

"You want to know how I feel about you?" His whispered words dripped loathing, and suddenly I wasn't so sure I did want to know. "Go ahead." The walls crumbled and a wave of power engulfed me, hot and suffocating like I'd opened an oven door. It took every ounce of physical strength that I possessed not to recoil. Electricity crackled through the air, causing the lights to flicker. Everything went still, as if time had actually frozen.

I didn't need to read Brand's mind; his hatred was a live wire, coursing energy painfully from him to me. The obvious issues between us were at the forefront of his mind: Penny's current condition and her mother's death; endangering the lives of Coalition soldiers; Crane choosing me over him. But I was right, there were deeper issues. Ones Brand had buried long ago and rarely let resurface.

The elder Meadows had been strong Talents and TOXIC operatives. The mandatory testing laws had just passed when Mrs. Meadows became pregnant with Brand. Shortly after he was born, the Meadows decided TOXIC's goals were no longer serving the greater good. They joined one of the more outspoken rebel factions who opposed the mandatory testing laws. This was where they met Ian Crane. It was agreed that they would continue working for TOXIC as double agents, now spying for the rebels.

Barely twenty-five, Crane organized the rebel factions and declared war against TOXIC. A fellow operative, a woman named Lanie Reece, who the Meadows had thought they could trust sold them out to TOXIC. Both of Brand's parents were taken into custody and tortured for information about Crane and the rebels. Neither cracked. Well, not exactly anyway. Brand's parents never gave in, never gave TOXIC the information they wanted about Crane or the rebels.

Crane and TOXIC struck a deal for the return of all prisoners as part of the peace treaty that ended the second civil war. Brand's parents were released to Crane, and returned to what became Coalition territory. But their minds were mush. Brand only saw them once after the war ended. The vacant expressions in their eyes haunted his dreams. The way they drooled when they moved their mouths but no words came out made him sick to his stomach. He hated himself for how disgusted the sight of his own parents made him. But the person Brand truly hated was the Mind Manipulator who'd robbed his parents of their minds, and him of a family.

Mr. and Mrs. Meadows died shortly after their only visit with their son.

I hadn't been that Manipulator, obviously, but whenever Brand looked at me, he thought about his parents and the person who'd destroyed them. What I'd done to Penny, providing the testimony that had sentenced her to death, reminded him of the woman who'd done the same to his parents. He hated me for what I was. He despised me for what I'd done.

Each new accusation sent a fresh shock to my system.

I tried to break the connection, except it was physically impossible. I'd heard about people being electrocuted, how their muscles tensed and they lost control of their bodies. That was how I felt now.

My mind and body were at odds, the former screaming to make the torture end, the latter unable to obey. But the panic, the true terror, that I felt was for how much I craved his power. Part of me was drawn to him, yearning to experience more of his Talents.

Abruptly the connection broke, leaving me empty and drained. I blinked rapidly to clear the fog. I reached out to steady myself, only to realize that I was on the floor. My skin still tingled, and I had an odd feeling that if I touched another person, I'd shock them.

"I didn't mean to hurt her," I whispered, barely managing to get the words out. My jaw was a vice, and I feared that I might have to physically pry the halves apart.

"No, Talia, you didn't. But you did nothing to stop it. Since the night your parents were killed, Ian has been willing to do anything to get you back. He let his sister die to get you back. Then he let Penny go through with that ridiculous plan to go undercover. I begged him to pull her out so many times. But he insisted that once she got close to you, she could convince you to run. After she was arrested, he thought for sure you'd see the truth. But you were too damn dense, too damn selfish to open your eyes! You let them take her!" Brand screamed.

The door to Erik's room burst open. I knew it was Crane, but I couldn't see him through the tears blurring my vision. The anger Brand's rant evoked helped me regain control of my limbs. I stumbled to my feet and ran.

He was talking about Penny, but the raw emotion that made his voice crack was for his parents. He didn't know who had tortured his parents, so he couldn't take out his anger on that person, which only left me. Had the Creation drug not been messing with my emotions, I might have been able to be reasonable, understand that he needed an outlet for his anger and I was his best option. I might have been able to commiserate with him. I, of all people, understood the need for revenge. But I wasn't in control. Brand's rage was contagious, infecting me, sending my temper northward.

In the days since I'd stopped taking the suppression drug, I'd been more in control of my emotions. That wasn't to say I didn't feel like I was losing control half the time, but I was better at keeping the struggle internal. As I rode the elevator and tore through the atrium, I felt like the ticking time bomb Brand had accused me of being. If I didn't make it outside before I exploded, I'd take out the heart of the Coalition. Victoria would have no choice but to contain me.

I tripped in my haste to get up the metal staircase to the main level, banging my shin against one of the stairs. Pain shot down my leg, and a small part of my brain registered the blood soaking my pants. Get outside, get outside, I chanted. The trapdoor blew open before I touched it. Hurtling myself through the opening, I dashed for the front door.

Black spots dotted the parts of my vision not blinded by a red haze. Navigating the path to the beach was near impossible, and I fell several times before I reached the sand. The wind picked up, sending grains of sand swirling around me. Brand's accusations ran around and around in my head, chased by the one he hadn't known to add: Donavon's death. Everyone I loved was hurt or dead because of me.

My mother and father died to protect me from Mac, and I repaid them by becoming his pawn. Crane tried to tell me the truth, and I attacked him. Penny risked her life to open my eyes, and I sat by while TOXIC sentenced her to death. I let Erik put himself in danger without even considering the ramifications, and now he'd been tortured and experimented on. Donavon gave his life for mine. It was my fault that Alex was now an orphan. Even Kandice's death could have been avoided. Hindsight might be twenty-twenty, but looking back I saw all the decisions I could have made for the situation to turn out differently. Had I not lost my mind, forcing Erik to waste time calming me down, Graham's team wouldn't have gotten antsy and acted on impulse. Had Kandice not been so frightened by my reaction to Alex, she wouldn't have been standing next to the window. She might still be alive.

Raindrops splattered the beach, soaking my hair and clothes until they were plastered to my skin. The waves swelled, cresting, before crashing feet from where I stood. I pushed them back before they could swallow me whole. I should let them drag me out to sea, I thought.

When the next wave stormed the beach, I stepped forward to meet it. I held my arms wide, closed my eyes, and welcomed the watery embrace.

I stood like that for a full minute before I realized that I was unharmed. The rain still poured from the sky, but the ocean hadn't claimed me as its own. Tentatively I cracked one eye. The water had retreated, and the waves were nearly back to their normal size.

Fatigue settled in every bone, every muscle, every inch of skin until I was liquid inside. I sank to the sand, incapable of stringing thoughts together. For several long moments I lay there uncaring, unfeeling like a zombie.

Anger lit up one corner of my mind. *"What is wrong with you?"* A voice inside my head screamed. Within the empty void where my brain should have been, the words echoed. Only instead of growing fainter with each reiteration, they grew louder. *"You are stronger than this, better than this! Killing yourself is a pretty shitty way to repay all the people who care about you!"*

I wondered if I'd finally buckled under the pressure. Was this voice inside my head a version of myself? She was confident and powerful. Above all, she was furious at the girl lying in the sand.

"We will get through this. We will stop Mac. We will make things right. But if you don't start acting like the girl I met two years ago, you won't be around to see TOXIC fall, or to avenge your parents."

We? Oh my god, I thought. I really am losing it. My multiple Talents were splitting my personality, and the various versions of myself were fighting. I should be put down like a rabid animal. That was what I was becoming, anyway. The Creation drug was driving me truly insane.

Next I knew, I was hauled to my feet with superhuman strength. I never saw her palm, it moved too fast. But I felt the sting, amplified by the wetness of my skin.

"Don't you ever do that again!" Penny screamed, her lime-green eyes bearing down on me until my knees went weak. Rage was not an emotion I'd ever seen her wear. It looked odd on Penny, wrong and out of place. I was the angry one, the unstable one. She was the fun-loving, easygoing one.

I stared blankly at my best friend. I blinked to be sure that she was real, although my smarting cheek told me that she was very real.

"What is wrong with you?" she demanded, shaking me harder than Erik had earlier.

"I-I-I-I don't know," I stammered.

"Do you really think the best thing you could do right now is die?" The air around Penny vibrated, shimmering in response to her palpable anger. I tried to back away from her, but her gaze seemed to pin me in place.

"I don't know," I repeated, sounding weak and defeated.

"Is this what you're going to do every time something goes wrong, or someone hurts your feelings? You have a lot of faults, Talia, but I never thought you were selfish." Penny's tone softened. "The rebellion needs you. Erik needs you. Alex needs you. I need you."

I didn't know what to say. Brand had called me selfish for letting everyone make sacrifices and take risks while I sat back. Now Penny was calling me selfish for trying to lessen the burden on those I loved.

"Mac killed your parents, Talia. He killed my mother. He killed his son. He strapped me to a chair and injected me with random drugs to see how they would affect me. And when I passed out because the power was too much, he had his men revive me. When I fought them, they starved me. I prayed for death because I knew what they wanted to do with me, they wanted to use me as a weapon. Just think, Mac said, you'll be the ultimate Talent. You'll be able to do anything and everything. He didn't mention what that much power does to one person. By the time Uncle Ian got there, I was half out of my mind."

Penny's shoulders began to shake. She stiffened her spine, standing a little straighter.

"But you know what kept me going? You know what kept me fighting?" she continued.

I knew it was a rhetorical question, but I shook my head no anyway.

"Now we had proof that TOXIC was manufacturing Talents. I knew if I died, it might be too late by the time Uncle Ian figured it out for sure."

"Penny," I began, but I didn't know what I was going to say. I'm sorry sounded lame. I wish that hadn't happened to you? That was obvious.

"Don't pity me, Talia. I knew the risk when I volunteered to go undercover. The Coalition has known for years that adding Mimic blood to the formula would make it stick. What we didn't know was that the Director was using a bastardized version to create more Talents."

"How did you figure that out?" I asked, finally finding my voice.

"Actually you did. When you told me about the amount of people you'd noticed with low level Talents, I looked into it. After a lot of digging, I noticed a high correlation between Talents who went crazy and low levels of ability. That's the opposite of what happens in natural Talents. It's no secret that extremely strong, natural-born Talents are at high risk for insanity. Particularly the mental Talents, but you know that. That's when I put two and two together. If so many low-level Talents were going crazy, they probably weren't natural."

"He's injected his operatives," I said quietly. "Mac already has his army of super-Talents. UNITED's too late."

Penny shook her head. "No, we can still put a stop to this. Once we do, we will find each and every one of the people Mac infected, and we will get them help."

"In a containment facility?" I scoffed.

"Dr. Patel is so close to a cure. Have faith, Tal. I do."

Twelve Talents. That was how many Penny said she'd been given. I'd just been given the one, and it was hard enough for me to handle.

"I know, right?" Penny said, laughing wryly. Clearly she was still in my head, reading my thoughts. "Lucky me, huh? Mac was right, I am the ultimate Talent now." Penny held up the hand she'd slapped me with. The air shimmered around it before her fingers went invisible.

I threw my arms around Penny, and she seemed so startled that she didn't hug me back right away. "I'm sorry," I muttered. "I'm so sorry."

"Don't be sorry, Tal. Be smart. We can win this war without you. But Erik and I can't survive without you. We're all in this together now. I need you to promise me that you won't give in to the urges. I feel them, too. The power inside you gets so intense that you feel like you're going to burst, and you just want it to end."

I nodded against her shoulder. She did know how I felt.

"But you, more than Erik and I, are able to fight them," she continued. "You've dealt with the overload of power your whole life. We haven't. We need your help to get through this. Uncle Ian is going to find a cure, but without you, Erik might not make it that long. I might not make it that long."

I hugged her tighter. "I promise, Penny. I'll be stronger."

"Good, now let's go inside. I'm freezing."

Chapter Fifteen

CRANE WAS STILL sitting in Erik's room when I returned. And to my dismay, Brand was there as well. The door was cracked just enough for me to see the three of them. Erik was on the sofa bed, and Brand and Crane had pulled their chairs over next to the bed, where the three were speaking in low voices. I knocked lightly to signal my presence.

"Come in, Talia. Brand and I were just leaving," Crane said without raising his head.

To my relief, Erik's mood was calm and relaxed, not agitated as I'd feared. Every time Penny recounted her story, the ordeal left her upset and exhausted. But Erik seemed like telling Crane and Brand had unburdened him. While I wished I'd been the one he confided in, I was glad talking to someone had helped him.

I waited by the door, dripping water on the stone floor, while Crane and Brand said their goodbyes. "I need to speak with you later," Crane said in a low voice as he passed me. He gave my soaked clothing a once over, but made no comment.

"Sure," I replied.

I watched the two men until they boarded the elevator, and then closed the door. Erik's gaze was fixed on me, his expression unreadable. Brand's words about giving Erik his privacy rang in my mind, so I refrained from reaching out to Erik mentally.

"Ian says my father and brothers are here," Erik said, breaking the silence before it became awkward. "Alex, too."

"Yeah. They, um, came back from Kentucky with us yesterday," I said, glad to have good news for him. "Your father was injured, but I don't think it's serious."

"No. Ian said he's already been patched up. He said he'll let them know as soon as I'm ready for visitors."

"You don't want to see them yet?" I asked. This concerned me. Erik loved his family. I figured he'd be desperate to see them once he woke up.

Erik shook his head. "No. I'm really tired. Maybe after a nap."

A thought occurred to me. "Do you want me to go? Ian wanted to talk to me. I was going to spend some time with you, but if you'd rather I not..." I let my question trail off. He'd already sent me away once today, I doubted I'd handle it well if he did so a second time.

"I'm not going to hurt you, Tals," Erik said, skirting the question.

"What?"

"You're still standing by the door. Are you afraid I'll hurt you? Because I won't. I really am sorry about earlier. I was so disoriented." I felt his agitation the moment it manifested, and hurried across the room to reassure him.

"No," I said, sliding into Crane's chair. "No, I'm not worried. I wanted to give you some space. You didn't seem to want me around earlier, and—" I caught myself before I let my emotions show, "I just didn't know if you wanted me close to you is all. And I understood about earlier, really. I know you're scared."

I reached to take his hand, and he let me, which I took as a good sign.

"I felt you in my head. That's why I asked you to leave. I didn't want you reliving my time at Tramblewood with me."

I smiled at him. Brand was right, as painful as that was to admit. Erik did need some privacy right now.

"I want you here now, though. That counts, doesn't it?"

"Counts for what?"

"You were upset when I asked you to leave. You're still upset. I can read minds too, remember?"

"No," I lied, "I'm not upset."

"Tal, come on. I heard you and Brand arguing. I bet everyone on this floor and probably the one above and below heard you two. Besides, just like you feel me, I feel you. So stop pretending. It's okay to be upset with me. You're my girlfriend, being mad at me is normal. Just because I'm hurt doesn't mean you need to tiptoe around my feelings."

Man, I am a shitty girlfriend, I thought. Everything I did was wrong.

Erik tugged on my hand, urging me to join him in the sofa bed. "I really do need a nap. Stay with me until I fall asleep?"

"Of course." Gingerly, I curled up beside him, careful not to disturb his bruises. He wrapped his arms around me, pulled me snug against his chest, and kissed the top of my wet, sandy curls.

I lay there, trying to clear my head of all thought. I was worried about projecting my pain onto him. Losing Donavon was awful, and Erik didn't need to see how much it was affecting me. I had no idea how much Crane had told him, but I doubted Erik knew.

Once Erik was asleep, I changed and left to find Crane. A quick peek into his head told me he was in the study. Thankfully, he was alone. Time had become relative. I had no concept of morning and night. It was light outside, so I figured it was daytime. Everything was happening so fast. Days were running together. Nights were often sleepless. The past several weeks felt like a never-ending nightmare.

Crane sat by the fireplace in a green armchair. His forehead rested in his hand, and he was using his thumb and forefinger to rub his temples. An electronic tablet was perched on his knee, and he appeared to be studying the screen intently.

"Hey," I said, tapping lightly on the open door. "You wanted to see me?"

Crane looked up and offered me a tired smile. He gestured towards the couch and I took that as an invitation to sit. A tray with a coffee canteen, two mugs, and a sugar bowl sat untouched on the coffee table.

"Help yourself," Crane said when he noticed me eyeing the coffee.

I did. Tired as I was, caffeine seemed like just the right thing to invigorate me. Mug in hand, I settled onto the sofa and waited for Crane to start talking. I had a lot of questions for him, but I wanted to get his out of the way first. If I had any energy leftover afterwards, I'd ask mine.

"We found out what is wrong with your friend, Mr. Daughtery," Crane began as he eyed me.

"Yeah, me, too," I replied. "Mental block."

Crane raised a questioning eyebrow, wordlessly prompting me to continue.

"Donavon told me about them," I explained. I had to bite my cheek to keep from crying when I said his name. The wound was too raw.

"Apparently TOXIC is using them on more disagreeable operatives. Anyone who might have a sympathetic inclination towards me, my movement, or you."

"Is it reversible?" I asked. I hadn't been able to reverse the effects, but maybe someone more skilled could.

"Usually. I find it is best to let them run their course. Eventually the drug will wear off. This is much better than the alternative," he added.

"The alternative?"

"When I watched UNITED's evaluation session with him, I thought a person had manipulated his memories. That would make his condition permanent. Chemical alteration is not."

"Thank goodness for the small stuff," I muttered.

"He has been injected with the Creation drug, which complicates matters. UNITED has declared him a threat. He's scheduled to be moved to a containment facility in Bern in three days."

"Isn't there something you can do about it? He can't, they can't, it isn't fair," I protested lamely.

"In his case, I agree with the decision. He will get the help he needs there."

"It's not fair," I repeated.

I sipped my coffee. It was hot and rich with the slightest hint of vanilla. Crane continued to study me as if he found every move I made fascinating. I felt small and self-conscious under his gaze.

"Penelope is with him now," he finally said.

I didn't bother to hide my shock. The mug slipped in my hands, and I was barely able to catch it before the entire contents poured into my lap. As it was, hot liquid sloshed over my fingers.

"He doesn't seem to recognize her, but he does seem calmer with her close by," Crane continued.

I nodded. Not that Harris needed to be any calmer. Besides the brief moment when he'd attacked me, Harris was so calm he was stagnant. Still, it was probably good for both of them to be around each other. I wondered how Brand was handling the situation. The thought made me smile. I'd have paid to see his face right then.

"TOXIC retreated completely after we left Kentucky. The Underground stations don't keep records of their inhabitants, so we have no way of knowing how many were taken. Frederick and Janelle have led a team out there and are assessing the damage and dealing with any operatives who failed to escape."

I breathed a sigh of relief. Frederick was okay. Better than okay, actually. He was obviously healthy enough to be running around and helping organize things, which meant he wasn't injured. I felt horrible about forgetting to worry about him until now. He was by no means an afterthought for me, but with so much going on, someone or something was bound to slip through the cracks.

Crane cleared his throat, alerting me that he was about to say something I wasn't going to like. Great, I thought, what now?

"Our casualties are being brought here. Well, not here to the cottage, but here to Coalition territory. They will be cremated, and a group memorial will be held in their honor. I regret this was not an option for those we lost in Gatlinburg." He paused and locked his gaze with mine. "If you wish, Donavon McDonough will be among them."

I let out a shaky breath. Funeral arrangements, memorial services, none of that had even occurred to me. Donavon deserved better than a mass memorial service. Maybe I'd arrange a private service, just Alex and me, I thought. That only seemed fitting. His father wasn't mourning his death. Gretchen popped into my mind. Did she know her son was dead? Did she know she had a grandson? Did she care?

"If you'd rather we do something else with his remains," Crane began.

"No," I said quickly. "Please, bring him here with the others. I'd like for Alex to have the chance to say goodbye."

There was no use pretending like I wasn't crying, so I just let the tears fall. At least these tears were for a valid reason. Donavon deserved to have someone who loved him grieve his passing.

"Your friend, Cadence Choi, I believe is her name. She and her brother are being relocated to San Lolito, a town not far from here. I am sorry we don't have space for them here, but between the UNITED council members and the extra soldiers, we're booked."

Another weight off my mind. Cadence and Randy were safe, and soon would be close by. I decided to arrange a trip down to see them as soon as possible. Maybe even Erik would be up for it. He'd like to see Cadence.

Crane leaned forward and began fixing himself a mug of coffee. Unlike me, the vanilla beans weren't sweet enough for him, evidenced by the unholy amount of sugar he dumped into his cup. He probably needed the energy. The only person sleeping less than I was seemed to be Crane.

"Is there something else you wanted to see me about, Ian?" I asked after he sat back in his chair and took several sips of his ridiculously sweet coffee. While I appreciated our little catch-up session, it hadn't been his purpose for summoning me. He was stalling, buying time until he felt he had the energy to ask me about something much more serious. Right now, Ian was practically tapped out. That was why his mind was so easy to read. For the first time, he wasn't actively letting me read his thoughts so much as not stopping me from doing so. Until that point, I hadn't known there was a difference.

"UNITED has given McDonough a deadline. It is clear to everyone he has no intention of meeting that deadline. According to intel, he's in D.C. All high-ranking TOXIC personnel are, which means D.C. is where UNITED will strike. The Underground station there could prove a valuable resource, and the tunnels will give our forces a way into the city undetected."

"Okay," I said slowly, feeling like I was missing a piece of the puzzle. "What's the problem with that? I think it's a great idea to use the tunnels."

"It's a maze down there. Very few Underground conductors know their way in or out, let alone all the twists and turns in the middle. Our forces could get lost. Frederick has a lot of experience with navigating the tunnels, so he'll be able to lead a team. The way I understand, so do you and Erik."

"Me?" I squeaked. "I've spent time down there, sure, but I'm no expert."

Crane's face fell. "And Erik?"

"He's your best bet," I admitted. "He's not the only one, either. The other Kelleys lived down there, too. I bet they'd be able to lead teams."

Crane arched an eyebrow. "Really?"

"Definitely," I agreed, warming to the idea. Leading a strike team through the tunnels made Erik invaluable to Victoria, which meant she'd be stupid to contain him. It also might push off the evaluation a little while longer. The only problem was, Erik could barely walk.

"Do you think they'd be willing to help?"

"I'm sure they would," I said, not sure at all.

"I'll speak with them before informing Victoria. We have three days yet before the deadline. If Erik agrees, I can have Dr. Patel speed his recovery. TOXIC isn't the only one with that capability. I prefer not to use it. The body's natural healing process is better than anything inorganic, but..." Crane held up his hands, palms out. "Sometimes we have to work with what we've got."

I understood why Crane was making the offer. He knew as well as I did: Erik needed to serve a purpose for UNITED. Like me, Erik's worth as an asset had to outweigh his threat potential. Skilled navigators being in short supply was a coup: it made Erik priceless.

"I'll discuss it with him."

That evening I had dinner with Penny, Alex, Henri, and the Kelleys. Spending the time with Penny meant Brand tagged along; he was like chewed-up gum always sticking to her side. Apparently letting out all of his lingering frustrations with me had lifted a great burden from Brand, and he was more polite than usual. It was too much to hope that he was actually repentant, so I assumed Penny had given him a stern lecture. Henri's shoulder was healing rapidly and, according to Dr. Patel, he would be good as new in a couple of days. Mr. Kelley's prognosis wasn't quite so cheery, but in time, he too was expected to make a full recovery.

Alex was subdued. He barely touched his food, some gamey-tasting meat with cooked vegetables, and was particularly clingy. Not that I blamed him. He'd lost his only family tie, and none of us were sure how he was coping. Drs. Patel and Kramer had examined him and determined he was physically unharmed. Beyond that, only time would tell.

The one thing Alex did get excited about was seeing Erik. After he finished playing with his dinner, he begged to visit Erik. I still had reservations about letting Alex around Erik until the latter had a better handle on his emotions. But, as Penny pointed out, I didn't have a handle on my emotions and Alex spent time with me. She thought the visit would be beneficial for both of them, and I reluctantly agreed.

So, all of us—Erik's family, Penny, Alex, and I—trooped through the maze of sublevels to Erik's room. Again, Brand insisted on accompanying our group. I pretended he wasn't there, which suited both of us just fine. Dr. Patel was there when we arrived, which turned out to be a stroke of luck since he'd woken up Erik to examine him.

Alex squirmed and demanded to be put down the instant we crossed the threshold into the bedroom. I set him on the floor, and he ran blindly for the sofa bed. His ability to navigate a room he was unable to actually see impressed me. He must've seen it in a vision, I decided. That concerned me. What little I understood about viewing was that strong Viewers were able to view anyone they'd encountered at will. Other, weaker Viewers, or those who had yet to master their Talent, were often pulled into a vision when someone they knew well was experiencing strong emotions. Alex, being so young, likely fell into the second category. I wondered how much he'd seen since Erik woke up.

"Erik!" the little boy exclaimed, trying to pull himself up onto the bed.

Dr. Patel lifted Alex the rest of the way and into Erik's arms. While Erik noticed the rest of us, his comfortable and calm demeanor was all because of Alex. The child gave him a peace that seemed to tamp down the ugliness swirling inside of him. He had that effect on a lot of people, I was coming to realize. Penny and I both gravitated towards Alex and were in better control of ourselves when he was around. Even Brand's mood and general disposition was better in Alex's presence.

"Hey, buddy," Erik whispered, situating Alex next to him in the bed.

The two of them talked about Alex's adventures since they'd last seen each other in D.C. Edmond and Alex had bonded quite a bit in their short time together, playing with blocks, learning how to whistle with blades of grass, wading in the stream in the woods behind Frederick's house. I couldn't help but feel a little jealous of Erik's brother.

Dr. Patel excused himself, claiming he did not want to intrude on "family time." I felt a little intrusive myself. Erik hadn't spent time with his father and brothers in so long. Penny, Henri, and Brand didn't have the same qualms, and found places to sit around the room. I, however, followed Dr. Patel. Erik was in good company for the time being, and I had some questions for the doctor.

"Talia, how is your shoulder? Is it giving you any trouble?" he asked pleasantly when he noticed me following him into the hallway.

"Huh? Oh, no. It's good," I said absently. "I actually had a question for you about the cure for the Creation drug? Ian said you've been working on one. Um, I just wanted to know, how's that going?"

For the first time in our short acquaintance, Dr. Patel wasn't overly cheerful and optimistic. He seemed regretful, almost. "I am afraid not as well as I would like."

"Oh, okay." Not the answer I'd wanted.

"Have no worries. With you, Mr. Kelley, and Ms. Crane here, I will be able to further my research. The three of you will be vital in perfecting the formula." He brightened as he talked, like the idea excited him. That made two of us. As much as I wanted to be rid of the taint of the drug, I wanted to reverse the effects on those Mac had infected as soon as possible. The encounter with the Mind Manipulator and the one with Captain Alvarez in Kentucky reinforced how imperative that was. Captain Alvarez seemed to be fighting his new power, but the guy in Gatlinburg had embraced it. He was the embodiment of UNITED's fears.

"Something else on your mind, dear?" the doctor asked.

"Um, yeah. Ian said you might be able to speed Erik's recovery? How badly would that hurt him in the long run?"

Dr. Patel sighed. "It is possible, of course. As I told you before, there are potential risks. In Mr. Kelley's case, I do not foresee any lasting issues, but I am still reluctant. So many chemicals are already in his blood. I fear putting more in will do more harm than good."

"But if Erik wants you to, you'd do it?" I pressed.

"If he so wishes, yes."

"Good. Thanks."

I was about to reenter the bedroom when Dr. Patel called my name.

"Ms. Lyons?"

I turned expectantly.

"Your friend, Mr. Daughtery? He is scheduled to leave for Bern soon."

"I know. Ian told me," I said.

"Maybe you could visit him again. I do not know whether it will help, but seeing friendly faces might draw out some of his memories. Should he not regain even some of his memories prior to his departure, I feel that waking up, so to speak, in the containment facility may cause irreparable harm. His mind is fragile right now, you see. I would hate to see him become so lost he cannot be found."

I wasn't entirely sure what Dr. Patel meant, but the gist was clear. He wanted me to see if I could help Harris while he was still here.

"Sure, I'll go see him now."

I wanted to spend every spare second with Erik. Our time together could be limited. It felt like that was becoming a theme in my life, trying desperately to cling to the present because the future was so uncertain. But Erik was with his family, and Harris was all alone. Deciding Harris's need was greater than my own or Erik's at that instant, I headed for the elevator.

The guards on the prison level were surprised to see me. One of them, Jared, was reluctant to let me see Harris without authorization from Crane. Pointing out that I'd already seen him once was an unconvincing argument since that visit hadn't gone well. But Jared and his partner, a middle-aged woman with hair so deep crimson it verged on purple, were easily manipulated. After a powerful suggestion on my part, the two practically rolled out a red carpet for me.

Interestingly, Harris was not alone. He sat on the small cot, his back against the only solid wall. Today he was dressed in clean black linen pants and a clean white t-shirt. He appeared to have showered recently, and his blond hair was still a little damp. A small folding table was sitting next to the bed with the remnants of his dinner. I was glad to see he'd eaten at least half of the same gamey meat Marin had served the rest of us. Next to the table, sitting in an uncomfortable metal chair was Janelle.

"Hey," I said softly. "What are you doing here?"

The dark-haired girl smiled at me over her shoulder. "Thought he could use the company. I feel so bad for him, you know? Want to come in?"

I wasn't sure about actually going inside the cage. With Jared and his partner preoccupied down the hall, nobody would come to my rescue if the situation turned ugly. With Janelle there too, I decided the odds were in my favor.

"Sure."

She stood and walked over to unlock the door. I entered the cage, keeping my focus on Harris to gauge his reaction. He followed my movements with little interest, which I found reassuring. At least he didn't tense up or immediately attack me. Still, I elected to lean on the bars closest to the door, just in case.

Janelle returned to her chair, crossing one long leg over the other. I took a moment to study her. She was wearing casual clothes today, jeans and a tank top. There were a few faint scratches on her neck, but any other injuries she sustained on either the rescue mission to Tramblewood or the evacuation in Kentucky had healed. Today she'd taken the time to fix her hair, and it shone even in the horrible fluorescent lighting.

"I was in one of TOXIC's low-level prisons for a while," she told me.

I stared at her. Seriously?

"Don't look so surprised." She laughed softly. "A lot of us weren't born here. A lot of us came from TOXIC states. Many were even at the School for a time."

Had I given it any thought before then, I might not have been so shocked. What she said made sense, of course. She was just so young, I'd figured she'd grown up in Crane's territory.

"How long have you been with Ian?" I asked. She seemed amenable to discussing the topic, so I only felt marginally nosy pressing her for the details.

"Ten years now. Came over when I was fifteen."

When she didn't elaborate, I became hesitant to push the issue, but I was curious. Few Talents left TOXIC, and being a teenager when she had made her situation even more unusual.

"What happened?" I asked.

Janelle shrugged. "My parents were sympathizers. They hadn't wanted to submit me for testing when I was five. But, they aren't big on breaking rules, either. I tested positive and was taken to the McDonough School. Let's just say, I never acclimated to my new surroundings. After a time it became obvious I was my parents' child. Except, I'm not great at following rules. I became very outspoken about my views on the testing laws. I was sent to see a therapist, Dr. Wythe."

Of course. The good doctor strikes again, I thought.

"He tried to convince me that my feelings were wrong and unnatural." Janelle laughed bitterly. "He actually said that, too. That a Talent being opposed to the mandatory testing laws was 'unnatural.' When his brainwashing attempts failed, I was carted off to Greenwood, outside of Atlanta."

I wasn't familiar with the low-security prisons, and Greenwood was not one I'd heard of.

"It's more of work camp, really. Most of the inmates are under eighteen. TOXIC likes to think they can rehabilitate problem children. With the number of Talents declining each year, the loss of one, even a low level one like me, is unacceptable for them. So, I spent my days doing manual labor. Assembling weapons, building furniture, stuff like that. Part of the package deal at Greenwood is a free mental block."

"They do it to all of the inmates?" I asked weakly. How awful.

"Yep. Part of the rehabilitation process. The drug wears off every couple of months, and you have to be injected all over again. It only takes a couple of weeks for some of your stronger memories to break through. By the time they re-up the injection, many people start to feel like themselves again. Before the doctor gives you another dosage, he evaluates you to see if you've gotten better. Like being opinioned is a disease or something. After a while, I learned what I needed to do to make the doctor believe I was better and ready to be an obedient little Talent. Of course, even after all of that, no one trusted me to be around other kids my age. They didn't send me back to the School."

"Where did you go?" I was so caught up in Janelle's story that I didn't even realize Harris had fallen asleep until she paused long enough to reach over and cover him with a blanket.

"To another work camp, essentially. Also in Georgia. Also doing manual labor. But there, no one gave me any drugs to keep me in line. I was given just enough freedom in the beginning to want more. After a couple of months without any trouble, they gave me even more liberties. I lived at the camp but was allowed to go into the nearest town on the weekends and stuff. There isn't much in the town, grocery store, bookstore, couple of restaurants, and this strange shop that sells really weird candles and jewelry. Anyway, it was there at the shop, Moonchasers it was called, that I met a member of the Underground. One thing led to another and before I knew it, I was on my way here."

When she finished speaking, I was at a loss for words. Janelle's story was no more tragic than many I'd heard. But it was heartbreaking all the same. How awful to be imprisoned as a child. And then to come here, to a place she knew nothing about, on the hope that life would be better. Obviously, her gamble paid off. Janelle seemed to genuinely enjoy working for Crane.

"Have you seen your parents since you left?" I asked finally.

Janelle shook her head. "Too risky. The people born on this side of the border have an easier time moving around in TOXIC territory. Faked identification and stuff like that helps them get in and out of anywhere without too much security. People like me, refugees from TOXIC, have a much harder time. Our stuff is on file. It's one thing for a fingerprint or retinal scan to show no match. It's another for it to come back belonging to an escapee. That's why Frederick has been so valuable to the movement. He can go just about anywhere in TOXIC territory. He's one of the few of us who can even get into the capital at all."

I thought about that. Frederick really had risked a lot for Crane's cause. That made me feel a little bit better about him keeping me in the dark about his connection to the Coalition. Telling me the truth, and me not believing him, would have had huge consequences. Not only for Frederick, but for the entire Underground movement and the Coalition. Had he chanced it and I ran to Mac, all of his hard work would have been for nothing.

After that, Janelle gave me a more detailed explanation of how the mental blocks worked. The one Harris had been given served two purposes. The first was that it kept me and others like me out of his head, which I thought was a pretty big risk, since it meant people like me couldn't manipulate his thoughts and feelings to their own advantage. And when you're trying to control someone, not being able to manipulate them makes that task pretty hard. But, as Janelle pointed out, a person given the mental block is a blank slate. They become easily suggestible to normal types of brainwashing, like mantras about TOXIC equaling good and Coalition equaling bad. Once their heads were filled with that sort of nonsense, and they made those ideas their own, a Manipulator like me would be unable to break through and change their minds.

The second purpose of the block was to prevent the recipient from accessing all or part of his own mind. They didn't remember how they used to think or feel. Again, making them easily suggestible to brainwashing.

Taking all of this in made my brain hurt. It also made me wonder to what extent Mac was using the technology. Was he not only creating his army of super-Talents, but also brainwashing them, too? UNITED had to be briefed on the possibility. This new development was a whole other layer of horrifying.

I left Janelle and Harris a little while later. I debated going to Crane with the information directly, but was worried that would lead to a long night in Victoria's company. No, telling them tonight wouldn't change anything, I decided. Tomorrow was soon enough.

The lights in Erik's room were out when I returned. He appeared to be sleeping in the sofa bed, but I felt his brain activity, so I knew he was awake. A quick read of his emotions told me his mood was darker than the deepest depths of the ocean. I wasn't entirely sure it was my fault, but felt I was the root cause. A fight was the last item on my agenda, and if it escalated and Victoria found out, I wasn't sure Erik's ability to expertly navigate the tunnels would save him. I let him continue feigning sleep.

I changed into pajamas, brushed my teeth and washed my face, and then climbed into the bed with Erik. I stayed on the opposite side of the mattress so I wouldn't accidentally kick him or roll over onto him in my sleep. Soon, I realized that wasn't going to happen because I wasn't going to fall asleep. Questions thundered through my head, demanding my attention. It wasn't long before I became so distracted with my own problems that I forgot Erik was pretending to be asleep beside me.

His touch was light on my back, his fingers cold as they brushed my curls aside. Gently, he began massaging the back of my neck with his thumb, making small circles that went a long way towards releasing the tension in my muscles.

"Why didn't you tell me?" he sent after a couple of minutes.

I tensed. There were so many things I hadn't told him yet, and I had no idea what he was referring to. He had his mental walls up. Not good.

"About what?" I asked.

Erik tugged on my shoulder, urging me to roll over and face him. Another bad sign. He wanted to read my face. I refused to budge. This conversation, whatever it was about, was better had with my back to him.

"Donavon," he sent.

Oh no, I thought.

"You should have told me."

"I didn't want to bother you with it," I sent stiffly.

Erik groaned as he scooted closer to my side of the bed. Snaking his arm around my waist, he pulled me flush against his chest. Erik wrapped his body around mine, and I began to shake with silent sobs.

"Shhh," he soothed. *"I'm so sorry, Tals."*

I cried harder.

"He's free, Tals. Donavon's prison didn't have walls, but that didn't make it any easier for him to escape. The guy was a mess. Don't get me wrong, I am sorry about his death. But however this war ends, Donavon's fate had already been decided."

Erik was right; Donavon was finally free. Free from his father, free from TOXIC, and free from the uncertain future his father had sentenced him to. That gave me some comfort.

"Don't hold things back from me. I'm not sick, Tals. Don't treat me like I am. Nothing has changed between us. I want to be here for you right now. But I can't if you don't let me."

"I'm sorry," I told him.

In Erik's warm embrace, I cried myself to sleep.

Chapter Sixteen

OVER AN EARLY breakfast of pink tomatoes and orangey-colored eggs, Erik and his father met with Crane in our bedroom. I'd prepared Erik for the meeting by filling him in on all I knew about UNITED's attack strategy. I'd told him about the evaluations, and how Crane and I were both concerned about his chances of avoiding containment. Erik agreed that his chances of passing were slim. He was naturally hotheaded, which didn't help matters. He also agreed that hurrying along his recovery so he could lead a team through the tunnels was a good solution.

Victoria and the rest of the UNITED council members still in residence hadn't been invited to our breakfast, since Crane was trying to keep Erik out of their sight until absolutely necessary. The three men talked over all of the different ways in and out of the tunnels beneath D.C. I listened, adding in an occasional comment, but not knowing enough to contribute any worthwhile information. Crane had gotten ahold of old blueprints for the ancient metro system and had them spread out across the sofa bed. Mr. Kelley's leg wasn't going to heal in time to go. Crane didn't offer him the choice of receiving any fast-acting drug. Edmond, however, was in prime condition and nearly as well-acquainted with the tunnels as his brother and father. Mr. Kelley reluctantly agreed to allow him to take part. Edmond still being a minor—he had a couple of months before his eighteenth birthday—Crane felt Mr. Kelley's acquiescence necessary.

Dr. Patel made his morning visit, and gave Erik a dose of the miracle cure that would further speed his unnaturally-fast healing.

"Councilwoman Walburton is very eager to meet with the young Mr. Kelley," Dr. Patel told us nervously. "I have impressed upon her how important his rest is at this crucial time. She is persistent, though. I am unsure I can hold her off much longer."

I was about to tell him that he'd better find a way to do just that, when Erik said, "It's cool, I'm ready."

"Erik," Crane began.

"No, seriously. I want to get this over with. Besides, I'm going to see her later today when we start talking strategy with the rest of the team, right? All the council members will be there, won't they?"

"Sort of," Crane said. "Victoria will be here with us, as well as the other members on site. The rest of the Council will be on teleconference from Bern. The council guard who have already landed in the U.S. will also be taking part in the planning sessions via teleconference. They're occupying many of the military bases on this side of the border."

"Has Mac even responded to the order for surrender?" I asked.

"Not so much as a peep from TOXIC or the government as a whole. Communications into and out of the capital have gone dark. We're having a hell of time trying to reach the Underground station there. Brand is still working on it, but I'm afraid we might need to send scouts ahead to alert them to the current situation."

"I can do that," Mr. Kelley piped up.

"Dad, no, your leg," Erik protested, gesturing to his father's bandaged limb.

"I can't fight. I can walk. I'll be able to get word to Adam so he won't be surprised. That will give him time to evacuate his people, at least the ones who don't want to fight."

"It's a good plan," Crane said reluctantly. I could tell he had reservations. "It would save us sending one of the few guides we have for the mission. Earon, if I sent two or three soldiers with you, would that do? Would you feel safe?"

"No more than that," Mr. Kelley said. "We'll attract too much attention."

"With TOXIC jamming the signals in and around the city, how will we know whether Mr. Kelley has made contact?" I pointed out.

"Faith, Talia," Earon Kelley told me. "Trust me to get the job done."

There was that word again: faith. Everyone wanted me to have faith. Trouble was, I was fresh out. I'd had faith in Mac, and look where that had gotten me. I'd had faith in Donavon, and that hadn't turned out so well either.

"If you're sure, Earon, I'll assemble a small team to accompany you," Crane said.

"Positive."

After Crane, his father, and Dr. Patel left, Erik was in a foul mood. He didn't want his father taking chances. I understood how he felt. I wasn't keen on Mr. Kelley risking infection, or worse, just to get word to Adam. There also didn't seem to be a plausible alternative.

The first of what promised to be many strategy meetings wasn't scheduled until the late afternoon. My sole objective between now and then was keeping Erik away from Victoria and her cronies. He might be ready to face them, but I wasn't convinced that it was a good idea. However, Erik was going stir-crazy being cooped up in the bedroom. A short stroll of the medical sublevel did little to mollify him.

"Let's visit with Henri," I suggested. "I think Frederick is back from Kentucky, so he'll probably be there, too."

"Whatever," Erik replied, limping along the stone corridor beside me.

Frederick had returned, we learned from Henri, but was busy doing chores for Victoria. She was using him to keep tabs on Mac. The Director of TOXIC was living like a king in the penthouse of The Hamilton, a posh D.C. hotel.

"City is on lockdown," Henri confided. "Frederick says only those affiliated with TOXIC are allowed in or out of the city. All civilians were evacuated as soon as the surrender order was issued. Even the senators who aren't in the Director's pocket have been banished. TOXIC's military personnel have taken over. They're patrolling the streets and skies around the clock."

"If we know Mac isn't going to surrender, why are we waiting?" I asked, exasperated.

I was sitting in an uncomfortable plastic chair with my legs flung over the arm. One of my feet started tapping against the metal leg impatiently. The noise was grating, but I found it impossible to stop the twitch.

"Diplomacy," Henri said. "UNITED gave him a deadline. They have to wait it out."

"Screw diplomacy," Erik said angrily and kicked the wall with the foot of his good leg. He'd been pacing back and forth since we'd arrived. "The longer the Director has to prepare, the worse off we are. He'll be ready for us."

"They're already ready for us," Henri said quietly. "Frederick's seen some conversations. The Director's injected all of the operatives with the drug. Shit's out of control."

I'd never heard Henri cuss. The swear word was odd coming from him. I'd have smiled had the situation not been so grim.

Sitting with the two guys felt like old times; the three of us against the world. Except it wasn't like old times. Too much had happened for us to pretend like we were talking strategy for any old mission.

A knock on the bedroom door pulled all of us from our thoughts. Erik stopped pacing and glanced at me, alarm radiating off of him. Even Henri seemed tense. Our visitor didn't wait for an invitation.

"Erik, I'm sorry. The time has come. Councilwoman Walburton wants to see you immediately." Crane stood in the doorframe, tall and imposing and extremely grim as he delivered the news.

"Ian, there has to be something you can do," I protested.

"I'm sorry, Talia. She is insisting that she meet with him before the session tonight. She's worried about him being in close contact with so many people."

Erik snorted. "What does she think I'll do? Go on a killing spree?"

Crane sighed and rolled his dark eyes. "She's just using that as an excuse to see you. Honestly, she's curious. She wants to see what you're capable of. Penelope doesn't embrace being Talented the way most of us do. She's reluctant to use her gifts on a daily basis, so she isn't actively using her new ones. You were taught differently. Your time with the Hunters is well documented. You'd already mastered so many other Talents as a Mimic, now that they're your own, she wants to see how good you are. That doesn't mean she'll hesitate to contain you if she perceives you a liability. Just answer her questions and try to remain calm."

That was the same advice Crane had given me before my evaluation.

"This isn't a full evaluation. It will be just the two of you talking. She's even agreed to meet with you in my study, alone. That shows how very interested she is. The session won't be recorded, so anything you say or do will be your word against hers. In case you're wondering, though, her word carries more weight."

"Let's just get this done," Erik said, his limp more pronounced as he headed for the door.

"I'll come, too," I volunteered quickly. "If this is informal, that shouldn't be a problem."

Erik paused halfway across the room. His shoulders sagged, and he let his head fall forward until his chin was almost touching his chest. *"No, Tals. You stay here. I can keep my head if I'm alone. If she tries to rattle me by using you, well, that's a different story. I'll be okay. Promise."*

I swallowed. *"I'll be waiting,"* I sent.

"Wait naked and I'll be back even sooner," he teased.

Crane cleared his throat, and I flushed crimson. Had he been listening in on our mental exchange?

"Come on, son. She'll be irritated if we keep her waiting."

I watched Erik and Crane leave, dread weighing me down. Crane better be right, I thought, Victoria better be trying to satiate her inane curiosity. Otherwise, she'd have me to deal with, and like she said, my threat level was off the charts.

Henri and I passed the time by going upstairs to visit Alex and Penny. Marin had put the child in the room I'd occupied until I'd moved below ground to be with Erik. It had been agreed that was the safest, most nurturing place for him. I was slightly miffed that I hadn't been consulted, but he appeared happy in the small, rustic bedroom that was next door to Penny's.

Marin had taken responsibility for Alex, and he'd grown attached to her in the short time he'd been at the cottage. He excitedly told me, in detail, how Marin let him help make cookies.

"He just stirred the batter," Marin assured me quickly when I stared at her in horror, assuming that she'd let the small, blind child near an oven. I couldn't be trusted near an oven and I had superior eyesight.

Every other minute, I glanced at an old-fashioned clock hanging on the wall over Alex's bed and willed the hands to move faster. What was taking so long? Seriously, how many questions did Victoria need to ask to know Erik was now one of the most powerful Talents alive? She'd have felt his power the instant he entered Crane's study. Had I let myself, I'd spend all day basking in the energy he emitted. I'd purposely been blocking the part of me that craved his power. The attraction was unhealthy, and my hormones were already on a constant upswing where Erik was concerned. There was no telling how I'd react if I opened myself up to him.

Fingers snapped in front of my eyes.

"What was that for?" I asked, staring at Penny, who was sitting cross-legged opposite me on the bedroom floor.

"You spaced out." She gave me an odd look. "You feel okay?"

"Fine," I said, the single word sounding harsher than I'd meant it to. "Just worried about Erik, is all," I added sheepishly.

"Well, Alex said he was hungry. And I asked if you wanted to go to the kitchen and fix a snack with us."

"Right, um, sure, let's go."

I got to my feet, feeling stupid. Alex held his pale arms up to me, and I hoisted him onto my hip. He buried his face in my neck like a puppy burrowing close for warmth. I hugged him tightly to me and breathed in the scent of fresh soap in his hair. Following my friends and Marin, I carried Alex to the kitchen.

That was where Crane found us two hours later. He had a pale and exhausted Erik trailing a step behind. Erik was too proud to lean on Crane for support, even though he was swaying on his feet.

I jumped off the bar stool I was sitting on and hurried to catch him before he fell. Under the pretense of hugging me, Erik wrapped his arms around my waist and practically collapsed. It took both Crane and Henri to get him through the trapdoor and down the metal stairs. Erik had all but passed out before we reached the elevator.

"What did she do to him?" I hissed at Crane.

"Not sure. Probably had him demonstrate some of his new abilities. It must've drained him. I'll send Dr. Patel by, but rest is likely what he needs."

"She better hope so," I snapped.

"Careful, Talia. I know you're angry. Making empty threats won't help the situation."

"My threats aren't empty."

Crane groaned but gave up his side of the argument.

Dr. Patel agreed that Erik just needed to sleep it off. Expending energy he hadn't had to begin with had drained him. The doctor also suggested he eat a high-protein dinner.

"I'll let Marin know," I said dryly.

Victoria excused us from the evening meeting since it was more of a state-of-the-world address than a strategy session. Via Crane, she'd sent word that Erik and I were to report to her the following morning.

Over a dinner of bison steaks and gloopy protein shakes that tasted like chalk, Erik recounted his session with Victoria. He said it actually hadn't been so bad. She was impressed by his control and mastery of the new Talents. I wasn't sure that was a good thing. Being valuable to her and UNITED had obvious perks—no containment. Being too valuable might mean a future spent under UNITED's thumb. Working for the Council had appeal, but once this was all over, I wanted to fade into obscurity and live the life I was meant to. Whatever that was. Maybe Erik and I could get a little house in the middle of nowhere and become hermits. Isolation sounded like heaven after being entombed in Crane's underground palace of wonders with so many other people.

"How are you feeling?" I asked him after he'd cleaned his plate. "You look a lot better." He did, too. Color had returned to his cheeks, ridding them of the sickly pallor. His bruises had faded from black and blue to greenish-yellow. Previously jagged cuts and gashes were now faint lines of red crisscrossing his chest and abdomen. The miracle healing drug was doing its job.

"Not so bad," Erik said. "My knee is stiff and my ribs are a little sore."

He was lying, underplaying his condition. All the physical activity of the day had caught up with him, and he was paying for it. I let him believe his ruse worked. Optimism and denial were the best paths forward.

I smiled and touched his cheek with the tips of my fingers. We were sitting side-by-side at a small folding table Marin had set up so we wouldn't have to eat in the bed. Erik leaned into my touch, nuzzling my palm with his cheek. His mind was open, and I felt how much he wanted to pretend life was normal, if just for a night. He kissed the inside of my wrist softly, causing my pulse to jump under his lips. I sat very still as he trailed kisses up the inside of my arm, my heart thundering in my chest. When his mouth found my collarbone, he glanced up at me through long dark lashes.

My breathing was uneven and when I returned Erik's gaze, the air shuddered as it left my lips. His mouth was on mine a moment later. I finally dared to move, wrapping my arms around his neck as he shifted in his chair to close the gap between us. Dark, silky strands of his hair tickled my fingers, and I pulled him closer until he was no longer sitting, but rather leaning over me.

I felt how badly his knee hurt and began drawing the pain from his body into mine.

"Don't," Erik sent.

"Why?" I replied, taking more of his pain with every breath.

"You need your energy. Don't want you getting tired on me." Erik's attempt at a joke—at least, I thought it was a joke—made me laugh.

"Are you sure about this? Dr. Patel wants you to rest," I sent, even though I knew Erik had already made up his mind.

"Tals? Stop talking."

I did. Erik left his mind open, so I did, too. While imprisoned, Erik had truly believed he was going to die. Every cut that healed, every bone that mended itself, only caused his resolve to plummet further. He, like Penny, had welcomed death while in Mac's custody. Now, all he wanted was to feel alive again. Being with me did that for him. Every touch, every kiss, reminded him why he'd never lost hope. I wasn't sure if leaving his mind open was his way of sharing the events of his torture with me or not. Embarrassment colored his emotions, and I realized Brand had been right. Erik wanted me to see him as strong and undefeatable, the constant stream of tranquility in my otherwise rocky life.

The more we touched and kissed, and the more skin became exposed, the hungrier he was for more. His urges were basic, just like the other day, but today he was driven by love. In the back of his mind, a dark cloud lingered on the horizon. For tonight, the storm would hold off. I wondered if he saw a twin cloud in my mind. That thought was quickly replaced by more primitive ones. The feel of his rough hands as they skimmed over my sides. A tingly sensation spreading across my skin when he traced my collarbone with the tip of his tongue. His emotions intensified my reactions. And for a little while, I truly believed the future held promise. As long as we were together, nothing else mattered.

Chapter Seventeen

AS IF BEING awakened by the way too cheerful Dr. Patel before sunrise wasn't bad enough, he had an entourage with him. The covers were pulled up to my waist, leaving the upper half of my body naked and on display. I was curled up next to Erik with my arm across his chest and his holding me against his side, a palm splayed in the middle of my back. The situation could've been worse. Not much, though.

Edmond snickered from the doorway. "Way to go, big bro," he called.

I wanted to throw a pillow at him, but that would expose more of me to his overeager eyes. Erik pulled me tighter against him, using his free arm to pull the covers up over my shoulders.

"Give us a minute," he told his brother and the others, who included Brand of all people.

"I wanted to go over some stuff with you before the meeting today. We can do it down here if you'd prefer. Doesn't make a difference to me." Brand's tone was bored, like catching us naked was an everyday occurrence.

I attempted to blend into my surroundings. Maybe shifting into a chameleon would help, I thought.

"I'll come upstairs," Erik replied.

"Command center in thirty?" Brand asked.

"Sure," Erik said.

Heavy footfalls signaled one less visitor.

"Edmond, leave," Erik ordered his brother this time, using manipulation to ensure compliance. Without another word, he too was gone.

Only Dr. Patel remained, and I considered using Erik's method to get rid of him, as well. Oblivious to my humiliation and impervious to the awkwardness of the moment, the doctor closed the door and continued towards the bed.

"Um, I'm not wearing any clothes," I pointed out needlessly.

Dr. Patel waved his hand and said, "I am a doctor, Ms. Lyons," as if that made it okay. Erik and I exchanged glances, his amused, mine irritated.

He has a point, Tals. Don't worry, he'll be quick, Erik sent.

I'm naked, I sent back, annoyed.

Erik slid his hand down my spine and around my hip, giving it a little squeeze in the process. *I know.*

"No need to check him out today," I told the doctor dryly. "He's back to his old self."

Only Erik wasn't back to his old self. Physically, even Dr. Patel was impressed with the rapid rate at which Erik's injuries were healing. But as the doctor lectured him on not exerting himself so soon, Erik grew agitated. When Dr. Patel suggested taking part in the attack was inadvisable, Erik's temper soared.

"I'm not an invalid," he snapped at the doctor.

"No one is saying you are," soothed Dr. Patel. "I am merely suggesting such violence at this time might stir up unpleasant memories and emotions that you are not ready to deal with."

"Then why did you give me the healing drug?" Erik shot back.

"I am merely making a suggestion, Mr. Kelley. As your doctor, I feel it is my duty."

The anger hit a breaking point, and I threw my arms around Erik while simultaneously sending him wave after of wave of calming thoughts before he attacked the doctor.

"Leave," I told Dr. Patel in a flat voice.

"It was not my intention to upset him." It wasn't an apology exactly. A part of me thought the doctor had been trying to trigger a reaction in Erik. It was like he was seeing what pushed Erik's buttons. If he felt what I felt, he'd know he was on very shaky ground.

"Leave," I repeated, firmer this time.

I returned my focus to Erik. He was seething. Currents of electricity transferred from his skin to mine at every point of contact. The sensation didn't hurt, but it was uncomfortable. I held him tighter, thinking happy thoughts even though I was quickly becoming scared. Not scared of Erik so much as what he might do if he didn't calm down.

"He's just worried about your health," I tried to explain.

Erik ground his teeth together. "No one tells me what to do anymore." The tone of his voice was low and threatening. He peeled my arms from around him and swung his legs over the side of the bed. "If I want to have sex with my girlfriend, I will. If I want to go to D.C. and kill McDonough, I will. I've earned that right."

I said nothing, fearing anything I did say would cause him to explode.

Erik struggled to his feet and swore when he put weight on his bad leg.

"Do you want help?" I asked timidly. I was nervous to speak mentally, since he hadn't. His mind was still open, so I felt the raw emotion and power fighting for dominance. Through the haze of rage, I saw how frightened Erik was. He didn't understand why he was so upset. He didn't like getting so worked up over something so stupid. He did hate being told what to do, though. It reminded him of Mac screaming orders at him as a doctor injected him with one needle full of serum after another.

"I don't want your pity, Talia," he grunted as he limped awkwardly towards the bathroom.

"It's not pity. I want to help you. Like you always help me. Like you helped me last night," I let the emotion show in my words, hoping my vulnerability would generate a positive response. He loved being strong for me, protecting me, defending me. Last night we'd done what we'd done because we wanted to. But being with Erik had given me comfort.

Erik paused when he reached the doorway to the bathroom and rested his forehead against the frame. He was completely naked and beautiful. The muscles in his legs, back, and shoulders were still well-defined. I bit my lip, trying to push back the thoughts I shouldn't be having in the middle of an argument.

To my astonishment and relief, Erik laughed. Not superficial laughter. Real laughter. The kind that started deep in his chest and shook his entire body. I wasn't sure what he found so funny, but the tension in the room evaporated like a fine mist.

"*Come here,*" he sent.

I scrambled out of bed, dragging the sheet with me. We might be alone, but I was still self-conscious about being sans clothing with the lights on. When I reached Erik's side, he gently untangled my fingers from the sheet, causing it to fall to the floor.

"You're beautiful, too," he told me.

Apparently I hadn't pushed those thoughts away so well.

Erik was half an hour late to meet Brand, who scowled and said, "You're late," when we finally joined him in the command center. The trek to the first sublevel had been slow and painful for Erik and even slower and more painful for me to watch. He blocked his mind, refusing to let me ease his suffering. I let him be stubborn. His pride was important to him, and I respected that. I worried that his body wasn't ready for the upcoming mission, and that he'd push himself into it anyway.

The meeting with Brand was brief. He just wanted to get his facts straight before addressing the entire Coalition and UNITED and their guard. It was agreed that Erik wouldn't speak during the meeting unless absolutely necessary. We were all worried he might become agitated if anyone questioned his knowledge.

Before long, Victoria and Amberly joined us. It was the first time I'd laid eyes on either councilwoman since my evaluation. Victoria appeared polished as usual, but stress was starting to take its toll on her. Her posture was more rigid than usual, and her painted lips were permanently pursed like she'd eaten something sour and was unable to get the taste out of her mouth. I almost felt bad for her, then I remembered that stupid tube. Yeah, she deserved a little stress in her life, I decided.

"Good morning, Ms. Lyons, Mr. Kelley. You are both well-rested, I see. Wonderful. We have a big day ahead of us," she said.

"I don't suppose McDonough surrendered during the night and we can bag this whole mission?" Brand asked.

"No, Captain Meadows, I am afraid not. Our sources indicate he has no intention of doing so, either. It is my plan to have the city surrounded and our forces on the ground in place and ready for action the minute the deadline expires," Victoria told him.

I wondered if Frederick was her source. According to Henri, he'd been her constant companion since returning from Kentucky. My heart ached for him. Having to spend so much time with Victoria was enough to drive anyone mad.

Both councilwomen took seats across the table from us. Amberly smiled at me as she bent to retrieve an electronic tablet from the brown leather briefcase she'd carried in. Victoria folded her hands on the glass tabletop and seemed content to stare at Erik, studying him like a piece of particularly fascinating artwork. It was off-putting.

The other council members I'd met previously filed in shortly thereafter, followed by Crane and Frederick. Coalition soldiers were next. I recognized most of them by now. Janelle waved hello to me. Jared even mustered a half-smile. I was growing on the guy. With only so much room around the table, the majority of the soldiers stood along the walls. They were different shapes, sizes, and colors, but they all had the same determined gleam in their eyes. Eager anticipation and nervous energy made them fidgety.

Next to me, Erik was gripping the arms of his chair with white knuckles. The heightened emotions in the room were getting to him. The angry mob mentally was sending his temper northward. I stared straight into his beautiful turquoise eyes.

"Block them," I sent.

"I can't." Erik's mental voice was strained.

"You've got to. You'll lose control if you don't. Concentrate on something soothing, something that relaxes you."

Erik's face transformed a moment later when he found his happy place. As it turned out, it was rather intimately associated with me. His irises danced and he drew his mostly healed bottom lip between white teeth.

My cheeks burned. *"Find another happy place,"* I demanded.

"That's the only place I want to be."

"This is crazy," an anxious voice said behind us.

We both jumped guiltily as Edmond stuck his head between ours.

"Did I interrupt something?" he asked, confused. "I know you guys have that whole weird mindspeak thing. Were you just talking?"

"Not important," I muttered.

"We're about to go live, people," someone called.

I turned my attention to the wallscreen at the far end of the room. It went from one large black rectangle to twenty smaller rectangles, each displaying a different image. One of the feeds was coming from UNITED Headquarters in Bern, Switzerland. At least twenty men and women sat around a huge round table with a holographic projection of Washington, D.C. in the center. The sound was muted, but I could see their mouths moving.

Another feed showed one lone participant, Councilman Michael Tanaka, the one council member I'd taken an instant liking to. He sat at a sleek mahogany desk in what looked like a personal office. The shelves behind his head were lined with moving pictures of a teenage girl who was his spitting image.

A third feed was from a lab. Glass vials, test tubes, and beakers were arranged in front of a terrifyingly pale woman with pastel pink hair and eyes that matched. She wore shimmery shadow on her eyelids that caught the light every time she moved her head.

Erik and I turned to look at each and exchanged a glance that said, "She's a scientist?"

The rest of the images were from military bases. Some were here in Coalition territory, while others were on foreign soil, if the flags flying in the background were any indication. At least one of the feeds was from a ship. The ocean peeked through behind the soldiers' heads.

"Councilwoman Walburton, the floor is yours when you're ready," Crane said.

Victoria smiled and pressed a button on the tabletop in front of her.

"Good morning, good afternoon, and good evening," she began, and her voiced echoed back at us a split second later from twenty remote locations. "As you are all aware by now, the United States government installation known as TOXIC is in violation of UNITED Mandate 1216.45, which prohibits use and experimentation involving the Creation drug. For those of you unfamiliar with it, the Creation drug is as the name implies, a drug for genetically engineering Talents.

"TOXIC Director, Danbury McDonough, has until zero hours Eastern Standard Time tomorrow to surrender to UNITED and submit himself for questioning. Failure to do so, and it is the belief of UNITED that he will fail to do so, will leave us no choice but to take action. The Director is currently residing at the Hamilton Hotel in Washington, D.C. along with top TOXIC officials and high-ranking members of the government. All civilians and non-essential government personnel have been evacuated from the city.

"Because we believe surrender is improbable, strike teams are being assembled and put in place to attack as soon as the deadline expires. TOXIC has an impressive military at their disposal, made even more impressive and deadly since we have reason to believe many of the operatives have been injected with the Creation drug. The battle will not be easy, but it is one UNITED is positive we will win."

Victoria spoke with so much confidence that she was awe-inspiring. Her calm demeanor left no room for doubt. Even I had to admit she was a master orator. I wasn't the only one who felt that way, either. Just in our small command center, the readiness for a fight was palpable. She had the soldiers' attention. Her words were mesmerizing. While I couldn't feel their emotions through the wallscreen, I saw it on their faces; she'd gotten to the others, too.

"Councilwoman Walburton," someone called from one of the feeds, and that rectangle zoomed to the forefront of the screen, dwarfing the other nineteen. A male soldier with a bald head and weathered face was larger than life as he addressed Victoria.

"Yes, Captain?" she replied, acknowledging him.

"Forgive my curiosity, but are we positive a violation has occurred? These are serious charges." His tone was clipped and he had a faint Irish lilt.

"UNITED has proof that at least four TOXIC operatives have been injected with the drug. Two of the four have suffered through rounds of experimentation at TOXIC's hands. I have personally evaluated each of the individuals. The evidence is irrefutable."

I thought this might be a cue and that I was going to be called upon to speak. But when I caught Victoria's golden eyes, she gave an almost imperceptible shake of her perfectly-styled head.

"Councilwoman," this time it was Councilman Tanaka's image that flew to the center of the wallscreen, "will our forces be facing super soldiers? What do we know about these Created Talents?"

"As of right now, not as much as I would like, I am afraid," Victoria responded. "For a more complete answer, I will turn the floor over to the Council's Head of Biomedical Research, Dr. Alexis Kramer."

I glanced around the room in surprise. I hadn't seen Dr. Kramer enter, but there he was, dressed in khakis and a blue short-sleeved button down. He moved away from the wall where he'd been standing between two Coalition soldiers.

The doctor cleared his throat and began explaining to all twenty-one locations that we should expect Mac's operatives to be stronger, faster, and all around better than our forces. Their healing abilities were likely to be far superior to our own, even those of us who were naturally Talented. They'd be harder to incapacitate for this reason.

I wasn't sure if I had the authority to speak, but a question was burning a hole in my mind. What about the operatives who were fighting against their will? Few, if any, had asked to be injected. Most had been against their will, or at least unbeknownst to them. Like Harris, many had probably been brainwashed. It wasn't fair to kill them. As soon as Dr. Patel found a cure, those people could be saved.

"Councilwoman," I started.

Victoria shot me a warning look, but I plunged forward before I lost my nerve. Speaking in front of this many people was new for me, and I found it extremely intimidating.

"Is the goal to capture as many of the operatives as possible so that they can be questioned?" I asked innocently.

Victoria's smile was for the cameras. Inside she was seething; I felt her annoyance like a slap across the face. "Only the high-ranking officials. Those are the individuals UNITED is most interested in interrogating."

"So we are to kill all the foot soldiers?" I asked like I was throwing down a challenge.

"Talia," Crane warned in my head.

I ignored him. "The Council is researching a reversal drug, right? So, we could conceivably uninfect those who've been infected. Not all of them chose this fate."

Murmurings from the soldiers in the command center, as well as the people on screen, filled the room.

"Good job," Erik sent, patting my leg under the table.

I wasn't sure if he was being sarcastic.

"The research is far from complete. The containment facilities are not equipped to handle the thousands, possibly tens of thousands, who have been infected." She met my gaze across the table and tried to stare me down.

I almost laughed. For all the notes Victoria had on my life, she'd failed to see the common thread: I was not easily intimidated. I opened my mouth to argue that she hadn't actually answered my question, when Crane *and* Erik invaded my head.

"You've made your point, Talia," Crane said.

"Don't start a fight, Tals. This isn't the time," Erik sent.

"Any other questions before I turn the floor over?" Victoria asked. "Ah, yes, Councilwoman Saito." The live feed from UNITED HQ took the center of the display, and I knew my window of opportunity had passed.

That was when I realized Victoria hadn't addressed me by name the way she had with everyone else. I studied her, wondering if that had been a tactical decision on her part. I knew why she'd refrained from containing me, but had she told her colleagues? Was she afraid if people knew who I was that she'd be forced to defend her actions? The Council was basically ordering the extermination of the Created, with the exception of Erik, Penny, and me. Harris was being taken away to be studied, which might sound to some like good fortune, but it wasn't. His future looked bleak from where I sat.

After several more questions about TOXIC and Mac and whether the Created could be killed—like we were invincible or something—Victoria introduced Captain Brand Meadows. He began a lengthy explanation of the underground metro system. I was keenly aware that he seemed to know a lot more than Erik had told him in our brief meeting beforehand. That's when I noticed Erik concentrating on Brand as the Captain spoke. Erik was feeding him the information mentally.

After Brand laid out the plan for both our ground attack and airstrike, Victoria introduced the men and women who would be leading the individual teams. She left Erik out. Again, I wondered whether the oversight was intentional. He'd be leading a team from here, so only the Coalition soldiers had cause to know who he was and what he was capable of.

My mistrust for her grew by leaps and bounds.

Days seemed to pass while I was stuck in that command center. Not that poring over blueprints and debating strategy wasn't important, or anything new for me; I just wanted to go already. I was ready to face Mac. I wanted to be the first one to reach him. Once UNITED had him in custody, the time for vengeance would be over. I wasn't sure what the penalty for his crime was, but a quiet, painless death was too good. Maybe that made me a monster. Maybe I was a monster. Maybe I didn't care.

Finally, we were dismissed with nothing to do but wait. Patience wasn't my strongest virtue, or one I had at all. My fingers twitched and my foot tapped the ground when the elevator didn't appear the instant I pressed the call button.

"Tals, it's almost over," Erik told me, placing a hand at the center of my back. "Just try to relax. I know it's hard."

"Relax?" I snapped and immediately felt bad about jumping down his throat. I sighed and tried to regroup. "I'm sorry. I just... it's just—"

"I know, Tals. I know."

The elevator arrived, and the two of us boarded. I pressed the button for the medical sublevel, and the doors closed.

"Maybe we could take Alex to the beach? I haven't been outside yet," Erik suggested, drawing me into his arms. He rested his chin on top of my head and worked my shirt up just enough so his hands were on my bare skin. "I bet Henri will want to come, too," he added.

The elevator arrived on our sublevel, but neither of us moved when the doors slid open. I tilted my head back and stared up at him through my lashes. Erik's eyes were hooded as he bent to kiss me. My lips parted as his touched mine, and the moment was starting to get a little intense when I heard, "Get a room!" echo down the corridor behind me.

I broke the kiss and turned to see Frederick jogging towards us.

"How'd you get down here so fast?" I asked grumpily.

"I wanted to see Henri before I return to being Victoria's personal Viewer," Frederick replied breathlessly. His cheeks were flushed, and he looked like he'd been the one caught making out. "Glad I ran into you two. Cadence and Randy have been relocated. They're in San Lolito. It's not far from here. I know there's a lot going on, but I bet if you wanted to go for a visit this afternoon, Ian would approve it."

"Really?" I asked hopefully. It was almost pathetic how excited seeing Cadence made me. "Wait, is she okay?"

Frederick shrugged noncommittally. "Physically, yes. Her injuries are healing. She's been through a lot and could really use a friend."

Suddenly I was desperate to get away from the cottage. War was everywhere here. The soldiers in residence rarely wore casual clothes, favoring fatigues and boots despite the hot summer air. Few people I encountered on a daily basis were devoid of physical reminders of the raids and attacks. I knew Cadence was probably still heavily bandaged, and Randy was definitely still too thin. But their new home wouldn't have constant reminders of what was happening throughout the country.

"You'll have to ask Ian," Frederick repeated. "He'll want to send an escort with you. Tensions are high, and we can't be too careful."

"Tal, I'm not sure this is such a good idea," Erik said.

"You're the one who wants to get out," I insisted. "Don't you want to see them? We can take Alex and Henri. It'll be good for us."

Erik hesitated and I continued to plead with my eyes.

"Yeah, okay. I guess if Ian thinks it's okay," he finally relented.

I squealed, actually squealed, and threw my arms around Erik's neck.

Crane thought the outing was a good idea. He thought it would prevent Victoria from trying to question Erik further and that I, too, should be kept at arm's length after my outburst in the meeting. Janelle and Marcel were tasked with escorting our entourage on the journey. Crane said he didn't expect any trouble, the guards were merely for protection.

I found Marin and collected Alex and a bag of snacks for the short trip. Henri decided to stay behind on the off chance that Frederick was able to extract himself from Victoria's claws long enough to spend time with him. Penny also declined my invitation, being evasive about the reason. A quick swipe of her mind told me she already had plans. Brand had asked her to spend the afternoon with him, and she was giddy at the prospect.

They'd been friends for as long as Penny could remember. Her crush on him dated back to early childhood. She worried his proposal of an afternoon hike and picnic was just a distraction for him, and not the date she was envisioning. I considered telling her Brand was head over heels for her, but decided she'd find out the truth soon enough.

I was happy for her. It warmed my insides to see their relationship going somewhere. Besides, maybe spending a little quality time with Penny would loosen Brand up and make him more pleasant to be around.

Hugging Penny, I told her to have fun. Her cheeks flushed pink as images of how she wanted to spend the afternoon filled her head. Exercise was on the agenda, but my best friend hoped it wouldn't come in the form of hiking.

Erik, Alex, and I stopped by to say goodbye to Mr. Kelley, who was getting ready to leave on his scouting mission. The three soldiers assigned to protect him were not names I recognized, but Mr. Kelley assured us they were competent. I had my doubts about how his leg would survive the expedition. Apparently Dr. Patel did, too, because he stopped by while we were there to reiterate his displeasure.

"I'll be fine," Mr. Kelley assured us. "I'm in good hands, and President Crane's contacts in Virginia are expecting us. There won't be any trouble."

"I could go instead, Dad," Edmond insisted.

"No, son, they need you for the hard stuff. You need to lead the soldiers in. That is more important."

"Then I'll go," Evan offered.

"You're too young," Mr. Kelley said sternly. "Besides, I know the tunnels best."

I hugged Mr. Kelley and wished him luck. He made me promise to keep Erik safe and to make sure he made it home alive. I heard him ask Erik to make the same promise about me.

All of us, Mr. Kelley, Edmond, Evan, Erik, Alex and I, rode the elevator upstairs together. In the cottage driveway, we said our final goodbyes. I watched Mr. Kelley board a small four-seater hovercar with his escorts and their pilot. Then Erik, Alex, and I crammed into the backseat of another small craft with Janelle and Marcel in the front.

Janelle took the pilot's seat, dark shades covering her marble eyes. She'd been sitting with Harris when Crane had called her away to go with us. The shades were more to hide her red-rimmed eyes than to block the sun. She kept sniffling and wiping her cheeks. From her mind, I learned Harris was being transported ahead of schedule, that evening in fact. Guilt gnawed at my insides. Janelle had wanted to stay with Harris until he left. Instead she was ferrying me around and all because I'd been somehow both too bored and too anxious to sit in the cottage for another minute.

Supposedly Marcel was there for our protection, but he kept eyeing Erik over his shoulder, and his thin finger never strayed far from the trigger of the handgun tucked into the back of his pants. He was terrified of Erik. He'd seen him attack the medic. Rumors had been circulating throughout the cottage, growing more and more absurd as they passed from one ear to the next. The soldiers thought Erik a living legend, a highly-trained, extremely dangerous one they preferred not to get too close to, but a legend all the same. Marcel was even convinced he couldn't be killed. Images of Mac's Created filled his head; he envisioned them all looking exactly like Erik, each one a carbon copy of the next. As attractive as I found my boyfriend, seeing him that many times over, all fierce and cold with dead eyes, made me shiver.

"Are you cold?" Erik rubbed his hand up and down my goose-bump-covered arm. *"It's like a hundred and ten degrees outside."*

"Cold chill. Weird, right?" I laughed it off since I didn't want Erik to pry into my head and see what I'd seen in Marcel's. He didn't need to know the other guy was terrified of him.

Upon arriving in San Lolito, Janelle brought the hovercraft low and wound through the center of town, pointing out various shops and cafes like a bored tour guide. Soon the quaint downtown gave way to a stretch of barren earth that time had forgotten. The earth was dry and cracked, with wisps of grass sprouting up in random places. It reminded me of my math instructor at school; he'd been going bald since forever but was determined to hang on to the three hairs he had left.

Several miles of hopelessness later, the world brightened and came back to life as a small city materialized. Unlike cities such as D.C. that had been retro-fitted to account for global warming, exponential population growth, and the technological break-throughs of the last two centuries, this California city was being built from scratch. Tall glass buildings lined the main street, which was cleverly named "Main Street." Solar panels were affixed to the top of each one to provide power to the inside. Oddly, I wondered what effect an Electrical Manipulator had on solar power.

Construction crews were hard at work, sweating their asses off, lifting beams into place and digging up earth. Only there was very little heavy machinery. All the workers were Talents, and they were using their abilities to build the new structures. This was truly using our gifts for the greater good.

Apparently Erik thought so, too. He whistled long and low.

"Impressive, huh?" Marcel asked from the front. "This is one of the first new communities President Crane has commissioned in a long time. Monies from some of the wealthier families on the other side of the border wanting to get their Talented children away from TOXIC paid for it. Those folks have deep pockets and are willing to use them."

"Wow." Crane really had been busy. Mac had painted him as the anti-Talent, when really he was a proponent of freedom and choice.

"This is us," Janelle said as she maneuvered the hovercar between two finished apartment buildings. The alleyway was narrow, and the car barely fit through. In the rear, there was a square parking lot with a handful of numbered parking spaces that I assumed correlated with the apartments they belonged to. Janelle parked in one marked "visitor" and turned off the engine.

Erik perched Alex on one hip and offered me his free hand. Janelle took the lead and Marcel brought up the rear. Neither soldier had any weapons visible, but both remained vigilant, constantly scanning the area for threats. I thought them a little paranoid, yet that didn't stop me from sweeping my gaze across the parking lot and checking over my shoulder.

The lobby felt a lot like the school dorms. A matronly woman with wispy gray hair and big brown eyes greeted us from behind a circular desk set off to one side. She was pleasant enough when she asked us to sign a guestbook. Janelle took charge, writing only her name and Marcel's in the visitor spot. Even in her beige sundress and shades, the matron seemed to understand that Janelle was a soldier, and didn't question her about Alex, Erik, and me.

The five of us rode the elevator to the third floor. Janelle led the way to Apartment 315 and knocked. It was Randy who answered the door an instant later. His face, now clean shaven and slightly fuller, broke into a smile.

"Talia!" he exclaimed. Then he peered past us, his expression becoming anxious. "How did you know we were here?"

"President Crane knows everything," Janelle answered mysteriously and pushed past him into the apartment.

"I'll be out here," Marcel said, taking up a post next to the door. I stared at him questioningly as I passed. Was that necessary?

"Can't be too careful," he said mildly, repeating the catchphrase I'd heard what felt like a hundred times that day.

Erik and Alex were a step behind me. The little boy had been silent most of the ride, munching on the dried fruit Marin had packed for a snack. He was shy and clung to Erik or me instead of interacting with anyone else.

"Did I hear you say Talia?" a female voice called from somewhere within the apartment.

"I'm here, too, Cadence," Erik called back.

"Erik, is that you? You're alive? You're okay?"

"Hold on, Cadence, I'll come get you," Randy called back to his sister. To us, he gestured towards the small living room and politely invited us to sit.

While Randy went to help Cadence, Erik and I sat on the sleek leather couch to the left of the entranceway, pushed up against the back wall. Erik tried to settle Alex between us, but the little boy whimpered, and Erik pulled him onto his lap.

Two matching chairs were arranged opposite the couch. Each had a folding table set up in front of it. The interior of the apartment was sparse and decorated in all neutral tones. Very calming, I decided. Thin walls made it easy to hear the neighbors discussing the merits of working for some shopkeeper named Rhea or Ray versus trying to get a job on one of the construction crews.

"This is temporary housing," Janelle explained in a soft voice. She'd situated herself in front of the window next to the couch. She drew the blinds closed and was using one finger to separate two slats just enough that she could keep an eye on the street in front of the building. "The residents are only allowed to stay here for three months. Gives them enough time to find work and secure permanent housing."

I nodded. That explained the dorm-like feel of the place.

"Can't this thing go any faster?" Cadence's impatient voice drifted into the living room.

"The wheels don't move so well on carpet," Randy responded calmly.

"Good to see a few broken bones haven't damaged her spirit," Erik sent, sounding amused.

I was glad we'd come. Maybe the visit had been silly in light of the upcoming attack, but Erik seemed to need this. I needed this.

"Cadence!" I exclaimed upon seeing my friend emerge from a short hallway. She was looking worlds better than the last time I'd seen her. Gauze no longer covered her face, and the cuts it had been hiding were scabbed over and healing. Randy stood behind her, pushing the wheelchair she sat in.

"It's great to see you, Cadence, really," Erik told her.

She actually blushed. It had to be a first.

Randy maneuvered his sister the short distance to the living room and got her situated next to the couch. I made introductions between Janelle, Alex, and the Chois. Alex had never been overly fond of Cadence, and he shied away from Randy, electing to bury his face deeper in Erik's neck.

Janelle made polite conversation with Randy and Cadence, asking them how things went at the induction center and whether they were comfortable in their new home, all the while keeping one eye glued to the outside world. Cadence had found the experience humiliating and degrading, but she was too uncertain of her place. Randy, on the other hand, had welcomed the large sleeping rooms with their bunk beds. Even the communal bathrooms and cafeteria-style meals were like heaven to him. After living in a damp, dank prison cell for years, I'd have agreed with him.

Erik and Randy had never officially met. Their shared time in Tramblewood had formed an unspoken camaraderie between the two guys that was undeniable. They talked about trivial things like the fact that San Lolito had no good bars, which I found amusing since Randy hadn't seen daylight, let alone a bar, in like six years.

Having quickly grown bored with our conversation, Alex fell asleep on Erik's shoulder. Randy excused himself to start fixing dinner. "Would you guys like to stay and eat with us? I make a mean sandwich."

"No," Janelle answered hastily. "I mean, thank you, but we need to be back at Headquarters before dark. Big day tomorrow."

"What's tomorrow?" Cadence asked, confused.

I bit my lip and debated how much to tell her. The attack was bound to be public knowledge within hours after it went down. Did it matter if she and Randy had advanced warning? Who were they going to tell?

I glanced sideways at Erik, who nodded, and then up at Janelle. She shrugged like it didn't make a difference to her one way or the other. So, I spared no detail of UNITED's plans to bring Mac to justice.

"Damn it, I want to go," Cadence swore and hit the arm of her wheelchair. Her dark eyes flashed with anger, and the air around her shimmered before she became transparent. Janelle's expression Morphed into one of surprise and unease. She wasn't alone. In her mid-twenties, Cadence was too old and too acquainted with her Talents for her emotions to impact them.

"Sorry," she muttered, becoming fully corporeal. "It's like hitting puberty again. I get upset and go invisible. Sucks."

I met Erik's turquoise gaze. The alarm in his irises mirrored my own.

"How long has this been going on?" I asked in what was supposed to be a casual tone, but came off a little frantic.

Cadence shook her short hair in annoyance. "I don't know. Since I got injured, maybe?"

I didn't want to scare her, so I kept my theories to myself. One look at Erik and I knew we were on the same page. Guilt was emanating off of him. He blamed himself and I didn't understand why. I dug into his head, and realized he was actually one page ahead of me.

Her inability to control her Talents led me to believe she'd been injected with the Creation drug, or some derivative of it, at some point. I was half right, if Erik was all right. He thought her condition was a result of the amplification drug she'd used to heighten her light manipulation.

Cadence was only a mid-level Talent, at least she had been. She'd amplified her abilities, using the same drug TOXIC gave children during testing, to allow her to hold her invisibility long enough to rescue the Kelleys. The drug was supposed to wear off in a couple of hours. If Cadence was still feeling the effects over a week later, that wasn't a good sign. It also meant Mac's super-Talents might be even more super than we'd thought. Not only was he injecting people with the Creation drug, he was probably amplifying their abilities on top of that.

His army would be on a power-high and might truly believe themselves invincible. Sure, actually being invincible was different than simply thinking it, but thinking it meant they'd take bigger risks, be bolder, know no fear.

"I'm sure it's just stress," I said tightly. "It does weird things to people."

"Right, once I get adjusted I'll be back to normal," she agreed half-heartedly.

My heart and mind weren't in the conversation after that. I wanted to get back to the cottage and tell Crane about Cadence and the possibility of TOXIC's army being super-super-charged. It occurred to me this might prompt UNITED to demand Cadence undergo evaluation.

The entire hover ride back, I mentally weighed the pros and cons. Erik, who wasn't fooled by the fake smile I'd been wearing for so long my cheeks ached, threw in his opinions every so often. He was firmly in favor of divulging the information. Better to be prepared, he'd said. Which was, of course, true. I hated condemning her to the evaluation, though. UNITED didn't need her as proof of Mac's crimes the way they'd needed me, Erik, and Penny. Studying Cadence wouldn't advance Dr. Patel's research into a reversal drug. Still, those reasons wouldn't stop UNITED from containing her if they thought it necessary.

Alex slept fitfully, sprawled across mine and Erik's laps like he had a desperate need to touch both of us. He relaxed some when I stroked his back, but continued to twitch every so often. In between worrying about Cadence and whether to tell Crane about her, I worried about Alex. He'd recently lost both of his parents in violent ways, so nightmares were only natural. It felt like more than that, though. I wasn't familiar enough with viewing to know if he was having a vision in his sleep, and I couldn't get a good read on his thoughts while he slept, either.

"*He's a tough little kid. Have some faith,*" Erik sent.

"*Not you, too,*" I grumbled.

Chapter Eighteen

THAT EVENING, OVER the oddest family dinner ever, I did tell Crane about Cadence. All the usual suspects were present, Crane, Marin, Penny, Brand, Edmond, Evan, Henri, Erik, Alex, and me. Even Frederick, looking disheveled and exhausted and like he wanted to hit someone, made an appearance. This meant there were a lot of opinions on the effects of the amplification drug on top of the Creation drug. After awhile, I sat back and just watched the shit storm I'd started.

We were sitting on the large back deck that jutted off the main level of the cottage. The breeze coming off of the ocean made the heat bearable but wasn't so strong we had to yell to hear one another. Seaweed-scented air reminded me of my childhood and my parents and stirred unpleasant thoughts about my father in my head. I pushed them aside; tonight wasn't the time to deal with them. There was probably never going to be a good time to deal with them, but the eve of an epic battle—one for the history books—was too dangerous. I needed to concentrate, focus on what we were about to do. Come to terms with my potential death.

This wasn't the first time, and hopefully wouldn't be the last, that I'd faced death. Maybe I was prone to drama or unlucky, but I found myself in life-threatening situations fairly frequently. This one felt different. When it was over, I'd be different. We'd all be different.

Speaking of different, Alex was distant, spaced out, over dinner, but not nearly so agitated. Now I understood why. Whether he was able to view in his dreams, I still didn't know, but he was viewing while awake. He was following Mr. Kelley to D.C. Through Alex, I was able to watch the journey in real time. It was fascinating, like watching TV but better.

I let Erik in on the secret so he, too, could watch and know that his father was safe. The group had just reached Virginia when I tuned in during dinner. After taking a roundabout flight pattern, they'd landed in a rural area approximately one hundred miles south of D.C., on the water. There they boarded a tiny submarine that was only spacious enough for the three of them to sit in. Three back-to-back-to-back chairs were positioned in the very middle of a round, clear bubble. I felt my chest tighten as I watched them lower themselves down through a hatch on top. It was suffocating to watch from a distance, being there in reality must've sucked.

"I was thinking I would take Alex for the evening, so you and Erik can be alone." Marin's voice snapped me out of Alex's head.

"No," Erik and I shouted in unison.

"Sorry," I smiled. "It's just, we'd really like to spend time with him tonight."

The lie made me feel icky all over. Obviously I did want to be near Alex, but more because I wanted to watch the scouting mission play out in his head. I was pretty sure Erik could've viewed his father, had he been willing to try. Viewing was too weird for Erik; he was reluctant to use it, which was odd since he had no issue with his other new gifts. I thought it might be because Mac had given him the ability to view solely to find me. That was when they'd beaten him the worst, when he'd refused to use the gift.

For the next two hours, the three of us tracked Mr. Kelley underwater, to an entrance to the old metro system in Alexandria, Virginia, and into the tunnels. Cat Eyes, the same man who'd helped Frederick, Alex, and me escape D.C. was the one who smuggled the scouting party through the padlocked gate. The trek through the underground tunnels wasn't terribly exciting, save the creepy-crawlies and enormous rats that called it home. One section of the tracks was surrounded by dank, slick walls that had large fissures running along the concrete.

"It's the section that runs under the river," Erik murmured. "Riskiest part. Structurally unsound."

I nodded and leaned back on the pillows decorating the sofa bed. Erik and I were lying in the bed with Alex between us. The little boy seemed anxious, but showed no signs of letting go of his link to Mr. Kelley. I wasn't sure this was healthy for him. In fact, I felt like we were using him. But when I voiced my concern to Erik, he said that Alex was going to watch whether we did or not. If the scenes turned ugly, one of us would attempt to pull Alex back.

At one point, Mr. Kelley and his team reached an impasse where a section of the tunnel roof had caved in. This slowed the group's progress as they took the time to clear a pathway through the rubble. I was glad they'd done so, now we wouldn't have to contend with the same obstacle tomorrow.

Finally, the threesome reached a familiar door, and I nearly wept with relief. They'd made it. Alex seemed relieved, too, and once Mr. Kelley limped into Adam's outstretched arms, he passed out from exhaustion.

When I blinked my eyes open and surveyed the bedroom, I found I was exhausted, too. Living through the journey vicariously had been draining.

I heard Erik exhale. "They're safe for tonight," he said, sounding just as tired as I felt.

"Yeah," I agreed. "For tonight."

"Let's go for a walk," Erik whispered into the dark room.

"What? Seriously? Aren't you tired?"

"Yeah, but I'm not going to be able to sleep. I want to stretch my legs."

"What about Alex? I don't want to leave him alone," I said.

"I'm sure one of my brothers will stay with him. Edmond seems fond of him. I'll ask."

Erik was out of bed and off in search of his younger brother faster than I'd have thought possible with his knee. The injury had healed mostly, but he'd been favoring his good leg after dinner. I stroked Alex's silky hair and let myself think about how much he looked like his father. Tears started to pool in the corners of my eyes, and I didn't hold them back. No more had been said about a possible memorial service, but I intended on forcing Crane to make good on his promise. Donavon deserved that much. Alex deserved better.

Erik and Edmond returned a couple of minutes later, and the younger Kelley was all too happy to sit with Alex, even if he pretended like it was an inconvenience. I thanked him.

"Yeah, whatever," he replied.

After our first encounter, Edmond had gone out of his way to either avoid me or be nasty to me. He and Brand had a lot in common, I realized. Since the rescue in Kentucky, he'd been worlds more pleasant. I still wasn't his favorite person, but that was okay. Blaming me for Erik's capture was fair and not unwarranted. And, for Edmond, it meant he didn't have to blame himself. He tried to hide the part of his mind that carried that guilt. I saw it every time he was close. I wondered if Erik saw it, too.

This was Erik's first foray to the beach. He'd never seen the Pacific Ocean, and I loved how excited the sound of the surf and the smell of fresh salty air made him. Even his limp was less noticeable as he hurried down the winding path to reach the sand.

Erik and I strolled hand-in-hand on the stretch of beach at the base of the cliffs, and it was easy to forget the chaos that tomorrow would bring. We'd both left our flip-flops at the end of the path, and the sand was warm and soft beneath my feet and between my toes. The moon was full, a round white orb casting a soft glow over the black ocean. I hated that my first thought was about how much light that would cast on D.C. the following evening. We wouldn't have the cover of darkness. Neither would they, I tried to reason.

In my prior trips to the beach, I'd kept close to the cottage except when in bird form. In the first days after my arrival, I'd been too keyed up to sleep, and had taken to midnight flights to burn off the excess energy. Tonight Erik led me far enough that the cottage was little more than a pinprick of light in the distance. Down here the beach was more rock than sand, and Erik gallantly offered to give me a piggyback ride to save my feet from the sharp edges. He was playful, tickling the backs of my knees to make me squirm and giggle. I kissed the back of his neck and blew in his ear, causing his pulse to quicken. He waded into the water up to his knees before attempting to throw me in. I clung to his back like a spider monkey, dragging him into the gentle waves with me.

With a fantastic splash, we landed in the surf in a tangle of limbs. Salt stung my eyes when I tried to wipe tangled curls from my eyes. Erik managed to twist his body around while still keeping my legs securely around his waist. He locked his arms around me as he moved deeper into the ocean.

"You're in a good mood," I said, smiling up at him.

Erik's turquoise eyes sparkled with what I'd come to under-stand was desire. The scar in his bottom lip was illuminated by the white moonlight. Instead of making him appear disfigured or deformed, the scar made him seem stronger, tougher somehow. I kissed his mouth gently, and he leaned me backwards until water lapped over my ears. The soft noises he emitted when I worked my hands beneath the navy tee that clung to him like a second skin were all I heard beneath the waves.

I stared up at him. Water droplets clung to my lashes, creating a prism effect and causing a rainbow of light to dance across his handsome face. He radiated vitality and longing, and all I wanted was to be with him. Tonight might be our last chance to be together, and even if we did both survive tomorrow, the future was uncertain. Once we'd lost our usefulness to Victoria, there was no telling what she'd do with us. Maybe we'd be neighbors with Harris in Bern. I'd been to Switzerland; at least I thought I had. So many of my childhood memories were fuzzy, sometimes it was hard to know if they were even memories at all.

"We can't control the future, Tals. Tonight I need you, and I don't care how selfish that makes me. I want all of you. I want your head here with me. I want to be the only thing on your mind."

"You are," I assured him, and gazing up at Erik, I meant the words. He deserved my undivided attention. He was the center of my universe, and I wanted him to know that. "I promise."

Maneuvering in the water was difficult at first. The waves provided a natural rhythm like nature was conforming and aiding in our escapades. When Erik or I shifted, the water swirled around us to accommodate our new position. Clouds appeared out of nowhere to block the moonlight the instant I worried we'd been seen. A tiny part of me knew that I was responsible, and maybe Erik, too. Between the two of us, our Talents were controlling the world around us to create the perfect atmosphere.

There was no cuddling afterwards. Instead of being exhausted from the exercise, I felt invigorated and alive. Already devoid of our clothes—no clue where they'd floated off to—we Morphed. In bird form, we played tag high above the forest floor. Chasing one another through the trees, we took back a small bit of the child-hood TOXIC had stolen from us. We were carefree and silly, and I knew that this was how I wanted Alex to grow up. In his short life all he'd known was violence. That was about to change, I vowed. I couldn't bring back his parents any more than I could bring back my own, but I'd give him the life every child deserved. I'd never be his mother, but I would be the best caregiver possible.

Chapter Nineteen

THE ATMOSPHERE ON the hovercraft was charged. The air so heavy with anxiety it felt like a boulder on my chest. I fidgeted in my seat and tried to block the others' emotions. It was a lost cause. Adrenaline was pumping too fast, sounding like white rapids to my oversensitive ears. Hearts were beating too loud. Thump, thump. Thump, thump. The stench of fear, sweet and pungent, made me gag.

"*Calm*," Erik soothed from beside me. He placed a hand over mine, the other gripping the armrest with white knuckles. "*You're stronger than this, Tals. Block them out.*"

Erik was wound nearly as tight as the other passengers, but he was making an effort for my benefit. We both knew that this might be it. The end. Mac and his cohorts would fight to the death; they'd already made that clear. And Mac no longer cared whether I lived or died; he'd made that obvious in Kentucky. Tonight Donavon would not be there to save me. And I wouldn't let another person die on my account. The blood spilled on my behalf was so much, at times, I felt like I'd drown in it. Even if my body survived the night, my psyche was already irreparably damaged.

"Talia, it's time," Crane sent from the front of the craft.

I sighed. No amount of time was ever going to adequately prepare me for this fight.

"Coming," I sent back.

I turned and met Erik's turquoise gaze. His smile was thin, but reassuring all the same.

"Ready?" I asked out loud.

He squeezed my hand by way of reply.

My fingers were numb as I unfastened the safety harness. I needed to get control of myself, and fast. Otherwise, I might as well spread my arms and declare that I was throwing in the towel now.

Erik slid his hand into mine as we walked between the rows of soldiers lining the back of the craft. Their eyes followed our every step, but no one said a word.

In the front of the craft, Crane sat at a glass tabletop depicting a map of the country, Victoria beside him. I'd been unable to hide my surprise when she boarded the hoverplane. She wasn't exactly the fighting type. She was more of the talk-you-to-death-with-big-confusing- words type. Seeing her dressed in a uniform identical to those worn by the rest of UNITED's guard—jumpsuits that instantly blended into the surrounding area—gave me a new respect for her.

"What?" she asked when I'd gaped at her as she walked onto the hoverplane. "You think I would miss this?"

Brand was standing to Crane's left, peering over his shoulder. Penny sat on Victoria's right, nervously twisting a loose strand of red hair around one pale finger. She was still so thin, so fragile-looking. Of all the people going into battle tonight, she was the one I feared for the most. But when she turned and met my gaze, the confidence in her lime-green eyes told me she was ready to end this once and for all. She was one of the many who had suffered because of Mac, and was clearly itching to repay the favor.

I wedged myself in the small space between Crane and Victoria's chairs to look at the map. Erik rounded the table to stand beside Brand.

"We're a thousand miles out," Crane said, never taking his eyes off the glowing red dot that marked our flight pattern from California to Virginia. We'd be landing in the same spot Mr. Kelley and his team had the night before. Then, we'd be using the same underwater approach, not something I was looking forward to. The other teams, those not entering the city through the tunnels, would take up positions surrounding it from above. It was vital that the tunnel teams go unnoticed as long as possible. Mac was anticipating the attack. But once he saw the twenty hovercrafts ringing the city on radar, he'd be less likely to consider we'd use the tunnels, as well. "We'll be within their radar range shortly. Brand, Penny, and I will do our best to mask the crafts until we are on the ground in Virginia."

As Perception Manipulators, Crane and Brand were going to hide our hoverplane, disguising it as a fast-moving cloud. Penny, and her new Talent for Light Manipulation, was going to add an extra layer of protection and try to keep our craft invisible for as long as possible. This, of course, was not news to me. We'd been over the plan so many times I felt like the details were carved into my frontal lobe.

I still didn't like it. The hoverplane was massive. It was one of UNITED's, and held several hundred people. The amount of energy it would cost all three of them would hamper their abilities once on the ground. Penny was the most vulnerable since she wasn't used to using so much Talent. There was no telling how her mind and body would react.

"Showtime," Crane said and stood. He towered over me, and I had to tilt my head back to meet his gaze. "No matter what happens, I'm proud of you, Talia," he said, his voice thick with emotion. "Your parents would be proud of you."

Tears welled up in my eyes, but I blinked them back.

"Thank you, Ian," I whispered. "For everything."

Without another word, Crane walked to stand directly behind the pilot—Donna, again. He placed a hand on her shoulder and squeezed.

Brand nodded to me, clapped Erik on the back, and then joined his mentor and leader. Penny stood next, throwing her arms around my neck. "We've totally got this," she whispered in my ear.

I laughed. Leave it to Penny to sum it up so eloquently.

"I love you, Penny," I told her.

"If I don't see you down there, I'll be waiting by the bar at the victory celebration," she replied. She released me, and turned to Erik. The look that passed between the two people I loved most in this world spoke volumes. They shared so much pain and understanding that I would never fully appreciate. If we all survived, I'd be thankful they would have each other to lean on.

"I'll take care of her," Erik promised in response to Penny's unspoken question. "And him, too." By him, we all knew Erik meant Mac. What Mac had done to my parents, to me, was inexcusable. What he'd done to Penny and Erik was unforgivable.

I sat in the chair Penny vacated, and Erik took Crane's seat.

"Touching," Victoria mused.

I'd almost forgotten she was there.

"Mr. Kelley, you are ready for this, are you not?"

"I am, ma'am."

I hated that he called her ma'am.

"Good, because I will be on your team."

"Excuse me?" I interjected.

"Close your mouth, Ms. Lyons. It is unbecoming on a lady."

Erik snorted and I glared at him. Neither of us had ever heard me called a lady.

"Aren't you afraid we're too dangerous to be stuck underground with?" I shot back.

"Precisely the opposite, dear. You two are the closest we have to TOXIC's Created. You are the strongest, fastest, and most powerful Talents on our side, which makes you the most likely to survive."

I eyed her suspiciously. Was that little speech supposed to make me feel better? Inspire me? Because it didn't. I kept quiet. Antagonizing her took energy I wasn't willing to waste.

The rest of the voyage took place in almost complete silence. No one in the pilot's cabin spoke unless absolutely necessary. It seemed as though we all shared the same fear that any noise would distract Crane, Brand, and Penny and break their concentration. I felt the power they were using, it was impossible not to. The air crackled and hissed with it. Their energies were live entities and even smelled like them. Crane's was rustic and reminded me of the cottage. Brand's was like dewy grass, just like his eyes. Penny's was sweet and syrupy, same as her.

Donna updated us on our progress every two hundred miles, which seemed unnecessary since we had a map in front of us. She was nervous, I supposed. At two hundred miles out, Victoria ordered Frederick to the cabin. He'd been resting in one of the broom closets that were allegedly sleeping quarters, since Victoria had kept him up viewing Mac for the last ninety-six hours straight.

"You are looking much better, darling," she told him when he and Henri entered several minutes later.

I disagreed with her assessment. Frederick looked like death warmed over. The bags under his warm brown eyes had bags of their own. His cheekbones were jutting out, giving him a skeletal appearance, and his skin was sallow like he was recovering from a terrible illness.

"Do you have a lock on Director McDonough?" she asked him.

"Yes, ma'am. He's still in his suite at The Hamilton. He's running operations from there."

"Is he alone?" she asked.

"No, ma'am. Same people as before are still with him. No one has gone in or out of that suite in twenty-four hours."

"That will be our team's initiative," Victoria announced. "Once we are through the tunnels, we will storm the hotel. Leave the operatives to the others. That is not a problem for any of you, is it?"

I smiled. "No, it isn't."

"I thought you would feel that way, Ms. Lyons. As you are aware, the Council wants Director McDonough alive for interrogation. But this is war. And war is unpredictable. Sometimes we need to adapt in order to survive. Should you find yourselves in a kill or be killed situation, you are authorized to kill him."

"Understood," I said, like I needed permission.

"Beginning initial descent," Donna informed us from the front of the hoverplane. "Get ready to move. Once they drop the manipulation, I don't know how long before we're spotted."

Crane, Penny, and Brand would be the last to leave. They'd stay onboard until the rest of the teams were in the water, and then their team, led by Edmond, would board the last submarine. The plan was for them to hold the manipulation until they were in the water. Then, Donna would head north to rendezvous with the other hoverplanes.

The whole process went off without a hitch. It was almost too easy, in fact. So when we made it off of the hoverplane, and into ten-person glass bubbles that were barely larger than the three-person glass bubble I'd seen the night before without even a stray bullet in our direction, I began to worry.

TOXIC had jammed all frequencies within a hundred mile radius of the city, so we hadn't had communication with the other hoverplanes in awhile. Had the fight started early? According to the clock on the circular dash in our bubble, we still had two hours until Mac's deadline expired.

"He's probably focused on the more immediate threat," Erik sent as our submarine started north. At least, that was the direction the compass in front of me was saying. It was really hard to tell, since it looked like we were swimming through mud the water was so thick with soil. *"There are a bunch of UNITED hovercrafts with torpedoes locked on the city, you know."*

"Yeah, I guess. Just feels wrong, like we're walking into a trap."

The uneasy feeling spread through me like a virus, multiplying in each of my cells until I was completely infected. We'd managed to surface on the riverbanks in Alexandria, troop the hundred yards to the metro entrance, and descend into the station without a peep from TOXIC. I'd seen the lights from our hoverplanes as I sprinted through the gates that were usually kept locked. I tried to tell myself Erik was right, that Mac had more pressing concerns than whether we'd pop out of the ground like moles.

Erik led our team—me, Victoria, Henri, Frederick, Janelle, and four UNITED guards—down a rusty escalator to the main level of the station. Earbuds were out of the question since the wireless signals weren't transmitting. We relied on hand signals and mine and Erik's mental communication abilities. This only allowed us to talk to each other, Frederick, and Henri, but it was better than nothing. I probably could've communicated with Victoria, but I wasn't eager to forge that bond. For her part, the Councilwoman appeared capable. She knew her way around an assault rifle, was agile, and followed orders surprisingly well for someone so used to giving them.

The ten of us had lowered ourselves over the edge of the platform and were already jogging towards the mouth of the tunnel when I heard the second team coming down the escalator behind us. This part of the journey was straightforward, literally. There were no offshoots or branches from the main tunnel, which made our trek boring and quick. I stayed in the front of the group with Erik. Despite the pain in his knee, he was setting a fast pace.

"I don't suppose you can talk to your father? Ask him if they've seen any signs of trouble up their way?" I sent.

"Never tried the mental thing with Dad," Erik sent back. He glanced down at me. *"You're paranoid, Tals. The trouble's above ground."*

"TOXIC uses the old metro system to move people around," I said. *"What if they're using it to get Mac out of the city?"*

I could tell this possibility hadn't occurred to Erik, and my idea worried him. The tracks we were on now were still in use. The area where Adam's station was located had been abandoned decades ago, as had many of the side tunnels on the D.C. side of the maze.

"Frederick," Erik called aloud. His voiced echoed in the tunnel. "Update on the Director's location."

"Still in the hotel suite," Frederick panted. He was more winded than the rest of us, and it wasn't because he was out of shape. The constant viewing wasn't good for him. I thought UNITED owed him a long, all-expenses-paid vacation after this was over.

"See?" Erik sent me. *"Nothing to worry about."*

I wasn't persuaded. Just because Mac wasn't on the move, didn't mean there wasn't cause for alarm. My gut feeling was that we were in for a surprise, and not a fun one.

An eerie feeling of déjà vu set in as we came upon the area where Mr. Kelley and the other scouts had moved the rubble aside from the long ago cave in. The path was clear for us, and we charged forward. I tried to recall how much farther until we reached Adam's station. Maybe a mile, I guessed. At our current speed we'd be there in eight minutes. My concept of time was off, though. Our communicators weren't working, and I was thankful Erik knew the way because the technological blackout meant we had no GPS if we got lost.

Stopping at Adam's station wasn't on our itinerary. The plan was to keep moving so we were in position at the McPherson Square station at the stroke of midnight. That was the station closest to The Hamilton. Other teams would be coming through various other stations throughout the city. At the same time we showed ourselves, UNITED's hovers would open fire on the city.

Once we'd cleared the underwater part of the metro system, the real test of Erik's navigational skills began. He didn't hesitate at the intersections, confident each turn was the right one. Frederick started to fall behind. His panting had turned into all-out wheezing, and he sounded like he was having an asthma attack.

"Keep moving," Henri insisted. "I'll hang back with him. He knows where we're going. We won't be far behind."

Erik and I exchanged uneasy glances. Leaving them wasn't appealing to either of us. The other teams wouldn't be using the same branches we were since their final destinations were different. The two guys would be vulnerable. I'd seen Frederick fight and knew, if healthy, he could hold his own. Henri, too, was a trained fighter. But they were both running on a half tank. Henri's shoulder was still stiff, and his mobility wasn't one hundred percent. Frederick was ready to collapse.

"Kent, Noelle, you two stay with them. The rest of us will go on ahead," Victoria barked, making the decision. "The Director is still in the hotel, yes?" she asked, focusing on Frederick.

He nodded.

"Good. Mr. Kelley, onward."

"What do you think?" Erik asked me.

"Do we have a choice?"

There wasn't a choice. Erik may have been the leader, but Victoria was in charge. Besides, I wanted Mac. I didn't want to risk someone else getting to him first.

With one last look at Frederick and Henri, I mouthed, "Sorry," and followed Erik.

Ten minutes later, the remainder of our team was huddled behind the padlocked gate that separated the McPherson metro station from the world above. We were just in time to hear Councilman Tanaka issue a final warning to Mac from one of the hoverplanes.

"Director McDonough, this is your final opportunity to surrender. You have one minute until UNITED will have no choice but to apprehend you using deadly force if necessary."

I was crouched next to Erik, ready to blow the gate wide open as soon as the final seconds ticked off the clock. Sweat stung my eyes and soaked through my hair. In the silence my heartbeat was audible to my own ears, and I worried the operatives on the other side of the metal barrier heard it, too. Erik's gloved hand covered mine where it rested on the cracked ground between us. He squeezed my fingers tightly. I stared into eyes that had gotten me through so much. I didn't care that we were packed tight as sardines against that gate with five other people, including the high and mighty Victoria Walburton. I leaned forward and kissed him. This was no peck on the lips either. This was full-on tongue to tongue contact. His palms cupped my cheeks, pulling me closer. I buried my fingers in his dark hair and opened my mind completely to him. I wanted him to know what he meant to me, how much I loved him, that he, not seeking justice for my parents, was my reason for living.

We were still entangled in one another when the gate exploded.

Chapter Twenty

ERIK AND I were torn forcefully apart. I was hurdling backwards through the air, spinning head over feet. Instinct took over, and I Morphed without giving the idea any thought. Suddenly I was the small black bird, and still spiraling towards the platform below. I got my bearings in time to avoid a beak-first landing, and managed to skid to a stop on my talons. Unused to fighting in animal-form, I started to Morph back to human when I saw the stampede of large black shadows on the tunnel's domed ceiling. There were too many to be our people.

I pushed off the tiles, flying high into the rafters to search for Erik and the rest of my team. Four bodies were scattered on the platform I'd just vacated. I zeroed in on each one, relieved when none proved to be Erik. Where was he?

From this vantage point, I could see the operatives pouring over the lower platform's edges. In no time, the first wave would be up the escalator and descending on my teammates. I didn't know what to do. By myself, in bird form, I was hardly a threat. And there were hundreds of them. I circled above the melee, trying to find Erik and still keep an eye on Victoria, Janelle, and the others. A tiny relieved squawk escaped me when I saw Janelle struggle to sit up. She was alive, for now. I dove towards her, squawking louder and louder to alert her to the danger headed her way.

Janelle had just managed to make it to her feet when the first operatives hit the top of the escalators. Blood streamed down the side of her face from a gash over her left eye. She opened her mouth to scream, but no sound came out. Next to her, Victoria was groaning and rolling side to side.

Operatives were now running down the second set of escalators that led to street level. Janelle, Victoria, and the remaining Council guard were surrounded. And where the hell was Erik?

I was still flying in a circle near the domed ceiling, debating my options. There were too many operatives to fight. I could fly myself to safety, but that meant leaving Janelle and Victoria. My other teammates weren't as much of a concern: none of them had moved yet.

Do something! I shouted inside my bird brain.

That's when the ceiling above me opened up, sending a powerful shockwave reverberating through the station. I was blown askew by the force of it. Miraculously the concrete and earth that had previously been overhead flew upwards instead of collapsing inward. It was like the bomb had detonated from inside the station.

A loud squawk caught my attention, and I sought its source. My feathered wings beat faster when I saw him. Sleek black head, iridescent tail feathers, big turquoise eyeballs: Erik. He'd been the "bomb" that blew apart the ceiling, I realized. And he'd controlled the blast to prevent rubble from landing on Victoria and Janelle. Sure, it would have been nice if a couple large fragments had smashed the operatives, but whatever.

There wasn't time for me to marvel at his impressive skills. Bird Erik was diving headlong for the platform, wings pinned to his sides to cut through the air faster. I followed without understanding his plan, but trusting that he had one.

And he did. He swooped low in front of Janelle. She appeared confused, and Erik prodded her with his beak and flapped his beautiful wings until she got the picture. This left me to get Victoria. By now I was positive the Council guards were dead.

The operatives were distracted with Erik and Janelle, who were performing a routine of aerial acrobatics. I took the opportunity to land beside Victoria. She was in much worse shape than Janelle, but caught on to what she was supposed to do much quicker. She wrapped her arms around my neck and managed to pull herself onto my back. I'd never carried a passenger before. I was surprised to find her added weight didn't slow me down much.

Victoria clung to my neck, her own talon-like nails digging in to my flesh, as I shot towards the chasm Erik had created in the ceiling. Bullets followed us, and I used the same bob and weave technique I'd seen Erik employ. I had a feeling mine wasn't as graceful; although, it was effective. We were through the opening and soaring into the night unharmed seconds later.

Our hoverplanes were still forming a perimeter around the capital city. Buildings were erupting in orange-red flames to my left and right. Below, on the square outside of the metro station, Mac's Created were showing their worth. Their movements were so fluid, like they were made of something other than flesh and bone. Our people were good fighters, great fighters even, but how did you defeat a person who was there one second and gone the next? Human and then not? Transforming into your mirror image, so you thought you were fighting yourself?

My first concern was getting Victoria to safety. Her grip on me was starting to weaken, and her chest was thumping against my back in an irregular rhythm. The Councilwoman needed medical attention—now. I caught sight of Erik and Janelle making a beeline for one of our crafts. I decided to follow. There, medics would be able to tend to her injuries before it was too late.

The underbelly of the hoverplane was still open from when our troops had exited. Erik soared through ahead of me. By the time my talons were skidding to a stop across the metal flooring, he was human and helping Janelle up a ladder to a second level. Like the enormous craft I'd flown across the country on, this one belonged to the Council and was large enough to carry the population of a small island nation.

Unceremoniously, I dumped Victoria on the floor of the craft. When she cried out in pain, I felt guilty. The transformation from bird to human was quick. I'd become very proficient in my short time as a Morpher. I helped Victoria to her feet and draped one of her arms around my shoulders just before she passed out. She so better not contain me, I thought as I hauled her dead weight to the ladder. Two sets of hands reached down through the opening at the top and relieved me of my burden.

I didn't recognize either person, but they were both wearing scrubs and those were good enough credentials for me. After Victoria went up, Erik came down.

"Quick thinking down there," I told him. *"You saved our lives."*

"Yeah, well someone had to," he sent back with a grin. Then he sobered. *"Did you see what's happening on the ground?"*

"You mean how our people are getting their asses kicked?" I asked.

"I don't know what to do. They're too... too much for us. UNITED should just obliterate the entire city. Victoria was right, the Created are too dangerous."

"You don't mean that," I said. *"They deserve a chance to be cured. Most probably don't even understand why they're fighting."*

"*There isn't a cure yet, Tals. We don't know that there ever will be.*"

"*There will be,*" I shot back angrily. "*There has to be.*"

Erik blew out a breath and folded me into his arms. He kissed the top of my matted curls. "*The Hamilton?*" he asked.

"*The Hamilton,*" I agreed.

"*You lead, I'll follow.*"

I stood on my tiptoes and kissed him softly. Then I turned and sprinted the short distance to the opening, dove headfirst into the emptiness below, and once again Morphed in midair. I felt him as bird Erik drew even with me. Together, we dodged stray gunfire, circled skyways, and managed to take out several TOXIC sharpshooters en route to The Hamilton. The luxury hotel wasn't hard to spot; it was one of the tallest buildings in the city. I kept my focus on the square rooftop so I wouldn't have to see what was happening below.

Get rid of Mac and this will all end, I kept telling myself.

I had no idea whether that was true. In my mind, it was, though. In my mind, Mac's death would set the world right again.

Five operatives were standing guard on the roof of The Hamilton. One stood at each corner like a gargoyle warding off evil; too bad the real evil was already inside. The fifth was stationed at the door to the inside. They followed us with their guns, but no one took a shot. I guessed that they weren't sure which side we were on. Erik answered that question when he suddenly darted forward, his right wing fully extended, and swatted one of the operatives over the side of the roof. The person toppled forward, Morphing from dog, to tiger, to horse, and finally backed to human in time to splat on the sidewalk below.

Guess being multi-Talented is only handy if you know how to use all those Talents, I thought.

Gunfire burst forth from the remaining four operatives, none of whom were exceptional shots. I used evasive tactics to avoid the bullets, but Erik met the challenge. He dove at one operative, catching the woman between his enormous wings and tossing her into the air. I knew this was a kill-or-be-killed situation, but I was having a hard time getting my body on board with that train of thought.

Now that the odds were slightly better for us, I considered Morphing back to human. One of the remaining operatives was trying to grab hold of Erik's feathers as Erik sunk his talons into the guy's adapti-suit. The operative who'd been blocking the roof entrance to the hotel charged forward, gun drawn, and fired at Erik's head. I landed on the roof, Morphing at precisely the right time so that my boots slid over the rooftop instead of talons. I deflected the bullets before they found the mark. Then, I tore weapons from hands and belts to alleviate one obstacle.

The two operatives not actively engaged in wing-to-hand combat, rounded on me. I took a deep breath and readied myself for a physical fight. One of them evaporated into thin air, and the next thing I knew, the heel of his boot found a home in my lower back. I screamed in pain as I pitched forward. His friend rushed forward and delivered an uppercut to my jaw with enough force to rattle my teeth.

A sick cracking noise that sounded a lot like a wooden board being snapped in half distracted me long enough for the rear attacker to land a roundhouse kick between my shoulder blades. All the breath whooshed out of my lungs. I was getting my ass kicked. I fully expected the front attacker to hit me again. Through blurred vision I saw Erik, now human, materialize in the minute space between us. With lightning-fast reflexes, Erik caught the operative's fist in his open palm and twisted. I shut down my auditory senses so I wouldn't have to hear another bone breaking.

I whirled around to go another round with the guy behind me. He stared me directly in the eyes, opened his mouth to say something, and then fell flat on his face. I gaped. What just happened? Without getting any closer to him, I looked for blood. There didn't appear to be any. I sniffed the air. No, no coppery scent.

"Come on, Tals. Gotta move if we want to get to the Director before he escapes." Erik's arm was around my waist, dragging me towards the rooftop entrance to the hotel.

"Did you see that?" I asked. *"That guy, he just... fell."*

"You have a guardian angel," Erik sent back, pausing at the door to listen and feel for signs of life from the other side. He looked to me for confirmation that no minds were buzzing close by. I shook my head no.

"That's not it. He isn't dead. I don't think," I said.

Erik tried to twist the knob. When it wouldn't budge, I disengaged the lock with my mind.

"He's not moving, which means he's not attacking. That's all that matters."

Erik held up a hand, signaling for me to wait while he made sure the stairwell was clear. I ignored his silent order and followed directly behind him, easing the door closed and reengaging the lock.

The stairwell was pitch black. I heard the hum of a generator somewhere deep within the building, and assumed it was being used to supply power to areas where it was necessary, like Mac's suite. My eyes adjusted quickly, and I was able to make out the faint outline of the steps and handrail.

"Take my hand." Erik reached back and wiggled his fingers at me.

"I can see," I sent back.

"*Yeah and you can also be seen. I'm going to try making both of us invisible. As long as you're touching me, it should work.*"

"*Should?*"

"*Cadence was able to do it. I'm not as experienced with light manipulation, but my Talent for it is stronger than hers ever was, even with the amplification drug.*"

I threaded my fingers through his and waited for something to happen. When it did, I wished it hadn't. I didn't like not being able to see myself. It was like I'd ceased to exist.

"*It's okay, Tals. You're still here, just invisible. Hold on to me.*"

I did as instructed and Erik started down the stairs. Our footsteps were quiet, but still audible. It seemed pretty silly for Erik to waste the energy making us invisible if our shoes were just going to give us away. I kept my opinions to myself, since Erik wasn't likely to appreciate them.

One short flight of stairs, and then a four by four landing, followed by another ten metal steps, and we were at the door to the penthouse level of The Hamilton. I found that I was holding my breath as the door eased open just a crack. A thin beam of soft yellow light shot into the blackened stairwell from the emergency bulbs in the hallway. I closed my eyes and concentrated on counting the minds on the penthouse level. Four. I counted just four. That meant only three guards stood between us and Mac. There were more on the lower levels, but the symphony of gunfire and grunts told me they were occupied.

Coward, I thought as Erik slipped into the hallway with me a beat behind him. Mac was a coward. His operatives, his people, were fighting and dying because he was too weak to accept punishment for his crimes.

"*Two at the door. One must be inside with him,*" Erik sent.

"*Yeah, I see them.*"

Two guards stood sentinel on either side of the door to Mac's suite. One, the male, was exactly what I'd expected. He was close to two feet taller than me, just shy of seven foot, and probably weighed as much as a small hovercar. Hard muscle rippled under his adapti-suit as he rolled his shoulders and then jogged in place.

It was the woman—a girl, really—who stopped me in my tracks. She was tall and thin with hair the color of milky coffee and eyes that matched. Kenly Baker. My protégé. What the hell was she doing here?

"Tal? What's wrong?" Erik tugged on my hand.

"I know her," I said, dumbstruck. *"That's Kenly. The girl I was training for her Hunters' tryout. She... she shouldn't be here. This isn't right."*

Kenly glanced in our direction and squinted her eyes like she trying to see something a great distance away. I stopped breathing. Could she see us?

"Do you see something down there?" she asked her partner.

Mr. Muscles barely looked before answering, "Nah."

I exhaled slowly.

Kenly wasn't convinced, but she let it go.

"What do you want to do?" Erik asked.

What did I want to do? I wanted Kenly to not be here. Her presence complicated matters too much. Killing the nameless operatives at Tramblewood, even the ones in Gatlinburg, had been hard enough. She was my friend. No way was I going to harm her. Unfortunately, she was also in my way. I'd have to go through her to get to Mac.

"Tals?"

"I'm thinking," I shot back.

"Not to be an ass, Tal, but could you think faster? The natives sound a little restless downstairs."

I bit my tongue to keep from audibly groaning. *"Fine. You take the big one. Let me deal with her."*

"I was going to suggest that anyway."

"How chivalrous of you." Sarcasm lost something when used mentally. *"Erik? No matter what, don't kill her."*

"No. No deal. If she gets the upper hand with you, I'm taking her out."

"Erik," I begged.

Erik started forward without another word, leaving me no choice except to follow unless I wanted to suddenly appear in the middle of the hallway.

Fine, I thought, I just need to incapacitate her before Erik finishes with the oaf.

We crept so close to the duo that I felt the big guy's hot breath on my face. Onions, he'd eaten onions recently. I stopped breathing through my nose.

"Count of three?" Erik asked.

"One," I said.

"Two," Erik added.

And on three we broke apart. My forearm was corporeal when it slammed into Kenly's throat. Her eyes bugged and she looked like she was going to be sick all over me. I didn't hesitate before using the heel of my other hand to knock her head into the wall behind her. This should've put her down for the count. Her eyes crossed and she wobbled like a newborn animal unused to her legs, but she remained conscious.

"Talia?" she asked, sounding confused.

I clapped a hand over her mouth and was about to slam her against the wall for a second time, when I felt a sharp jab between two of my ribs. I glanced down. Kenly had the tip of a knife jammed directly below my heart.

"Kenly," I said in a voice barely above a whisper, "You don't want to do this."

Indecision flickered across her gaze, and the knife went in a little farther. The fabric of my suit was bearing the brunt of the force, and I was pretty confident the blade wasn't going to actually penetrate.

Before I could plead with her further, Erik's hand shot between us, knocking Kenly's hand and the knife upwards. The weapon flew across the hallway, skidded across the polished floor, and smacked into the wall with a thud. Erik had Kenly by the throat and was squeezing the breath from her.

"Erik, please. I don't think she knows what's going on."

"Get the Director, Tals. He'll have heard the commotion."

Kenly was clawing at Erik's fingers to no avail. I noticed that while he had her pinned to the wall, he wasn't actually strangling her.

"I'll be right behind you," Erik added.

He glanced down at me with murderous rage that made his irises glow. It scared me. He scared me. Even more terrifying was that I saw the same rage reflected in Kenly's eyes now. When she'd looked at me, she seemed confused, maybe a little lost. Now... now she looked like something not quite human.

"Go," Erik growled to me.

I didn't hesitate any longer. Mac was so close I could practically smell the expensive cologne he sometimes wore. And Erik didn't want me to see what he was about to do. He was trying to spare me the pain of watching Kenly die. His patience was wearing thin, though. Erik wanted Mac as much as I did.

He stood alone in front of a glass wall, arms crossed over his chest, and watched as the capital burned. Shoulders rounded, head hung, Mac kept his back to me as I slowly closed, and locked, the door to the suite behind me. I saw his reflection in the glass, superimposed over the fingers of orange flames that reached higher and higher until they gripped the top of the building directly across from The Hamilton and tore it to the ground. There was no sound to accompany the chaos; it was like watching a muted wallscreen.

"Natalia." Mac's tone was flat, lacking even the tiniest hint of inflection when he said my name.

"It's over, Mac," I told him, taking three more steps into the opulent suite.

Mac laughed humorlessly. "No, no, Natalia. 'It' is far from over." He turned, slow and deliberate, to pierce me with cold eyes the same silver as the blade Kenly had nearly shoved into my chest.

"You're trapped, Mac. You can't escape," I told him, even though I wasn't sure that was technically true. I had no idea who was winning the fight outside The Hamilton's walls, or within them for that matter. I wasn't even sure that anyone could be called a 'winner' in the wake of so much destruction.

My bluff fell on deaf ears. Mac kept talking as if I hadn't spoken.

"My vision has been realized. Others understand and agree that the Talented are superior to the rest of the population. We are more than human, Natalia. We are a class unto ourselves. And this new breed of Talents, well, they are superior still to you and I. They can and will take over the world."

"You're crazier than they are," I told him.

"You must have seen that for yourself," Mac continued, ignoring me once again. "If nothing else, you have seen what your own boyfriend is now capable of."

Mac raised a questioning eyebrow, finally seemingly to truly acknowledge my presence. I said nothing. I had seen what Erik could do. Before Mac's interference, Erik had been lethal. But he'd been controlled, too. Now that control was slipping. My own control was only hanging on by a frayed thread. In the past, I'd been quick to defend, but rarely was I the aggressor. Since being injected with the Creation drug, I was more willing to let my more basic instincts guide my actions, instead of my conscience.

"Why?" I asked Mac.

"Why?" he parroted. "Our race was becoming extinct, Natalia. Each generation has far fewer Talents than the one before it. Those that are blessed with gifts, are weak. Half the children at the School are unable to move a pebble with their minds, see further into the future than tomorrow, or view a person not related to them. The Created?" Mac's eyes lit up with unabashed glee. "The Created can move mountains. They can bend armies to their wills. They do not just see the future; they are the future."

My blood ran cold. Mac had just confirmed my worst fears. A dull ache started behind my eyeballs, causing the right one to twitch. My hands, fisted at my sides, started to shake. Mac grinned.

"Don't you want to be a part of that future, Natalia?" he asked. "The Created do have a flaw. I am sure you have heard. The power makes them unstable, unpredictable. Given the right environment and guidance, they are easily controlled. The weaker their minds become, the more nurturing they need. You, though, were born with more Talent than can be engineered in a lab. You have lived with the power your entire life. You could teach them how to control it, help them cultivate their abilities, lead them into tomorrow."

The pressure inside my head was building. It felt like air was being pumped into both of my ears, and I had no way to let it out. There were voices, too. They seemed to be struggling to be heard over one another. And then, without warning, my head emptied. I sagged and tried to focus on the reason I'd come to the hotel room in the first place, only I couldn't remember why that was.

A solitary thought sprang up from the blank landscape inside of my brain, like the first flower to bloom after a long winter. I thought, maybe Mac was right. Maybe I could help the Created.

Maybe, like me, they could learn to control their Talents. Who better to teach them? Not only was I naturally more Talented than most, but I'd been blessed with an extra gift more recently. Sure, it had been difficult at first, but now, now I was great at Morphing. The mood swings were easier to cope with now, too.

Mac had uncrossed his arms and he was holding a hand out in my direction. The smile on his lips was inviting, concerned, and, most importantly, loving. I smiled back.

"This is what Francis wanted for you," Mac told me.

I froze mid-step.

"He saw your potential. Just like I saw Donavon's. It was such a shame that my son wasn't born Talented, like you. That is why I had to help him along. He was so even-tempered, so wonderful at maintaining control. The two of you were so perfect together, Natalia. If not for the tragedy in Kentucky, he could have helped you lead the Created."

The voices were back, too many to count. They invaded my mind simultaneously, each demanding something different from me. I couldn't think, couldn't focus. My own thoughts were like stars, too small and too distant to touch. I shook my head and tried to regroup. Concentrate, I ordered myself. Inhaling deeply, I picked the brightest star and willed it closer until it formed an image in my mind.

"You killed him," I said. "He was your flesh and blood, your son, and you killed him." Each accusation came out uglier than the one before it, and suddenly I remembered why I was here.

"No, Natalia, it was an accident," Mac said calmly. "Don't you remember?"

The pressure started to build again, but this time I was ready for it. I slammed my mental walls into place as realization dawned on me.

"Where is he Mac? Where's your new pet Manipulator?" That was the fourth mind Erik and I had felt. The stupid Manipulator from Gatlinburg.

Mac applauded me. "Bravo, Natalia. Except, it isn't a 'he'."

Three things happened simultaneously: the door to the suite blew off of its hinges, the glass behind Mac shattered into millions of tiny icicles, and Gretchen stepped out from the shadows.

"Both of them. Secure both of them," Erik barked from behind me, as Coalition soldiers and UNITED guards poured into the suite.

"Danbury McDonough, you are under arrest," a voice boomed through the loudspeaker of the hoverplane now shining its spotlight through the nonexistent window. "Down on your knees, or we will shoot."

"Gretchen? No," I whispered, shaking my head. Not the woman who'd been so nice to me, so much like a real mother.

I watched as UNITED guards surrounded her. Thick metal cuffs were clamped around her wrists.

"Tranquilize her," Erik ordered. "She's too dangerous."

"No," I repeated dumbly.

I felt numb. This couldn't really be happening. I'd come to terms with Mac being corrupt a long time ago. But Gretchen? I pinched the delicate skin on the side of my neck, hoping that would jolt me out of this parallel reality and back to the one where at least part of the last eight years hadn't been a lie.

One of the guards held a small, strange-looking gun up to Gretchen's neck and pulled the trigger. I winced and she swayed. Her eyes rolled around in their sockets like marbles before latching onto me.

"You could've been great," she sent, and then her lids fluttered closed, long mascaraed lashes resting on sharp cheekbones.

"You are great," another voice told me, as a familiar arm drew me into a familiar body.

He wasn't a lie. He was real and good and all that I needed in the world.

Erik held me as another group of guards led a shackled Mac from the hotel suite. I wondered if this was poetic justice. My parents had been murdered in a hotel suite not so different from this one, and now their murderer had finally been caught.

Chapter Twenty-One

THE DAYS THAT followed were hazy. After Gretchen and Mac had been taken into custody, the battle died quickly. Some TOXIC operatives surrendered, while others fled. Those identified as Created were immediately contained. The McDonough School had been turned into a makeshift containment facility, and anyone and everyone still living who'd worked on the Creation Project was being called in to help deal with the problem. The real problem, though, was how many of the Created had escaped. Even more troubling? The Council had no idea how large that number truly was. If Mac had kept records of all those he'd injected, he'd hidden them well.

Crane, who'd been there to see Mac and Gretchen apprehended, was helping the Council question the TOXIC higher-ups and rebuild the capital. It was his belief that as long as the Created were still running rampant, my life was in danger. This meant I was under twenty-four hour a day protection. I thought the measure unnecessary, but Victoria, who was making a speedy recovery, agreed. Personally, I thought she was more concerned with me running rampant around the world than Mac's experiments, and was just using the whole life-in-danger angle as an excuse to keep an eye on me. I didn't much care.

Councilman Michael Tanaka had a Virginia home that was located close enough to the capital that Crane and Victoria could use it as a temporary residence, but far enough that it hadn't been obliterated along with most of the rest of the northern part of the state. That was where I was hidden away. Erik, of course, came with me.

Mac had been tipped off about our plan to use the tunnels for a ground attack, which was why we'd been ambushed. No one in TOXIC who'd been questioned so far knew who the mole was, and Mac wasn't talking. But I had my suspicions. Truthfully, it could have been anyone. Every Coalition soldier and UNITED guard present during our strategy meetings knew about the plan. For some reason, I felt confident none of them had been the source of the leak. Two others had been informed of our plan to use the tunnels. One of whom had spent six years in a TOXIC prison, and was probably willing to do anything for his freedom.

Randy Choi was at the top of my suspect list. I didn't share these concerns with Crane or Victoria. I wasn't worried about what they'd do to him; he deserved the punishment. Cadence was the one I cared about. She'd be devastated to learn her brother had betrayed us. Until I was certain, I would keep my theories to myself. With everything else going on, it wasn't exactly a high priority.

Frederick's knowledge of the old metrorail system was all that had saved him and Henri from being killed after the rest of our team had gone ahead. The two of them, along with the two UNITED guards who'd stayed behind, had hidden in one of the branches. Three days passed before the four of them were found. Nearly dehydrated and totally exhausted, Frederick had been taken to a medical facility to recover. The other three had been treated

316

for minor injuries and released. Victoria, though reluctant at first, had given Henri permission to stay at the Councilman's house with Erik and me.

It was Adam and his people who had suffered for our arrogance regarding the tunnels. TOXIC had found the camp and used it as a base for their counterattack. Many of the inhabitants had been killed, many more unaccounted for. Mr. Kelley was among the missing. Much of the fight had actually occurred beneath the ground, causing massive cave-ins and total destruction of several sections of the system. UNITED had formed a search-and-rescue team to locate the survivors. Every morning, Erik and I watched the giant wallscreen in Councilman Tanaka's office for the updated list of names of both the living and the dead. I constantly reminded Erik that it was a blessing his father hadn't turned up in the casualty column.

The Councilman's estate was impressive, like a palace out of the history books. It was post-Contamination era. The white marble foyer was covered in swirls of black and gray, that brought to mind images of smoking buildings and scorched earth. A ballroom, large enough for three of the Council's huge hoverplanes, was through a short hallway lined with moving images of Michael's daughter and wife back in Fujisawa. The floors were polished to gleaming perfection, and the chandeliers looked like vines of diamonds suspended in midair. I tried to avoid the cavernous space; it gave me the creeps.

The guest wing was in the back left corner of the mansion. That was where Crane and Victoria slept, when they did sleep. They spent most nights questioning TOXIC personnel who'd been captured or surrendered, and planning ways to locate those who hadn't. Erik and I had rooms in the family wing. Councilman Tanaka thought that would make us feel more at home. I wasn't sure I'd feel at home anywhere. It had been years since I had a home.

Joy Tanaka, the Councilman's teenage daughter, and her mother were at their Bern house near UNITED Headquarters, under the protection of the UNITED guards. I was offered the use of Joy's bedroom. The room was not small, but the abundance of furniture made the space feel tight. A double bed was pushed into the far left corner, the length of which ran underneath a bay window complete with a window seat. There was a sleek wooden desk with neatly-stacked piles of books and a free-standing computer monitor. A purple velvet throw hung over the back of a gray chaise lounge that was covered with beautiful silk pillows. Most notable were the picture collages hung on the walls. When I was alone, I studied the pictures of Joy and her friends and wondered whether I'd ever have ones like them. The girl was happy, always smiling and carefree. She was probably two or three years younger than me and made me think of Kenly.

I hadn't asked Erik what had become of my protégé. Part of me was scared to hear the truth. Her body hadn't been slumped outside of Mac's hotel suite like her partner's. I liked to think she'd escaped; although, that prospect was upsetting, too. On her own, hiding during the day and running under the cover of darkness, she'd be easy prey for all sorts of creatures. At the School she'd been sheltered, and I doubted her survival instincts were all that great. Mine weren't, and I'd spent nearly a year with the Hunters developing them.

"Ready for this?"

I looked up from a photo album of Joy's I'd found in her two-level walk-in closet. In it, she had beautiful prints of exotic locations all over the world. It had occurred to me that I'd been to many of these same places. The landmarks were vaguely familiar, yet I had no actual memory of visiting them.

Erik stood in the doorway of the bedroom, more handsome than ever in a dark gray suit and button-down three shades lighter. He appeared calm, but I felt his unease with the formal attire. Normally he enjoyed dressing up; Erik was fully aware of how well he wore a suit. Today, though, under the circumstances, he felt like it was all for show.

"Ready as I'll ever be," I said, snapping the album shut and tossing it aside.

I uncrossed my short legs and slid off the bed. As I stood, I straightened my own suit jacket self-consciously. My jacket and slacks were black and fitted, with faint white pinstripes. Victoria had delivered the garments the previous evening, along with an invitation to accompany her to UNITED's maximum security prison colony, Oceania. Currently, only two inmates were in residence.

Erik held out his hand to me, and I slid my fingers seamlessly into his.

"You don't have to go just because she asked for you," Erik told me as we started the hike through Councilman Tanaka's winding hallways.

The house was a maze, and I normally took one or two wrong turns before getting out of the family wing. On my first late-night visit to Erik—the Councilman said us sharing a bedroom was indecent—I'd ended up in this bizarre indoor rainforest. The air was soupy and smelled like rain, and the trees were brown with lush green leaves and looked like the ones found in textbooks from before the Great Contamination. There were even insects and birds and species of snakes that hadn't been seen on earth in over a hundred years. Erik had found me using our mental connection, and we'd spent the night making out by a mossy pond.

I smiled at the memory. We'd had little opportunity to make good ones lately. Besides getting to talk to Alex and Evan on the huge visual communicator in Michael's home office, the past week had been pretty depressing. Seeing Alex's smiling face and knowing he was safe was a daily pick-me-up that I craved. Watching Evan's hopeful expression fall when Erik told him we still didn't know whether their father was alive, I dreaded.

"I need to," I said, coming back to the present.

"Figured you'd say that."

Victoria wasn't alone in the foyer. Penny, dressed in a suit identical to mine, appeared polished and mature. As where I'd chosen flats so I wouldn't fall on my face and make a fool of myself, Penny was in four-inch black leather heels with a silver toe. She wiggled one in my direction when she caught me gawking.

"Brand went to Bern to meet with some of the Council; he took a day trip to Milan just for these."

Brand turned a brilliant shade of oxblood and muttered something about it being no big deal. Penny beamed. I hated Brand a little less.

"We should get going," Crane said. "I want to get this over with."

"You?" I asked. "I'm the one she wants to talk to."

Despite the best efforts of UNITED's interrogators, Gretchen was keeping her vault of secrets locked. Enough TOXIC researchers were spilling theirs that her testimony wasn't strictly necessary. Nothing she said could help her now anyway. But after over a week of silence, she'd agreed to talk, on one condition. She wanted to talk to me. From an unauthorized peek into Crane's head the previous night, I'd learned that Victoria, Crane, and the other powers-that-be had given this request lengthy consideration before finally relaying it to me.

"I know. It worries me," Crane admitted. "She's used her Talent to control several interrogators already, and nearly escaped because of it. I don't want her doing that to you."

He didn't add that she already had, twice.

"We have been over this, Ian," Victoria said sweetly. "Ms. Lyons is prepared and will be taking precautions to prevent Mrs. McDonough from doing the same to her. Right, dear?"

I nodded. Precautions weren't how I'd put it, but I was aware Gretchen could manipulate me, and I figured that was one step towards preventing it from happening again.

The flight to Oceania took an hour. We flew on a sleek hovercraft that looked more like a luxury passenger plane used for civilian travel than a military vessel. Had it not been outfitted with attack lasers—better than standard guns, according to Victoria— I'd have thought she'd stolen it from one of the private hoverlines.

The main cabin was fashioned to look like a living room. Semicircular couches sat on either side with bolted-down glass tables in front of each. I'd hoped for some privacy to collect my thoughts and figure out what I wanted to say to Gretchen. That was not an option. Instead, Victoria gave us a history lesson.

The Oceania had not been designed as a prison originally. It had been built as a safe haven for Talents approximately twenty years after the Great Contamination. At the time, Talents were being persecuted, and the newly-founded UNITED worried a time would come when they would need a place to live, separate and apart from the rest of society. The Oceania, and other colonies like it, had been built in the one place the non-Talented were unwilling to go: the middle of the water. Because many had believed the nuclear waste floating around in the waterways was what had led to our Talents in the first place, no one wanted to risk infection by getting too close. Entire island nations had been quarantined, cut out from the rest of the world, just in case Talents were contagious. This gave UNITED the idea to build floating islands in the middle of the oceans.

Few of these colonies had ever been inhabited. With UNITED's help, most countries had instituted laws to protect the Talented.

To date, five such colonies were active. They all held refugees from the more conservative nations, the ones who still ostracized the Talented. UNITED used others of these floating meccas, like The Oceania, as operation bases. Victoria didn't elaborate on what operations UNITED ran from them.

I found myself fascinated by her story. All of this was new information for me. At the McDonough School—I wondered if they'd rename it—students were required to take the History of Talents. Interestingly, this part of our history hadn't been covered.

"They probably worried we'd go live on one if they told us," Erik sent.

"I might have," I agreed.

The colonies were news to Crane, Penny, and Brand, too. All three of them sat wide-eyed and at attention as Victoria explained that, even though scientists had failed to find a direct link between contaminated water and the mutation that makes us Talented, few conservatives were willing to dip a toe in the water.

"Has UNITED maintained all of the colonies for the past eighty years or whatever?" I interrupted her at one point.

"Yes we have," Victoria said proudly.

"Isn't that expensive?" Erik asked.

"UNITED has deep pockets, Mr. Kelley. Besides, the time may be fast-approaching when the colonies will once again be necessary."

"What? Why?" Penny asked.

"The Created are a danger to the progress the Talented have made in the more reluctant nations. You all forget, the United States is a progressive nation. It was the first to grant Talents equal rights and pass protection laws."

"Yeah, that mandatory testing law really protects us," Erik muttered.

Victoria eyed him coolly. "UNITED does not agree with the mandatory testing laws as they are interpreted today, Mr. Kelley. But when they were first crafted, the purpose was to identify Talented children so that they could be sheltered from those who meant them harm. You have no idea what it was like for the early generations," her eyes flashed with barely contained anger, "what it is still like for many in other countries. If the Created are not caught and contained, we, the Talented, may be forced into exile."

Chapter Twenty-Two

FROM ABOVE, THE Oceania looked like a titanium island. It was huge, one mile in length and half as wide, according to Victoria. Like Crane's cottage, the sublevels were the heart of the structure. Two hundred floors stretched miles underneath the water's calm, crystalline surface.

We touched down on a small runway on the east end of Oceania. A crew of UNITED guards were waiting on our arrival. The head guard, Captain Klegg, was a man of few words and even fewer strands of hair. His mocha skin had been turned to dark chocolate by the sun's rays. Tour guide was not in his job description, apparently, so I was left to wonder about the strange glass pods that littered the main level.

Erik matched my short stride, keeping a firm grip on my hand despite Victoria's pointed glares at our twined fingers. Neither of us cared about professionalism or whatever; we both needed the comfort only physical contact could provide. Even Brand seemed to understand how difficult facing Mac and Gretchen would be, and he took hold of Penny's hand and didn't let go as we followed Captain Klegg to the elevator.

The inside of the car was three walls of thick glass, all tinted aqua. I felt like a curtain had been draped over my head, casting a watery haze over the world. There were no buttons or control panels on the walls.

"Captain Johan Klegg," a mechanical voice with a faint British accent announced once we were all aboard. "Identify your companions."

"High security," Erik mused.

"Agreed," I sent back.

Biometric identification was common in TOXIC's secure facilities. Coalition Headquarters had palm scanners outside certain doors. So, this was nothing new for me. Victoria had said that the Oceania wasn't strictly a prison. They'd only taken Mac and Gretchen here because it was one of the few places where escape was futile. Even if either McDonough managed to break free from their captors, there was nowhere to go. The hovers were all programmed for specific individuals with limited override permissions. The fleet of minisubs moored at three locations around the island was the same way. Only those assigned to The Oceania could leave The Oceania. Mac and Gretchen were decent swimmers, but the closest land was hundreds of miles away. Apparently, making it up the elevator was unlikely, too.

Each of us was directed to say our full names in clear, concise tones. The computer took its time processing our voices and matching them to voiceprints stored in some unseen database. I wondered when Victoria had compiled the information, but decided that wasn't important right now.

After the computer was satisfied that we were all authorized personnel, Captain Klegg instructed the elevator to take us to AF3.

My ears popped, and my chest felt like a small child was sitting on it. The farther we descended into the ocean, the worse the sensation became. AF3 turned out to be the deepest sublevel of The Oceania—the ocean floor. The sublevel was made entirely of thick, transparent plastic, and I could easily see all of the individual rooms that covered the mile-long floor.

"Freaky," Erik sent.

I nodded, too awed to speak.

Down here everyone wore white. Doctors were in one room to the left of the elevator, and were busy measuring colorful liquids in tube-shaped vials. I recognized the woman with the pink hair from the strategy meeting. Today she wore big goggles that obscured her eyes as she worked with the chemicals.

"That is where our researchers develop drugs and medications for the Talented," Victoria said, catching my eye. "Many of the compounds they work with are highly volatile. Much like many Talents themselves." Victoria gestured towards me, but I let the comment go. "Each sublevel can be locked and segregated from the rest of the levels in the event of an accident." There was a note of pride in her voice.

Captain Klegg was leading our group down a long corridor. Most of the rooms held hospital-style beds and state-of-the-art medical machines. None were occupied, but all appeared to be clean and well maintained.

"This is our sick bay. The clear walls make it easy to observe the patients," Victoria explained.

"Are you thinking of using this as a containment facility?" Brand asked.

It was the first time he'd spoken since we'd landed on The Oceania, and he sounded just as fascinated by the island as I was.

"Quite likely, Mr. Meadows," Victoria answered.

We reached the end of the hallway. To the left was another see-through hallway, lined with more rooms. The closest looked like a cafeteria. To the right was a solid, steel-reinforced door marked, "Authorized Personnel Only." A lone guard, a woman with the name Mashburn sewn over her left breast, saluted Captain Klegg.

"Mashburn, these are the visitors I was telling you about," Captain Klegg told her.

Mashburn had olive skin that appeared ashen, like she'd spent a lot of time down here as opposed to on deck. Her dark hair was cut short and threaded with blue highlights. Bags hung under her reddish-purple eyes that were heavy with exhaustion and devoid of any makeup. The most notable thing about Mashburn was the power she emitted. She was an extremely strong Talent with energy practically pouring off of her.

"All preparations are in place, sir," she said. Her accent was thicker than Victoria's, and not as polished.

Captain Klegg turned to address our group. "The prisoner has asked to speak with you alone, Ms. Lyons. Obviously the decision is yours. President Crane or Councilman Walburton may accompany you, or two of my guards can."

I exchanged glances with first Erik, and then Crane. We all knew these were Gretchen's terms. I was willing to speak with her alone, but neither man thought it was a good idea.

"I'll go by myself," I told Captain Klegg.

He nodded his balding head. "Very well. Mashburn will take you to the pod. The rest of you may join me in observation."

I released Erik's hand. He bent down and kissed my cheek. *"Remember, you can end this whenever you want,"* he sent.

"I know," I sent back.

"We will be watching, Ms. Lyons. If things get out of control, we will get you out," Victoria told me. Even she sounded nervous.

Not good, I thought.

"I understand," I said.

The group waited while Mashburn went through the necessary authorization protocols to open the heavy steel door. Finally, after what felt like hours, the door swung outwards with a loud whoosh. Without looking at my friends, I followed Mashburn through. The moment I crossed the threshold, the door closed, the locks settled back into place.

I looked around and found myself in a giant plastic tube, just wide enough for me to skim my fingertips along the sides if I stretched my arms out and tall enough even Henri would have been able to stand up straight. Dark sapphire water cast an eerie blue light over the entire tube, including the guards lining both sides. Large fish swam by in a neon rainbow. The walkway beneath my feet was several inches off the bottom of the tube, which sat directly on the seafloor. Plants swayed with the movement of the water, brushing against the sides of the tube as we walked.

"Our researchers have been working on restoring the marine life that lived in this region before the Great Contamination." Mashburn spoke in a soft voice, but it echoed loudly in the tube. "Using DNA from fossils, they have been successful in restoring the ecosystem in this area. As you can see, the scientists have taken some liberties." She shrugged her thin shoulders sheepishly. "We don't have a lot to look at down here. The pretty fish spice it up a little."

Under different circumstances, I would have found this all very interesting. But confronting Gretchen dominated my thoughts, and I found I had little room in my head for any others. So, I simply said, "Cool."

"Mrs. McDonough is in a pod at the end of the hallway," Mashburn said.

"Pod?" I asked. Captain Klegg had called it a pod, too. I'd thought maybe I'd misheard him, but now that Mashburn had used the same term, I was sure I hadn't.

"When The Oceania was built, the architect put in several prison pods. They're glass bubbles located on the ocean floor. Each one is self-contained with a bed, bathroom, and enough dehydrated food to last a year. It's worse than solitary. We can observe the prisoner at all times since the pods are entirely transparent. Zero privacy. Both the McDonoughs are in pods. Not together, of course."

We came to a three-way fork in the hallway. Mashburn indicated the right prong, and we entered another tube. This one was identical to the last, except approximately ten meters down, the hallway ended at a steel door with a black square where a handle should've been. It was marked, "Prison Pod Two."

"The door only opens from this side," Mashburn advised me as we neared the entrance to Gretchen's pod. "Should you need help, we can have it open in under ten seconds. For safety reasons, we don't allow weapons in the pods."

"I understand," I said.

The no weapons rule was smart. If Gretchen overpowered me and got her hands on a gun or something, I'd be dead before the door was open.

"I'll be right here," Mashburn said, and then gestured to the other guards stationed in this prong of the tube. "They'll be here, too. You have nothing to worry about."

That's what you think, I thought.

"Ready?" she asked me.

I nodded.

This time the authorization protocols seemed to go through in the blink of an eye. Before I knew it, I was standing inside the pod, face-to-face with Gretchen McDonough.

"Talia, dear, so good of you to come."

Gretchen stood in the middle of the pod between a twin bed with crisp, perfectly straight white sheets and a small rubber cabinet. Behind Gretchen was a toilet, sink, and shower stall. The ceiling was sloped. Where I'd entered the pod, it was low enough my ponytail touched the plastic. In the center of the pod, where Gretchen was standing, the ceiling reached its peak of about seven feet. The diameter was no more than ten feet long. All-in-all, extremely claustrophobic.

"You wanted to talk to me," I said stiffly.

Staring into Gretchen's bright blue eyes made my chest ache; they were nearly identical to Donavon's. Only his eyes had been warm and caring. Hers were like icebergs, giving off the same frigid air that Mac's did. Gretchen's hair was neatly styled in a bun, and even though she wore no makeup, she was beautiful. Prison seemed to agree with her. Even the shapeless white pants and tunic looked chic on Gretchen.

Gretchen gestured to the bed, an invitation to sit like this was a social visit.

I ignored her hospitality. "What do you want, Gretchen?

I wasn't sure how I felt about her. Hating Mac had been easy, but it hadn't come over night either. I'd remained willfully ignorant for so long that when I finally accepted the truth about him, I was ready to hate him. Still, I never was confident that I could kill him when the time came. Gretchen, well, her betrayal hadn't really sunk in yet. Even seeing her in this pod prison, it was hard for me to believe she'd been a part of creating Talents. Maybe that was why I'd agreed to speak with her. Maybe I needed to hear the truth from her mouth.

Gretchen wrung her hands in front of her. "Talia, dear," she began, and the pressure started to build in the back of my skull.

"Stop it," I hissed through gritted teeth. My mental walls were already in place, but that didn't stop Gretchen from trying to invade my mind.

The pressure lessened slightly. It was now more like an itch on my brain.

"Why, Gretchen?" I asked. "Why'd you do it?"

I didn't know what exactly I expected her to say. Did I want her to tell me Mac had forced her to do it? Did I want her to tell me she was sorry?

"At one time we, the Talented, were plentiful. Strong Talents, like you, were the norm. Now?" She laughed that bitter laughter I'd come to associate with her husband. I shivered. "Now we're a minority. A minority, Talia. If we let nature run its course, the Talented will be extinct before too long. The Created are the answer. The Created are the way our kind will continue to thrive in this world."

"They aren't like us, Gretchen," I said. "The Created aren't natural. They aren't born with the power, and they can't control it."

As I watched her blue eyes grow wide and unfocused, I wondered if even those of us born with the power were able to control it.

"They are easily controlled, though. You, me, people like us, we can control the Created. That's why we wanted you, Talia. Few Mind Manipulators are strong enough to control so many people at once. Together, you and I could have led Danbury's army. We could have spread our gifts to all of the citizens of the United States."

"So that was your big plan?" I asked. "You wanted to make everyone Talented? Why?"

"Not everyone, dear. Just those who deserve it. Like my son. Donavon deserved to be Talented. His lineage was excellent for it. Yet somehow, he was born ordinary. But, you, you with two ordinary parents won the genetic lottery, and were born the strongest Mind Manipulator since the first generation of Talented. It's not fair. Well, the Creation drug takes genetics out of it. Now all the worthy can be Talented. As to the why? Given the choice, wouldn't you rather be Talented than not? I would. So would many of the ordinary."

Of course I would, I thought, but stopped the words before they slipped passed my lips. I wasn't willing to give Gretchen the satisfaction of agreeing with her. She knew I loved being Talented, that I craved the power my gifts brought with them. She'd been the first person to warn me against abusing my Talents, about taking advantage of others using them. I laughed humorlessly. Ironic, I thought.

I rubbed my temples. The headache had spread from the base of my skull, around the sides of my head, to settle above my eyes. I squinted; the dim light in the pod seemed to exacerbate the pain inside my head.

"Did you ask me here to prove you're the stronger Talent now?" I snapped. She was pounding on my mental walls, doing everything in her considerable power to break them down. It took everything I had to keep her out. She was more powerful than I remembered.

"No, dear." Gretchen's smile was somehow both sickeningly sweet and bitterly cold. "I asked you here because you are the strong Talent."

My heart skipped a beat. What the hell was she talking about?

The ache in my head reached a breaking point. It felt like my brain was fracturing. I closed my eyes, and tried to block the pain. A sound, like ice shattering, filled my ears. The air in the pod seemed to become thinner, making it harder to breathe. I started gasping for breath, but got a mouthful of water instead.

That was when I realized that the shattering ice noise wasn't in my head, and it wasn't ice. The dome top of the pod had splintered, allowing streams of ocean water in.

Ten seconds.

Ten seconds, that was how long Mashburn said it would take for the guards to open the pod door.

The cracks in the dome ceiling became larger. Ten seconds might be too long.

Streams of water turned to raging rivers. Water was filling to bottom of the pod. Cold and wet, it swirled around my ankles, soaking through my suit pants.

"What are you doing? Trying to drown us?" I screamed to be heard over the rushing water.

I started backing towards the solitary door. As soon as the guards had it open, I was out of here.

Gretchen said nothing. Her eyes started rolling around in their sockets, one blue orb going clockwise, the other going counter-clockwise. Then, a huge chunk in the center of the ceiling fell inward, flooding the pod.

Chapter Twenty-Three

THE IDEA TO Morph into one of the brightly-colored fish swimming nearby did occur to me. But before I had the opportunity, the door to the pod opened, sucking me towards it like a gigantic vacuum. The water and I rushed into the tube, knocking over Mashburn and the other guards trying to close the door behind me. I was tossed head over heels through the tube before finally being slammed into a wall, shoulder first.

I swore when my head followed my shoulder into the wall, and I received a mouthful of saltwater for my troubles. Splashing and the sound of my name followed. Then, pounding from the other side of the wall caught my attention.

Disoriented, I tried to put my feet down. At least, I thought that direction was down. Immense relief filled me when my flats found the metal walkway of the tube. With my feet firmly underneath me, I stood, and was surprised the water was only waist high.

Mashburn was wading through the seawater from the opposite end of the tube.

"Talia? Are you okay? We had to seal this part of the tube to prevent contamination in the other areas. We'll get it open as soon as we drain this tube." She was out of breath by the time she reached me.

"I'm good," I said, shrugging out of my suit jacket since it was weighing me down. "Did, did, Gretchen get away?" I asked through chattering teeth. The water was freezing.

I pushed past Mashburn, frantic to go after Gretchen. Mashburn grabbed me by the wrist. I whirled to face her, my dripping wet ponytail smacking my cheek.

"She's dead, Ms. Lyons. It's over two hundred miles to the surface. No one can hold their breath that long."

"What about the other pods?" I asked. "What if she got to one of them? Could she be running loose around The Oceania?"

"The pods only have one door. None of them have been breached. She's gone."

I stopped struggling. Gretchen was dead. I felt numb, and not just because my clothes were soaked through. Mac's death I'd envisioned. Hers, not so much. I'd thought watching Mac die would provide me with closure. I still didn't know for sure whether it would. But Gretchen's did not.

Slowly the water level in the tube started to go down.

"Mac?" I asked Mashburn. "Is he ...?"

"Like I said, none of the other pods have been breached. He's still in custody. At least we still have the mastermind of this whole fiasco."

The water had retreated almost completely. Only the small space beneath the walkway still held standing water.

Mashburn smiled, her lips thin and blue from cold. The other guards were walking towards us. "I'll get this door open," Mashburn said.

She tapped on the divider that had come down to section this tube from the others to prevent contamination. It looked like she was just hitting random spots on the divider, but I had a feeling it was interactive. As if to confirm this, the divider shot upwards a moment later, and Erik rushed into the tube.

He wrapped his arms around me, unperturbed by my wet clothes. He rubbed his palms furiously up and down my back to warm my skin. I buried my face in his jacket, pressing my cheek to his chest to siphon his body heat.

"I'm sorry," I murmured. "I'm so sorry."

"You couldn't have known this would happen," Erik muttered back.

"There are towels and dry clothes in the sick bay you can borrow," Mashburn said.

Erik and I followed Mashburn through the tubes, the other soldiers who'd gone for an impromptu swim bringing up the rear. Erik kept his arm around me, lending me his warmth while we walked.

"I can't believe she's dead," I sent. *"I mean, why'd she do it?"*

"I don't know, Tals," Erik replied. *"She was a very sick woman."*

"Right. But suicide? Seems extreme. And did she want me to die with her?"

"She'd been given the Creation drug. Maybe a lot of it. Her brain might have already deteriorated beyond repair. Crazy people do crazy things."

"I guess," I agreed.

After what happened with Gretchen, my request to visit Mac was denied. Honestly, I was sort of relieved. I had no idea what I wanted to talk to him about. He'd said all I needed to hear in that hotel room at The Hamilton. Gretchen had reiterated and expanded on their vision for a Talented world. I hated that whatever Mac's punishment, it wasn't going to be sufficient. But there was also nothing I could do about it now.

In the days following my visit to The Oceania, the area surrounding the island was searched for Gretchen's body. It wasn't found. The currents were unpredictable, and the ocean too vast to search all of it. I understood the difficulty with searching the entire Atlantic Ocean, but until her body was found, a part of me wouldn't be convinced she was dead.

Erik and I returned to Councilman Tanaka's Virginia home to a hero's welcome. Evan, Alex, Marin, and Edmond were all at the estate when we arrived. We soon learned the welcome wasn't for us. Mr. Kelley had been found. He was in bad shape. There was talk of amputating his injured leg. But he was alive. And that was all that mattered. Dr. Patel had made the trip east along with Erik's father, Alex, and Marin, and would be caring for Mr. Kelley at the Councilman's home. The preferential treatment was authorized by Victoria since Erik and I were the ones who, technically, captured Mac and Gretchen.

For the first time since his father had gone missing, Erik cried. He sat beside Mr. Kelley's bed and wept. When I tried to leave him alone to cry in peace, he insisted I stay. Mr. Kelley was my family now, too, Erik said.

Penny and Brand stayed the night at the Councilman's estate. Penny insisted it was because she was tired of flying. I knew the truth. She wanted to make sure I was okay after the emotional day with Gretchen and the return of Mr. Kelley. We even had a sleepover in my bedroom and pretended like we were back in our pledge days at Elite Headquarters. We painted our nails with polish we found in Joy's giant closet, and ate cake that Councilman Tanaka's chef had prepared.

Erik and his brothers and Alex spent the night in Mr. Kelley's room. Alex had put up a fight when Marin tried to take him away from Erik's father, so it was agreed he could stay. With no family left, we'd all made an agreement to share in Alex's care. Once Erik and I figured out where we were going to go after we left the Councilman's, I planned on taking Alex with us. I wasn't ready to be a parent, but I'd promised Donavon and Kandice.

Brand spent the night talking to Crane and Victoria. That was one party you couldn't have paid me enough to attend. Yet, when Penny and I went down to the kitchen to get more cake and got lost on the way, we heard them laughing hysterically in the Council-man's study. A quick peek—mental on my part, through the crack in the door for Penny—told us they were drunk. The three of them and the Councilman were sitting on plush leather sofas, drinking scotch and smoking cigars.

I smiled. They all deserve it, I thought. I considered recanting my previous statement about not wanting to attend their party. I was honestly curious whether Brand was less uptight when he was drunk. I wondered whether Victoria said funny British words and dropped the whole regal act. Instead of crashing their festivities, Penny and I agreed that overconsumption of decadent confections was the better option.

Penny and Brand left two days after our trip to The Oceania. Gretchen's body was still missing. Erik and I fell into a domestic routine. It was easy to pretend the Councilman's house was ours. We ate breakfast with Erik's brothers and Alex every morning, then I'd take Alex to play outside while Erik, Edmond, and Evan visited with their father. Mr. Kelley was awake but bedbound until further notice from Dr. Patel. Normally we ate dinner with Mr. Kelley in his room, one big strange family affair.

I waited up most nights to talk to Crane and Victoria about what, if anything, they'd learned from the day's interrogation sess-ions. Usually they had little to report. We still had no idea how many people had been infected with the Creation drug. There still wasn't a cure.

Nearly a week after our visit to The Oceania, I woke well after midnight to someone with sharp nails shaking my shoulder.

I blinked sleep from my eyes to find Victoria's golden irises staring down at me. I sat up. I'd fallen asleep in the study, waiting for Crane and Victoria to return home.

"We need to talk, Ms. Lyons," Victoria said. She had a crystal tumbler of scotch in one hand and was swirling the ice cubes around so that they made a clinking noise against the glass.

"Sure. What's up?" I asked, yawning.

"Some of the Created have begun to show themselves, make nuisances of themselves," she said. She selected an armchair across from the sofa I was sitting on and settled in. Crossing one long leg over the other, she sipped her scotch.

"What's that mean?"

"They are causing problems. Displaying their new Talents for the world. Some are harmless, using their gifts like magic tricks to amuse crowds. Others, well, others are terrorizing people. They must be stopped. UNITED still does not have the names of all those infected, but the ones stupid enough to openly abuse their power will be easy to track down. I am assembling a taskforce of highly skilled Talents to do just that. I would like for you to be a part of that taskforce."

"Me?" I asked, a little surprised.

"Yes. You have experience as a Hunter. You are a trained fighter. And you know what to expect from them."

"Do I have a choice?" I asked, my surprise turning to suspicion.

Victoria had been friendly since I'd saved her life, but I didn't think she was so grateful she'd conveniently overlook the fact I'd been infected.

Victoria smiled coolly. "There is always a choice, Ms. Lyons."

"Right. But my options are what exactly? I join your taskforce or you contain me?"

Victoria sipped her drink. She set the tumbler down on the coffee table between us. "No. You join because you want to. While UNITED's policy is to contain all the Created, I have to say I am very impressed by your ability to control yourself. If you agree to monthly checkups with one of our doctors, I do not believe containment is necessary."

"What about Erik?" I asked. There had to be a catch.

"I've made him the same offer."

"Did he agree?" I asked, starting to get uneasy that he hadn't discussed it with me beforehand.

"No, not yet. He felt this was a decision the two of you needed to make together." She rolled her eyes. "Very noble, that one."

I smiled. "Then that's my answer, too. I need to discuss the matter with Erik."

Victoria sighed. "I figured you'd say that. Take the next day or so to think it over. Watch the news feeds from around the world. I am sure you will you agree with UNITED. The Created must be contained."

I did agree with her. At least, I agreed that something needed to be done about them. Containment wasn't the preferable option, but if we found a cure soon, then the drug could be reversed.

I stood and started for the doorway, to go in search of Erik. This was a decision we needed to make together. Our future wasn't the one to consider. Alex. I needed to make sure Alex would be taken care of.

"Oh, and Ms. Lyons?" Victoria called after me.

"Yeah?"

"Gretchen McDonough was spotted in Florence last night. If that makes your decision any easier for you."

Epilogue

TO ERIK KELLEY, the flight from northern Virginia to the Oceania seemed longer the second time around. He had only two companions today. The girl sitting next to him on the UNITED hoverplane was nervously chewing her thumbnail with animal ferocity. He gently tugged her hand away from her mouth when he noticed blood on her lower lip.

"He can't hurt us anymore," he told her quietly.

She nodded jerkily. "Yeah, I know. I just, I don't." She shook her head from side to side, wisps of her orange-red hair skimming his cheek. "We should've told Talia."

Lying to Talia that morning had been one of the hardest things Erik had ever done. Not just because she was a mind reader, either. He never lied to her. You didn't lie to people you loved. But this was the only way. If he'd told her about the trip, she'd have wanted to come. Talia wanted the Director dead; Erik knew that from their bond. He also knew she wasn't prepared to do the deed herself.

Erik had no such qualms. Neither did Penny. Sure, she had some hesitation, but Erik felt her hunger for the Director's suffering. It was ugly and primal and matched his own.

Victoria, the third member of their group, had agreed to this visit because she, too, felt prison was better than Danbury McDonough deserved. Also, Victoria wanted Erik, Talia, and Penny to join UNITED. This was one of Erik's conditions for agreeing to do just that, and for convincing the girls to do the same.

Erik smirked. Victoria thought convincing Talia was hard. Really, Talia had been more on board with the idea than he had. Erik wanted away from UNITED and the politics and all the bullshit that came along with it. He wanted to spend time with his family and Talia and Alex, who were both part of the Kelley clan now, too.

"No cameras. That was our deal," Penny reminded Victoria as the trio deplaned. "I don't want any evidence."

The first thing Erik had done after striking his deal with Victoria was comm Penny in California. He'd known she would want to be a part of this. And, no surprise, Penny had jumped at the opportunity.

Now that they were on the Oceania, Penny's nerves had turned to steel. She was cool, calm, and collected, and ready for revenge.

Erik's smile died on his lips. This wasn't the Penny he knew. Talia's best friend was sweet, goofy even. The Director had created the bloodthirsty monster that was driving Penny to become a killer. Erik considered offering her the chance to back out.

"*He tortured me,*" Penny sent Erik. "*He doesn't deserve to live.*"

"*If you're sure.*"

"*Positive,*" Penny replied.

Victoria led them to the glass elevator that would take them to AF3. Erik was so focused on what he was about to do that he barely noticed the lack of people. It wasn't until the three of them actually boarded the elevator that Erik began to wonder where Captain Klegg and his team were.

Plausible deniability, Erik thought. If there was any backlash, the guards would be able to claim they didn't know what had happened. There wasn't likely to be backlash, though. UNITED wanted this matter taken care of quickly and quietly. A public trial would be an international fiasco, set on a global stage for the world to witness. Crazies would come out of the woodwork to defend Director McDonough, UNITED wanted to prevent that. Victoria had told Erik and Penny as much on the flight.

Like the main level of the Oceania, the deepest sublevel of the facility was practically a ghost town. Mashburn, a guard they'd met on their last trip, was the only one waiting for the three of them when they exited the elevator.

"I have not told the prisoner you are coming, just as you asked, Councilwoman," Mashburn said, addressing Victoria. Then, she turned to Erik and Penny. "We have divers in position. If he manages to escape somehow, he won't get far."

Another reason Victoria, and by extension UNITED, had agreed to let Erik and Penny handle the Director was because of Gretchen's escape. No one understood how she'd managed it. Talia was beside herself with guilt. She blamed herself, even though no one else did. UNITED was trying to track Gretchen, but they didn't have a Viewer familiar enough with the Director's wife to find her. She'd kept out of the public eye, kept her role strictly behind the scenes. There had been sightings of Gretchen all over the world. UNITED was drowning in false leads and dead ends. They worried she'd rally the Created and come for her husband—another reason to take him out of the equation.

No one spoke as Mashburn led the way through the transparent hallways to the tube that would take them to the prison pods.

Erik let his mind wander back to the time he spent in Tramble-wood. The memories he'd repressed made their way to the surface. Anger and hatred turned to fury and rage as Mashburn performed the necessary security measures to unlock the door to the tubes. Penny took his hand and he felt the same storm brewing inside of her that was in him.

The two of them hadn't discussed how they were going to dispose of the Director, but Erik felt they were on the same page. Danbury McDonough would suffer before his life ended. He would get to experience the fruits of his poison. He would be like the magician's assistant, an active participant in the greatest display of power on earth. He would be the puppet of the two strongest Talents the world had known.

"Are you ready?" Victoria asked, pulling Erik from his mental tirade. Her hand was on his shoulder. Her smile was cool, detached, but her golden eyes were pure understanding. In that moment Erik liked the councilwoman a little better.

Erik blinked. He'd been so consumed with his hatred that he hadn't even noticed that they were now standing outside the door to the Director's prison pod. Only one barrier stood between him and the man who'd stolen so much from him. His mother had died because of the Director's greed. His brothers and father had lived like prisoners for years, their safety on his shoulders. They'd been the pawns the Director had used to keep Erik in line.

No more, Erik thought. His family was free. After the Director was dead, he would be free, too.

Erik met Penny's lime-colored eyes. They nodded in unison.

As Mashburn unlocked the last obstacle standing between Erik and revenge, Erik sent Talia a message across the thousands of miles of ocean that separated them.

"Don't hate me. I'm doing this because I love you. His death isn't worth your sanity."

Erik knew that no matter how much Talia wanted the Director, she wasn't a cold-blooded killer. She would have come with him. She would have helped Penny and Erik make him pay. But she would've hated herself afterwards. The guilt would drive her crazy. She'd never taken the life of another when the other was helpless. And the Director was helpless now.

He hadn't expected Talia to answer him. The mental communication didn't have such a long reach. So when her voice filled his head, Erik froze.

"Just make sure Mac pays for my parents, too," she sent back. *"I'll always love you."*

Relief washed over him. Erik hadn't realized how heavy the weight of his guilt over lying to her was until that instant. There was so much more he wanted to say to Talia just then, but the door to the Director's prison pod was opening. He blocked Talia instead. She might want the Director to suffer, but she didn't have to witness it.

Penny stepped through the doorway first, Erik only a step behind her.

Former TOXIC Director Danbury "Mac" McDonough was sitting on his twin-sized bed. He looked up as the door closed behind Erik and Penny. Fear sparked in his gray eyes. Erik thought he'd feel satisfaction at seeing that emotion from this man. He didn't.

Reflexively the Director scooted backwards on the bed. His back was literally against the wall.

Erik stepped forward so he was even with Penny.

"Hello, *Mac*," Penny said, her voice cold enough to freeze boiling water. "Surprised to see us? Don't worry, we have big plans for you."

Dear Reader,

Thank you for joining me on Talia's journey so far. I really hope you've enjoyed the books! As an independent author, I rely heavily upon readers to spread the word about my books. Writing an honest review on your retail site, and even copying it to Goodreads, is a small way for you to make a big contribution. Your support is greatly appreciated. Keep an eye out for Exiled and Inescapable, coming soon!

Xoxo, Sophie

Inescapable

THE FIFTH INSTALLMENT IN THE TALENTED SAGA
COMING SUMMER 2014

AND LOOK FOR . . .

Exiled

KENLY'S STORY
COMING JUNE 2014, PRE-ORDER AVAILABLE NOW!

Signup for Sophie's Sweethearts on
www.sophiedavisbooks.com for the latest news
on the Talented Saga and Sophie's other series.
You'll be the first to receive release announcements and cover reveals!

For more information on Sophie Davis and the *Talented Saga*, visit Sophie's website, www.sophiedavisbooks.com

To contact Sophie directly, email her at sophie.davis.books@gmail.com.

You can also follow Sophie on twitter @sophiedavisbook.

Thank you for taking the time to read *Created*. Sophie loves feedback, and any reviews posted to goodreads.com, amazon.com, Barnes and Noble, or any other retail site where *Created* is sold, are greatly appreciated.

42202406R00201

Made in the USA
Charleston, SC
21 May 2015